A DANGEROUS DANCE

Remington watched the blades move, analyzed them. "There's a space between them in the arc of their swing. If we time things just right, we should be able to make each beat and move between them."

He grabbed her hand and crouched into a running stance. "We'll make a run for it on the count of three. One. Two."

"No!" She yanked her hand from his. "There's no clear path. Our movements have to be to a precise beat to make it through the blades." She began to hum a tune as she watched the blades.

He crossed his arms. "And you have a better method?"

A glint of amusement lit her eyes. "I think we should go *dancing*."

He glanced at the blades and frowned. "Dancing? Now?"

"It'd at least make death a bit more fun."

Remington sighed, grasped her hand lightly, and spun her about, putting his hand at the base of her spine and holding her arm extended to the side to waltz with her.

"This what you had in mind?"

"Well, it'd be better without the swinging blades of death, but I suppose it's the only chance we'll get."

He tracked the movement of the blades. "Keep humming that tune."

She obliged, and together they began to sway. Remington glanced at the blades, counting silently in his head to the time of her tune. One. Two. Three. One. He moved them forward. Two. Their feet came together, and he pressed his hand against her waist signaling her to quickly turn as the first blade came swinging back. Three. He took a quick step backward as the blade finished passing behind them, waiting a beat before moving forward on the next step. The stream of air caused by the blade ruffled the back of his hair. That was close. Too close.

Books by Theresa Meyers

THE HUNTER
Book One of the Legend Chronicles

THE SLAYER
Book Two of the Legend Chronicles

THE CHOSEN
Book Three of the Legend Chronicles

THE INVENTOR
A Legend Chronicles Story

Published by Kensington Publishing Corporation

The Chosen

BOOK THREE OF THE LEGEND CHRONICLES

THERESA MEYERS

ZEBRA BOOKS
KENSINGTON PUBLISHING CORP.
http://www.kensingtonbooks.com

ZEBRA BOOKS are published by

Kensington Publishing Corp.
119 West 40th Street
New York, NY 10018

All Kensington titles, imprints and distributed lines are
available at special quantity discounts for bulk purchases
for sales promotion, premiums, fund-raising, educational
or institutional use.

Special book excerpts or customized printings can also be
created to fit specific needs. For details, write or phone the
office of the Kensington Special Sales Manager: Kensington
Publishing Corp., 119 West 40th Street, New York, NY 10018.
Attn. Special Sales Department. Phone: 1-800-221-2647.

Zebra and the Z logo Reg. U.S. Pat. & TM Off.

ISBN-13: 978-1-4201-2126-1
ISBN-10: 1-4201-2126-X

First Printing: March 2013

10 9 8 7 6 5 4 3 2 1

Printed in the United States of America

This book is dedicated to my California family.
Some family you get by birth.
Others are added in as you live,
but all are a special part of your life.

To my Uncle Perry, Aunt Julie, and Sabrina.
Thanks for always being the ones to
remind me what true family is all about and
how wonderful it can be.

To my grandparents, Helen and Jack Stokes.
You are truly one in a million.

To Aunt "Sister" a/k/a Liz Freeman.
Thanks for making sure we all stay in touch.

Chapter 1

1883
Bisbee mining camp, Arizona

"What can I do for you, stranger?" A stout, pot-bellied sheriff stirred out of his afternoon nap and sat up at Remington Jackson's approach. Remington closed the jailhouse door and stepped into the dark interior. The place smelled of dust and body odor, but the welcome drop in temperature from the desert heat made his mission suddenly more bearable.

"I'm here to see Miss McGee."

The sheriff eyed him suspiciously. "You her husband?"

Remington nearly choked on the thought. The whole idea of being tied to one thing for the rest of his life was loathsome enough, but to a Darkin was unthinkable. He cleared the sour thickness out of his throat and grasped the lapels of his black gentleman's jacket. It had been foolish to wear his court clothing on a trek such as this, but he had no idea who he'd have to convince to let the Darkin thief go once he arrived, and a good attorney used all his assets, not just his silver tongue. He needed to be prepared to sway anything from a local sheriff to a federal marshal to a territorial judge.

"No. I'm her attorney."

"Name?"

"Remington Jackson."

The sheriff's gaze sharpened. "Have we met before?"

Remington was about to throttle the man, but he kept his face placid and his manner cool. Maintaining control was key in these matters but the sooner he got Miss McGee released to his custody, the better. "No."

"You look awful familiar, mister."

"I assure you, had I met such an outstanding officer as yourself before, I would recall the moment."

The sheriff sniffed, wiping the back of his hand across his nose, then hitched up his pants. "This way."

As Remington approached the cell, even in the gloom of the jail, he could see her propped up against a wall, her hair a golden tumbled halo about her head, her curvy body accented by form-fitting buckskin breeches and a matching fringed jacket over a faded, pale blue chambray shirt. His body jolted with a hit of pure, intense attraction. Colt had said China was a looker. He'd lied.

From the light filtering in through the barred window of her cell, Remington could see even coated in dust she was something crafted out of pure male fantasy made real. Her creamy smooth skin, tinted with pink, delicate features, and the glass-like clarity of her silver-gray eyes reminded him of an expensive china doll. The normal taint of sulfur that hung about Darkin was softened by the scents of black tea and vanilla.

Colt had once bragged this woman could steal the rails out from under a train and no one would be the wiser. If Colt was right, directions to a missing piece of the Book of Legend were within his grasp. If Colt was wrong, well then Remington figured he'd have wasted his time and considerable skills as an attorney getting this shape-shifting female thief out of jail.

Why Colt would work with a supernatural being like

China, Remington couldn't figure, except his little brother had a penchant for running on the wrong side of things and liked pretty females. All their lives they'd been raised to hunt the Darkin down, protecting the unsuspecting population from the likes of vampires, demons . . . and shape-shifters.

Working with one just seemed a shade too desperate for Remington's taste, but then he wasn't much like either of his brothers. Not the older one, Winchester, who detested Hunting, and not the younger one, Colt, who reveled in the life.

Remington fit into neither category. He sat firmly in the middle. He liked to play both sides of the tracks as it suited him. Some days he was safe behind a desk, living a normal, respectable life. And others he was out hunting down Darkin and getting in a taste of adventure and danger.

The plan was simple and foolproof. Get in. Get her out. Obtain the material from Diego Mendoza's safety-deposit box by legal means, if possible. Illegal if necessary. Head back to Tombstone and send the information on to Colt who could take care of things from there. Go back to the nice little life he'd carved out for himself as a part-time attorney and part-time Hunter. The only variable he couldn't count on was the female Darkin.

He knew she'd worked with Colt before. He knew she'd cheated Colt a time or two. In fact at one time he and Colt had come to blows and gunshots over the matter. And he knew she'd been in Colt's bed. Not an easy matter to untangle, but he'd dealt with worse.

But after taking a second long look Remington suddenly had a new understanding of his little brother's assessment of this Darkin's assets. Colt had never brought her around Winn or him before because his brother didn't want either of them being sucked in by her like he was. Altruistic of him? Probably not. But Remington was made of sterner stuff than his little brother. He at least knew how to resist a Darkin's charms, even one as pretty and deadly as China McGee. The trick was

never to get emotionally entangled. As long as he treated her
like the Darkin thing she was, everything would move along
slick as oil.

Blowing up the bank had seemed like a sensible thing to do
at the time. Colt Jackson had claimed the map in a Hunter's
safety-deposit box in the bank would lead them to a piece of
the Book of Legend, giving China a way to gain favor from
the Darkin archdemon lord Rathe. He was part demon, part
vampire, and all powerful, and she'd do just about anything to
ensure she stayed in his good graces permanently.

Of course now that her dirty skin pimpled up in gooseflesh
as a black cockroach skittered up the stone of her cell wall
next to her head, she had changed her mind about her methods and crossed off blowing up banks and working with
Hunters.

The stench of stale sweat and fumes of liquor and urine
from the drunkard in the next cell sleeping away his intoxica-
tion made even breathing an unpleasant experience. The crust
of rock dust from the explosion still coated her skin, making
it itch. Being cooped up in a cell made her chest tight. She
needed to get out, soon. Shifters didn't do well in confined
spaces.

In retrospect, it had been stupid of her to trust Colt even
marginally. Their rocky, on-again off-again relationship over
the years should have given her enough experience to know
better. The only reason she'd been willing to give it another
shot was because she had usually come out better than he did
whenever they'd crossed paths before.

Maybe it had been just her pride talking a bit too loudly,
but she'd truly believed she could take the map, leaving him
behind to take the punishment for the robbery. So much for
well laid plans. It had turned out just the opposite. He'd
double-crossed her and made the fuse on the dynamite shorter

than she realized. She'd been the one caught in the blast and hauled off to the pokey.

China frowned and crossed her arms over her chest, making her fringed buckskin leather jacket creak. Once an apple went bad, it was bad to the core, and their seeds were soured too. She'd never trust another bad-seed Hunter again as long as she lived. Colt had seen to that. As much as she found him physically appealing, if he ever dared cross her path again, she'd scratch those blue eyes right out of his head.

The heavy thumping step of the sheriff, accompanied by the jangle of brass keys, grew louder. China leaned forward, trying to see who was coming.

"She's down here. I'll give you five minutes."

"Ten." The deep male voice wasn't familiar, putting all her senses of self-preservation on alert. Ten minutes alone with the wrong sort of man could be an eternity. China pushed away from the wall.

The sheriff huffed. "All right then, ten, but not a tick longer. I've got to get to lunch."

China pressed her face against the cool metal of the bars to get a better look at the man the sheriff was leading to her cell, but all she could see in the shadows of the long hall were his hands. They were an odd mix of smoothness and size. Big and powerful, but so well-manicured it had to be a fancy man who hadn't done a lick of hard work in his life. What in the world could he want with her? A brothel owner? A card sharp?

She stepped back, pressing herself against the wall, the rough texture of the stones digging into her back. The sheriff rattled the key in the lock and opened the cell door. China stiffened her shoulders, smoothing her damp hands along the legs of her buckskin pants.

In walked the spittin' image of Colt Jackson, all jet hair, superior blue eyes, sexy mouth, and broad shoulders, gussied up in a black suit and tie. The cell door clanked shut behind him, leaving them locked in together. All the words China had been holding in her mouth crumbled into a gritty dust that coated her throat and made her choke.

She bent over double with a coughing fit, and the man laid one of his smooth hands on her shoulder, his touch burning right through the leather to sear her skin.

"Are you all right, Miss McGee?"

China blinked back the tears in her eyes and glared at him for an instant, slapping away his hand. His features were nearly the same as Colt's, but his chin held a cleft that Colt's didn't, and the blue of his eyes was just a shade lighter. She didn't trust him any more than she trusted the man he resembled. Less. She didn't know just how far *this* one would go to get what he wanted.

"I thought you were Colt."

The man tugged at the impeccable white cuffs that peeped from underneath his suit jacket. Expensive sapphire cuff links winked in the light. Nothing like Colt would've worn. "People often mistake us at first. I'm his older brother, Remington."

China drew back from him as though she'd been branded. "Get him out of here!" she shrieked.

The sheriff came at a run, his breath in short gasps, his hand on his chest. "What in tarnation is goin' on in there?"

Mr. Jackson ignored the question and stared at her, his blue eyes piercing straight through her. "Miss McGee, may I at least explain why I'm here?"

China shook her head, making her hair, still dusty from the explosion, swing in limp hanks about her face. "I don't want nothin' to do with you, or your brother, or whatever other kin you have out there. Colt's the reason I'm stuck in this cell, so no. I don't want to have any kinda conversation with you. Just git."

The doppelganger's face turned nearly as smooth and unreadable as blank paper. "I'm here to get you out. I'm your attorney." He turned to the sheriff. "We're fine here; you may go. I'll be taking Miss McGee with me."

The sheriff's eyes narrowed. "I don't think so."

Mr. Jackson's jaw ticked. "And may I ask why?"

The sheriff held up a yellowed "wanted" poster of a face very like Remington's. "Said your name was Jackson, didn't ya?"

Remington frowned. "If you would check the name on that poster, you'll find it's a *Colt* Jackson—my brother."

The sheriff eyed the paper, glancing from it to Remington's face and back again. "Yep. It is. But as close as you both look, it could be an alias. I can't let you out until we track down your brother and can prove you ain't him."

Remington grabbed the bars, bringing his face as close as he could to the sheriff's. "You have no right to hold me," he said, his tone cool, calm, and lethal. "You have no evidence. I demand to see a federal marshal or at the very least a judge."

The sheriff smirked. "Well, that'd be long about Friday three weeks from now. They don't come by here but once a month, and you just missed them. Unless, of course, you can tell me where I could track down your brother."

Jackson's body remained deadly still. His icy cool façade frightened her more than Colt's gun-blazing anger at a time like this.

"Just tell him!" she urged. He blasted her with a bone-chilling stare that was colder than an icicle through the heart. China about swallowed her tongue. Clearly he wasn't about to turn in his little brother to the authorities to save his own skin—or hers.

"Do as you must," he told the sheriff without a hint of emotion. "And I shall do the same."

The sheriff turned on his heel to walk back down the hallway. China rushed to the bars. "Wait! I didn't hire no attorney," she spat, but the sheriff wasn't listening. He kept his back to her and kept walking, whistling some inane tune under his breath. She turned and glared at Colt's look-alike brother. "I didn't ask you to come here."

"No, but Colt did."

China didn't know whether to laugh or cry. Her plans had already failed. She'd needed to get the piece of the Book of Legend. But Colt had ditched her before they'd recovered it. "Why would he do a fool thing like that?" But she already knew the answer.

He felt guilty for leaving her to be arrested when he robbed the bank. He needed her skills to get to the missing piece of the Book of Legend that he'd been searching for during the last two years, said he'd need a Darkin thief to get to it. He might even still be attracted to her. She hoped.

She had a thing for Colt Jackson. He'd somehow gotten under her skin. While their relationship had been brief—and neither could trust the other farther than either could pick the other up and throw him or her—it didn't mean he wasn't attractive as hell.

China eyed the other Jackson brother. He was just as devastating as his little brother, perhaps more so because he had the polish and an air of sophistication that Colt lacked. A keen intelligence sparkled within the depths of his blue eyes that she found intriguing. They looked so much alike she could see how the sheriff would be damn certain he had the outlaw with an alias behind bars.

"Maybe he was concerned you knew too much and wanted someone to keep an eye on you."

China frowned. Now that sounded like Colt. No trust. But with good reason. Colt was a man who liked to win. But what about Remington Jackson? Was he cut from the same cloth as his brother? Just how hard would it be to outsmart him and get away from him once they were out of the jail? She wasn't about to stay in this cell with him any longer than she had to. She had a job to do. And she was going to recover a piece of the Book of Legend for Rathe one way or another.

She lifted her chin and looked down at her fingernails, dirty around the rims since the bank explosion. "And if you get me out, then what do I owe you?" She wasn't stupid enough to believe he'd do this out of the goodness of his Hunter heart—if he even had one. She glanced up.

His firmly sculpted lips tilted into a calculating half smile that made her shiver. It reminded her of Rathe. Dead certain you were gonna do whatever it was he wanted because he had you by the shorthairs. "You'll give me what you retrieved from Diego Mendoza's box."

Out of habit her index finger went into her mouth, and she nibbled at her nail. "What if I don't have it?"

All traces of humor suddenly vanished and his blue gaze turned to ice. Out of sheer will, China forced herself not to squirm under his scrutiny. "Don't bother lying to me, Miss McGee. I've learned to spot lies easily enough in my profession. The deal is simple: your freedom in exchange for whatever you recovered from Mendoza's deposit box. Agreed?" He held out a hand to her.

For a second China hesitated. The hand-scrawled page from Diego's safety-deposit box was burning a hole in her shirt pocket right over her heart. What choice did she have? She'd already tried to shift into something small enough to crawl out of her cell, but each time she touched the iron bars either at the door or at her window, she shifted back to her human form. Iron was a pain in the ass to shifters, neutralizing them back to their original form and sapping their other Darkin powers.

She slipped her hand into his to shake on the deal, but the first contact of his warm, dry skin against hers sent a shock of awareness up her arm. Her heart went from a trot to a gallop. China sucked in a startled breath and got hit with the scent of expensive Bay Rum aftershave with its distinct blend of bay leaves and cloves. It reminded her of wood warmed in the sunshine, but spicier. He not only looked nice, he smelled nice. She stopped herself from taking another deep breath.

Remington Jackson was trouble, plain and simple. He'd ruin everything she had planned.

China went to yank her hand back and found his grip suddenly tightened while his other hand placed something cold on her wrist. An iron bracelet! He released her, and for a second she stared at it. She tried prying it off, but it was locked.

China glared at him. "How dare you!"

He didn't seem the slightest bit ruffled by her anger. "You're a shifter. Did I really have a choice? You were planning on shifting into God knows what the second we got out of this building and leaving me without honoring our agreement."

China's eyes narrowed, even as her fingers fought to pull off the hated manacle. How had he known? "I said I'd go with you," she gritted between her teeth, wishing like hell she could have transformed into a mountain lion right then and there and bitten his head off.

Remington had the balls to grin at her, which only pissed her off more. "Yes, but you never said how far you'd go with me. My guess is to the front door. The bracelet is just to insure we're on equal terms until I have Diego's information, then you can be on your way."

She muttered some choice curses beneath her breath. Remington Jackson was a snake. A slippery, loathsome snake of a Hunter who was too smart for his own damn good. She didn't have a damn map. All she had was Diego's chicken scratches on a patch of paper that Colt claimed were supposed to lead them across the border. On one half was a jumbled series of numbers that made no sense to her and on the other a few scrawled lines that looked like a trail through some mountains. No well drawn roads, no place names. Nothing to help pinpoint where it was or what it meant. She figured Diego didn't intend for anyone but himself to understand the dang thing. But the bit of the Book of Legend it was connected to was her ticket to redemption in the Darkin realm, and she wasn't going to let any fool Hunter,

Jackson or otherwise, take away that opportunity to regain her standing with Rathe.

"So how are you planning on getting me out of here? They've got a price on my head. And you ain't a judge, and now you're stuck here in the pokey same as me."

Remington Jackson's eyes sparkled with a mix of mischief and determination. "You didn't think I'd walk in here without an alternative exit plan, did you?" He pulled the right side of his jacket back to reveal not just a holstered revolver and gun belt filled with silvery bullets, but also a couple of glass vials of clear liquid topped with cork stoppers.

China snorted. "It's gonna take a lot more than that little bit of water if you want to get through those walls. They're at least two feet thick."

He gave her an arch look. "It would, if it were water." He picked up one vial and glanced at her. "But considering it's nitroglycerin, I'm assuming it'll be much more effective. Toss that mattress up on its side and hunker down behind it for cover." She didn't question, just did as he said.

Remington crouched down behind the mattress with her in the corner of the cell, their backs to the bars. He threw the glass vial as hard as he could at the outer adobe wall, then ducked.

The explosion rocked the jail, sending down a shower of dust and chunks of stone and mortar. Miss McGee coughed, then frowned. "Blowing up the jail? That's your solution?"

He shrugged. He really didn't care what she thought of his methods. "It works." His life wasn't a black or white proposition. It was more like a smorgasbord. He took what he needed, when he needed it, to get the job done. Being a Hunter, even part-time, meant he didn't always have the luxury of doing things by the book.

Judging by the narrow-eyed look and pinched mouth on

Miss McGee's pretty face, he'd been right to bring the iron bracelet along as a precaution. Colt said she could change into many things, including a mountain lion, and he had no plans of getting shredded to pieces on the way back to Tombstone.

Remington didn't waste any time. He hustled Miss McGee out of the jail as quickly as possible, assisting her with his hand as she crossed the rubble, aware that the sheriff and half the town would likely be on their heels at any moment.

They dashed around the outer edge of the jail and waited for everyone to disappear inside. He grabbed hold of her hand. "Let's go."

He rushed to his horse, Joe, grabbing on the reins that swung about the horse's legs. The explosion had spooked the chestnut gelding and he'd pulled free from the hitching post.

China's mouth dropped open. "How are we gonna get out of here quick on that? Don't you have a mechanical horse like Colt?"

"No. Hate the damn thing. Now are you coming or not?"

China snapped her mouth closed and nodded. Remington mounted in one smooth, swift motion, then hauled the Darkin up to sit in front of him. Well, really, given the confines of the saddle, she sat more in his lap than in front of him. She was far softer than he'd anticipated. Somehow Miss McGee's prickly exterior didn't change how very feminine she felt. "Hold on to the pommel." She gripped it hard, and he grasped the reins in each hand.

"Is this really necessary?" she growled as he kicked Joe into motion.

"Until I have clear access to Diego Mendoza's information, absolutely." That was a half-truth. He could have just taken whatever she'd gotten from the safety-deposit box and left her there, but his gut had told him that wasn't the safest path. And if there was one thing Remington did, it was always listen to his gut. Besides, everything Colt had him meticulously research indicated a Darkin was needed to access the hiding place of the missing pieces of the Book. No, he didn't intend on letting Miss McGee out of his sights any time soon.

He wheeled Joe around and sped up the hill, making quick tracks out of Bisbee before anyone figured out what had happened and where they'd gone. A hot breeze, tainted with the ozone of heated metal and the acrid stench of woodsmoke belching from the stack on the Copper Queen smelter at the base of the hill, blew hard as they crested the hills around Bisbee and powdered his coat with a fine layer of grit. But he didn't stop or slow until Bisbee was completely out of sight.

"I can just give you the page. That's all there was. No map. Not a decent one anyway. Just a bunch of squiggly lines. No place names. No directions." With her right hand she reached beneath the edge of her leather jacket and pulled a folded page of yellowed paper from the breast pocket of her faded pale blue chambray shirt. "Here. Take it. Then you can just drop me off at the next town. Deal?"

Remington smiled. She was just as anxious to get away from him as she was to get back at Colt. He could tell by the nervous way she fidgeted. "No deal. How do I know that paper will lead me anywhere?"

She shrugged, the movement causing her back and the curve of her shoulders to rub up against his chest. Remington grit his teeth. He was a Hunter, not a monk, after all. And despite the taint of being Darkin, she was a beautiful creature.

"You don't. But I don't have anything else, so it doesn't matter."

"Oh, I think you have a bit more than that. You were working with Colt to help find the lost piece of the Book Diego knew about, weren't you?"

She heaved a sigh. "I don't know anything."

"That's not what Colt said."

A fine tremor worked its way through her body. Remington

wasn't sure if it was anger or desire. There was an exceedingly fine dividing line between hate and love, and it didn't take a whole hell of a lot to push some folks from one to the other.

"Colt knows everything I do."

"Yes, but he's bent on finding Cadel's piece of the Book, which my father hid. That means I'm collecting you so you can help him find the piece Diego is rumored to have discovered."

She twisted in his lap. The leather stretched across her finely curved ass was not nearly enough of a barrier between them. Remington grunted. China gazed up at him. "You're trying to put the Book of Legend back together, aren't you?"

They started down the rugged hills surrounding Bisbee, and Remington weighed the options of telling her the truth versus telling her only what he wanted her to know. His gut told him to trust her when every bit of Hunter training told him he was a fool to do so.

"Yes."

Something changed in her eyes. A flash of silver, like lightning streaking across a stormy, cloud-covered sky. It was a breathtaking sight. "I'll help you on one condition."

Remington was tempted to tell her she wasn't exactly in a position to bargain, but his curiosity got the better of him. In the courts, sometimes what people told you when trying to bargain revealed far more about their intentions than they realized. "And what's that?"

"If you do find all the pieces, I want to be there when you put it together."

Remington frowned. "Why?"

"'Cause if what the Darkin legends say is true, it's gonna be one hell of a show."

In Remington's opinion deals were made to be remade. He didn't see the harm in agreeing to it if it could get the information Colt needed out of her. "Sounds like you have a personal stake in the matter. Is that true, Miss McGee?"

She shifted uneasily. "You've got your secrets, Hunter. I've got mine. Do we have a deal, or don't we?"

"Your help in securing whatever Diego's map leads to in return for being there if and when the Book of Legend is re-united?"

"Yes."

He paused for a moment, letting her believe he contemplated things. "Deal."

She relaxed a little, her back curving into his chest as she handed him the paper she had retrieved from Diego's box and he unceremoniously stuffed it into his pocket.

"Ain't you even gonna look at it?"

He shook his head. "Not yet. I'll look at it when I have the time and space to properly analyze it. Maybe you've just missed something and I can figure out Diego's intentions."

"And maybe you can't."

He gave her an enigmatic smile. "Never bet against an educated Hunter, my dear. You won't win."

She grumbled, the sound of it vibrating through her body and into him. Remington resisted the urge to laugh at the absurdity of it all. He knew Colt liked women with spirit; he just hadn't realized his brother liked them hardheaded too.

The horse huffed. As the white hot sun bore down on them from overhead, heat rose up in shimmering waves from the parched earth. Joe was growing tired carrying a double load. Only the large saguaro cacti, their tall, prickly bodies topped with multiple arms reaching toward an endless blue sky, offered meager shade. They rode on in silence. Remington didn't want to get too chummy with the shifter.

Finally China broke the endless shuffling sound of the horse's hooves in the dirt. "You ever get tired of being a Hunter?"

His gut contracted. It was too personal; too close to something he might have discussed with his brothers, but never with a stranger, and certainly not a Darkin. "That's an odd question."

"Why?"

"It's like me asking if you ever get tired of being a shifter. You're just born to it. It's not a matter of if you want to be one or not."

"I do."

"Do what?"

"Get tired of being a shifter."

Remington frowned, the sweat on his forehead making his hat slide a little lower. He'd never thought about a Darkin in that way—that they could possibly not like what they were or want to change it. It made them seem almost, well, human.

Curiosity bit at him. "If you weren't a shifter, what would you be?"

China twisted and gave him a brilliant smile that took him by surprise, making his stomach flip-flop. "I'd be a high society New York heiress."

He chuckled. "Of course you would." He had to give her points for being both practical and smart. Had he been a woman and not a Hunter, he might have chosen the same. A life completely different than that of his brothers. One with proper society, wealth, and privilege—not worry, sacrifice, and death.

But Hunting wasn't something one elected to do. He didn't get a choice in the matter. It was his birthright. He'd been trained since he could talk about what Darkin were, how to defeat them, and how to defend innocent bystanders against their attacks.

He couldn't help but muse about how the shifter sitting on his lap didn't quite measure up to his idea of the ruthless, depraved monsters he hunted.

In the heat of the afternoon when everything fell silent, a rattling from the creosote bushes up ahead caused the horse to raise its head, perk up its ears, and come to a sudden halt. It whickered, an uncertain, unhappy sound. Both China and Remington peered into the desert scrub.

"Sounds like a snake," Remington muttered.

"But it doesn't smell like one." China's body turned hard and tense against his.

He reached for his hip holster, pulling out his revolver and cocking it in one quick, smooth motion. Darkin, shifters and vampires in particular, had a keen sense of smell. If China said it didn't smell like a snake, then in his Hunter experience it was likely something far worse.

Amorphous forms, fast and dark, came streaking out of the desert. The shots of black smoke caused the horse to rear. Demons?

Remington did his best to hold the reins in one hand and his gun in the other and maintain his seat in the saddle by gripping his thighs tight around the sides of the horse. China held fast to the pommel. The rattling turned to hissing as the forms coalesced into solid matter. Boots and dusters, beefy shoulders and craggy, scaled olive-green faces with yellow, vertical-slitted eyes. Black forked tongues flicked from openings where their mouths should be.

The six creatures were shaped like men, but Remington knew they sure as hell weren't human.

He did his best to get Joe to settle down before he and China got knocked to the dirt, or worse still, knocked down, then trampled. The animal huffed and snorted, its nostrils flaring. Its soft brown eyes were now liberally surrounded by white as it shied and sidestepped backward from the creatures surrounding them in a loose circle.

China had gotten even stiffer, if that were possible, her back now ramrod straight. If the horse and the Darkin were scared, they were in deeper shit than he'd first thought. He'd never seen anything like this described in Pa's Book. "What the hell are they?"

"Viperanox. Snake demons. Usually you don't see them this far north of the border. The Indians down in Southern Mexico thought they were gods, but they're just Rathe's rustlers."

The hissing of the strange creatures garbled into words Remington could understand. "Give usss the map."

China spat in the dirt. "Go to hell, you bastards. You know the way."

They exchanged quick glances, a few of them hissing and barring sharp, dagger-length fangs. One moved in to grab the reins from Remington. He didn't hesitate. He shot the creature point-blank in the forehead, knocking it backwards into the dirt. It writhed and shrieked, its scaled hands pressed hard to its face. The creature twisted in upon itself until it was once again dark, undulating smoke that sank into the earth.

China turned in his arms, her gray eyes fierce. "What the hell are you waiting for? Shoot them all!"

That was easier said than done. He was down to only three more of Marley's special bullets, and there were five, now very pissed off, viperanox left.

Chapter 2

Remington squinted against the glare of the sun and popped off another three shots, taking down three more of the scary as hell snake demons that were after their asses. Joe skittered sideways and whinnied as the remaining viperanox tried to pull China from his back. China growled and kicked at them.

Remington grabbed hold of the pommel with one hand, his arm braced around China, and spurred Joe into motion. The horse didn't wait to be told twice and took off at a full-out gallop. The hisses and snarls of the viperanox faded for only a moment as they turned into two dark streaks of smoke hot on their heels.

"Get this damn bracelet off!"

He hesitated for only a moment. He knew it disrupted her ability to change her shape. "Know something you can shift into that can fight these things off?"

"Hell yes."

He slowed Joe to a stop and grabbed her wrist with the bracelet. His brilliant inventor friend Marley Turlock had created a tumbler lock in the bracelet. Only Remington knew the precise arrangement of numbers to unlock it. As he rolled the last tumbler into place and gave a slight push to the hidden button, the bracelet opened, falling from China's wrist.

"About damn time," she muttered as she massaged her wrist. The hair around her face was damp with sweat. "Get off the horse and hold him; otherwise he might run off." Her no-nonsense tone brooked no argument.

They both slid off of Joe's back as the dark twin, sidewinding, sulfur-tainted smoke trails surrounded them. The viper-anox began reforming into their solid snake-man bodies as China began to shift.

Remington had seen a shifter make the change a time or two, but never without fear for his life, so it wasn't as though he'd paid all that much attention. She blurred, like liquid being poured across a watercolor painting, her form becoming indistinct and at the same time larger and darker. He didn't have time to stare. He cocked his revolver, his gaze locking on the two circling snake demons. The viperanox froze, baring their fangs; at the same time a powerful and vile stink like nothing he'd ever smelled before made Remington's eyes water and bile rise up the back of his throat. What the . . . ?

A deep, throaty growl from beside him reverberated straight through him from spine to navel and caused him to throw a quick glance in China's direction. He jerked back, shocked by the sheer size and malevolence of the hellhound beside him. Black as sin and the size of a buffalo, it was far larger than any of them. A string of saliva dripped down from one of the hound's bared canines, which were the length of a dagger in the grizzly bear-sized maw; the saliva caught the light and glistened before it dropped and was absorbed by the thirsty desert floor. Red eyes glowed like embers, and a ridge of dark hair along its back completed the hound's malevolent stance.

Joe whinnied in panic and thrashed his head, trying to pull back away from the triple threat. Only Remington's grip on the horse's reins kept it from rearing up. Miss McGee hadn't been kidding when she'd told him to hold onto the horse. Holy hell. He'd had no idea shifters could change into other Darkin forms. He'd only seen them change into animals or impersonate people they'd touched before.

The hellhound, ears pressed back tight against its massive skull, advanced on the viperanox. Its growl, a hot, stinking sulfur wind, rumbled low and deep, vibrating straight through Remington's chest. It lashed out, snapping at the snake demons, biting one in half, the black gore nearly indistinguishable against the blackness of the fur. The other viperanox dashed beneath the hound and sunk its fangs into the inner side of the hound's hindquarter, piercing its thigh. The hound howled—an ungodly roar that echoed against the mountains—and kicked back, flinging the viperanox twenty feet out into the desert.

China bounded over to the snake demon and squashed it beneath her massive paw, its innards oozing black into the sandy soil. She bit off the head for good measure and flung that in the opposite direction. Remy didn't wait for her to change back. He figured if she bit off the head she had good reason. The same that applied to rattlers might well apply to viperanox. He pulled a machete gauntlet Marley had made him from his saddlebag, slipped it on his hand and forearm, and stalked over to the top half of the snake demon she'd left behind.

It reared up, one arm clawing at him as it hissed. Damn thing was still dangerous. Remy lopped off the head, letting it roll to the ground. "Never did like snakes," he muttered.

"That so?"

He glanced over his shoulder. China was limping toward him, a trickle of scarlet dripping down her leg. "Damn it. I knew it! That thing got you." Considering she'd just been a hellhound only a few minutes before, he was frankly surprised her blood ran as red as his own. Most Darkin had black blood.

She shrugged, then winced, turning slightly so he could

see the rip and twin gash marks on the inner part of her thigh. "Looks worse than it is."

"You really aren't good at lying, you know that?"

"That's not what I hear from most people."

He gave her a sly smile. "I'm not most people."

China sat down on a rock, stretching her injured leg out in front of her, gripping the upper part of her thigh so tight her fingers turned white. She blew out a harsh, slow breath and was shaking.

"Those damn things have poison like regular vipers?" he asked, trying to keep the concern from his voice. She was in shock, her body already shutting down.

She nodded, then squeezed her eyes tight. Her skin had turned unnaturally pale and waxy, a sweaty sheen glistening on her face. His worry increased. She was not doing well, and they both knew it. The sun beat down on them from above, and Remington wished there were some way to find her shade. Heat made poison move more quickly through the bloodstream.

"What do we have to do?"

"Suck out the poison," she said between gritted teeth.

Not what he had planned. Not even close. Somehow his well-laid plans of in, out, nice and quick, had all been effectively blown to hell. His boots scraped in the dirt as he crouched close by her, gently nudging her knee aside with the back of his hand so he could get a better look at the wound. Her breath came in shallow pants laced with agony.

He pulled back the torn pale brown leather. Twin jagged slices in her skin ran red with blood. The open gashes were far enough apart he couldn't do both together. The one closer to her heart was also farther up the inside of her thigh.

He swallowed hard. The sweet, musky, distinctly feminine scent of her invaded his airspace. Definitely not what he had in mind in this position with a female. He glanced up at her. "This'll just take a minute. Grip on my shoulder if you need to."

She let out a harsh bark of laughter, her skin now greasy with pain and her pupils slightly dilated. "I've heard that bef—"

Her words were cut off by a grunt, as he placed his mouth on the creamy silk of her thigh and sucked hard. She sunk her fingers deep into his shoulder, bruising him. The thick, hot, metallic blood laced with something horribly bitter filled his mouth. Remy spat it out and quickly took another draw on the wound, then swiftly switched to the other puncture.

Her body shook, but from pain, not from pleasure. Remy had the dark thought cross his mind that he was sure Colt would be far more welcome than he would in a similar situation. He sucked on the wound until there was no more bitter tang. Satisfied he had removed everything he could, he wiped her blood from his cheeks and chin onto the sleeve of his suit. At least the suit was black, so the blood didn't show. "I think we got it all."

Remington rucked the bottom edge of her shirt out of her pants and tore it away, leaving her midriff bare.

"Hey! What do you—"

He put a finger to her mouth and found it softer to the touch than he'd anticipated. "I'm going to use it as a makeshift tourniquet and bandages for your thigh." He quickly tore and twisted the fabric, putting it into place and tying it tight. "That should hold you until we can get to a town." They were between Bisbee and Tombstone. Not a hell of a lot lay in between.

China's loose blond hair blew in the warm early evening breeze, sticking honeyed strands of it across her very enticing lips. She lightly brushed her fingers through his hair, starting at his temple, causing an electric jolt through his system. "Thank you, Mr. Jackson."

"Call me Remington. Since there's more than one of us, I'd hate to think you were talking to me when you meant Colt."

The soft warmth in her eyes slowly evaporated, turning cold. There were purple smudges of color beneath her eyes that hadn't been there earlier. The poison, even though gone now, had taken its toll, and she was weak.

"Do you think you can still ride?"

"Darkin heal quicker than you think. I'll be fine, as long as the poison is out."

Remington nodded. There were plenty of things he could have said, but he held his tongue. The moment had been awkward enough for both of them. There was no reason to make more of it than it was. And yet, something still nagged at him—a small, persistent voice in the back of his head that itched and annoyed like a mosquito bite. Why had she fought against the other Darkin? And what exactly had she and Colt done when they'd been together?

He clenched his jaw until his teeth ached, determined not to say something he had no business saying.

Breathe in. Breathe out. Focus.

It helped in heated arguments in court to be cool, calm, and collected. It helped as a Hunter to maintain a level head and disciplined control, even in the heat of battle with things that could scare the living daylights out of ordinary folk. Remington drew on every ounce of that ability now to re-focus himself and his thoughts back to the matter at hand.

"Let me help you up."

China slipped her hands into both of his and unsteadily stood, putting her weight on her good leg. Her injured leg still burned, a slow fire crawling through her veins. She sincerely hoped Remington had gotten out all the poison. The last thing she needed was to become paralyzed from the stuff and die as her lungs ceased to function. Viperanox were nasty creatures.

"Those weren't no ordinary bullets you shot at them viperanox. I've never seen one disintegrate like that from a gunshot. What do you have in them things?"

"Powdered bone, ash, gunpowder, bit of silver in the casing. The usual."

She quirked one brow. It didn't sound like anything she'd heard of before and certainly nothing you could buy off the shelf. "That's usual?"

"It is if you're a Hunter who works with Marley Turlock. He wouldn't have us load with anything else."

That only confirmed what she'd known all along. First, Hunters were dangerous, and second, they couldn't be trusted. Just as Rathe had said.

She was certain she'd hear about tearing apart those creatures later. Most Darkin didn't go after one another. It was an unwritten rule among the children of the night. But there were exceptions. Apparently she'd become one, now that she was clearly no longer on Rathe's good side—if he actually had one. He wouldn't tolerate her working with the Chosen. Message received loud and clear. But that didn't mean she planned to listen, especially since she now had the opportunity to get her hands on the *entire* Book of Legend, not just a single piece of it. Rathe would have to take her back into his fold then.

"Why did they come after you?"

"They were after Diego's map," she hedged. She wasn't about to trust another Jackson simply because he'd pulled her from jail and sucked poison from her thigh. Now that she wasn't in such blinding pain, the image of his dark head against her thigh made her insides squirm a bit. She didn't want to imagine what other skills Remington Jackson had with regard to that part of a body.

He peered at her, his clear blue eyes fixed on her in an unflinching stare. "No. The map was just an excuse. They wanted you. Why?"

China shrugged. "How should I know? Just because we're all Darkin doesn't mean we get along like some big happy family."

Remington's face hardened, the strong line of his jaw ticking as the muscles worked. "There's something you're not telling me. And as long as you're working with me, you need to be completely up front."

That was one way Remington and Colt were alike. They both could sound so damn imperious at times—givin' orders like they owned the whole damn world. "I'm not working for anyone but myself."

"You still have a tendre for my brother, don't you?"

Her eyes narrowed. The fact that he'd been able to tell that Colt had crossed her mind bothered her. "I don't have a single tender part of me, not for your brother, and certainly not for any other man."

Remington closed his eyes and pinched the bridge of his nose for a moment, before locking gazes with her. "You can't paint all us Jackson brothers by the same brush."

"Why not? You're all Hunters, ain't you?"

His strong hands spanned her waist and lifted her up into the saddle. She flinched as her sore thigh settled against the hard leather. He climbed up behind her, his chest broad and firm against her back. She was so damn worn out, both from the massive shift and the fight, that she wanted to sink back into him. But she didn't let herself. Not now. Not when she was vulnerable.

"That's like my saying all Darkin are the same—and I know enough about your kind to know that's patently false." His words were hot against her ear.

China steeled her resolve, seeking some way to put a wedge

in between them, regardless of their sitting body against body in the saddle. She latched onto the first thing that came to mind she could needle him about. "You like those big fancy words, don't you?"

The planes of muscle pressed against her flexed slightly, growing more tense. "Words are my weapon of choice."

Good. She'd found a soft spot that irritated him. She deliberately prodded it again. "Don't you ever get tired of using dollar words when penny words could do?"

"No."

"Well, you're right about one thing then. That's where you and Colt differ. He always speaks his mind, plain and loud."

"I thought I was being extremely direct."

"You talk like I'm a judge. Your fancy words don't impress me, Jackson, any more than those highfalutin' britches and coat you got on."

His voice dropped to a lethal whisper that brushed through her hair, sending an unwarranted shiver down her spine. "And what exactly does impress a woman like you?"

"Honesty."

"Ah. You see all this as not being honest. But ask yourself this—what if it is completely honest? What if what you see is precisely what you get?"

China snorted. "Not a chance. You hide behind those fancy clothes of yours because you think it'll make the ugly truth harder to see. But deep down, you know and I know you're nothing but a murderer—for your principles, but a killer nonetheless."

From the cool wash of air against her back she could tell he'd pulled away from her.

"And what are you?" he asked without a fleck of emotion in his voice.

Good. Wedge in place. Mission accomplished. Jackson

brothers were far easier to deal with and more predictable when they were prickly.

"That's easy. I'm a thief."

A harsh grate of laughter rasped from him. "And that's honorable?"

"I never said I was honorable—just honest. I know what and who I am, and I don't care what anyone else thinks about it."

But that wasn't totally true. China would admit to being a thief. She could admit to being a liar. But there was one thing she hadn't openly admitted to Remington or another soul; nor would she.

A dreaded secret she both held close and despised: she was Rathe's estranged daughter.

Not that it mattered. She was going to save her own skin and finally prove to the sadistic archdemon who'd infected her mother and marked her early as his spawn that she was worthy to be a princess of the Darkin realm—worthy of his attention. All she needed was a little more time and the completed Book of Legend.

Remington Jackson didn't need to know *any* of that. Her family issues weren't his or anyone else's business.

They rode on in silence, which was just fine by her. Between the viperanox venom and the thoughts swirling about in her head, she felt sick. The sun was sinking by slow degrees to the west, and the cacti began to throw shadows across the landscape.

"I'm not Colt you know."

The statement both surprised her and stung like a barb.

"I know. But you're still a Jackson and a Hunter."

"True." A brief stretch of silence followed, but China could almost hear the gears grinding inside Remington's head. "How'd you and my brother ever begin working together in the first place?"

China winced. She didn't like to think on it too much.

She'd actually been sent to find Colt and kill him, but she'd ended up being seduced by his charms instead. That had been the first thing that had put her on her dear daddy's not-so-well-behaved list. She wasn't about to make the same mistake twice. "We both happened to be in the same place at the same time to steal the same thing." It was the truth—from a certain point of view.

"And?"

She twisted in the saddle and gazed up at him. "You talk a lot for a man, you know that?"

He gave her the famous Jackson smile, that lazy, sensual grin that reached in and stole one's ability to breathe or think straight. The same one Colt had that could lay a woman flat on her back in a heartbeat. If they'd had any sense at all, they could have patented it and made a fortune. "There's a simple reason for that."

"There is?"

His blue eyes sparkled with mischief. "Attorney, re-member?"

China turned away from him. Outfoxing Remington was going to be harder than outwitting Colt. Overhead a hawk cried out, a keening wail, as it circled, looking for prey far below. The blue of the sky it wheeled in was so like the clear, breathtaking color of the Jackson brothers' eyes.

"So who'd the blue eyes come from in the family?"

"That would be my ma. We got her smile as well."

China thought on that for a moment. "If Colt's the charming one in the family, and Winn's the law and order type, what does that make you?"

"I'm the brains in the family."

"Uh huh."

"You doubt the veracity of my claim?"

"I find if a man has to brag about it, chances are there's less to what he's selling than advertised."

He leaned in close, the contact of his body suddenly hot against the length of her back, causing a snap of awareness to crackle along her nerve endings. "Is that a challenge, Miss McGee?" Intrigue laced his tone.

China stiffened. Damn it. So much for the wedge between them. She'd gotten so caught up in their verbal sparring she'd let down her guard for just an instant. "Why?" she shot back, feeling prickly and unable to stop herself.

"There's nothing I love more than a challenge."

Double damn.

She might want that Book, she might need that Book, but getting it meant working with a Hunter. This Hunter. And she suddenly lost a little faith in her abilities to escape from the association unscathed.

Chapter 3

True to her word, China was tougher than she looked. She lasted through the rugged red canyons dotted with green scrub along the valley floor and the endless empty miles between Bisbee and Tombstone without a single complaint. The setting sun was no more than a line of red and gold just over the horizon, the cacti surrounding them reduced to silhouettes. A light evening breeze stirred her loose hair, sending silky tendrils of it spinning about his cheek and neck in a most distracting fashion.

How much pain was she in? Fool woman was too stubborn to complain. Her body was still ramrod straight and unbending despite the heat and the dusty miles traveled. He'd never seen anything like it in a human. But then she wasn't human, and he'd best remember that, he chided himself.

"Are you absolutely sure you don't want to stop?"

China sighed. "Can you please stop asking me that? These small town doctors wouldn't know how to patch up a shifter anyway."

Feeling her feminine form against him, he couldn't figure out how shifters were really all that different. "Aren't you basically human?"

She snorted. "No Darkin is basically human, just like no angel is basically spirit and no human is basically an animal."

He frowned at that. He'd had it drilled into him by his pa that Darkin were creatures of the night, an unholy amalgam of otherworldly powers and in many cases human flesh, creatures that ought to be unilaterally destroyed. But the rational and questioning part of his mind couldn't reconcile that. Nothing was completely black or white. Their world was infinite shades of gray, and it was only logical that the Darkin realm would be as well.

"You don't bleed black like the other Darkin—" He stopped short of saying I've killed.

"Darkin that bleed black are corrupted. They've taken life or souls to feed themselves rather than just in defense."

"Huh. Never was taught that."

"There's a lot more to Darkin than you think you know, Jackson."

Well. She had that right. But that didn't mean he couldn't learn.

By the time they were nearly to Tombstone, dark had descended on the desert. It was a heavy, warm darkness, deep like velvet sprinkled with sharp, diamond points of white light. Heat still seeped from the rocks, but the air had cooled, carrying with it the scent of creosote and night-blooming cactus flowers. As the gibbous waning moon rose, it washed the valley in pearlescent light, making the new lumber buildings in Tombstone seem to glow from a distance like some magical city. Every now and then the swift dark forms of bats would dart past the glowing moon, their tiny squeaks and flapping wings a contrast to the sounds of humanity laughing and carousing growing louder as they neared Tombstone.

"In the morning, if you are able, we'll decipher Diego's map."

Joe's plodding steps went a little faster as they approached town and the prospect of feed and water. Remington tried to slow him down to keep from jostling China.

"Where will we be spending the night?"

Remington didn't see the need to keep a house in town. He rented rooms at the Occidental Hotel, just as he did his offices across Allen Street from the hotel. It meant less to cope with if he were gone for a time hunting. He could pay his rent in advance, and others took care of the premises. But he could hardly take China to his rooms without there being some notice and talk of it, and he had his reputation as an upstanding attorney to maintain.

"I'll get you a room at the Occidental."

There was a discordant charm to Tombstone. It was a city in the midst of wilderness. As the dark of the desert gave way to civilization, everything changed. Gas lamps lent a flickering light to the adobe and wooden buildings lining the heart of Tombstone, but their light didn't reach beneath the wooden awnings that protruded here and there over the boardwalks. With eight saloons in just his block of Allen Street alone, the din of tinkling piano, drunken laughter, and off-tune singing seemed overwhelming compared to the soft silence of the desert at night. But China was not some sheltered little society miss, and her wide gray eyes drank it all in. Secretly Remington was pleased she found it inviting.

"You've got quite a town here, Jackson."

"It's Remington, and I should think you'd seen enough of the world not to be so impressed."

She gave a huff of laughter. "Oh, I seen plenty of towns, but not this size."

He pulled Joe into the Pioneer Livery across the street from the offices of Bartel & Jackson, Attorneys at Law. There was no actual Bartel, but Remington had thought having a partner, even in name only, gave it a bit more influence. The familiar odors of horse and hay, leather and saddle soap were prominent in the livery yard as they dismounted and put Joe in his assigned stall and removed his tack. He told the stable hand on duty to rub his horse down and feed him. Remington tried to stretch the kinks out of his shoulders and neck. "You're certain you don't wish to see a doctor?"

"I'm as right as rain, Jackson." She did a soft-shoe shuffle there on the wooden sidewalk. "See?"

He chuckled. She was every bit as flamboyant as his brother. No wonder the two got on like eggs and bacon. The thought of food made his stomach grumble. "Let's go get you a room and something to eat."

"I haven't got any money—"

He cut her off with a raised hand as they walked side by side out of the livery yard. "No need. I am your attorney after all. You can always tack it on to my fee."

The scent of seared steak and fresh bread from a nearby restaurant filled the air during the short walk, not even half a block west, to the Occidental Hotel. It might have been a trick of the shadows, but he thought he saw China's nose twitch.

She glared at him. The gaslight caught her eyes in such a way that they glowed green, like a cat's. "You really going to charge me for being my attorney? If you should charge anyone, it should be that fool brother of yours who sent you."

He chuckled. "You can always pay it off by going with me on the trek to wherever Diego's map leads."

She grumbled under her breath. "I planned to find what's at the end of Diego's map with or without you, anyway. I'm not working for a Hunter." She placed her hands on her hips, making the fringe on her jacket sway.

"You don't have to work for me, just with me," he murmured. He grasped one of her hands, even though she was reluctant to let him. "Now let's get something to eat."

A hearty steak dinner and a good night's sleep in a clean bed hadn't improved matters much by the next morning. It was early. Too early, but the quick loud rap at her hotel door wouldn't stop. *Damn.* Remington was serious about her helping him locate whatever was at the end of Diego's map. And he was an early riser. *Double damn.*

She cracked open the door and peered outside, getting the view of one piercing blue eye, a long nose with just a hint of a bump, a bit of stubborn lip, and a devil's divot in a freshly shaved masculine chin.

"Ready?"

His tone was far too cheerful. Didn't he know she was a child of the night? Night being the operative word here. Mornings were not her best time, and she preferred to nap now and again throughout the day.

"Do I have a choice?" she grumbled. She walked away from the door, letting him swing it open as she yawned and stretched the length of her body. He was dressed this morning in a well-tailored gentleman's coat over a crisp white shirt with a red paisley vest. A small black ribbon was tied at his neck and matched his fancy black pinstriped pants. Hell, even his boots were shined. How in the world did someone look that fashionable this goddamn early in the morning? It simply wasn't natural.

He quirked one dark brow at her. "Did you sleep in your clothes?"

She shrugged, plying her fingers through her tousled mane to work out the knots. "It's not like I got to go home and pack a traveling trunk when they hauled me off to prison."

He gave a quick nod. "What size are you?"

China crossed her arms. "No. No man is picking out my clothes. I can do that my own damn self."

He shrugged, but his eyes lingered a second too long on the buckskin that encased her legs like a second, comfortable skin. "Fine. But first thing after we get some breakfast and go to the office, we're getting you some other clothes."

China didn't bother to argue. She needed clothes. Her shirt

and pants were torn and dirty. He could simply add it to her tab. They ate a quick breakfast. His included eggs and toast. Hers included as much protein as she could pack on her plate, eggs, sausage, sausage gravy and biscuits, and bacon.

Remington paid their bill, and they headed out into the bright sunlight across the dirt street to his office. It looked completely benign from the outside. The two-story adobe structure was covered over with boards on the front and painted brown with white trim around the four-pane windows on either side of the fancy-cut double glass doors. Overhead a sign swung from the wooden awning. Painted in a flourish of black and gold lettering were the words BARTEL & JACKSON, ATTORNEYS AT LAW.

"Home sweet home," Jackson murmured as he opened the door for her.

China glanced down the street and then at the door. "Don't you ever worry about this fancy glass getting broken in a street fight?"

Jackson shrugged. "Like most things, it's replaceable. Offices are on the second floor."

China clenched her hands and stalked up the staircase. Remington Jackson had better not think for one second that he could replace her. Without her he couldn't get to the Book. And since she'd been the one to alert Colt to the potential marker of a piece of the Book of Legend, she had a claim to it. Which she'd remind Remington every time it became necessary.

The office door marked BARTEL & JACKSON swung open. Lined with oak filing cabinets and bookcases crammed with volume after volume of leather-bound books, Jackson's office smelled of lemon and beeswax wood polish, leather, paper, and the faint, sour chalky scent of india ink. In short, the very kind of place she preferred to avoid. It had a large oak reception desk, with another door behind it that led farther back into what she assumed was Jackson's private domain.

"You got a secretary?"

"No. It's mainly to add an additional veneer of legitimacy to the practice, as is the name Bartel." Jackson bent, retrieving a folded telegram page that had been slipped under his door. He flipped it open, frowned, then crumpled it in his hand.

The fact that Jackson tricked even his own clients into believing something that wasn't wholly true about him didn't sit well with her. If anything it confirmed that Remington was far more devious than his brother. Far more like her father than she'd anticipated. Smart, sophisticated, and deadly.

"Didn't like the news?" she prodded.

"It was from Colt. Nothing important." He dropped the crumpled yellow paper in the trash near the reception desk and went through the direct door to his office where he sat down behind his desk. China leaned up against the doorframe.

"What do you want me to do?"

He didn't look at her when he responded, just kept his head down, sorting through the papers on his desk. "Just wait a bit. I've got a few things to arrange before I can leave to go tracking down whatever's at the end of Diego's map."

She sighed. She hated sitting around and waiting. Indoors no less. Why couldn't he just have come to get her when he was ready to leave and given her a few more hours of recuperative sleep? She glanced out the big glass windows to the street below, watching the people, horses, and carriages go about their business before the air got stiflingly hot.

The scratching of an ink pen against paper was all the noise that came from Jackson's office. Casting a quick glance through the open door, she crept over to the trash bin and fished out the crumpled telegram.

Jackson hadn't lied. It had been from Colt.

WATCH YOUR BACK STOP DON'T TRUST MCGEE
STOP GET A DIFFERENT THIEF STOP SUSPECT SHE
DOUBLE-CROSSED ME STOP CONTACT MARLEY
WHEN YOU RETURN FROM BISBEE STOP COLT

A little pang ached in the middle of her chest. China flung the telegram back into the trash and crossed her arms over her chest. Somehow knowing Colt didn't care if she got out of jail made things worse.

Remington—she refused to think of him as Jackson now that Colt had angered her—sat in his office in silence, scratching away at something for another hour. Which gave her time to try all the drawers on the desk and use her special tools to pick open the ones that were locked. She only found a fountain pen and a few gold dollar coins worth taking. A good thief always looked for items that could be useful.

Rather than grow antsy, she decided to try and relax. She propped up her dirty cowboy boots on the reception desk and watched a fat fly buzz in lazy circles along the glass of the window. It was still shady and cool in the adobe office building, but come afternoon, the sun would shift enough to bring in the heat.

Remington listened intently the entire time he worked. He knew that she'd peeked at the telegram from Colt. He knew she'd rummaged around in his desk drawers. God only knew what she'd taken, but he didn't expect any less. As long as she was occupied it gave him time to analyze the page she'd taken from Diego's safety-deposit box.

While crude, it was the gross approximation of a map. An unlabeled map, but certainly one he could follow if he could decode the string of seemingly random numbers listed on the back right hand corner of the page. It had to be a code of some type. Hunters used coding for anything that could be potentially intercepted. And something that could lead to a hidden piece of the Book of Legend was far too valuable to leave uncoded.

He worked through the string of numbers again, adding, then subtracting, multiplying and dividing them to see if he could come up with something that made sense. He tried to see if they matched up with letters in the alphabet as some kind of alpha-numeric code.

Remington scraped away with his Waterman fountain pen at the paper he'd set beside Deigo's page. Sometimes doodling gave his brain a chance to think. He drew a globe and began to criss cross it with lines. His eyes drifted back to the numbers. Perhaps the numbers weren't related to the alphabet at all. Perhaps they weren't coded as he thought. But it couldn't be as simple as longitude and latitude, could it?

Then again, Diego obviously never intended anyone to look this page over and realize first, that it was a map with no names, and second, that the locations on the map indicated here and there by dark blobs of ink, were directly related to the numbers scribbled in the corner. If the numbers were what it thought, the hodgepodge of lines and dots looked like a trail from Tombstone down into Mexico and then further down the coast nearly to South America.

His thoughts were interrupted as downstairs the door to the building opened and closed and footsteps came clomping up the stairs.

She'd just begun to drift off, letting herself dream of exactly what she might buy for clothes once Remington was done with his arrangements, when the sound of approaching footsteps on the floorboards outside the office snapped her eyes wide open.

The knob on the office door turned, and the door creaked inward. In walked Colt.

Her heart gave an extra beat as his gaze slid quickly over the front of her faded blue button-down chambray shirt that stretched tight across her chest. Colt Jackson was the kind of man who could have a woman in a lather just with one look.

Behind him a fiery redhead stared China down, her emerald eyes narrow and her lips pinched tight. As close as she stood to Colt, she seemed mighty possessive. A single sniff pegged her as Darkin. Succubus if China had to guess based on the girl's assets. Well, well, perhaps Colt wasn't as opposed to Darkin lovers as he'd led her to believe.

China gave a slow, heated gaze in Colt's direction before she spoke just to tick the prissy woman standing next to him off. "Hello, Colt. It's been a while." Her drawl was lazy with a heavy dose of sensuality.

Colt grunted with a curt nod, but his eyes instantly darted to the open doorway behind the desk. She heard the sliding scrape of shoe leather against the floorboards in Remington's office a second before he appeared in the doorway behind her.

Perhaps Remington had been right about being nothing like his brothers. They certainly looked nothing alike now, except for the dark sweep of hair, and those piercing blue eyes. Both were extremely attractive, but Colt was more ragged and rough, his overgrown, shaggy hair curling against his collar and his clothes dusty, while Remington looked every inch the well-heeled gentleman. With his shorter hair-cut and spotless, tailored clothing, he looked wealthy, power-ful, and alluring to China.

"Did I just hear you say—" Remington's blue eyes widened along with his mouth into a giant, heart-stopping smile. "Hey, little brother!" He rushed forward and swung his arms around Colt in a bear hug that knocked a huff out of Colt. "Good to see you. Especially all in one piece."

The fancy miss next to Colt grinned, and China tamped down the prickle skating over her skin.

Colt pulled out of his brother's arms. "Good to see you too, Remy." His glance connected with hers, and that familiar heat rose to the surface. "See you've got China working with you."

Well damn, at least he'd noticed her, she thought smugly. China stared at him, willing him to remember what her body against his felt like, how she'd bested him, leaving him tied buck naked to the bed in Silver City. Her blatant attention made the woman next to him antsy. Good. The no good sonofabitch deserved it after abandoning her at the bank to climb her way out of the rubble. But the presence of two Jackson brothers in one room was almost more than any normal female could take. Good thing she was far more than a mere mortal—or an average Darkin.

But perhaps this could be entertaining. A cat-like smile curled her lips as she glanced from one muscular Jackson to the other. For a second China wondered just how closely the two brothers resembled one another without their clothes on.

"Yep. Got her out of the Bisbee camp jail, no thanks to you." Remington nudged his brother with his elbow, but his face went soft and his blue eyes out of focus as his attention settled on the redhead. Every hair on China's head rose up sharp and stiff as the air filled with the scent of male attraction. "And who is this charming young lady?"

China didn't give a damn who the bitch was. She didn't like her. Just a whiff of her cheap perfume and the look of her confirmed her suspicions that she was a succubus.

"Certainly you'll introduce us," Remington persisted.

Colt glanced back over his shoulder, his brows knitting together slightly and his jaw flexing as if he'd rather do anything but that. Damn, China knew that look. Colt *did* like her. Far more than he wanted to. "This is Miss Lilly Arliss. Lilly, my brother Remington and Miss China McGee. Lilly's helping me find Pa's part of the Book."

She bet. Based on the subtle way Miss Arliss touched Colt practically every damn chance she got, they'd shared more than just a trip from Bodie together.

An inexplicable ache started in her chest as Remington pushed past his little brother, purposely knocking him aside with his shoulder. He bowed slightly from the waist, never taking his eyes off the unnaturally green eyes of Miss Arliss, and lightly grasped her hand in his smooth one, brushing a warm kiss over her knuckles. "A *pleasure* to meet you, Miss Arliss."

China bristled. He'd never done that with her, and he continued to hold Miss Arliss's hand a moment longer than propriety demanded.

Certainly the succubus was absolutely stunning. Tempting men was her job. That didn't mean China had to like it. Or her. Tension crackled between the Jackson brothers.

Miss Arliss blushed at Remington's attentions, and Colt quickly wedged himself between them, breaking his brother's hold on her hand. The jealous coil of tension in China's gut twisted a little tighter. Colt clearly had enough feelings for the little Darkin to go head-to-head with his brother over her. China's dislike of her increased another notch.

"I didn't haul us all over God's creation to watch you kissing hands and sweet-talking ladies. Pa didn't leave pages. He left a *riddle*. The kind of thing you're so good at. Need you to solve it so I can go find what we're looking for and not waste any more time."

China resisted the urge to snort. That was rich coming from Colt who flirted with ladies as naturally as he breathed.

Remington turned to his brother. "You didn't find his piece of the Book?"

Colt shook his head slowly, his jaw tight. "Nothing in the damn box but a scrap of paper with a riddle written in Navaho."

"You don't speak Navaho, let alone read it. For that matter, neither do I."

"Yeah. But Balmora apparently does."

"Balmora? You mean Marley's analytical decoder machine? You saw it?"

Colt's lips twitched. "I think he's going to have a hard time letting her go to the queen, when the time comes."

"Her?"

"I'll explain later. Right now, can you make heads or tails of what Pa meant?"

Chapter 4

Colt fished a single piece of paper from his pocket and unfolded it, handing it to Remington. In the light pouring through the office windows Remington scanned the page, his lips moving as he read to himself. He had nice lips, China thought, very close to the same sculpted shape as Colt's. But did they kiss the same way? She bet they didn't. Remington was more polished, and far more reserved, than his brother.

Remington brushed his fingers back through his short dark hair. "Well, the first part is pretty straightforward. We're going to need the whole damn Book of Legend to close the Gates of Nyx."

"I figured out that part myself, thanks," Colt said sarcastically. Even as he leaned close to his brother looking at the cryptic message, China kept Miss Arliss in the corner of her vision. The woman stepped lightly around the office, running her fingers over the fine leather volumes in Remington's library, and cast a cautious glance in China's direction. The air in the room eddied with agitation between them. One Darkin in cahoots with Hunters was more than enough for China's taste. Two was overkill.

She and Colt shared the same wild, predatory nature, and she could hardly see this fancy little bit of skirt having the wherewithal to be able to keep up with bred-to-the-bone Hunters. She looked too damn dainty for that. China flipped her long hair over her shoulders and leaned forward, her elbows on her knees, feet braced wide apart like a man's.

Her gaze darted from Remington to Colt and back again, assessing, weighing them against one another. Colt was fire; Remington, ice, but they both had the potential to burn away her common sense. What was she doing attracted to another Hunter anyway? She should have learned her lesson the first go-around. Hunters and Darkin didn't mix, at least not romantically. Physically . . . well, that could be a whole other matter.

The two brothers, their dark heads close together, kept picking at the message. "At the height of the mountains, where legends are born and reborn from the ashes . . . Phoenix birds are reborn out of ashes," Remington murmured. "Legends— another word for myths and superstitions. It could be the Superstition Mountains outside of Phoenix."

"What about the eye part?" Colt pressed his fisted hand to the top of the desk.

"Alone it doesn't make any sense, but see where it says sew and tapestry in the rest of the line?"

"Yeah?"

"Ever heard the story going around of the Lost Dutchman's Gold Mine?"

Colt snorted. "Who hasn't?"

China made her move. She slid, swiftly and silently, between the brothers, standing as close to Colt as she could get, but resting her hand on Remington's surprisingly muscular shoulder. Let the little succubus suck on that, she thought.

The heated glare Miss Arliss threw back at her could have burned the fringe off her buckskin jacket, but instead it sent sparks of pride shimmering along her veins. China liked to win, no matter the cost. She glanced up long enough to lock stares with the succubus and give her a self-assured smirk along with the silent message: *Mine. Back off.*

The Jackson brothers were oblivious—absorbed totally by their riddle. "Well, legend has it Jacob Waltz used the rocks called the Eye of the Needle and Weaver's Needle as landmarks to the mine," Remington said.

"So you think Pa was in cahoots with Waltz?"

Remington turned away to face the windows, his shoulder slipping from beneath her touch. She closed her hand reflexively against the loss. He looked out at the dusty street and shrugged his broad shoulders. His expensive suit hid far more than it revealed, China thought. He was every inch as handsome as Colt, and that was saying something, since she'd been certain she'd never meet another man who could wipe Colt out of her mind as her greatest misadventure.

"Maybe. Maybe not," Remington said. "Point is that if you were looking at those mountains or Phoenix, I'd think the Eye of the Needle is the place to start."

"You're leaving something out," the succubus interrupted. Miss Arliss deliberately strode up to Colt, placing her hand on the broad expanse of his back, and leaned between the brothers, pointing to the paper they were looking at.

Nearly in unison both brothers turned their identical blue eyes to her brazen show of bosom. She was practically falling out of her corset, China thought bitterly. They were probably magically enhanced breasts. That would just figure for a succubus. Colt's eyes widened a bit, and he swallowed hard, while Remington colored slightly. Colt cleared his throat and gave Lilly a heated look that could have melted a solid gold bar. China silently fumed.

"You missed the last two words." Miss Arliss leaned her shoulder into Remington and threw a "take that" glance at China. China resisted the prickles of heat washing over her skin. She'd mastered her power to shift long ago and refused to give in to the automatic response her body had to her intense annoyance with the other Darkin. Cool. Collected. China refused to give in to the pulsing heat beneath her skin. She spun away on her boot heel to look outside and calm herself.

"Chosen destiny," Colt grumbled, crossing his arms. "So what? Means we get to choose how it all turns out by our actions."

The sexy redhead tilted her chin up. "No. 'Chosen' is capitalized."

"Yeah, so?"

Miss Arliss's hand curved around Colt's bicep and Remington's muscle ticked in response. Even if she was working with his brother, he'd have to have been deaf, blind, and dead not to be attracted to her, even if she was clearly Darkin. And from the sexually-charged aura rolling off of her thick as fog off of water, he could tell she wasn't just any Darkin, but a succubus.

His little brother was in some deep water with her, and Remington wasn't certain Colt could swim. It was hardly fair that the ladies were so attracted to the outlaw image Colt liked to flaunt. They were drawn to it, bees to honey. Even China, despite her earlier protests, still perked up when Colt had walked in. That irritated him.

"Do you really think your father would have done that if he didn't mean you three boys?" Miss Arliss said. "You are the Chosen."

Colt pulled away from her touch and rubbed the back of his neck, frowning with discomfort. "Ah, come on, Lilly, don't start up with that again."

Remington chuckled. Oh yeah. He had it bad for the succubus already. Poor bastard. "I hate to say she has a point, but perhaps she does."

Her unearthly green eyes sparkled. "It's your destiny to reunite the Book of Legend, and all of the Darkin know it."

Colt cast a serious glance his way. "I've got something you need to see."

"More important than the clue?"

"Could be."

"Well, let's have it, then."

Colt pulled a worn leather journal from his pack and handed it to Remington. The leather was smooth from use beneath his fingers. Familiar somehow. He'd seen this before when he'd been a small child, but he couldn't place when or where. "What's this?"

"Ma's diary. Had it with me all this time. There's clues in there, like the one I found about Diego's map. Things that Pa should have told all of us, but didn't. Soon as you can, read it."

Behind the three of them came the clearing of a throat and the tap of a boot against the wooden floorboards. "Excuse me, hate to break up this little tea party, but didn't you say you'd need to reunite the whole Book of Legend?"

They turned, and all looked at China. "That clue you got out of the safety-deposit box. That's to a map that leads to one of the pieces, isn't it?" she said as she shifted her piercing pale gray eyes between him and Colt.

The brothers glanced at each other. Pa's number-one rule had been "never trust a Darkin," and they both knew it. Neither of them were absolutely certain Diego's map led directly to the hidden piece of the Book. They turned, united, back to China. Colt shrugged. "Could be."

China threw up her hands and growled, her smooth pink lips tightening over her even white teeth. "Great. A bunch of idiot Hunters out to save the world and it 'could' be the key to the next piece. You know, it's a wonder that we didn't both get caught in that last heist."

Remington stepped over, unable to resist the odd pull China had on him, and leaned in closer to her. "I did tell you that I tend to be the brains of the family."

China huffed, brushed the fall of her blond hair off her

shoulder in irritation, and turned away from them. Remington gave a lingering look at the tight spread of leather over the shifter's derrière, then noticed his brother did the same. For a second he wondered if Colt had sent his message to stay away from China only because he didn't want Remington too close to his past lover. He also wondered if Miss Arliss were already his brother's next flame and realized Colt's *old* flame was in the room tracking every move they made with cat-like precision.

"Let me know when you actually want to do something about finding what you're after, instead of just cackling about it like a bunch of old hens," China threw back at them as she stared out the window. While she stood motionless, her anger pulsated, prowling about the room like a living thing.

"I think your analysis of the riddle was wonderful," Miss Arliss said as she grasped his arm.

The skim of her touch over his arm ignited the tension China seemed to cause in him. He turned back to Colt's Darkin and deliberately gave her a sinful grin that made even a succubus take a second long look. "Thank you. Nice to know someone appreciates my efforts."

"Oh, I'm glad you can make sense of it," Colt said gruffly. "But that doesn't change the fact that we still don't have a single piece of the damn Book in our hands."

"True." Remington grasped and held the lapels of his long coat as if he were in court debating. "But we do have a good lead to the second piece. The clue in Diego's safety-deposit box starts just outside Tombstone."

Colt took off his Stetson and smoothed the edges of the firm felt brim between his fingers, then locked his familiar blue gaze with Remington's. "We're running out of time, Remy. I can't go to Phoenix looking for Pa's part of the Book and go on a hunt for the piece Diego heard about at the same time."

Remington glanced over at China. He'd only gone to Bisbee as a favor to help Colt in his quest to reunite the Book of Legend, but it seemed his little brother wasn't out of the woods just yet. He needed further help. "What if China and I were to go after it?"

China shifted, cocking her head like a cat, listening to them. But she remained steadfastly gazing out the window. He damn well knew nothing too interesting was happening on Allen Street. She was as stubborn as his brother.

Colt's gaze softened. "You'd do that?"

"I'd be willing to sacrifice a few weeks in the office for you if it meant saving the world," he answered, his words laced with sarcasm. They both knew going after the pieces of the Book required both a Hunter and a Darkin to access the hiding places.

Colt's mouth twitched, and he gave him a brotherly slap to the shoulder. "That's mighty big of you, Rem."

"Nobody asked me if I'd be willing," China interrupted as she turned away from the window and strode slowly up between them and directly across from Miss Arliss.

The succubus glared at the shifter. Remington wasn't sure he'd ever seen two female Darkin go after one another before, but the two might as well have had pistols out and cocked the way they glared at one another.

"Do you have any idea of what will happen if you *don't?*" Miss Arliss said.

China glared back. "The end of annoying Hunters?"

"How about the start of a new world order, featuring a sadistic archdemon lord at the helm?" she volleyed back.

China stood up a little straighter and glared at Remington, as if somehow her misunderstanding of Miss Arliss was all his fault. How? What the hell had he done?

"Well, why didn't you say so?" China groused.

Remington put up his hands in defense. "I just found out, like the rest of them." He jerked his head toward the window. "What the hell is that nois—?"

A mixture of screams, the whinny and galloping of spooked horses, and the thunderous crash of wood splintering came from the street outside the office. A shadow darkened the interior of the office. As one they ran to the windows.

Miss Arliss's mouth dropped open. "What *is* that . . . thing?" she demanded.

He glanced upward at a most unusual sight. The silver fabric skin of a giant dirigible, at least two hundred feet long and fifty feet across, glittered in the afternoon light as it descended over Allen Street, scattering the citizens and animals below. "It's a dirigible, a class A, I'd guess from the size of it," Remington answered over the din coming up from the street.

"That better be good news," Colt said. Remington heard him slide the revolver from his hip holster and slam the hammer back. "I've just about had my fill of bad news."

But Remington's attention was fixed on the dirigible. Near the front, across the silver skin, was an image of a red castle turret bracketed by black bat wings. "You ever seen that insignia before?" he asked Colt.

"Nope. You?"

Remington shoved back the edge of his long coat and pulled his gun from his hip holster. "You packing silver?"

"Marley's special bullets."

Remington nodded. "Then let's join the welcoming party, shall we?"

Miss Arliss grasped Colt's shoulder. "I've seen that insignia before. That's vampire. European or Russian royalty."

"You tellin' me we got a vampire nobleman just deciding to drop in for a visit?" Colt grumbled.

China snickered, crossing her arms. "Since when would that be so strange for you two? You are Cy Jackson's boys, after all." She had a point.

Miss Arliss pointedly ignored her. "Based on the size of

their dirigible, I'd say it's either a very small vampire nobleman with a very big inferiority complex or an entire battalion
of vampires."

"Have any idea which royal house it might be?" Remington asked.

Miss Arliss squinted in thought. "Could be Petrov, or the
house of Drossenburg. Both have bat wings in their insignia."

"Nothing like a little subtlety," Colt muttered. His brother
caught his gaze, and Remington knew Colt was thinking the
same thing he was. Colt turned toward the female Darkin.
"You two stay put. We're going to check this out."

"And miss all the action? No, siree," China spat back, her
face hard with determination. Blast. Remington tensed.

In a flash her form began to change. Everything grew
smudged and shapeless for a moment as the particles re-
arranged themselves into the form of a great golden mountain lion. The mountain lion roared, baring an impressive set
of white canines, and everyone took a big step back. He'd
only seen her transmogrify once into the hellhound, and he
still found it impressive and a bit surreal.

Miss Arliss was pressed against the wall, her porcelain
complexion a definite shade paler than normal. Maybe she'd
never seen a shape-shifter like this before. Only a desk stood
between the two of them, and the big golden beast began to
pace his offices, its head bent low and ears pinned flat to its
enormous head. All that stored up hostility between the
Darkin females was plain and out in the open now. He didn't
have time for this, not with vampires outside his office doors.

"If she wants to go out and greet the vampires, I think you
ought to accommodate her," Miss Arliss offered, a tremor in
her voice.

Colt grimaced. He pointed at the cougar. "Fine. Come
along, but don't attack unless they provoke. Got it?"

"We need to know exactly what we're dealing with first,"

Remington added. The big cat growled low and deep and blinked in acknowledgment.

"We'll be right back," Colt said to Miss Arliss, then opened the office door.

"Unless there's trouble," Remington said with a smile. "Then we'll be back in about thirty minutes."

Chapter 5

Remington's mind reeled as Colt cursed under his breath. Remington wasn't sure if his brother's reaction was to the vampires looming overhead or to China dogging their footsteps in mountain lion form.

Through the leaded glass doors they could see the dark shadow of the dirigible on the street. It meant the sun was at its zenith. No chance the passengers would come out unless they were fully covered in protective clothing, which left them vulnerable as far as Remington was concerned. So why park the thing smack dab over the center of Tombstone in broad daylight instead of waiting for dark? Clearly this wasn't an attack. In his estimation as an attorney, they needed something.

"What do you reckon they want?" he muttered as they clomped down the stairs, guns at the ready, the golden mountain lion trailing behind them with soft, padded thumps.

"Hard to say. But make no mistake, they'll want something," Colt answered as they swung open one of the double doors to the sidewalk. "You know vampires. They *always* have an agenda."

A wash of dry heat, smelling of horse, dust, and the oily scent of creosote, tightened the skin on Remington's face. The heat shimmered in the air, distorting everything beyond the massive shadow of the dirigible overhead that blotted out the desert sun.

A ladder, constructed of rope and wooden rungs, hung down from the topmost of the three decks of the airship. It swung perilously close to the building, threatening to break a window or two. Remington muttered a curse beneath his breath. He'd already had to repair his office building last time Colt had visited. This was getting to be a bad habit, and one that would get him ejected by his landlords if it continued.

Colt shaded his eyes with his hand as a dark form emerged, then started to descend the swaying ladder. Remington tugged his hat down a bit to make it easier to see against the backlit shadow, but couldn't make out who or what it was, though from the shape and the boots it looked to be a man. He kept his hand on his revolver, just in case.

"About time you made it out," a familiar voice shouted. *Winchester.* "I was beginning to wonder if Marley had told me wrong about you coming here." A pair of tight-fitting, dark-lensed brass goggles obscured Winchester's face, and he was wearing his black oilskin duster and his favorite black Stetson.

Remington slid his revolver back into the holster just below his hip, relieved it was his older brother. Colt did the same.

"What in tarnation are you doing on a vampire dirigible, Winn?" Colt called out.

China rubbed her furry cheek and chin up against Colt's leg, and he shooed her off with a flick of his hand. She answered with a low rumble in her chest and padded away to sit closer to Remington. He resisted the urge to comment and tightened his hand into a fist then released it, letting go of the urge to hit something. Clearly the shifter still wanted his little brother's attention, but Colt was no longer interested. The realization that she'd sparked an emotional reaction in him—against his brother no less—stuck thick and hard in his throat. He'd have to be more mindful around her.

Winchester made it farther down the ladder and hopped the last few feet to the ground. The dust billowed up in a cloud around him as he pulled the dark goggles down to rest around his neck. "Was made an offer I couldn't refuse."

Remington gave their older brother a narrowed-eyed look, glancing upward at the dirigible. Offers unopen to refusal were dangerous. "You in trouble?"

"No. Not yet. Seems the vampire royalty in Europe think they could use our help in tracking down a missing third of the Book. The contessa says they sent her here to request our assistance."

"Who *they?* Vampires? They want *our* help?" Disbelief tinted Colt's tone and echoed in Remington's thoughts. In general vampires didn't need anyone—ever—unless it was for dinner.

Winn shrugged. "Simple matter of survival. If Rathe wipes out humanity, their food supply disappears."

Just as he suspected. Remington grimaced, and his hand tightened reflexively on the butt of his revolver. "Hardly seems like the best of reasons for us to forge an alliance with them," he muttered. Working with Darkin was an iffy proposition. It could always go either way, which was why he'd avoided doing so until now. Winn never did. Colt seemed to find dancing on that fine line between what was easy and what was right rather addictive.

People were beginning to peek out from behind their closed doors. Across the street the tinny sound of a piano started up again. As odd as the dirigible was, nothing could get the hardy souls of Tombstone ruffled for long. It was part of the reason he'd settled here. The oddity of being a part-time attorney and part-time Hunter didn't faze the residents of Tombstone any. Not when they'd already had the likes of Wyatt Earp and his brothers as the law in their town.

A gust of wind blew, kicking up dust along the mostly

deserted street and making the rope ladder sway. Colt peered up at the windows to the law office, and Remington followed his longing look. The succubus, silhouetted behind the glass, looked down at the unfolding tableau on Allen Street, her arms crossed, nibbling her lip.

He considered the irony. Their pa would be twisting in his grave if he could see his boys working side by side with the very supernaturals he'd trained them to kill without compunction. But at least in his case, Remington didn't consider the arrangement to be anything more than temporary. Especially not with a Darkin who'd been his little brother's lover. Somehow knowing she and Colt had shared a past hadn't been such a big deal before. He and Winn had even enjoyed teasing Colt over it. But now—now he wasn't so sure.

"Considering how little time we've got, if Marley's calculations are correct, I don't see much of an option," Winn answered. "If we want to discover where all the pieces of the Book have been hidden, we'll have to split up. You two any closer to decoding Pa's message?"

Colt caught Remington's gaze for just an instant, then turned his attention back to Winn. "Remy thinks it's got something to do with either the Weaver's Needle in the Superstition Mountains or a place called the Eye of the Needle on the outside of Phoenix close to McDowell."

Winn rolled the sharp, waxed end of his mustache between his fingers, his dark brows bending together in concentration. Winn was calculating in his head. Remington had seen him do it a thousand times before. "Phoenix," he paused for an instant. "I could get you there in about an hour."

Raw-arr. From behind them the mountain lion growled, and Winchester gave it a pointed look. "What is that? And what is it doing here?"

"You mean *who* is that," Remington corrected him.

Winn nodded with understanding. "Shifter?"

"China McGee," Colt and Remington said in unison.

Winn's eyes widened slightly in recognition, and his gaze darted to Colt. He at least had the decency not to let his jaw drop. "Not the same one who—" He waved his hand as if shooing the thought away. "Never mind. I don't want to know."

Remington tried to hide his amused smile, but Colt saw it and punched him in the arm. That was the thing about brothers. They never let you forget anything, especially if it was embarrassing. There was certainly no way he or Winn were apt to forget that Colt's first run-in with China had been a whopper. It wasn't often that a woman could best their little brother, leaving him tied up to a bed naked, and get away with stealing his stuff.

"It wasn't my fault," Colt growled.

Raw-awrr, the mountain lion growled again in retort.

Remington couldn't understand cougar, but he understood the gesture. "She begs to differ." He holstered his guns and flipped his long jacket back over them. Once upon a time, the story of China and Colt had been something amusing to poke him with, but now that Remington had spent some time in China's company, it gave him all sorts of unsettling ideas he didn't have any business thinking about, about exactly what she might do to him in a bed.

"Despite that, she's agreed to go with me down to follow the clue Diego left about the map in Mexico."

Colt gazed up at the dirigible. "You sure the contessa would be all right with extra company?"

Winn smiled, and it lifted the ends of his mustache. "We already have Tempus on board. Thought we might drop it off for you. We're flying to Europe."

"And now Phoenix is on the way to Europe?"

Colt had a point. Winn would be doubling back for a distance, but air flight was faster than train no matter how you sliced things. "It could be. Are you up for it?" Winn answered.

Colt nodded. "Let me go and fetch Lilly down here from Remy's office, and we can get going."

Winn's face darkened. "You still hanging on to that demon?"

Colt pulled back his shoulders a bit and set his jaw. Winn had a hell of a nerve throwing it at him when they all had uneasy alliances to deal with at present. "She's with me until we find Pa's part of the Book."

The look in Winn's eyes changed. There was only so far he could push as a big brother, and Colt had long ago passed the point of taking anyone's advice but his own. Remington usually just watched from the sidelines, preferring not to be the punching bag in between them—literally. "Just watch yourself," Winn said simply.

As quickly as the tension amped up between them, like a static charge, it instantly dissipated. Colt jibed back, "Look who's talking. You better consider wearing extra starch in your collars. You might need it, considering the company you're keeping."

Winn's mouth tipped up at the corner. "Fair enough, little brother. Go fetch your demon, and let's be on our way."

Colt took the steps two at a time back up to the office. Winn waited until the door closed behind his little brother, then speared Remington with a glance, and jerked his head up toward the second-story office window. "What do you think of the demon he's with?"

"Nice enough looking." Beside him, China in cougar form chuffed and growled deep and low, the tip of her tail twitching. He certainly hadn't taken China for the jealous type, but perhaps she was. Regardless, her behavior only confirmed what he'd suspected. She was still pining for Colt. It was good to know, even if it stung a bit. Okay. More than a bit. But that was nobody's business but his own. And why did he suddenly feel any different about it? She was just a Darkin. Just a thief.

They would get the job done, and then he'd never have to deal with her again.

"Wasn't what I meant and you know it. Do you think Colt is in danger?"

"Well, on one hand, I think he's as safe as he lets himself be. He's got good hunting instincts, and he seems to have struck a fair bargain with the demon." Although considering how well Colt's relationship with China had fared, Remington sincerely doubted Colt could escape from his deal with the succubus unscathed.

Winn frowned.

"On the other hand," Remington continued, "he seems agitated around her, and I'm not sure if it's because he's so damn attracted to her or because he doesn't trust her."

"Can't you ever give a straight answer, boy?"

That was his older brother—black-and-white to the bone. Seeing anything in shades of gray didn't happen for him. "Attorney, remember?"

Winn tugged on the left side of his mustache. "Well, I don't trust her. Not yet."

Remington snorted. From the time Winn and Pa had started teaching him about the Hunter life, Winn had been a parrot of Pa's lessons, taking them literally. "You've *never* trusted a Darkin."

"With good reason." Winn's hand strayed to his left thigh, brushing the thick, rope-like scar beneath his pants. Remington counted himself lucky. He'd been the only one to escape undamaged the day the demon had visited their homestead. Winn had nearly lost his leg and Colt had nearly drowned. But Remington knew better than to assume all Darkin were cut from the same cloth.

"At least give her a chance."

"I will. But that doesn't mean I won't have a backup plan in place."

Remington's eyes narrowed. Colt wouldn't like knowing

they were worried for him. In fact most times if he caught on they were watching over him, he became even more reckless, as if to prove himself. So how would they know if their little brother was safe with the succubus?

Finally Remington spoke. "China, you can change into just about any animal shape you want, can't you?"

She instantly shifted, her blond mountain lion fur retreating, her body blurring completely until she was a woman with waist-length blond hair. The fringe on her pale brown leather jacket swung slightly as she stood up, bracing her legs apart. Tight brown buckskin pants again hugged her long, lean legs and fitted over her cowboy boots. He swallowed hard against the thickness in his throat. China McGee was a beautiful woman.

"Human too, if I'm in the mood," she grumbled in reply as she crossed her arms over her ample chest. Remington snapped his attention away from her lovely cleavage and focused instead on her intense gray eyes.

"Do you think you could hitch a ride up the ladder and check things out to make sure the vampires aren't just setting a trap for my brothers?" Winn asked.

China shrugged. "I could," she said, then made a show of inspecting her nails on her long, slim fingers. Remington was already familiar enough with the gesture to know she wanted something. Everything China did came at a price. Exactly how much did he have in the safe upstairs that he could easily part with? "But I don't see what's in it for me," she continued.

"How about two hundred dollars?" Remington offered, trying to stay one step ahead of her. Keeping her off-balance seemed to be the best way of dealing with her.

"And half of whatever we find off Diego's map?" she countered. Damn she was good.

"Half of everything but the Book," he countered.

China reached out her hand. "Shake on it, Jackson."

Remington grabbed her hand and locked gazes with her.

There was something more than just a keen intelligence in those silver eyes. A shower of sparks and a wave of heat ran up his arm like an electrical connection from the point where they touched. He might need her to get to whatever Diego's map led to, but he would be damned if he was going to let his guard down around her.

China glanced at Winn and gave him a very cat-like, self-satisfied smile. "Seems I'll be going along for a ride on your vampire's dirigible as well."

"She's not *my* vampire."

Remington chuckled.

"That funny to you, boy?" Winn shot back.

"Yeah. Never seen you so agitated about a woman before."

"You haven't met her," Winn grumbled.

"Uppity?"

"Yep."

"Know-it-all?"

"Yep."

"Sounds like a typical vampire to me."

Winchester ignored his last statement and focused on China. "Look, I want you to wait until Colt and that demon are at least halfway up the ladder before you try to get on board the airship."

China nodded. "That's easy enough."

"Can you change into something inconspicuous?"

China sighed in exasperation. "Would a mouse do?"

Winn smiled. "Perfect. Colt won't suspect a thing. Much better if he doesn't see you."

"Can't handle being looked after by his big brothers?" she jibed.

"Yep," Winn and Remington said in unison.

Colt and Miss Arliss came out the double glass doors and stepped out from under the shaded walkway into the bright Arizona sunshine. Even though Remy gave one last look at the succubus's truly exceptional form, he didn't miss the heated gaze Colt gave China or the deep throaty growl that rumbled behind China's pursed lips, even though now she'd transformed back into her human female form. He was treading a dangerous path with China, because while she professed what happened between her and Colt was in the past, Remington wondered if she were simply lying to herself.

Winn had snapped the dark goggles back into place, the brass edges of them glinting in the afternoon sun. He dug deep in the pockets of his duster and fished out two pairs of similar goggles, handing one to Colt and the other to Miss Arliss. "You'll want those once we get up in the air. The sun seems even brighter up there, and there's some dust."

Lilly and Colt dutifully pulled the goggles on, and Colt made sure his hat was down good and firm on his head before all three of them ascended the rope ladder.

Remington speared China with a glance. "You don't like that succubus much, do you?"

Her lips twitched. "What gave it away?"

He didn't bother to answer; he wanted to get to the point of the matter at hand. "Is it because Colt's taken with her?"

China glared at him. "You seem to spend a lot of time worried about your little brother's love life."

"I watch my brother's back no matter what the situation."

China snorted and turned her gaze upward as the froth of Miss Arliss's petticoats smacked Colt in the face. "Family first with you Jacksons. That's the way it works, ain't it?"

"Why does that seem to irritate you so much, Miss McGee?"

A flash of darkness clouded the silver shine in her gaze for just a moment. "Maybe we just have different definitions of family."

Remington let that thought roll around in his head for a bit. He really didn't know all that much about where China had come from before she'd met up with Colt. What exactly made her so prickly when the subject of family surfaced? There was more to her story than she was telling any of them. The attorney in him could sense it—and the danger it posed to him and his brothers.

"Looks like they're preparing to pull up that ladder. I'd better get on quick."

He grasped her by the upper arm, and she turned those unnerving silver eyes his way. "How are you going to get back here safely?"

"Don't you worry about me none. I've got my ways."

Her silver eyes blurred as her form dissolved, changed shape, and shrunk in size. The tiny golden mouse sat up on its haunches, its front feet clasped before it, impossibly small nose and whiskers twitching. Remington crouched, holding out his hand in the powder-fine dirt of Allen Street. China scampered into his hand, her little mouse feet tickling his skin. He scooped her up and held her level to the rope ladder.

China ran off his hand and clung to the rope as the ladder was hauled upward. Her golden color blended in perfectly with the tawny color of the rope, and after a few feet he couldn't even see her any longer. He watched as the props on the airship began to spin faster and faster and the ship lifted higher into the piercing blue of the desert sky.

There was nothing left for him to do but wait. And pray.

Chapter 6

China dug her tiny mouse feet into the rope for all she was worth and bit her teeth into it too for good measure. The last thing she needed was an errant hawk spying her and ripping her off the rope before she made it to the decks above. She could shift quickly, but not fast enough to defend herself from a bird of prey.

Distance seemed to infinitely increase when her size changed to something so small. She was just grateful they were pulling the rope ladder up so she didn't have to climb the whole damn thing. The dark wood of the teak deck hovered into view, and China jumped off the rope before she was crushed in the tangled heap of the ladder.

She glanced to the side and saw the tips of Miss Arliss's scuffed and dusty black boots right beside a pair of knee-high black boots that were polished so highly they gleamed like Oriental lacquer. Each shoe seemed the size of a train car. Her gaze traveled up an equally shiny expanse of blue-black taffeta the color of raven wings that stretched upward as far as she could see. China took a sniff. Definitely another Darkin; she would bet her whiskers on it. Likely the vampire noblewoman Winchester had mentioned.

"Another Mr. Jackson, I presume?" Blue-black taffeta

asked. Her Eastern European accent made "Jackson" sound more like "Yakson." Definitely vampire.

China scampered for cover when Colt nearly squashed her beneath the heel of his cowboy boot as he sprung up from the deck where he'd landed after clambering over the edge of the dirigible. He dusted off his hands on his denim pants before taking the woman's hand, which was covered in fine black kidskin. He kissed it lightly on the back, then flashed her *that* smile. The one that could make women melt. "The youngest, and the most handsome, at your service, your ladyship . . ."

China squeaked in indignation. Colt was still the same cocky bastard with the ladies he'd always been. At one time she'd thought he found *her* special. How stupid of her. His charm was just how he related to women—all women. What she wouldn't give to sink her tiny needle teeth into his ankle right about now. 'Course with his boots on it wouldn't do her a damn bit of good.

She grinned, as much as she could as a mouse, when his older brother unceremoniously took the young woman's gloved hand out of Colt's. "Lady Alexandra Porter, Contessa Drossenburg," Winchester said, his tone tinged with a ripple of irritation. "My *little* brother, Colt Jackson."

China didn't miss Winchester's emphasis on "little," as if it somehow referred to Colt's anatomy and not just the age difference between them. It was a pity mice couldn't belly laugh, but she squeaked and headed toward the edge of the wall and from there toward the double glass doors. Her legs were burning. What was only a few feet for the humans, vampire and succubus was a long run for her.

"So this is the contessa."

The woman gave the slightest inclination of her head. "It seems we are to transport you to Phoenix, along with your charming companion." Her voice was like warm, rustling silk, smooth but husky and inviting at the same time. China bet the contessa could throw one hell of a glamour on people with a voice like that.

"Yes, we're much obliged, ma'am, um, Lady Drossenburg," Colt corrected himself.

She smiled and another burning curl of jealousy ignited in China's gut. Was there not a single female on this planet who didn't just trip over herself when he smiled? Well, it wouldn't be her. Never again. At least not with Colt. Now, Remington's smile was a whole other matter. China cursed silently. What was she thinking? No. Hunters had to be off her list of interests completely, especially if she wanted her plans for getting back in Rathe's good graces to be successful. She could be as helpful and as pleasant, even enticing as she wanted, as long as in the end she got the completed Book of Legend in her hands and gave it to Rathe.

"It is my pleasure to help the Chosen," the vampire contessa answered, then turned away from him without missing a beat, expecting them to follow.

Colt frowned. Her head snapped around, her tawny eyes narrowing in warning, the air bristling with distaste. She looked down her long aquiline nose at him. "Fair warning, sir, this ship is filled with vampires. And we can hear your thoughts as clearly as if you'd spoken them out loud."

China watched Colt's Adam's apple bob in his throat. "Yes, your ladyship." At least the man had enough sense to know when to back down from a dangerous Darkin.

The vampire gave him a curt nod and turned back, heading for the large, intricate Tiffany stained glass double doors that adjoined the deck. The motif of the red castle with black wings swung past Colt's nose as Winn opened the door to let the ladies enter the interior of the dirigible first. China skittered in right behind them, nearly getting lost in the shuffle of skirt fabric before the door could close.

"Mind your manners, boy. No sense in offending the vampires before we know if they can help us find the missing

part of the Book," Winn whispered harshly into Colt's ear as
he passed.

The top level of the dirigible looked immense. Perhaps it
was her diminutive size, or just that she'd never been anywhere so grand before. It was surprisingly modern, like a
plush hotel lobby, surrounded by windows. Huge potted
palms scattered throughout the space were like giant jungle
trees to her, their long, fringed green boughs ruffled by the
breeze coming in the open doors, and the sunlight filtering
through them from the windows above.

China skittered from behind the heavy, elegantly carved
mahogany foot of one of the stuffed chairs and settees to
another. They were grouped to create areas like small parlors
for gentle conversation or drinking tea, making it easy for her
to maneuver about without being spotted.

From her vantage point on the plush, thick Oriental carpet-
ing in rich burgundy and gold interspersed with the black
points of the vampire's crest, it all looked immense and especially grand. Even the roaring fire in the grate of a marble
fireplace at the far end of the room looked four stories tall
from her inch-high viewpoint.

Colt paced over to the fireplace and stared deeply into the
flames. He looked so utterly out of place in such an elegant
setting that for a moment she felt sorry for him. But she had
mere seconds to act.

Scampering behind one of the potted palms, she allowed
the shift to take her. The heat of it, like hot water running just
beneath her skin, always invigorated her. Nerve and muscle,
skin and bone stretched and grew as she took mortal form
once more.

She rarely changed into the form of a man, but when she
did, it always felt a bit off. As if she were wearing clothing a
size too large or had a head cold when she spoke in a voice
too deep. With animal forms it was different. Each one had
a special feeling to it. They were like different colors—all

together producing a single rainbow, yet distinct enough on their own to be easy to identify. All of them resided within her, and yet they were each different parts of her. She just hoped Colt would be more receptive to talking to an old friend than to an ex-lover.

China pulled on the lapels of the lab coat, trying not to trip over her larger than normal feet as she approached Colt. "Fascinating, isn't it?"

He spun around and stared hard at her in her male guise. "Marley?"

China grinned. Maybe she was even better than she'd thought at this if she could fool Colt at such a close range. "So good to know that I can occasionally surprise even you Jacksons."

"What are you doing here?"

"Your brother and the contessa offered to assist me in delivering Balmora to Her Majesty." China thought that sounded right. She'd only picked up bits of their conversation in Remington's law office because she'd been too distracted by that succubus sniffing around Colt's heels and the fierce tangle of confusing emotions roiling around in her. Something in her still hung on to the possibility that she and Colt had a chance. She'd always been an outsider and felt that he was one too. Once upon a time she'd thought they were two of a kind in that respect. Now she wasn't so sure.

Colt's nostrils flared slightly, and he drew his revolver and cocked it in one swift motion, pointing it an inch from the center of her forehead. Her heart stopped, then kicked up beating twice as fast.

"Who are you really?"

She sighed dramatically, rolling her eyes, and let the change take her, melding back into her normal mortal form. "What gave me away?"

"First, Marley don't like supernaturals, so I seriously doubt he'd take an offer of riding aboard a vampire's dirigible.

Second, I think it's going to take half of the Queen's army to pry Balmora out of Marley's hands. He's not going to give her up willingly. Third," he wrinkled his nose, "I can still smell the sulfur on you."

"So I'm a little rusty," China groused with a shrug.

"You're sloppy. There's a difference. You should know who you're impersonating better than that. And you didn't answer my question." The bite to his words and the cold, all-business tone of his voice suddenly made China feel brittle.

"I attached myself to the ladder as a mouse when they hauled it up. Remington wanted to make sure it wasn't a trap. And, for your information, at least I'm not heartless like you. I can't believe you left me behind."

She wanted him to acknowledge her. To wrap his arms around her and tell her it was all a joke. He was just using the succubus to get to his father's piece of the Book like they'd planned all along. But Colt didn't so much as budge an inch toward her. His frame was still stiff and solid. China frowned, and Colt turned back to the fire.

All of a sudden it hit her like a bullet mid-chest, a hot sting, piercing to the core. He was done with her. Done with them. Whatever spark had smoldered between her and Colt was gone. Somehow, he'd moved on.

"Look. If I'd had any chance of getting us both out, I would have. As it was, Remington came to get you. If anybody could talk you out of that jail cell, I knew it would be him, not me."

"Regardless, you still owe me." She didn't like the petulance in her voice, but she wanted no doubt left that she intended to collect on the debt. "And by the way, I'd watch that demon if I were you. She's already got you hooked."

Colt's sensual lips hardened into a flat, firm line. "Tell you what, you protect my brother's back if you two go out searching for Diego's map and make it back, then we'll talk about what I owe you."

Anger, hot and seething, spurted in her gut. How dare he cast *her* aside—a princess of the Darkin realm. Sure, she'd never told him as much, but still the disregard stung her pride. A low growl started deep in China's throat. How dare he try to weasel out of what he owed her! For a moment she contemplated shifting into the cougar again, but then the flicker of movement behind him caught her attention. The succubus was back.

China had had enough. She was done with Colt Jackson.

"We'll talk when we get back," she said between gritted teeth, then turned on her booted heel and stalked off across the lobby of the airship to find the nearest exit.

Indignation made her steps quick and determined. Windows were everywhere on this airship, but where was the damn door?

"I am Enric. May I be of service?" China whipped her head around. She hadn't heard anyone approaching. The blond vampire, in his fancy uniform accented with gold buttons down the left side, held his hands loosely clasped in the small of his back and stood there staring at her.

China refused to let him ruffle her. When it came down to it, he was just another Darkin like her. "You got a door out of this place?"

He quirked one brow in question and lifted his right hand, indicating a small hall that angled off to the right. "This way."

China marched off, not waiting to see or caring if he tagged along or not. She just wanted to be as far away as she could get from Colt Jackson. *Now.*

Once she rounded the corner of the wall she spied the double doors leading to the outer deck that circled the gondola at this level. Coming up, she'd counted three decks. They were on the top.

"Is there anything else?" Enric asked politely, his expression bland.

"Not unless you can arrange to have Colt Jackson or that red-haired hussy dropped off this thing."

Enric's lips twitched. "I'm afraid not."

China nodded and pushed the door open, stepping out into the brilliant sunlight. The vampire didn't bother to follow. She closed her eyes, letting the orange glow of the sunlight filter through her eyelids as she took several deep, measured breaths. Slow in. Slow out. Deep and steady. The heat began to flow in her veins, her body shrinking again. The hairs on her body enlarged and stiffened as they transformed into large black feathers; her toes and heels spread backward into thin clawed feet; and her face hardened and pulled forward, making it impossible to move her lips as they turned into a beak.

She hopped up onto the railing, flexing her wings, and glanced back for only a second at the bemused expression of the vampire behind the windows before she dropped off the edge of the airship and let the wind take her.

Flying under one's own power was the most glorious thing of all. Well, next to sex, but it was pretty damn close. First the sensation of falling, then of being perfectly buoyant in the air, lifted by the warm slipstream of wind that caressed her body like a lover.

At least flying didn't break your heart.

China circled down slowly toward the small dot she saw waiting on the streets of Tombstone below. As the buildings grew larger, so did Remington. He held his hand over his eyes, shielding them as he looked upward at her.

For a second she had the silly notion to show him what she could do. She dove, head first for the ground, her wings tucked in neat and tight against her body, and then, at the last moment, expanded them fully, circling in a wide arc above Allen Street.

Remington's sculpted lips lifted in a smile as she settled down to earth. She shifted, letting the heat fuse her body back into its human form. A wave of dizziness washed over her, and for a second she lost her balance.

A firm, warm grip circled her upper arm. "Whoa there. You all right?"

China held the heel of her hand to her temple to steady the teeter of the landscape in her vision. Her body swayed. "Just a might dizzy. Must have shifted too many times today." She tried to stand steady and ended up sagging into Remington. He settled his arm around her waist and locked her against his side.

"How about we get you back up to the office and out of this heat. That might help."

China shook her head. Big mistake. The world swirled even faster into a dizzying blend of color. "Need to eat," she murmured. Darkness crept in on the edges of her vision.

Remington caught her before she fell to the dirt. He'd never known a shifter to faint like that, but then he supposed there were lots of things he'd not learned about them on a personal level, since the only time he'd come close to them was in a kill or be killed scenario.

"Miss McGee? China? Can you hear me?" He shook her slightly, patted her cheek with his hand, and when she didn't respond, swept her up into his arms to carry her back up to his office. Her body was as soft as it was firm, smooth skin over sleek muscle. He cleared his throat and readjusted his hold on her, doing his best to ignore exactly how she felt. He pulled open one of the double doors with two fingers and gazed at the stairs.

Remington groaned. That was a lot of steps carrying the dead weight of a woman. But there was no choice. He couldn't very well leave her down here, and he couldn't get her to his office without climbing the stairs. As he walked up each step, her hair tickled his neck and chin. The strangely feminine scent of black tea laced with vanilla lingered in her hair.

A spark of image flashed across his field of vision of what she would look like tangled in white sheets, her shoulders bare except for the fall of honey silk. He frowned. He had no business thinking about what it would be like to bed a Darkin. It had been reckless of Colt to do so. Remington wouldn't make the same mistake.

Both of his brothers had had near-death experiences with Darkin. So far he'd been lucky enough to escape the same. But the odds were not in his favor.

By the time he reached the second-floor landing outside the hall where his offices were located, his legs and arms were burning. He kicked open his door and settled China on the brown leather couch in his personal office. Having slept there a time or two, he knew it would be comfortable enough until she woke.

A nagging itch pestered the back of his mind. He wanted to know what had transpired on the airship. Did she think Colt and Winn would be safe? Did the vampire seem intent on helping as Winn had said, or was it a ruse? She would know.

He waited a few minutes, and when she still hadn't woken, he jogged down the stairs and across the street to the Occidental to get a couple of sandwiches and iced drinks. What he returned with was cold roast chicken, coffee, and milk. The lunch rush had left them out of fresh bread until evening, and there was no more ice to be had until the special machine the hotel had ordered from Wickenburg made more. Remy was just profoundly glad he wasn't the cook having to bake bread in this heat.

The moment he brought the food into his office, he noticed China twitch, first her nose, then her eyelids. He settled the meal down on his desk and turned to find her sitting up slightly on her elbows, her eyelashes fluttering, a confused expression on her face.

"What am I doing in your office?"

"You fainted."

China snorted. "Shifters don't faint."

Remington removed his coat, sat against the edge of the desk, and crossed his arms. If she wanted to argue with him, so be it. But he would win. He'd made a career of winning at such things. "I object. You are a shifter. Clearly you fainted, and I had to catch you before you planted your face in the dirt. Therefore, shifters not only can but *do* faint."

Her faced puckered in a sour look. "Most shifters don't try to make three to four different shifts in less than twelve hours on an empty stomach either."

"But you ate an enormous breakfast."

She cocked her head to the side. "Shifters burn through food faster than humans."

He pulled the white linen cloth off the plate of sliced cold roast chicken. China immediately sat fully upright.

"You mentioned something about being hungry before you passed out. I thought you might want something to eat when you woke."

She glanced first at the chicken, then at his face, then back to the chicken. "I think you may be right."

He handed her the plate and China dug in, not even bothering to ask if he had a fork. Remington chuckled. He'd yet to lose an argument.

"Get your strength back, then you can tell me what happened up there."

China swallowed a mouthful of chicken. "Your older brother has a good sense of the situation. Seems to me the vampires really want to help, but the contessa is none too happy about it. She doesn't like having to work with Hunters, but she ain't got a choice. She's following orders."

Remington frowned, his lips twisting as he thought it through. "A break in the ranks of the Darkin is very unusual."

China snorted. "Unusual? How about unlikely. There's got

to be a lot more going on than just the vampires wanting their food supply safe—no offense."

He waved a hand at her. "None taken." He paused, glancing at the worn leather of his mother's journal sitting on the top of his desk. He hadn't bothered taking it down with him when the airship had come, and he hadn't cracked it open yet. But Colt had been very direct. There was information in there Remington needed.

"If the loyalty among Darkin to Rathe as their leader is faltering, it could mean far greater things are at stake than merely control of humanity."

"Well, that ain't no small thing," China hedged.

"True, but Earth alone isn't the entire universe, now is it?"

China frowned. "Don't you ever just talk plain and say what you mean?"

"I say precisely what I mean," he shot back. "Just because it isn't simplistic doesn't mean I'm obfuscating."

"Ob foo what?"

"I'm not trying to hide my intentions."

China shrugged as if it didn't matter to her either way and licked her fingers. Her shiny pink tongue curved around her digits in such a way that Remy's gut and groin tightened in response. He looked away.

There was certainly no reason to tell her what he was thinking. It had no bearing on their efforts to recover the missing piece of the Book of Legend, wherever it was hidden. For a second he wondered if cleaning her fingers with her tongue was the only cat-like quality she possessed.

China sighed, a contented sound, and blinked lazily at him. "So now what?"

Remy picked up his mother's diary and flipped it open. "I think it's time we find out precisely where Diego's map will lead us."

China touched her index finger to the center of her full bottom lip, rubbing the slight indentation there in a most distracting fashion. "Colt said the bit of paper out of Diego's safety-deposit box would lead us to the hiding place of the Book."

"It will, when combined with this." Remington held up the diary. "If Colt is right, what was in Diego's box was only half the clues we need. The rest we might find in here."

China frowned. "You aren't gonna sit here and read it out loud to me, are you?"

Remington put his hand to his chest with a bit of dramatic flair, as if he'd been wounded. "My dear Miss McGee, don't you enjoy being read to?"

She gave him a saucy grin that shot straight through his veins like a good gulp of bourbon. Holy hell. He was going to have to watch himself around her.

"I'm more a woman of action myself."

He laughed. "I'm beginning to see why Colt both liked you and feared you, Miss McGee."

Remington pulled the paper from his pocket and spread it out on top of his desk; it was a series of numbers and markers, along with what looked like trails and mountains. A map with no details, no place names. But now that he knew the numbers were longitude and latitude, he could begin to piece it all together. It would get them there, but he wanted to know what lay at the end of the line because X never marked the spot, and if Hunters had hidden the last remaining piece of the Book of Legend in the jungles of southern Mexico, then they hadn't simply dug a hole and buried it there.

It would be well protected—and that meant booby traps. He brushed his finger back and forth against the binding of the diary in his hand as he thought. "The numbers that run along the side are latitude and longitude correlating to the markers on Diego's map and begin just outside of Tombstone. The next leads to Nogales."

He opened the diary where the ribbon marker was lodged

and began to skim the flowery, handwritten script faded with age.

> *Diego came to the homestead today. He's returned from checking on the security of the piece hidden in his mother's homeland. He brought back an Indian relic with him. It looks like a squat, smiling square of a man. He says he pulled it off of one of the temples when he finally made it out. His tale of discovering the hiding place of the Spanish gave me goose bumps. His ancestors are protecting the Book now. Only the keys his ancestors left him will get it out of the temple safely.*

"Diego's page never said nothing about keys," China grumbled.

Remy gazed into her eyes. "Sometimes a key isn't a physical thing. Sometimes it's merely a legend on a map. Sometimes it's a hidden knowledge that answers a riddle."

"And sometimes," she added in a caustic tone, "it's a real key."

"Indian relic," he murmured. "I wonder if she meant that little stone smiling face that sat near our fireplace."

Remington turned and went to his bookcases that lined the walls behind his desk. There, at the top corner sat the squat little stone his mother had told him never to part with. He'd been using it as a bookend, and now he pulled it down from the shelf.

"Here is our first key, Miss McGee. Let's go find the rest."

Chapter 7

Remington Jackson was a man who liked to be prepared. And as far as he could tell from his sources, including his mother's diary, Diego was still alive somewhere near the border. Perhaps he could tell them precisely what the markings on his map meant. That was a lot of desert to cover. Little if no water, little shelter, and a Darkin for company. Lucky him.

They'd left that evening, preferring to make the trek in the coolest part of the day. As promised, he'd procured China new clothes, as well as provisions before leaving Tombstone.

They had food. They had equipment to camp out. He'd packed one of the water distillation devices Marley had created to use should they come across an accessible source of water out there. He'd also loaded up with a number of Marley's custom Hunter weapons that were as unconventional as they were effective—rather like Marley's special bullets. Remington had tried to think of everything both he and China might need. Once they were out there, there'd be no popping back to town for supplies. It would be a grueling, dangerous trek, and their lives would depend on his not forgetting anything vital.

China hadn't even bothered to open all the brown paper parcels she'd brought back from the dry goods store before they'd left. She'd just pulled out clothing from the first two things she'd opened and put on whatever was in the package. She rolled her dirty clothes, with the exception of her fringed leather jacket, into a ball she stuffed down into her saddle packs. The stiff, high white collar of the shirt was too prim on her. He realized that now. But at the time he'd been thinking it would keep the sun off the pale skin at her nape. She'd folded her jacket carefully and tied it over her bedroll and blankets at the back of her saddle.

She'd been less fortunate in the second package she'd selected. While split down the middle, with buttons that ran up along the leg on either side, the garment was more or less a skirt. She'd frowned when she'd held it up. "Well, at least I can ride in it," she'd muttered. The store hadn't carried pants that would fit a woman, and the smaller boys' sizes wouldn't accommodate the curve of her hips.

"What about my gun?"

Remington had balked at that. "I think you're well-armed enough between your wit and your barbed tongue and whatever claws you can create out of thin air, don't you?"

She'd grumbled. "I *want* a gun."

He could just see her shooting him in the back and taking the piece of the Book of Legend along with whatever else they discovered along the way. "We'll wait on the gun."

She'd balled her hands, resting them on the curve of her hips, and had spoken plainly and firmly. "You get me a gun or we ain't leaving."

"We don't even have a horse for you yet. I'll go to the livery and—"

"I already got one."

"Where?"

"Tied waiting at the hitching post downstairs in front of the hotel."

He'd narrowed his eyes. "And where did the horse come from?"

"Why does that matter?"

Remington had plowed his fingers through his hair and muttered, "You stole it, didn't you?"

"I prefer to call it borrowed without asking."

"As far as folks around here are concerned I'm on the side of the law. And horse thieves get hanged. You can't just go around taking what you want."

She'd arched one brow. Remington had gone to the window and glanced down into the street. Down at the hitching post was a beautiful palomino. Its deep golden coloring and flaxen mane and tail reminded him of the color of China's coat when she'd been a mountain lion. "Holy hell, woman, you took the mayor's horse?"

She'd shrugged. "If you are going to borrow without asking, you might as well borrow exactly what you want."

There hadn't been time to debate things further. In the end he'd tossed her one of his revolvers and replaced it with one Marley had modified to include a sight scope, then had hustled her out of the hotel and gotten them out of town on the double.

He'd briefly toyed with the idea of putting the iron shifter restraining cuff back on her, but thought better of it. Doing so only would have broken the fragile sense of trust beginning to build between them. And he did have to admit, she'd been both a mountain lion and a hellhound and hadn't ripped him apart either time. That had to count for something.

"Is your mount suitable, Miss McGee?"

She turned for a moment and looked at him. "You know you ain't got to be all stiff and formal with me; you might as well call me China."

An unwanted wash of something hot and acidic roiled in his gut. "Colt called you China."

She huffed. "Well, it's my name, dammit. What else was he supposed to call me?"

He raised a brow. "I take it by your tone that you are no longer enamored of my brother."

"If that means I ain't after him no more, then you got it right."

Interesting. And dangerous. For both of them. "And why is that?"

"Colt made it plain he don't have no more use for me. He's got that red-headed tramp Darkin of his now to help him find the piece of the Book he's hunting."

Remington resisted the urge to chuckle. Clearly China was feeling scorned, and his amusement would only add to her humiliation and pain. Neither of which he wanted to do. He needed her to be focused.

He needed to be focused.

He'd long ago determined the best course of action with a woman who was heart hurt was to reassure her of her desirability. *Wait.* The horse slowed, sensing his hesitation. *What the hell did he think he was doing? And when had he started thinking of China as a woman rather than a Darkin?* He shook his head to clear it. She *was* Darkin, and a powerful one at that. He'd do best to remember it before something dreadful happened. He shouldn't be worrying about her emotional state, and he'd damn well better get his own under firm control.

"Something wrong?"

Remington swiveled his gaze to her. The hot evening desert wind caught her hair, sending it into a swirl of blond satin ribbons behind her head as she rode beside him. Her sun-kissed skin gave her a healthy glow and made the gray in her eyes turn at times a silvery sage green color. He realized with a start the point he'd been duped into thinking of her as female—the moment he'd seen her in the cell, dirt, grime, and all. She'd been too angelic looking to be something damned and vicious as he'd been raised to believe all Darkin were.

"Why you lookin' at me like that?" Her words came out velvet soft, very nearly a purr.

"Pardon?"

"Why you lookin' at me like I'm the last swig of water in the canteen? All needy-like."

He gave her a tilting half smile, nothing serious, nothing too comic, so she'd believe he made light of the situation. "A man can't enjoy a beautiful view?"

A delightful pink color suffused her cheeks. "Is that all? 'Cause I could've sworn you looked like you had thoughts running through your head."

Remington knew better than to bait her, but he could hardly help himself. Letting anyone get the last word just wasn't in his nature. He liked to win. "What kind of thoughts?"

"Thoughts like you were wondering what exactly happened between me and Colt."

Remington frowned. "Frankly that's the last thing I'd like to discuss."

China snorted. "Hit a sore spot?"

Remington centered himself, shoving down the boil of emotion until he was calm, cool, and collected. "What happened between the two of you is immaterial to our mission. I need you, and you need me to locate and obtain the Book. Simple. Easy. Neat and clean. End of story."

She snorted again and muttered under her breath. "Ain't nothin' *that* simple and easy."

Remington looked at the crude directions they'd constructed from a combination of Diego's handwritten map and the additional information he'd uncovered in his ma's diary. He'd need Diego himself to understand what risks lay at the end of the trail. He peered up over the flat wash of scrub and cacti, looking at the rim of blue hills to the southwest.

She leaned toward him, looking over his arm at the map. "Where we headed, exactly?"

"Southwest until we hit Nogales. Probably get there by morning if we ride through the night. Then we'll keep going west until we hit Caborca."

"What's in Caborca?"

"If I've interpreted the clues correctly, I'm hoping Diego."

"And if he ain't there?"

My, she was a persistent thing. "Then perhaps there is another key."

Her lips pursed. Remy could tell she was holding something back. "You have something to add, Miss McGee?"

She glared at him. "China."

"Very well, China, do you have something to add?"

She frowned. "What do we do if Diego doesn't want to give us the information you want?"

Remy hadn't really considered that. He'd assumed he could convince Diego, or whomever else he needed to, that they should give them the information. "What makes you think it could be a problem?"

China shrugged. "Nothin' really. I just figured if Diego had gone to all the trouble of hidin' his map and then puttin' only half the directions to it in a safety-deposit box, he might not hand it over without gettin' something in return. That's how I would be."

"Diego knows the stakes if Rathe takes over."

China snickered. "You think he's gonna care? If there's one thing I've learned, it's that people don't much care what happens to the rest of humanity if they think there might be an end to the world right around the corner. They get grabby, and it's every man out for hisself."

Remy tightened his grip on his reins. "You have an awfully low opinion of humans."

"Don't have a much better one of Darkin."

That surprised him. He was beginning to wonder if China really had loyalties to anyone or anything besides herself.

They rode on in silence. China didn't see much point in making conversation with him. The more he found out about her, the less likely he was to trust her. And the more likely he was to stumble across the fact that she was related to his arch nemesis. More important, she needed his trust if she was going to get her hands on the Book and hand it over to Rathe.

Her new clothes weren't nearly as soft and comfortable as the old ones she'd been wearing. They had too much store starch in them. A few dunkings and they'd be right as rain, but for now they made her feel suffocated. She also wasn't certain she liked wearing a skirt. Even with it being a split skirt, she wasn't used to the wash of air she got against her lady bits now and again. That just didn't happen in well-fit britches. Not that she'd tell Remington.

There was a comfortable wedge of wariness in between them. Ever since he'd seen her with Colt, he'd backed away a bit, which gave her room to breathe. When Remington focused the full force of his attention on her, it seemed to suck all the air out of her lungs. No, this was far easier—on both of them.

As the dark blue bowl of the sky became rimmed with purple, and finally bruised a darker color, she looked at him, really looked at him. Remington Jackson was exactly the temptation she didn't need. Her shifter eyes could detect far more light in the darkness than mere human eyes, giving her excellent night vision.

His big, blatantly male body rolled easily with the steady

walk of the horse beneath him. Remington had the dark good looks, the intelligence, and the air of danger about him that was as addictive as any opiate, but it was cleverly cloaked in civility. In so many ways he was more dangerous to her than Colt.

Colt had been wild and reckless, but their relationship had been equal parts of mistrust and mutual physical attraction—never anything serious. He was a womanizer, and she knew it. It wasn't as if she'd ever thought that Colt would give up his life as a confirmed bachelor Hunter to settle down with a Darkin. Was. Not. Going. To. Happen. He just wasn't made that way.

But Remington was a far different man. That veneer of civility promised, if not in words in implication, that he'd do right by a woman—in short he seemed more the type to settle down with one woman once he'd made up his mind to. And for some reason that was so much more alluring to her than it should be.

He was more than just her type; he was exactly the kind of man that intrigued her most. Strong. Polished. Unattainable. Maybe it was because she'd seen her mother struggle for so long by herself. Maybe it was because she'd always felt as if she were set adrift in the world of the Darkin—part of it, but utterly alone without family or friends to cling to in stormy times.

In fact, looking at him objectively, if it hadn't been for her miserable experience with Colt, she'd probably have already found a way to wrap Remington around her little finger. If she wanted to. If she could.

She wasn't a succubus, and she couldn't throw a glamour to gain a man's compliance like a vampire. If she wanted him, she'd have to resort to old-fashioned womanly wiles. Or powerful Darkin binding magic—the kind that worked both ways.

"How long do you think it'll take to get there?"

He glanced at her, his blue eyes clear in the moonlight. He smiled, his teeth a flash of white in the darkness. "Likely all night and a good part of the morning. Why, you petering out on me?"

She took it as a jab to her pride. Shifters, even among Hunters, were known for their stamina. "'Course not. Just trying to figure out when we're going to eat next."

He chuckled. "You shifters really need to eat a lot to keep up your strength, don't you?"

China sniffed. "At least we don't need as much sleep as you humans."

"Touché."

"I'm *not* touchy."

Remington shook his head and chuckled. "You always this prickly, China?"

She looked at him full on. "No, sometimes I'm worse, especially when I'm hungry." She dug her heels into her horse, pushing it into a trot so she could move ahead of him on the trail.

He clicked to his horse and quickly caught up. "I don't know a single animal alive that doesn't get ornery when it's hungry."

"Are you calling me an animal, now?"

He slid her a sideways glance. "No. You're too smart for that."

China decided to change tactics. He was obviously used to being around prickly people and that didn't push him away any. She feigned shock, placing a hand over her heart. "I do declare, Mr. Jackson, was that a compliment I heard?" The subtle, sugar-sweet tone of her voice made him raise one brow.

"Perhaps," he answered with caution in his tone. "But I wouldn't take it as a sign of acquiescence if I were you."

China changed the subject. "You ever met Diego? Might be good to know exactly who we're looking for."

"Just once, when I was young, before Winn bowed out of Hunting for the Legion."

Thoughts tumbled around over one another in China's head like stones crumbling off of a bank, one overtaking the next until it was a jumble. She knew powerful little about the Jacksons beyond what Colt had told her. And when he wasn't busy hustling or stealing, or killing Darkin, he was gambling, drinking, or womanizing—which left no time for just sitting and talking.

So she'd done some research of her own, talking to fellow Darkin, those that would talk to a marked one—the name for those Darkin unfortunate enough to be physically branded by Rathe as his personal property.

Some said that the three Jackson brothers were the Chosen—three Hunter brothers in the Darkin lore prophesied to bring a balance back to the world between Darkin and humanity, so that neither wiped the other out completely. She really didn't care much either way about balance or prophecy. She did however care a great deal about being on the winning side no matter what it took. What she saw was an opportunity to gain Rathe's approval for good. And when it came to an archdemon lord, *that* wasn't an opportunity that came around every century.

"What'd he look like?"

Remington pulled his hat from his head and scratched his scalp. "You know I don't really remember much. He was one of those people who are easy to forget. Nothing overly distinct about them."

"Then how will we know if we've found the real Diego?"

He threw her a knowing smile. "Don't you worry; I've got ways of telling."

"And do these secret Hunter skills extend to detecting Darkin as well?"

He gave her a secretive smile. "Of course."

She couldn't help herself and smiled back. "And exactly how does that work?"

"Would you like a demonstration?"

Her heart thudded harder in her chest. China wasn't sure she actually said yes, or anything at all for that matter, but she did nod her head.

Remington brought his horse to a standstill, and China came to a stop alongside him. He dismounted and gallantly offered his hand to assist her from her horse, even though they both knew she didn't need it.

After several dusty hours of traveling, the night air was cool, crisp, and clean. In a word, romantic. The cloying sweet aroma of cactus flowers seasoned the night, and out in the desert a lone coyote bayed at the moon. His call was met by yips and howls from others who joined him in singing to the night.

Remington gently brushed a strand of hair off her forehead as he locked his eyes on hers. "A well-trained Hunter uses all his senses when detecting a Darkin."

"Such as?" she asked, her voice soft and a little breathless.

"He can smell a Darkin." He bent low, his nose lightly skimming a trail along her neck, right beneath her ear. She heard him inhale and felt the brush of air as his chest expanded, nearly touching hers. Her knees wobbled a bit.

He pulled back and gazed deeply into her eyes. "He can see a Darkin by looking for that telltale glint in the eye." His warm hands slid over her upper arms, and he turned her just slightly, so the moonlight caressed her face.

"Anything else?"

His devastating smile flashed white in the darkness. "A great Hunter can even taste a Darkin." He leaned in, his mouth gently sealing over hers in a searing kiss that rocked her to her toes. Her whole body responded to the intimacy of his touch, and while it was innocent enough, it made her yearn for far, far more.

She'd told herself once, and she'd say it again—Remington Jackson was trouble.

Remington let himself get so caught up in the sensations that his common sense had to reel him back in. She smelled sweet and felt both soft and sleek beneath his touch. But it was the kiss that knocked him for a loop. Until that moment he'd still been in control of the situation. Of himself.

Her lips were honey on rose petals, slick and sweet and oh, so soft. And when they parted, he tasted the flavor of her mouth. He'd been wrong, so very wrong to think a Darkin female might taste worse than a human one. China McGee tasted like vanilla ice cream. She wound him up in knots so tight, it took every ounce of willpower he had to release his hands on her and step away.

Both of them were breathing hard. Her luminous eyes were dilated at the centers, big and dark, and rimmed in brilliant silver.

"If we're going to make Nogales by noon, we ought to get going," he said absently. Part of him already regretted that he hadn't kissed her longer. But it was better that than to let the physical stray into some emotional connection and begin sharing true Hunter secrets with her. "That would conclude my demonstration."

China bit her bottom lip, her teeth worrying the soft pink fullness. Now that he'd kissed her, he knew precisely the texture of her there and how slick and warm her lips could be. "You're very convincing." Her voice was a bit breathless.

He turned away from her and found something to occupy his hands, checking the cinch and buckles on his tack. "Do you need a moment to take care of anything before we mount up again?"

She nodded and handed him the reins of her horse, then hurried off between the rocks. He didn't follow. Didn't even try.

China McGee was temptation, pure and simple.

They rode on through the night, and as the dawn broke golden over the mountains, the sky becoming a paler blue, they spied Nogales. Thankfully it was closer than he'd thought. They'd make it before noon.

The sleepy little village was no more than a few squat adobe houses clustered together around a central well. The smell of freshly cooking beans, onions, and peppers spiked the air with a delicious scent that made his stomach rumble. What he wouldn't give for a stack of freshly made tortillas and a bowlful of good beans. A few chickens scratched in the shade, and a dog lay panting just outside the front door of a home, but there was nary a person in sight. It seemed eerie, as if the people had simply evaporated and left everything behind.

"Where is everyone?" Remington asked.

"Exactly what I was wondering," China responded in a hushed tone.

He spied a pale wisp of white smoke coming from a hole in one of the adobe houses. Someone was home in this village; they just weren't open and friendly to visitors. He dismounted and went over to China, grabbing the bridle of her palomino. He intentionally lowered his voice so only she could hear it as she dismounted. "There's people here. They're hiding out. Watch yourself."

She gave him a barely perceptible nod and pulled out the revolver she had holstered at her hip.

* * *

Slowly they walked through the village, looking first in the half-opened door of one house and then another. By the time they reached the fifth house, they were across the small square from their horses. *"Hay alguien en casa?"* Remington called out, hoping whoever lived here would be more willing to show themselves to the gringos if they knew they could communicate with them.

Before they'd had time to turn around in the doorway, a chorus of clicks sounded as multiple guns cocked and pointed at them. "Put your hands up on your heads and slowly turn around, gringos." The deep, gravely male voice sounded as if it had choked on dust for years.

They complied, and Remington took care to keep his face and manner as calm and unruffled as possible. There was no reason to increase the tension already sparking in the air. "We're looking for Diego Mendoza."

"There's lots of people who look for Diego. What's your business with him?"

"He worked with my father, Cyrus Jackson. I'm here to see him about a map."

The older man who seemed to be leading the others spat out a dark stream of tobacco juice into the dirt. He squinted one eye against the brightness of the sun as he looked them over. "Who's the Darkin?" he said with a jerk of his head in China's direction.

"She's my scout. I'll need one where I'm headed." At least Colt had said as much. Diego might know where to find the missing piece of the Book, but only a Darkin could gain access to it.

The old man chuckled. "You don't need a Darkin to show you the path to Hell, boy. A Hunter can find that all on his own in good time."

Remington struggled to maintain his control when the old man shifted the aim of his rifle to China's head. "Diego will know why she's here."

The old man's gun lowered a notch. He glanced back at the group of men gathered on his right and nodded. One of them took off running to an adobe house set apart from the others and came back a few minutes later. "Diego says he'll see you."

They were led at gunpoint to the adobe house. "How do you know Diego and your father weren't enemies?" China whispered as they walked.

"I don't."

Chapter 8

The dim interior of the adobe house momentarily left Remington sun blinded, and his hand automatically went to his gun. It came up empty. His hand reflexively fisted at the loss. Their weapons had been confiscated while they were marched at gunpoint to what he supposed was Diego's home. Their welcome party was still behind them, now blocking their only means of escape, guns pointed at their backs.

At least they hadn't separated him and China. He glanced at her, and she seemed more curious than upset. Perhaps she could see better in the dark room than he could.

As his eyes adjusted he could see the place, no bigger than fifteen-feet square. Slats of light from the shuttered windows slashed across a dirt floor pounded flat and hard from the wear of many feet.

A single bed covered with a colorful, handwoven wool blanket, a small table, a couple of chairs, and a chest of drawers on which sat a chipped enamel washbasin took up pretty much all of the floor space, leaving little room to maneuver. The place smelled of cooked meat and beans, gun oil, and the pungent tang of strong alcohol.

A bent figure, hand resting on his cane, stood in the shadows beside the table. Remy noticed out of the corner of his eye the abandoned, half-eaten plate of food and the liquor bottle. But his attention was fixed on the elderly, white-haired man dressed in light clothing who at first glance looked more like one of the locals than a Hunter ready to fight.

"Diego Mendoza? I'm Remingt—"

"Where's Cyrus?"

Remington reached up to remove his hat and found the cold rounded muzzle of a gun pressing into his back. He realized he'd been rude to interrupt breakfast uninvited, but that didn't warrant the gun. Obviously Diego was expecting trouble.

"Easy now," Remington murmured. He slowed his actions so they couldn't be mistaken. As his eyes adjusted the man's features became clearer. His face, tanned by the sun into a wrinkled brown leather, sported a wide jawline obscured by a scraggly salt and pepper beard. Thick white hair was combed straight back. Deep-set dark brown eyes peered at him from beneath bushy black brows. Diego was older than Pa. Or perhaps they'd been the same age, but Pa hadn't lived long enough for Remington to have a memory of him like this.

"Cyrus has been gone for five years. I'm his middle son, Remington."

He found the tip of the cane, which he realized was actually the barrel of a rifle, pointed in his face. "If you're really Cy's boy, then tell me why he named you boys what he did."

"He named us after his favorite hunting guns. Winchester, Remington, and Colt. Ma didn't like it, but she couldn't fault him for it because those guns had saved him so many times."

"And what branch of the Legion are you descended from?"

"Cadel, the lion of the Legion."

Diego nodded and lowered the tip of his cane/gun. "If your father is gone, why are you seeking me out, boy?"

Remington swallowed hard against the dust coating the

back of his throat. The smell of Diego's breakfast tweaked his nose and made his belly grumble. It had been a long ride all night through the desert, and a hot meal sounded divine. He resisted the urge to glance at the half-finished plate of beans and tortillas on the table. First things first.

Pa had always taught them duty came before one's personal needs. Winn followed the advice to the letter, Colt rarely, and Remy did when it suited him. China shuffled her feet as she stood beside him but kept quiet. At least she knew enough not to attract unwanted attention as a Darkin in a Hunter's home. Smart girl. He glanced at her for a moment, then turned back to Diego.

"We're searching for the southern European portion of the Book of Legend—the one that came to the Kingdom of Navarre with Elwin, then was brought to North America by the Spanish searching for Aztec gold. My pa believed you knew where it was located and what it would take to get it."

The old man's hands shook for a moment, and he clutched one of them into a fist as he swayed, then sat down carefully in the chair behind him. He looked away from them, his eyes unfocused, as if he were reliving memories in his head. He picked up his empty glass and rolled it between his twisted brown fingers. "Your father and I didn't part on the best of terms."

"But he saved your life once. My mother wrote of you in her diary. And you know this is bigger than just a grudge between him and you."

Diego's gaze shifted back to Remington, piercing in its intensity, the dark of his eyes bottomless.

He still wasn't budging. Remington pushed harder. "The Gates of Nyx could be opened permanently, leaving a bridge between our world and that of the Darkin that could allow them to overtake us. It would be a global disaster."

Diego cursed under his breath and pulled at his grizzled beard. "Who leads them?"

"Rathe," China interrupted.

A hiss of breath escaped Diego's lips, and his eyes narrowed into hate-filled slits as he glared at China, as if just recognizing she'd been standing there. Perhaps he'd taken no note of her before because she was a woman—easily dismissed by a Hunter like Diego. "Darkin dross, you have no business here. It's because of your kind I have no right leg."

Remy stepped slightly in front of her, just enough to let the old man know that she was under his protection. "She's here to help us defeat Rathe."

Diego gave a dry bark of laughter, devoid of humor. "When a Darkin rises up against her own kind, that will be the day Hell freezes over. She's fooling you, boy. She means to take the Book from you and give it to Rathe the minute she kills you."

China shoved past Remington, her body shaking. "Hell's iced over right now, and I'm not the only Darkin resisting Rathe. So are the vampires. Now are you going to help or let the world come crashing to an end?"

"Hunters don't work with Darkin." Diego spat into the dirt floor at her feet, then turned to Remington. "Get her out of here, and I'll talk to you."

China growled. Remy could sense the frustration and heat coming off of her. She fairly vibrated with it. He might not know China well, but he knew her well enough to see she was good and pissed off—enough to shift and take a bite of Diego's ass, literally.

He grasped her lightly about the wrist. "It's best if you wait for me outside."

She locked her glare on him, the angle of her jaw defiant. "I don't have to go anywhere."

"I know." He slid his hand down grasping hers and gave it

a slight squeeze. Her eyes widened slightly then softened for an instant.

He was asking a lot of her, especially for her to trust him. It was a hell of a lot more than he should ask of her, considering they knew so little of each other. He knew he couldn't secure the piece of the Book alone, but he also knew he needed the information Diego possessed, and the old man wasn't about to give it up with her standing there. He was old guard—the kind that saw the world in black and white with no room for Darkin of any stripe. "I'm asking you, wait for me outside."

She threw one last withering look at Diego, lifted her chin, and then turned on her heel and sashayed between the men gathered just outside the doorway, without a single look back. Colt and Winchester could both learn a little bit of grace and how to make an exit from her, Remington thought. He knew she wasn't backing down, just being strategic.

He turned back. Diego indicated with a nod that Remington should join him at the table. Diego had obviously been drinking. Remington dropped into the other chair and leaned back. Diego ignored the plate of food in front of him. The beans now had a dark, drying crust, streaked with bits of hardening white fat. It didn't look nearly as appetizing as it had when Remington had first come in. Perhaps Diego had lost his taste for hunting just as he had lost his taste for his meal. Hunters, like his brother Winn, sometimes did. Always fighting, each battle never the last, wore on a man.

Diego grabbed the brown bottle sitting in the middle of the table about the neck and shook it. A slight sloshing sound indicated it was almost empty. The old Hunter motioned to one of his men who promptly brought a fresh bottle and another glass and set them down in front of Diego.

Diego poured them each a measure of the dark caramel liquor. "You'd better drink."

"I didn't come to socialize."

Diego's brows pinched together. "Nothing social about it. You're going to need it for what I'm about to tell you."

Remington took the glass and sniffed. Tequila. Aged tequila. Good stuff if he had the time, which he didn't. He downed it in a long, slow swallow, letting it burn a path down to his stomach. It was awfully early in the morning to be drinking, but if it made getting information from Diego easier, then what the hell.

"The journey you seek is a dangerous one." Diego took a sip of his drink and shook his head. Fear flickered in the old man's eyes. "You likely will not survive. I barely made it out myself, and we never made it all the way in."

Remington's heartbeat stuttered, then picked up the pace double-time. He set his glass down with a *thunk* on the table. "When were you there? How?"

"You don't think you're the first Hunter to go after Elwin's piece of the Book of Legend, do you?" Diego poured out another measure of the tequila and took another drink. "How many are going with you on this journey?"

"Just me and the shifter."

Diego kicked back the rest of his entire glass in one swift swallow, then grimaced and looked down into his glass. "It can't be done. I lost thirty men when I went to search for it. You and a shifter? Alone? You won't survive."

Remington leaned in and waited until he made eye contact with Diego. "I don't have a choice. We have until the new moon before Rathe tries to open the Gates of Nyx permanently."

The spark in Diego's eyes died, turning the brown flat and lifeless. "You're asking me to give you a death sentence."

"I'm asking you to help me save the world."

Diego shook his head sadly and sighed. "Show me what you have. Then I will tell you the rest of what you need to know."

Remington pulled the scrap of paper from his breast pocket and carefully unfolded it, spreading it smooth with the palm of his hand.

Recognition flitted across Diego's face. "My map." He peered intently at Remington, his eyes narrowing. "Where'd you get that?"

"I guess you haven't heard yet that the Bisbee bank was blown up."

One of Diego's dark brows arched upward. "That Darkin you're with have anything to do with it?"

Remington nodded. "She was working with Colt. Pa told him he could find the map in your safety-deposit box."

Diego muttered under his breath. "I should have known Cyrus would send one of you boys after it."

Remington glanced down at the paper before him. "What exactly is this?"

"Back in 1519 Cortez and the Spanish Hunters on his crew brought Elwin's piece of the Book of Legend with them to Mexico. It had been captured as a spoil of war when the southern half of the Kingdom of Navarre was taken by the Crown of Castile in 1513. The king sought to keep it hidden and sent it with Cortez to be secreted in a place where no one would find it." A fine tremor shook Diego's hand as he traced the lines on the map with his outstretched fingers. "This was a journey to hell and back. We thought we'd take Elwin's piece of the Book . . ." He locked gazes with Remington. "We were wrong. It takes a Darkin to make it past the final barrier Cortez had the natives call on the Darkin to erect."

The adobe bricks were digging into China's back as she leaned against the outside of the house and surveyed the town. The men stationed just outside Diego's door eyed her warily and kept their weapons at the ready. Even though she was in the shade, her skin was still hot with anger and the urge to shift.

She would not be dismissed, not by some old Hunter, who should have known better, and not by a Jackson brother. The only reason she hadn't shifted into a mountain lion, shoved Diego to the floor, and taken a bite out of him was because of Remington.

His eyes had said what his mouth could not. *Please trust me. He's just an angry old Hunter.* And God help her, she had given him her trust. If Diego didn't explain the squiggly lined map to Remington, she could just come back later that night and steal it and figure it out herself.

A thin trail of pale dust kicked up into the air as a group of men approached. At the center was a young man in military garb with Diego's men flanking him. He looked barely out of puberty, and his face was far too smooth to be that of a seasoned soldier.

It took a moment for China to realize the rider was not male at all, but a proud young woman. Her skin the color of milky coffee, her thick, dark hair bound at the nape. A heavy military jacket buttoned up the front disguised most of her shape.

Her gaze flicked to China as the small group dismounted, leaving their horses in the hands of the men stationed outside, and she passed by her with a confident stride to enter Diego's home. It was just a glance, but enough to connect them. It was as if the young woman had said, this is a man's world, but that doesn't mean you must accept what is given to you. Just then it hit China. There was no reason for her to stand out here exiled. If Jackson hadn't gotten what he needed out of the old man by now, then chances were they'd worn out their welcome anyhow.

She let the warmth seep through her bones, like hot water, as her form squeezed and compressed, growing smaller. Her skin hardened into overlapping scales, and her tongue and jaw elongated until she was a lizard. The men guarding the house were so busy talking to the new arrivals, they didn't even notice her shift. She skittered into the home and zipped up the wall.

Diego gestured to the young woman. "I told you my submarine crew was coming soon. This here's Monica Nation, the daughter of my submarine captain, Karl Nation. She'll take you to Caborca and from there to the coastal waters where the submarine is kept."

Clearly Diego and Remington had discussed a great deal while she'd just been hanging about waiting. The man had a submarine? Why? He lived in the damn Sonoran Desert.

"And you're sure the submarine can take us to the location on the map?"

"Ain't no way faster." Diego leaned down and pointed to the map. The remnants of breakfast had been cleared away, and the folded paper spread out like a cloth that hung over the edges of the small table. Diego's gnarled finger traced the coastline along Mexico until he hit a bay just above Guatemala. "It's as close as you'll get. You'll need to walk in the rest of the way. And once you get to the Veracruz province, you'll need this to decipher the rest of the map." He scooted back on his chair and pulled a small steamer trunk from beneath his bed.

"That's a bit large to pack on the back of a horse," Remington said.

"Not the trunk, boy. What's in it." Diego hid his movements as he worked the lock on the front of the trunk, opened it, and pulled out a thick book bound in odd brown leather.

Remington seemed pragmatic, all except for the slight lift in his shoulders. "What is it?"

"A translation of the Mendoza Codex. The writings my Spanish ancestors put down about the Aztecs, the tribes they subjugated, and their lore. Them Indians know what's down there, and they worked with the Spaniards to hide it. I tried my best with an interpreter to make a coded map that can guide you through to where the piece of the Book of Legend was hidden. You have that. But once you get inside the temple there's two rivers and trials you'll need to pass before you can get to the Aztec hell itself where the bone gods wait to strip the flesh off of you."

"That sounds encouraging."

Diego grumbled. "This ain't just some hunt boy; this is the Aztec land of the dead. You ain't meant to come out alive. So listen up. The River of Scorpions is a pit filled with the critters. Wide enough you can't step across it and deep enough that if you step into it, you'll drown in them."

Remington swallowed hard. China made a note that Remington appeared not to be fond of scorpions. One never knew when information like that would give a girl an advantage.

He glanced up at Diego. "And the other river you've mentioned is more of the same?"

Diego looked grim and drank straight from the bottle. China watched his throat work as he stared at Remington with bleak eyes. "The next is called the River of Blood. It's an acidic river that flows rust red from the heart of the caves and reeks of Darkin. It'll strip the flesh right off your bones. We lost three men crossing that alone."

China bet it was sulfuric acid. Underground caverns could be full of them. And these were just the river crossings? She couldn't wait to hear what other fiendish Hunter traps and natural barriers they'd be up against.

"And the trials? Are they varied as well?"

Diego nodded and took another drink. "Each one represents a fear meant to challenge your brain as well as your mettle."

Remington gritted his teeth and looked deep into the old man's brown eyes. "If Elwin's piece of the Book has been there that long, how do we even know it hasn't moldered away?"

"We don't. But you tell me how else the Chosen is supposed to put it back together and close the Gates of Nyx if we don't get it out of there?"

Remington's shoulders stiffened, and his face turned dour.

"There is no other way except by reuniting the Book. Marley and I have researched Hunter lore a thousand times over looking for anything else that might work against Rathe."

China shifted back into her human form, and every eye turned in her direction as she seemed to sprout out of thin air. Weapons were drawn. She straightened up from her crouch on the dirt floor. "There is nothing else."

Diego's face darkened with fury. His narrowed eyes flicked from China to Remington. "I can't stop you from going on this death march, but are you sure it's wise taking this Darkin?"

Remington stood. "Wise, no. Necessary, yes."

China grumbled. "Thanks for the vote of confidence in my loyalty, Jackson."

He gave her a half-tilted smile. "You're welcome."

"How large is your party?" the captain's daughter asked.

Remington braced his feet wider apart, mimicking the military woman's stance, putting them on equal terms. He did it so effortlessly, China had to appreciate it. Like her, he understood the importance of knowing the mind of both your ally and foe alike. "Just the two of us."

The captain's daughter nodded. "It'll make it easier on the submarine if you are taking fewer people and supplies, but ultimately a harder journey."

"Doesn't look as if we have a choice, Miss Nation."

"First Mate Nation, if you please. I've earned my rank."

China respected the woman in a way she didn't Miss Arliss. She liked how the captain's daughter hadn't even flinched at the mention of her being a Darkin. Perhaps like Remington, First Mate Nation understood that there were differences among Darkin just as there were among humans. Some were good, some were bad, and some just were.

"How long will it take to get to Caborca and the submarine?" China asked.

Monica's shoulders straightened slightly. "At least a day

and a half by horse to Caborca, another to the coast where my father has the submarine moored."

China knew enough about Rathe to know that if he thought his greatest advantage would be at the new moon, he wouldn't delay. By the time they reached the coast, they would have already used nearly one of their three precious weeks until the moon disappeared in the sky.

Beneath their feet the earth began to tremble. At first China thought it might be an earthquake, but the tremors were too even and regular, almost like gigantic footsteps. She knelt, pressing her fingertips to the compacted dirt. There was no roll and pitch to the earth, but she could feel a grinding sensation.

Screams and the whinny of frightened horses echoed outside. Her preternaturally sharp sense of smell picked out the dirty scent of machine oil and the greasy stench of coal smoke. And the sulfur of another Darkin. Rathe had sent more of his minions to stop or kill her and Remington.

One of Diego's guards burst into the house. "*Pardon, senõr*, a large machine has entered the village." An explosion outside shook the adobe house, sending down a shower of grit and dust on top of them. Everyone crouched low.

"What the blue blazes was that?" Remington growled.

China didn't wait; she didn't hesitate. She'd grabbed the codex while everyone was distracted and tucked it beneath her jacket, then turned and dashed for the door to look out. A giant scorpion created from metal, gears, and pulleys was ripping through the houses with a massive brass claw. It crushed the adobe walls as if they were sandcastles.

In a second Remington was by her side. "What is that?"

"It's a message from Rathe. See that man atop the driving platform?"

* * *

Remy squinted. Between the bulbous glass eyes of the mechanical monster he could barely make out the driver in his red jacket and black broad-brimmed hat. "You know him?"

"That's Dr. Adder Morpheus, a snakeoil peddler turned demon who works for Rathe." The tone of disgust in her voice indicated they weren't allies.

The metallic shell of the machine flashed in the sunlight as it drew closer, ripping a path of destruction through town in a beeline for Diego's house. "What does he want?"

"I reckon he's here to stop us, kill us, or both."

There wasn't time to think things through or create a plan. Remy swiveled back to Diego, First Mate Nation, and the other men under Diego's command. "Get out now!"

Shutters flew open as men scattered out of the adobe house through the windows. First Mate Nation helped Diego to the doorway. It was clear to Remy the old hunter was in no condition to run. He hoisted him up over his shoulder and prepared to make a dash between the scorpion's legs. A shadow fell across the doorway, and Remington looked up to see a big brass claw descending toward them.

Chapter 9

There were two things of which Remington was absolutely sure in a blinding instant of clarity: one, bullets weren't going to do a damn thing to stop this machine from crushing them, and two, he needed to act fast.

"Follow me!" He rushed forward. The bulk of Diego lay heavy on his shoulders and back, slowing him down. The two women ran beside him. With a low-pitched mechanical groan, the claw came down where they'd been standing only moments before. It smashed straight through the center of the tile roof, collapsing it inward with a crash. A cloud of dust and debris shot up into the air, blinding them for a moment and sending bricks and bits of shattered tile and stone shrapnel flying everywhere.

Remington squeezed his eyes shut and coughed, unable to shield his face from the cloud as he held on to Diego. "I hope everyone got out," he muttered as he gasped.

Monica had tucked her chin, mouth, and nose down beneath the edge of her military jacket collar. She popped her head upward, leaving a pale line over the bridge of her nose where the dust coated the top half of her head. "They did. We were the last ones out." She coughed against the dust still thick in the air.

Remington tried to twist around, searching the area. He caught a glimpse of China, clearly spitting mad. First things first. Find somewhere to stash Diego out of harm's way. "Where's a safe place we can put him?"

There was a pause. It stretched out too long to be good.

"I don't think that's going to be an issue." Sadness laced Monica's tone.

"What happened?" Remington leaned up close to the building, allowing Diego to slip slowly from his back. He propped the old man up against the wall. Bright red seeped from Diego's temple, staining his face, and caking with the dust and dirt into a sluggish dark mat in his beard.

Monica put her fingers to his neck. "There's no pulse. A chunk of brick must have hit him."

"Damn. Where's the codex?"

Monica nodded at the rubble. "Probably still in there."

"Now how in the blue blazes are we going to unravel the rest of Diego's map?"

The dust cloud was beginning to clear. Soon their cover would be gone. The machine was on the move. The ground shook beneath their feet. The clinking of metal against metal, the shoosh of pistons, and the clunk of gears as the machine repositioned itself grew closer and more ominous.

Remington glanced at China. It was a chance, a slim chance, but one he had to take. They couldn't outrun the machine either on foot or by horseback. "Maybe if I can keep Morpheus busy telling me what he wants, you and First Mate Nation can escape, and we can all meet up in Caborca. He seems like the type that I could cajole into bragging about himself for ten to fifteen minutes, enough to give you a decent head start."

China grimaced. "Stand there and talk him to death. *That's* your plan?"

Remington glared at her. "You have a better one?"

The machine appeared out of the dust cloud, a metal menace, belching steam, claws snapping.

"Hell yes. Let's rip that sonofabitch apart! Here, hold this." She pulled the codex from her jacket and handed it to him.

His eyes widened slightly. "You took it?"

"Thief, remember?"

In just a few seconds China had transformed into a rather large desert rat. With pale brownish-gray fur, her foot-long body and small oval ears blended in quickly with the desert colors of the adobe rubble and dirt. Only her darker brown tail could be seen as she skittered off directly toward the mechanical scorpion.

He shot up from his crouch. "Wait!" He didn't know exactly what she planned to do, but Remington knew he had to give her time. He clasped his hands about his mouth and yelled up at the driver of the machine with all his might. "Dr. Morpheus!"

The scorpion stopped mid-motion, a hiss of steam escaping from the valves in clouds of white. It was easier to see the man now, up this close. His dark, elegantly waxed mustache curled at the ends and matched his precisely trimmed goatee. He touched the brim of his black plantation owner's hat with a gray-gloved hand, nodding toward Remington in acknowledgment. "The very same. And you are?" His Southern drawl made the words sound so much more polite than negotiations with a demon bent on killing him, China, and the rest of the village.

"Just a traveler trying to find out why you are destroying this village," Remington replied. There was no reason to reveal his true identity or give China away if he didn't need to.

"Then, sir, I have no reason to speak to you. I'm here for Diego Mendoza." Another hiss of steam was accompanied by the ratcheting sound of gears as the pulleys and metal components of the brass claw lifted it up into the air to strike a final blow to Diego's home.

"Wait!"

Dr. Morpheus pulled on a lever, leaving the claw suspended over what was left of the crumbled walls. "You begin to irritate me, sir."

"Mendoza is dead. You must have crushed him with the last blow."

In the corner of his vision Remington watched as China scampered up the leg of the mechanical scorpion and vanished between chinks in the monster's armored metal plating with a swish of her tail. Her flag of triumph, Remington thought, amused in spite of the situation.

"Where's the body? Mendoza has something I want, and he'd never give it to anyone for safekeeping."

"Are you certain?"

Faster than Remington could move, the huge brass claw swung down and pinned him against the building behind him. It knocked the air out of his lungs and pushed so hard on his ribs, he was certain a few of them cracked.

"Do not make the mistake of toying with me, son. I've made a living out of selling charades to folks, so I know how to spot one. Tell me where Mendoza's codex translation is, and I'll let you live."

A sudden spurt of steam and the crunching grind of gears seizing up came from the scorpion's claw as it went slack, slamming to the ground, inches from Remington's boots. Free, he stepped clear.

From the metal deck between the scorpion's eyes, Dr. Morpheus muttered a string of curses as he pulled levers and prodded buttons on his control panel. *Retchetchet. Crack! Scree!* Suddenly the articulated legs of the scorpion began to collapse down upon themselves, becoming shortened stubs. Remington didn't need any encouragement to slip away as swiftly as possible.

He rounded the corner of the building and found Monica along with Diego's body. She'd dragged him out of eyesight, away from Dr. Morpheus and his mechanical monster.

"We won't have much time once China gets back."

Monica nodded. "If we take the horses out through the arroyo, he won't be able to see us. It's deep enough to hide us."

Remington frowned. Arroyos were dangerous and unpredictable places. Water could rush downstream from a monsoon storm miles and miles away in the mountains, washing down the gulley so fast that it swept away everything in its path. "What about the chance of a flash flood or an ambush?"

Monica peered up at the cloudless blue sky. "We only need it for cover long enough to reach the tip of the Sierra Madre mountains to the south."

Remington considered the plan. It was as good as any, and a damn sight better than anything he had in mind. There was no telling how long it would take for Morpheus to get his machine working again. He peered at Diego. It wasn't right to abandon a Hunter in this way, but the others would have to see to his funeral. They simply didn't have time to wait. Monica whispered softly in Spanish to Diego, pressed a kiss to his forehead, swiped the back of her hand quickly against her eyes, then made eye contact with Remington.

From the look in her dark brown eyes he could tell she was hurting, but determined. "I'll wait for China and bring her down to the arroyo with our horses. We'll meet you there."

She nodded. "I'll be there as soon as I make sure Diego will be taken care of by the others in the village." She stayed on alert and crouched low as she disappeared between the buildings.

Remington turned his attention back to Diego. "I'm sorry you didn't get to see the Book of Legend for yourself, Diego, but your efforts won't be in vain. I will find it. I will bring the piece back, and I will defeat Rathe with my brothers."

"You know it ain't doin' him a bit of good to natter on like that." China's voice caused him to whip around.

"You're back!" He stepped close and lightly brushed the smear of dark grease away from her cheek. Her skin was silken to the touch. Truly China was more than she appeared, no matter what shape she took. Her mouth opened slightly at his touch, making Remington remember what kissing China was actually like. Her eyes grew round, and the gray color turned a dreamy, misty slate blue. But he had no business kissing her. Not now. Not ever again.

"How'd you disable it?"

She blinked and snapped her mouth shut, clacking her teeth, then cleared her throat. Her skin turned slightly pink. "Oh, you know how it can be when rats get chewing on wiring. It can cause all manner of things to short-circuit." If he hadn't been watching her eyes, if he hadn't observed her pupils dilating with the same desire he felt himself, he would've been fooled that she didn't reciprocate his feelings.

With a start Remington realized she was just as affected by him as he was by her. The connection between them was more than just both of them knowing Colt. There was a chemistry that percolated and bubbled just beneath the surface that neither of them had acknowledged. And never would if Remington had anything to do with it. His life was complicated enough without getting sweet on a Darkin who was anything but. He needed China, but that didn't mean he trusted her farther than he could spit.

Remington cleared his throat and dropped his hand, realizing he'd been stroking her cheek long after the grease had disappeared. "The first mate is waiting for us down in the arroyo behind town. We need to find our horses. I'm sure Dr. Morpheus's machine scared them off their hitching post. It would be best if we separate to find our mounts and meet there. There will be less chance of being noticed that way."

China nodded and headed off in the direction Monica had

gone. Remington stared down at Diego one more time. He could hear the hissing, spitting sounds of the boilers in the mechanical scorpion and the gritty grind of the gears. Dr. Morpheus wasn't getting his contraption going anytime soon without a good mechanic. He tucked the codex into his pack and hauled ass toward the arroyo.

The arroyo cut like a jagged, deep scar through the desert. He scrambled down the steep incline, his fingers digging, when he could, into the loose earth and rock that lined the edges. The slick bottoms of his boots gave him little purchase as he half slid, half trotted down toward the horses.

Monica was already mounted, as was China. "Everyone okay?"

Both China and Monica nodded.

He took the reins in hand and swung up into the saddle. "Where'd you find them?"

"It wasn't hard; they were drinking out of the fountain," China answered, her tone a bit smug. "You didn't think Hunters were the only ones with tracking skills, did you?"

Remington wheeled his horse around so it was facing south. "How long do you think it'll take him to fix that machine?"

"Depends if there are other Hunters in town beside Diego who realize Dr. Morpheus is a demon."

"Diego was the only one," Monica interrupted.

The rapid report of gunfire from the direction of town was their cue to exit. They kicked the horses into a steady gallop, weaving as the path of the arroyo twisted and turned down the length of the valley. Remington knew there was only so far they could push the horses as the sun and heat grew more intense, trapped by the narrow, airless ravine. The deep sides of the arroyo provided a slight bit of shade from the rim until the sun reached its zenith.

They came to a rest at the base of the mountains where the arroyo spread into a wider plane. His horse was shaking, its sides bellowing in and out.

"We've got to be careful not to push them too hard, or there's no way we'll make it to Caborca," Monica said with a matter-of-fact tone, leaning down to run her hand over the horse's neck as she slowed her mount's pace to a steady walk.

Remington followed suit, and China came trotting up to his other side before she slowed too. "How did you know Diego? You seemed more tore up about his death than a normal henchman would have," Remington asked as casually as he could manage.

Monica kept facing straight ahead, her back military straight. "He was my uncle."

Now that Remington looked at her, he could see the slight family resemblance around the eyes. The first mate's dark eyes were just as intense and piercing as Diego's. Which made him wonder something else.

"Were you raised a Hunter?"

If it was possible, her ramrod straight spine stiffened even further. It was a wonder it didn't snap in two. The corners of her mouth turned downward. "Women are not allowed to be formally trained as Hunters in this part of the world."

Remington snorted. "Don't take it personally. They aren't anywhere."

"Why is that?" China cut in.

Remington twisted around to face his Darkin. "It's too hard a life."

China snorted, then leaned forward to make eye contact with Monica. "Do you think what you've endured is any different than the experiences of the men in your family?" she asked.

Monica gave a heavy sigh and shook her head. "Absolutely not. No offense, Miss McGee, but in the heat of battle most Darkin care not if their victims are male or female, young or old. Child, old man, woman, it's all the same to them if we are after something they want."

China nodded and leaned back in her saddle. "Can't fault you for speaking the truth."

Remington had the uncomfortable sensation of being caught between the frying pan and the fire. They traveled on through the desert, often single file through the most treacherous parts of the mountain passes. The more he stewed on how the women had talked, the more he realized how little he knew about China—where she'd come from, her upbringing, how she'd come to despise Rathe enough to fight against her own kind.

All afternoon and into the evening his rational attorney mind began to play through different scenarios, until he was as agitated as a frog on a hot skillet. It was all he could do to keep sitting in his saddle. He was hot, irritated, and damn hungry.

"What's eating you, Jackson?" China called from behind him. "Got sand in your shorts?"

Remington clenched his jaw hard enough that he could hear his teeth grind in his skull. He brought his horse to a stop. China was obliged to do the same since there wasn't room for her to pass him on the trail. He turned in his saddle and locked his gaze on her.

China's skin seemed to shrink a size under the piercing blue stare. It was the same intense look Colt had given her that could shake her confidence and strip away her bold as brass attitude in a heartbeat. Perhaps it was a Jackson family trait. Maybe it was just a Hunter skill.

"I've got something eating at me, if that's what you're implying."

She swallowed and flicked a glance up ahead of Remington long enough to see that the first mate had kept on going. "Sorry, I shouldn't have pried. If you don't want to talk about it I—"

"Get off your horse."

"What?"

"Off."

"Why?"

He swung down from his horse and stalked toward her. China's stomach flip-flopped. "It's just occurred to me that I don't know you very well, Miss McGee, and before we go any farther, I'm going to get some answers from you."

Her grip on her reins tightened until her knuckles were hard and white. "This ain't court, Jackson, and you ain't a judge. I don't have to talk if I don't want to." She turned and lifted her chin, staring pointedly ahead. As long as she did not look at him, she'd be fine.

He stood there, quiet, brooding, the energy pulsing off him in annoyed waves. Her sharp sense of smell detected a whiff of what she called male pride—peppery and strong with a hint of musk. It always grew stronger when men faced off against one another, or when they were showing off.

"If I talk to you, will you leave me alone?"

Remington remained silent.

China counted to five before she turned and hazarded a glance. He was still staring at her, his arms crossed over his broad chest.

She gestured with a hand at the trailhead where Monica had disappeared. "We're going to lose her if we don't get going."

"And we're not going anywhere before we have a little talk."

Night was coming swiftly, the mountains had long turned a bruised purple behind them, and the sun had set, leaving a smear of pale golden light behind the peaks to their right. China sighed and swung her leg back, sliding down out of her saddle. It was a silly move on her part that left her smack dab between his massive body and that of her horse.

"Say your piece then, so we can get going before the wild things come out."

"Why did you agree to help Colt find the missing piece of the Book of Legend?"

"He told me he'd pay me. I'm a good tracker and an even better thief."

He stared at her.

She narrowed her eyes back at him. "Did you have another question?"

"Wrong answer."

Her anger kicked up a notch. China crossed her arms and didn't give a damn that they bumped into his. "Then perhaps you ought to do a better job asking the question."

Quicker than she could blink he'd grabbed her about the upper arms and lifted her to the tips of her toes. "What's in it for you? What do you get out of coming with me? Out of risking your life?"

Her entire body stiffened. China tried hard to swallow past the sudden hard lump swelling in her throat. Her eyes burned. "Revenge."

Remington frowned. "On who?"

"Rathe."

He set her down so her feet were back on solid ground, and his hold on her softened slightly, but not enough for her to twist easily out of his grasp. "What'd he do to you?"

She started to shake. She couldn't control it. Images came of her mother, frail and worked to the bone, trying to scrape by to feed and clothe her. Of her mother being hunted down by man and Darkin alike when she wouldn't just blindly hand over her six-year-old to the demons who came for her. Of the torture her mother endured as they raked her flesh with their claws. "It's not what he did to me; it's what he did to my mother." As much as she craved Rathe's approval and feared him, she also hated part of him for hurting her and her mother as he had.

Remington's hands slid from her as he folded her into his arms. China couldn't hold back the heat or the tears any longer. It hurt to think on it. It hurt to remember. She wanted to shrink within herself and escape, but she couldn't. When she thought about the past there was nowhere to go where it didn't hurt. Where it didn't burn her to the core, knowing she could've saved her mother if only she'd never been born. It hurt even more to know that once they'd killed her mother and handed her over to Rathe, over time she'd come to love her father, to crave his approval and small kindnesses.

She knew he was capable of horrible things—had seen it with her own eyes. The severed heads of his enemies were shrunken and gilded, becoming macabre fobs on the elegant watch chain he wore. It had horrified her and yet made her grateful each time she was not the object of his sadistic behavior. And when she was, she knew it was somehow her fault. Even now she knew Rathe's ending the world as it was couldn't be right, and yet she couldn't help herself. She needed to get that completed Book of Legend to him. She was compelled to. And she hated that weakness within her.

She curled into the solid warmth of Remington's chest. He didn't tell her not to cry. He just held her while she did. Silent. Strong. He offered her what no one else had, the safety to crawl within herself for a moment, to work through the despair and confusion that she stuffed down daily. China dug her fingers into the fabric of his shirt and inhaled the scent of him as her body shook with sobs.

He rested his cheek on the top of her head. "I'm sorry," he murmured against her hair, the heat of his words soft and soothing against her scalp.

She pulled back and looked into his face. "For what?"

"Bringing up the past."

China sniffled. "It's not your fault." *It was hers. Always hers.*

He stiffened slightly, putting his finger beneath her chin,

Chapter 10

For a moment he just stood there and stared at China. Her revelation of her past gave Remington pause. "Are you certain you want to take on Rathe this way?"

"You have a better idea than joining with the Chosen and putting the Book of Legend together to close the Gates of Nyx?" China demanded, her cheeks flushed.

Warm desert wind funneled down the canyon, buffeting them as the temperature of the desert continued to drop. Their horses shuffled uneasily as they waited to continue their journey. It was still light enough that if they got back on now and continued riding at a decent speed, they could reach the mountains by dark. But then where? Remington realized getting off the horses had been an error in judgment. They needed Monica's knowledge of the terrain to get to Caborca.

Dark came swiftly out in the wide open spaces, and the minute that sliver of red hid behind the mountains, they'd be plunged into darkness with just the moon to light their surroundings.

"Give me a minute to think it over, and I might come up with something better."

He didn't like depending on anyone, and First Mate Nation was an unknown entity. He still wasn't sure if he was willing forcing her to look up at him. "What did Rathe do to your mother?"

China pulled back from the warmth and turned away from him, her stomach suddenly sick at the thought of telling the truth to him. Once he knew, he wouldn't forget. Once he knew, he wouldn't forgive.

She turned her gaze back to him, stricken. She didn't want to do this. Didn't want to ruin things between them. But she would, just like she'd ruined things with her father by falling for Colt. A mistake she didn't intend to repeat. She'd get on Rathe's good side and hope it was enough to remove the curse of being Marked, even if it meant stealing the complete Book of Legend away from the Jackson brothers once it was put back together.

His eyes narrowed, reading her face. "Never mind. It doesn't matter. It's in the past." He pulled her back into the warmth of his arms.

But deep down in her chest an icy chill took hold, making her shiver. It might not matter to him now, but soon, very soon, it would.

to entrust his life, and China's, to a woman he knew so little about. Other than his father's relationship with Diego—and that was rocky at best—he didn't have a reason to trust her. Or China.

He had no idea how far Monica had gone on without them in the few minutes they'd been talking, if she'd double back for them, or if she'd abandoned them. Hell, for all he knew this could be a setup designed to leave them vulnerable or dead so she could retrieve the codex for herself and keep Elwin's portion of the Book hidden. There were Hunters who didn't believe in the whole hokey-pokey prophecies about the Chosen. He and his brothers among them.

If she'd left them high and dry, he figured he was no worse off than he'd been before he'd contacted Diego.

China's Darkin connections and revenge plan should probably give him more grounds to distrust *her*. That, coupled with her frequent, and sometimes shocking, propensity to shift at the drop of a hat certainly had him on his toes.

He glanced at her now, the wind blowing her long hair around her shoulders like a veil. The heat and exertion of the day had pinked up her cheeks and made her unusual gray eyes sparkle and shine.

She looked, Remy thought, somewhat discombobulated by the observation, far too touchable and pretty to be a Darkin.

While it was true China hadn't done anything to harm him yet when she'd shifted into her various forms, that didn't mean that under the right circumstances she wouldn't turn on him as Darkin were wont to do. It wasn't in a Darkin's makeup to be good friends with humans, and if he or she did extend a friendly hand, a man would be smart to make sure there were no claws or other lethal appendages attached.

Revenge made people stupid and unpredictable. Revenge made people take risks they would never take under normal circumstances. They'd make choices they normally wouldn't, and do things they found abhorrent, if the chance came to make the object of their revenge suffer.

Just how far would China be willing to go to get back at Rathe? Remington's brain spun. Unlike his brothers, he liked to look at a situation from all sides. Sometimes he found looking at a case from the defendant's point of view much different than looking at it from the eyes of the plaintiff, or even the judge.

"So getting the Book of Legend reunited isn't as important to you as getting the Gates of Nyx closed?" he asked. Her answer would tell him how far she'd be willing to go to achieve her objective and how much he, and his mission, were at risk.

Sparks fired up in her eyes as if metal were grinding against metal. "It'd be even better if you could close them on his damn neck."

"Vicious little thing when crossed, aren't you?" Remington observed dryly.

And just that quick the spark in her eyes winked out. "I don't like being hurt," she murmured softly, the words slipping like a breath past her full, kissable lips.

Damn it. He didn't want to know that she could be hurt, either physically or emotionally. She was a Darkin. Darkin didn't *have* human emotions, did they? "And have I hurt you?"

She shook her head. Light from the moon illuminated her golden hair, making it gleam like moonbeams. Now that darkness had settled in like a blanket across the landscape, the air grew cooler, making him that much more aware of the heat of her body beside him. The scents of night-blooming cactus flowers, sweet and potent, mixed with the clean fragrance of vanilla coming off her skin. His body went where his mind couldn't, soaking up the sensations and humming with it.

She did something to him all right. She near turned him inside out with just a glance. And now that he knew more about the real China, he thought his brother either a complete fool or exceedingly brilliant. He saw how she could easily sneak her way under a Hunter's thick skin. She was charming and bold, with just enough sass to make sparring with her an enjoyable pastime.

"What do you think is happening?"

"Monica's run off and left us here to die?" China retorted, sounding surprisingly belligerent.

He had no idea, but wished he knew. "She's probably riding ahead to scout." He hoped.

"I don't trust her." She made a rude noise. "We're the crazy ones. Off to seal ourselves in a tin can of a boat with a strong possibility of drowning."

He used his index finger to push her chin upward so she was forced to look at him. Her eyes looked like mercury in the moonlight, all shining and liquid silver. Just looking at her like this was enough to make him want her. But there wasn't a damn thing he could do about it. Not here. Not now. Not ever.

"You know I wasn't asking about the submarine, or the Book, or Rathe."

"Then perhaps you ought to rephrase the question, counselor."

"I keep getting mixed signals from you. I want to know if you are as attracted to me as you were to Colt."

She nibbled at the base of her rosy lip, and his famous control crumbled. He wanted what he wanted, and right now it was her.

"I don't think—"

Remy crushed his mouth down upon hers, cutting her off. He didn't want to think about what it all meant, or why they were here, or even what might happen next. He wanted to kiss the beautiful woman in front of him in the moonlight. To get the crazy simmering interest she sparked in him under control.

But it all went sideways. Instead of calming his irrational impulse to kiss her, the smooth, slick slide of her lips on his spiked his temperature, and he instantly found a simple kiss was not enough. Like a damn laudanum addict, he craved more.

Remington deepened the kiss. He tasted her and found the flavor of coffee, mixed with the sweet, wild taste of prickly pears from their improvised dinner on the trail. His hand slowly caressed the slender channel of her spine. China shivered, the small soft sounds she made in the back of her throat stoking the fire already burning in his belly. His pulse roared in his ears. There weren't any words he could summon in a moment like this. All he could do was be carried along by it.

Her tongue was wet and warm, her teeth slick and smooth. He speared the silk of her hair with his fingers, letting it slip against his skin as he cupped the back of her head with one hand and wrapped the other around the curve of her ass, bringing her closer. God, she was soft where he was hard. And she smelled good. Too good. She reminded him of warm cookies straight from the oven. A feather-soft bed. Especially the bed. She softened against him, the plump pillows of her breasts pressing against his chest. In his mind he could see the glorious curves of her.

"Mr. Jackson! Miss McGee!" The sound of Monica's voice over the clop of her horse's hooves broke the spell weaving between them. The horses whinnied, and China pushed back from him. She was breathing hard, her eyes glazed and bright with desire.

Remy ran a finger along the rim of his shirt collar, finding it suddenly hard to get enough air with every breath. Holy Hannah. No wonder Colt couldn't resist her. Despite his little brother's assumptions, Remington probably knew women just as well as his little brother. And China McGee, Darkin or not, was one hell of a woman. Remington cleared his throat and flexed his hands.

He didn't want to apologize. In fact, given half the chance and an hour longer, he'd likely go a lot further. But he did owe

China an apology. And he ought to give it before Monica came within earshot.

He pulled at the rim of his Stetson. "Apologies, Miss McGee. I shouldn't have taken advantage of you like that."

China simply stared at him, a sexy as hell smile playing about her lips.

He waited for her to say something, anything.

"Well?"

She shrugged. "Don't see why you're apologizing. If I hadn't wanted you to kiss me, I would have kneed you in the balls."

It took Remington a moment to process that before he burst out laughing. So she had wanted him to kiss her. That brought a whole new level of danger to his attraction to her. "Remind me never to piss you off."

Monica's black gelding came to a standstill in front of them on the trail. "Well at least you're in good spirits." She glanced at the two horses standing aimlessly in the middle of the trail. "What happened? Horse throw a shoe?"

Remington and China turned and answered in unison. Unfortunately he said yes and she said no, which made Monica frown. "Well, which is it? Did the horse throw a shoe or can we ride on?"

Remington glared at China, and a small part of the happy glow that filled her dissolved instantly.

"We can ride," China quickly answered. She didn't know why Remington didn't want Monica knowing what they'd been up to, but an insistent little thought pestered her. Perhaps he was ashamed to be working with her—ashamed of his attraction to her. It made perfectly logical sense. He was a Hunter after all. But that didn't mean it hurt any less. The kiss should have been a fond memory, not a wicked barb.

China's skin contracted, but not from the cold alone.

Perhaps she should focus more on getting them to the Book and the Gates, and less on how Remington Jackson was far too tempting for his own good.

Rathe could still reach her here. He could reach her anywhere. And she'd do well to remember how displeased he'd been last time he'd found her focus had tilted. She needed to remember Remington Jackson was only a means to an end. The important thing was to get to the piece of the Book so the whole thing could be reunited. Then she'd tail along to the Gates of Nyx and ensure Rathe got the entire thing handed to him. He'd be pleased then. He'd forgive her. The sooner that happened, the better. She didn't like walking on eggshells and living under the cloud that at any moment he might call her to his domain to question her progress and deliver appropriate discipline if he didn't like her answer.

"How far are we from Caborca?" she asked Monica.

"If we rest for an hour or two, then keep riding, we can be there by tomorrow."

Remington mounted his horse. "I'd rather travel by night. It'll save the horses' strength if they don't have to fight the heat."

Monica gave a single nod. "Shall I go slower this time so you two can keep up?" China didn't miss the sarcasm in Monica's tone. She nearly rose to the bait, but then glanced at Remington. He was perfectly calm, as if nothing had sparked into a full-fledged inferno of a kiss between them.

"We'll manage just fine," he said, his tone even and unflustered. He turned and glanced at her. "Ready?"

China mounted her horse, and they set off once more. China fell behind Remington, Monica in the lead. China stared at his broad back. Well, damn. Maybe the kiss hadn't impacted him half as much as it had her. The moment his lips had met hers, China had just about split out of her skin. His clever hands set off a shimmer in her blood, and his even more clever tongue had caused her bones to liquefy and turned her knees spongy. The man could flat-out kiss a girl senseless.

But then he'd gone and ruined the whole sensual haze he'd put her in by apologizing. Apologizing! What the hell did the man think she'd been offended by? A few minutes more and she would have started peeling the clothing off of him and taking him right there in the moonlit dirt, regardless of the consequences.

They rode on in silence. The moon rose higher, casting the rocks of the mountain pass into stark shapes. Light and dark mingled freely, the shadows playing with the moonlight. China didn't see why it couldn't be the same between Darkin and Hunter. She and Colt had been a team of sorts, hadn't they?

She worried her lip between her teeth. Damn. The more she thought about it, the more she realized Colt had just been using her. Fair enough. She'd just been using him as well. But at least it had been a symbiotic relationship. They both had gotten something on occasion out of the deal.

But with Remington things were different. He was more complicated than Colt. Hell, he kissed better than Colt. He made her want things she had never considered before—like a long-term relationship. Maybe even lov—no she refused to contemplate it.

Pop. Ping. Pop, pop. Ping. Ping. "Gunfire! Get to cover!" Remington yelled as he pulled and cocked his revolver in one quick, smooth movement. He swung his horse around on the trail, trying to block the shots from hitting either her or Monica until they were all hidden safely behind a jagged outcrop of rock.

"Where's it coming from?" China swung her leg over her horse's back and slid to the ground, pulling her own gun.

Monica pointed to the silvered edge of the mountains just above them. "Up there, on that ridge. We're getting close to where the trail narrows into a pass."

China sniffed the air, trying to see if their attackers were human or Darkin. There was the taint of body odor, woodsmoke, and cooked meat, but no telltale hint of sulfur. "They aren't Darkin. I'd bet it's banditos."

"We aren't carrying anything of value save Diego's book," Remington muttered as he switched his revolver for the rifle strapped to his saddle. He handed his reins to Monica.

"Yes, but they don't know that," Monica retorted. "We're probably too close to their hideout. They're just seeing an easy target."

China snorted and tucked her revolver back in the holster. "Easy target, huh? We'll see about that." She handed her reins to Monica as well. "You might want to hold on tight to the horses."

"Why?"

Remington glanced over his shoulder, then hunkered down against the rocks, setting his rifle in position to shoot anything that moved at the rim of the mountains. "I'd do what she says."

China smiled. This was going to be easy as pie. She hiked a bit above where Monica and Remington hid with the horses before she let the heat shimmer through her and her shape smudged into that of a mountain lion. Shots continued to ring out, keeping them pinned down, unable to go forward in the canyon and unwilling to go back.

China in her mountain lion form padded down to where the others waited and went up to Remington and huffed, rubbing her cheek against his thigh.

Monica jumped, pressing herself against the rocks. She crossed herself and kissed her hand. "Please tell me that's China and not a pet mountain lion that's followed us."

"Rawrr," China growled.

Remington grinned at the first mate. "It's China. Mountain lions don't generally have gray eyes." A small curl of pride

welled up inside her that he'd noticed that about her. She
blinked at them both and chuffed softly.

Remy turned and looked down at China. He had the crazy
urge to pet her fur to see if it was as silky as her normal hair.
It certainly was just as golden. But this was no housecat, and
he didn't know enough about shifters to know if they still
maintained all their human instincts when they transformed.
It was better to play this one safe.

He looked into her familiar silver eyes. "Find out where
they are, and we'll make a plan from there."

She growled low in her throat, the rumbling sound of it
pricking his skin into gooseflesh. It was the sound of a wild
animal, powerful and close enough to bite. He figured that
was a grudging agreement, but it could have been her grous-
ing about the idea. It was hard to tell.

She padded away, her golden shoulders rolling as she
stalked up the rocks, the darker tip of her tail swishing, an
animal on the hunt. She looked back over her shoulder only
once before she sped off and disappeared into the darkness.

Monica inched closer and kept her voice low. "Are you
sure you can trust her?"

He flicked his gaze to Monica before returning it to scan
the top of the mountains. "No."

From above them there was the rattle of scree tumbling
down the rocks. Remington and Monica both shifted their
gazes up a moment too late.

Pop. Ping. Rock chips flew, nicking his face. A hot trickle
of blood streamed down his cheek. Dammit. They were
getting closer. But in the night with the deep shadows cast by
the rocks, it was damn near impossible to discern movement.
The horses shied and whinnied, making it hard to control
them. He narrowed his eyes, trying to improve his vision.

What he wouldn't give for a pair of Marley's special goggles about now with all those fancy changing lens and scopes.

Click, click, click.

From the sudden itch climbing up his scalp Remy knew there were three cocked guns pointed at them. He turned and saw the glint of moonlight on steel.

They were barrel facing barrel in the narrow confines of rock. Nowhere to go. Nowhere to hide. A true Mexican standoff.

"I don't have to miss you, gringo. I could have shot you in the head."

Remington gave a silent prayer of thanks for small favors. A bandito with a conscience.

"Put down the guns. Kick them to me. And raise your hands." Remington slid a sideways glance at Monica and saw that she was already complying. He did the same grudgingly, flicking his gaze up for a moment to the hills, looking for a flash of golden coat, but saw nothing but moon-streaked darkness.

The banditos moved down the rocks toward them, their guns still poised to shoot. "What is it you want?" Monica asked.

The bandito leader pinched her cheeks between his hands, making her mouth squeeze into a pucker. "With you, *chica*, there are several things, but mostly we want your horses and whatever you have of value. Then we will ransom you."

Remington, his hands on his head, huffed out a dry laugh. "That's not going to get you much. We're on our own. There are no relations to write to."

The leader's dark brows drew together, and in one swift motion he butted Remington in the side of the head with the end of his rifle. Monica gasped. Pain exploded in Remington's temple as streaks of light and stars filled his vision, and he toppled over to the dirt. He tried to breathe through the fire.

The leader kicked him in the ribs to roll him over, then

stuck the cold metal of the barrel against his cheek. "Talk out of turn again, and I start cutting off pieces." He gave a vicious smile, his teeth a flash of bits of yellowish white in the night.

"Bind them. Get them up. Take the horses back to camp."

Remington was dragged to his feet, stripped of his other revolver and ammunition belt, and his hands were lashed behind him with rope. They did the same to Monica, only the man who worked on her bindings stopped for a moment to reach out and grasp one of her breasts and squeeze it. Monica cursed and kicked out at him with her foot, landing a solid kick to his knee. The man yelped and backhanded her across the mouth hard. Her head snapped to the side.

Remington's blood boiled. He hated men who treated women like worthless trash. His fingers itched for a trigger to pull. Damn. Where the hell was China?

The banditos marched them down the trail, horses tied pack-style in a line behind the last bandito, then up the hills along a winding animal track until they reached what looked like a semi-permanent camp. The smell of unwashed bodies, woodsmoke, and charred meat became stronger in the air. Shacks created from stacked rock, with roof coverings made from salvaged Saguaro ribs, sat clustered around a large central campfire surrounded by boulders for seats. There were eight more men in the camp. All of them peered with dark eyes at Monica and Remington as they were summarily marched into the middle of the rough clearing.

A corral had been created from a cave blocked with barbed wire stretched across posts of dried wood. The horses shifted and pawed, sensing the tension in the air.

"Put them in the cell," the leader called out. "Pietro, you look through their packs, and Manuel, put their horses with the others." The men shuffled off away from the warmth of the fire to do his bidding.

They were put in a makeshift cell. Really it was more of an

outcropping of rock that formed the roof and three sides of a cramped space, blocked along the entrance by a door made of wooden boards and leather hinges. There was barely room to sit, and the ceiling was too low, at least for him, to properly stand.

The moment the cell door was latched in place, Monica started to wriggle against her bindings. "Well this is a fine kettle of fish you've gotten us into."

"Me? How am I responsible for the banditos?"

She glared at him. "If you hadn't been so busy kissing with your Darkin mistress, I wouldn't have had to double back, and we wouldn't have been caught in the canyon. So it *is* your fault. Both of you," she said with asperity.

"She's *not* my mistress," he muttered.

"You telling me that because you want me to think it's true or because you wish it were?" she shot back at him, but Remington was only half listening to her complaints. He had better things to focus on. Like how to get them the hell out of this. He used the sharp edge of the stone behind him to cut through the bindings at his wrists. The banditos had taken his guns, but not the knife tucked down into the side of his boot, which he couldn't manage with his hands tied behind him. If he could get out, he could slit the throat of one, take his gun, and get them their horses and packs.

The low sound of the men's voices was abruptly cut off by high-pitched male screams. Remington shot up from his crouch between the outcropping of rocks and smacked his head on the rock ceiling. Shooting stars whizzed across his vision, and for a moment his world wobbled with a case of vertigo. He rubbed at the spot on his head. It was swollen. Clearly his head was still tender from the blow the leader had given him.

Monica shot up too and turned shaking, her hands behind her. "We have to stop her! Hurry and untie me."

A cold feeling slid through his gut like icy water from a

high mountain stream as he pulled the small knife from his boot and started hacking away at Monica's bindings. The dark made it difficult. He didn't want to slice her hands, but he was trying to be quick.

The shrieks and agonized screams rose in intensity, accompanied by hair-raising growls, and the unmistakable sound of bodies slamming into the ground, and the sick, wet sound of flesh tearing.

China was killing those men.

Every Hunter instinct within him urged him to rush in and defend them, but the other half of him, the one focused on the mission to reunite the Book at all costs, hesitated. Those men were an obstacle to their path. Remington held the knife tighter. He should have tried to reason with them before letting China go forth as a Darkin bent on defense via destruction.

Monica ripped the loosened ropes from her wrists and started shoving and kicking against the cell door.

He frowned in the darkness. "It's too late."

"You can't mean that." The disapproval in Monica's tone was clear.

"You don't know China." Remy tried for a no-nonsense tone. "She's obeying a primitive instinct to protect. Besides, we can't kill her. I *need* her."

The screams cut off, leaving the camp ominously quiet.

"Yes, but banditos or not, *they* are human." Monica insisted, her voice getting higher and higher. "She's . . . not. Hunters and Darkin aren't meant to mix. You know that. It's you who's crossed the line. You need to reevaluate your priorities."

Acid swished uncomfortably in his stomach. He wished he could. Remington closed his eyes for a moment and let out a heavy sigh. She was right, but there was more than one side to all of this. This wasn't simply black and white, human versus Darkin.

From what he'd witnessed, China was clearly on the human side of the equation when it came to taking down Rathe. At least she seemed to be. God, these kind of mental gymnastics wrecked havoc on him. They made him mentally and physically tired when he hadn't even moved a muscle.

He opened his eyes and turned in Monica's direction, willing her to understand the gravity of what they faced. "Yes, but I doubt those banditos would have been so kind in how they handled you once they'd killed me."

Monica frowned, her throat working as she swallowed hard. "True. But that doesn't make it right."

"This isn't about right or wrong. Unless I have her to help me break through whatever Darkin protections there are in the temple and get back Elwin's piece of the Book of Legend, all of humanity can kiss its ass good-bye. Rathe will win. That's not an option. In this case we side with the Darkin shifter."

For a moment they just stared at one another. Monica's mouth pressed into a firm line, and she gave him a single, curt nod. She didn't like it, but she accepted it. When it came to battling Darkin, the loss of a few to save the many was sometimes the best they could do.

"The only way we're going to get that door open is to take a run at it together," he said.

They both squeezed as far back as they could in the cell. Remington glanced at her. "On the count of three. One. Two. Three!"

In unison they ran at the door, butting it with their shoulders. It cracked at the assault, but didn't give way.

Monica rubbed at her arm. "We'll have to do it again."

They ran at the door once more, and this time it tumbled outward, landing them on top of it in the dirt.

A cloud of dust rose up around them, and he and Monica both coughed and swung at the swirling dirt, trying to breathe and see what was happening.

"Dear Mother of God," Monica rasped as she stared at the shambles of the camp and what was left of the banditos. "What kind of monster are you working with, Jackson?"

Chapter 11

The stink . . . the blood . . . the slaughter . . . the sheer brutality of the kill made Remington's stomach churn as he took in the destruction China had wrought. Bloody gore splattered the rocks surrounding the camp. Men, their throats ripped out, their bellies torn open and innards glistening in the moonlight, lay scattered in the narrow confines between the shacks and the fire pit where the coals glowed red.

He gritted his teeth, trying to keep the cold fury within him at bay. This was the very kind of thing he was born, raised, and trained to defend against, and yet he couldn't summon sympathy for the men. What the hell was wrong with him?

He tugged Monica's shoulder. Her eyes were slightly dilated, and her breathing was off. Perhaps she hadn't seen this violent a scene before. Perhaps she was just stunned at the ferocity of it. But for Remington times like this caused him to drain of all emotion. He became cold inside. Dead. There was only the mission. No feeling. No thought. "You get our horses. I'll see where our packs are and if there's anything useful we can take."

Monica stared at him, dumbfounded. "She murdered them!"

"They died in battle," he argued calmly. "And there was only her against many of them. I'd say the odds were in their favor."

Monica's face hardened. "Look at what she's done. Do you really think her help will be worth it?"

"Absolutely."

The soft shuffle of a leather shoe over dirt turned Remington's head. China was back. Her shirt was blood spattered, her face and hands a mess, smeared with red, and she looked bone tired—somewhat dazed, her feet barely lifting off the ground.

He pulled off his jacket and handed it to her. "Here, use this. Let's see if we can find you some water to clean up." China slumped down and leaned against a rock, clutching the jacket to her chest. She was still breathing hard.

"I'm getting the horses," Monica grumbled, then spun on her heel and headed off to the corral.

Remington crouched down beside China. There was enough blood that he wasn't certain she'd made it through the battle unscathed. "Are you hurt?"

Her head lolled to the side, and she gazed up at him. "I hate blood. Did Colt ever tell you that?"

Remington shook his head. His emotions began to return as he focused on her rather than the carnage around him. "If you hate it, then why'd you kill them?"

"They weren't going to let you and Monica go. I heard them. They were going to have their way with her and kill you both. It was only a matter of time. What I did, I did for you."

The words hit Remington with the force of a sucker punch. And the emotions he'd bottled away came back with a rush. He didn't know what to say. If there'd been any doubt about China's loyalty he laid it to rest right then and there. She'd more than proven herself.

A canteen hit the dirt with a thud beside him. He glanced

up and saw Monica there with the horses. "There's your water. Get her cleaned up, and let's get out of here. We've only got a few hours before daylight."

Remington found their packs, and took out her worn chambray shirt, and tore off a strip off it. He wet it from the canteen and handed it to China.

She took it from him, her eyes troubled. "Thank you. I'm sorry—"

He held up a hand. "Don't be sorry for doing what needed to be done. We've all had to do battle before. And what's at stake is far bigger than this."

China bit her lip. "I don't think Monica feels the same."

Remington crouched down beside her. "There are some Hunters, and their families, who can't accept Darkin, no matter what is done to prove some Darkin are not our enemies. I know you want to get rid of Rathe. I know that look I saw in your eyes. We're on the same side in this quest, you and I. And I won't forget it."

Her pale pink lips turned up into a slight smile that didn't reach her eyes. "Neither will I."

It took them another ten hours to reach Caborca. The city spread out in the valley below. The open-air markets lining the streets were bright and alive with activity, even in the wee hours of the morning. Vendors were setting up stacks of fresh melons and bright green ears of corn, their silks still pale and golden. Chickens squawked in the cage at the butcher's stall, and a goat tied to the post of his cutting block bleated loudly. The smell of roasting chilies, fresh spices, and cooking corn wafted in the air, making their trail dinner seem long ago and far away. China's stomach rumbled loudly.

"I sent a messenger bird to my father regarding our arrival. He'll be expecting us," Monica informed Remington. She hadn't said a word to China since they'd escaped the bandito

THE CHOSEN 139

camp. "He usually sends me up to talk with Diego before a shipment leaves and again when it returns. Our next trip was supposed to begin today. I'm back late as it is."

"Do you think he'll let me into his home?" China asked.

Monica flicked a glance in her direction. "It's hard to tell. He's a Hunter, so there's a natural aversion to your kind, but he's also been reciting the prophecy of the Chosen to me since I was a child. He might be so thrilled to meet Mr. Jackson that he won't care if you're a member of his party."

That hardly seemed encouraging, China thought. But they had little enough choice in the matter. If they were to reach the temple where the piece of the Book was hidden according to Diego, then they'd have to get there by the fastest means possible. And since she hadn't seen any other airships beyond the one the vampires had hovered in while over Tombstone, and the rail lines were sporadic, the submarine seemed the fastest way.

They were all dog tired and hungry. Remington didn't think imposing on Captain Nation's hospitality a good idea, so he arranged for rooms at a hotel nearby in town. After a good meal, and a hot soaking bath with lots of soap, followed by a siesta, China felt almost human again, which was really as close as she ever got.

A knock sounded at her hotel room door. Given their situation she was overly cautious and cracked the door only enough to peer at who was on the other side. She let out the breath she was holding and couldn't believe her eyes.

Opening the door wider, she grinned. Remington Jackson was a fine-looking man, and he cleaned up *very* nicely. Although she eyed his pristine, stiff, starched appearance with some amusement.

He carried a large parcel wrapped in brown paper and tied with string in one hand.

China ran a self-conscious hand over her unbound hair and

inhaled the delectable smell of Bay Rum and clean male. "Well, don't you clean up nice?"

He glanced down the corridor as someone came out of one of the rooms down the hall. "Are you going to invite me in?"

"Yes, sir. Please come in, Mr. Jackson, sir." China stepped back and waved an expansive arm, inviting him inside.

A pulse beat at his temple as he surveyed the shadowy room, the crumpled sheets, and the cold hip bath near the window. His gaze returned to glide, as physical as a touch, over her damp hair, which hung down her back to dry. "Good," he muttered, voice thick. "You got some rest."

China felt a blush heat her cheeks, foolish really. She had nothing to be ashamed of. She went to pull open the drapes, then stood with her back to the window, waiting for him to speak. How silly of her to have sweaty palms and an elevated heartbeat just because this man had bathed and used a little scented water.

He'd changed his rumpled black coat, pinstriped dark pants, and dirt-smeared, once-white shirt into a crisp uniform of off-white jodhpurs and matching military jacket with tall collar and a row of shiny brass buttons marching down the middle of his broad chest. He had exchanged his black cowboy boots for knee-high brown military boots that accentuated the length and strength of his legs. And perhaps most shocking of all, he'd given up his black cowboy hat for a cream-colored pith helmet.

He would have looked dashing if she'd been in England, or if she'd never seen him in his other clothes. But he looked so starched, so formal, she nearly felt sorry for him.

"What on God's green Earth are you wearing, Jackson? And *why?*" China waved a hand from his head to his boot tips and back again.

Remington simply stared at her, his hand on the lapels of his crisp explorer's uniform. "I was informed this was proper attire for jungle exploration."

China shook her head and ended up laughing until she doubled over. When she caught her breath and wiped her eyes, she took a deep breath. "There is no way you're gettin' me into a getup like that."

He raised one dark brow. "What's wrong with it? Don't like the hat?"

"You look like an Englishman on holiday, not someone about to go head-to-head with a dark, unexplored jungle and the Aztec version of Hell."

Remington sighed as he walked farther into her room. "It was the only clothing the man at the outpost had in my size."

"Probably because no one else wanted to buy it." China snickered again. "Sorry." She forced her face into a more serious look. "It should work fine, as long as you don't expect it to stay clean for more than five minutes." And given the dusty streets right here in Caborca, maybe not even that long.

A hint of a smile lifted the corner of Remington's mouth, making the divot in his chin that much more enticing. "I don't mind getting dirty for the right reason. Your turn to change. Are you ready to meet the captain?"

"Almost." She looked down at her clothing, which was rumpled beyond repair. After her bath she'd changed into the other set of clothes Remington had purchased back in Tombstone. It'd been crammed in the bottom of their traveling packs. There'd been so much blood on her other clothing she figured it was unsalvageable. "I don't have anything to wear but this."

He shook the brown paper parcel he was holding. "You're in luck. I've brought you something."

China snatched up the parcel and hugged it to her chest.

"Sure you don't need any help?"

She threw him an arch glance. "I can undress myself quite well, thank you."

* * *

But he'd enjoy peeling her out of her clothing a lot more, Remington thought, sitting in the only chair as she sashayed behind the changing screen. As long as he remembered this was only a physical thing and didn't get emotionally involved, it could prove entertaining. Silently, he began to count down the impending explosion he knew was coming. Five. The rasp of string being untied. Four. The impatient rip of paper. Three. Two. One.

"Remington Jackson! What the devil is this?" China came barreling out from behind the screen, shaking the garment in her fist at him. "This is a dress. A dress! How on earth do you expect me to go hiking through the jungle in this?" She lifted it by the shoulders in both hands, glaring at it in disgust.

It was really a very nice dress. Something elegant. Perfect for visiting the captain and making a proper impression. It would show off the slope of her shoulders, and if she wore her hair up, the arch of her neck. Now it was Remington's turn to chuckle. It had been a choice between this dress and another one, red calico. He'd thought the black would be less apt to show wear and dirt during their journey. "I thought you would look lovely in it."

She gave him a sour look. "It's black. I'll look like I'm in mourning."

"Only for your dignity and mine."

"It's downright awful, that's what it is. If I hadn't ruined my leather britches fighting those viperanox, I'd be back in them in a heartbeat."

He stared at her, thoughts running through his head of exactly how tight those leather pants would have become if they'd become wet. An uncomfortable heat swirled low down in his belly, turning to pressure. He didn't need her as a distraction on this trip; too many lives hung in the balance, and he couldn't afford to lose focus.

China huffed. "You know, if I changed into a mountain lion, I wouldn't have to deal with this damn dress at all."

Remington wanted to say, run bare naked through the jungle if you like, but he didn't dare. She might take it as a challenge and do precisely that. The idea of seeing the flash of her bare, pale skin, forehead to toe, dashing through the forest brought to mind things he'd do best not to contemplate.

Focus. Naked. Focus. Good God, now he was arguing with himself. "It'll do while we meet the captain." A little of his frustration with himself leaked into his tone.

China gave a reluctant sigh. "Fine. For meeting the captain. But I'm giving you fair warning; the first opportunity I get, I'm finding me another pair of britches to wear."

Remington smothered a smile. That was just fine by him.

They met Monica in the lobby of the hotel and followed her to her father's house. The home of Captain Nation was far different than he'd expected.

"Does that look like a porthole to you?" China whispered as they passed through the wooden gate with the unusual brass fixture in the high adobe garden wall. Early evening light filtered buttery and yellow through the pale green boughs of the mesquite trees. The soothing sound of running water greeted them as they entered a tropical paradise. Hand-painted tiles rimming the fountain reflected light onto the water as it sprayed and tumbled over the body of a mermaid. A sparkling silver stream poured from the upraised conch shell in her hand, overflowing two levels before filling the tiled basin at the bottom.

"My father doesn't like to be away from the ocean for too long," Monica said with a hint of amusement in her voice. "He finds the water soothing."

He probably would need more than soothing water when he learned he had a Darkin in his home for dinner, Remington thought.

All around the paving stones surrounding the fountain

were tropical plants, their wide-leafed foliage lush and many shades of green. Exotic flowers dripped like purple water from a small shrub, and small yellow flowers danced on slender stems along the walkway. The sweet fragrance of honey and something spicy was strong in the air, and the buzz of insects mingled with the soothing sound of running water. "This is magnificent." Remington waved an expansive hand around the courtyard. "I've never seen such a vast variety of tropical foliage in anyone's home before. Did your father bring the plants back with him from his travels?"

Monica glanced at Remington and gave him a secretive smile. "The plants . . . and other things."

China nudged him, her sharp elbow finding a niche between his ribs. He huffed, not so much from the sharp jab as from surprise. He frowned at her.

She crooked her finger at him to come closer. Remington bent down. "Look at those." Her harsh whisper was hot against his ear. Her breath smelled of the peppermint tooth powder he'd found at the mercantile, and her hair like vanilla cream as it brushed his cheek.

Along one wall of the garden was a small alcove with three squat statues. They looked like ugly little dwarves to him, but there was something about their squared stone faces and the unusual carvings of snakes and scorpions and skulls surrounding them that was intriguing, and he paused to inspect them. They looked remarkably similar to the squat little statue he and China had brought with them.

"Want to bet he and Diego snagged those from some ancient ruins?" China said softly.

She was probably right. From the calculations he'd made from Diego's map, their goal lay far to the south on the eastern coastline near Veracruz. He wasn't sure how Captain Nation planned to get them there without sailing all around South America, but he'd learned that often just going with a situation could yield better results.

Monica clanged the large brass ship's bell by the front door of the adobe house. The door opened, and a wiry man greeted them. His skin, weathered nearly to the shade of dark cherry-wood, made his white hair and the bright white stubble on his face seem brilliant in comparison. He wrapped his arms around Monica in a tight hug.

"Father, I would like to introduce you to our guests," Monica said softly, pulling herself out of her father's arms to stand at military attention beside him.

Captain Nation's nostrils flared, and his eyes narrowed. "What is this? You've brought a Darkin to my home?"

"She is part of Mr. Jackson's exploration party."

The old man's gaze shifted back to Monica, the harsh lines in his face smoothing some. "Jackson? Part of the Chosen?"

Monica gave him one curt nod. "The very same, Captain."

Captain Nation turned back to Remington and looked him up and down. "Well, he certainly looks like an ex-plorer." He extended his hand in greeting. "Welcome to my home, Mr. Jackson."

"Thank you, Captain Nation. This is not a social call, how-ever. We were told by Diego Mendoza that you could take us with your submarine to the place where they hid the last piece of the Book of Legend from the Kingdom of Navarre."

Captain Nation pulled at his whiskered chin and glanced about the walled garden. "Where is the rest of your party?"

"It is just myself and the shifter."

The captain cast his dark gaze in China's direction. "And you, shifter, are you indentured to him?"

It was laughable. She'd never been indentured to anyone in her life and was damned if she'd start now. Only her father held any kind of lasting hold over her, and that was by a mix-ture of equal parts devotion and fear. But China also realized they needed to humor the captain if they were going to use his boat. She hitched her thumb at Remington. "No. I'm in it to help him recover the missing piece of the Book of Legend so the Chosen can reunite it." It was the truth. She just didn't bother explaining what she planned to do *after* they'd reunited the Book.

The old man's mouth split into a wide smile. "Excellent," he said, rubbing his hands together. "So the rebellion has begun, then?"

His change of demeanor took China aback. "Rebellion?" She knew the vampires were rebelling against Rathe, but perhaps there were others as well. The thought sent a chill through her. Perhaps there was a way to escape him after all. She'd never considered it possible before, but the tantalizing idea sparkled and fizzed in the back of her brain.

The captain looked around the garden and into the darkening evening skies. "It's not safe to discuss it out here," he murmured, as he tapped his ear in a silent gesture to meant others might be listening. "Please, come in."

The inside of Captain Nation's home looked like he'd gutted an old sailing ship and then had an adobe house built around it. Even the wood-lined walls curved, bowing out. Old wine barrels, topped with colorful blue pillows, constituted the chairs he offered them.

He settled into a leather chair and glanced at his daughter, who'd shut the door behind them. "Monica, be a good girl and fetch our honored guest some refreshments."

China noted that he said guest, singular, but she decided at this juncture it was better not to comment on it. If Remington were indeed part of the Chosen, then he was indeed an honored guest, whereas she was, well, she was just his sidekick.

Captain Nation leaned forward, his elbows on his knees, a manic gleam in his dark brown eyes. "One of the signs, foretold centuries ago by a vampire prophet named Kostick, was that a rebellion would begin among the Darkin in the days before the Book of Legend would be reunited by the Chosen."

"Well I don't know that it's a full-fledged rebellion. I just have a personal interest in seeing the Book reunited by the Chosen."

The old man took the glass of amber-colored liquor his daughter offered him and passed the silver tray of glasses to Remington. He raised his glass at them. "To the rise of the Chosen and the Book of Legend reunited."

China took one of the glasses and glanced at Remington. He shrugged as if to say, what the hell. She lifted the glass in salute to Captain Nation's toast. "To the Chosen," she said.

The tequila was a damn sight stronger than she'd anticipated, but as smooth as could be.

Captain Nation smacked his lips with satisfaction, then pointed one of the fingers holding onto his glass at her. "You may be only one Darkin, but it is the smallest loose thread that causes a whole blanket to unravel," Nation said. "If you are in rebellion, then there will be others."

"The vampires are moving against him as well," Remington added.

"What else was in the prophecy?" China pushed.

"There's to be a blood price paid when the Book is reunited. The codex was specific about that. The Aztecs believed strongly in the power of blood." Captain Nation's brows furrowed in thought. "Things are moving faster than I thought." He locked his gaze on Remington. "How close are we to the closing of the Gates of Nyx?"

"We have a little more than two weeks until the new moon."

Captain Nation stood. "Monica! Why didn't you say so? We have no time to lose. We must make for the coast tonight."

Monica saluted him. "Aye, aye, Captain." Her hand lowered

slowly, and her face dropped. "There's more, Father. Uncle Diego is dead."

Captain Nation wobbled a bit, then fell back in his chair. "I am the last of us then. Cyrus, Diego, Bart, and me. We went after the pieces of the Book, the four of us. We wanted to know where they were hidden so the Chosen could find and reunite them." He looked down at his wrinkled hands. "Am I that old?"

Monica grabbed him by the shoulder. "Rest now, father. I will see that we get the ship supplied and the horses ready."

Captain Nation shook his head, the air of sadness thick around him. "You will go in my stead on this voyage, Monica."

"But father—"

He held up a hand, cutting off her protest. "It is time we all do the things that must be done. I will take the statues north to Sir Turlock. You must take our adventurers south. We will meet, daughter, at the Gates of Nyx."

Chapter 12

They rode through the night. By the time they reached the western coast of Mexico, the sun was rising. It shimmered on the water like gold coins scattered across a vivid field of aquamarine blue.

"It's beautiful, isn't it?" China said a bit breathlessly.

Remington shrugged. "I don't know. I thought it was rather homely to be honest. Looks like a metal shark."

China stared at him stunned. "The sun on the water?"

"No, the submarine." He pointed at the dark hulk that rested near the shoreline. The dark iron ship did indeed look like a shark, with the higher arch of a back in the middle tapering down at either end to a finer point. A large screw propeller at the rear end of the machine gave the impression of a tail.

"Think it actually floats?"

Monica trotted up beside them. "It's not supposed to float; it's supposed to dive beneath the waves. Running under the water makes it harder for our enemies to spot us. It has compressed air ballast chambers to aid our descent and ascent. My father commissioned it after the Civil War from a builder named Simon Lake and had it loosely based on the design of Julius Kroehl's *Explorer,* although on a much grander

scale. Come this way, and we'll get you aboard the *Chipirón*."
She dismounted, and both Remington and China followed her
lead, handing the reins of their mounts off to a waiting crew
member.

"You named your submersible ship after baby squid?"
Remington sounded slightly appalled as they walked toward
the machine.

Monica's mouth split into a wide smile. "I thought it fit.
She's small, but fast in the water, and has a few surprising defenses. We'll have you down the coast in no time."

China watched with fascination as the front of the submarine seemed to open like a large mouth onto the beach.
The waves lapped at the metal gangway. She wasn't that
comfortable with the notion of walking into the metallic
machine, or with being in the water for that matter, but what
choice did they have? Time was ticking away. The sooner they
got to the temple Diego had told Remington his map led to,
the better. They still needed to join the Book of Legend together before it could be of use at the Gates of Nyx. She followed behind the first mate and Remington into the belly of
the beast.

It was immense and reminded China a bit of hiding out in
an empty water tower. "This serves as our cargo hold and
loading dock for larger objects," Monica explained as they
trekked past wooden crates and large objects covered over in
thick duck-cloth sheets.

"What's under that?" China asked out of curiosity.

"Sensitive equipment. Mostly experimental, but some of
it is for travel."

Remington pulled off the ridiculous pith helmet and ran
his hand through his hair as she looked around at the machine. "Your submersible is very impressive. Will it ride near
the surface or can it run at deeper depths?"

A spark of excitement lit Monica's eyes. "Beneath, to
depths of sixty feet. It has both a pressurization system and

air scrubbers to ensure we have recycled air to breathe for trips beneath the surface."

She began to babble about things that held no meaning for China, who was feeling sicker by the second surrounded by this much metal. It sapped her powers, leaving her feeling woozy and weak. She pressed a hand to her cheek. A strong hand steadied her as her steps faltered and she wobbled.

"Looks like you don't have your sea legs yet," Remington commented. A clank followed by a loud suctioning sound made them both turn.

"That's just the cargo door sealing," Monica said with a flick of her hand as if it were something to be easily dismissed. For China it was anything but.

Being cooped up in any closed environment, even one as big as this, played havoc with her senses as a shifter. The metal was bad enough, but the overwhelming sense that the walls were pressing in on her, that was something she couldn't control—hadn't been able to since she was locked at regular intervals in a box by Rathe as a child whenever she displeased him. The box at least had been blessedly made of wood. It had taken time, but the box had allowed China to learn to change at will, and taking the shape of something small had allowed her to survive the confines with her sanity intact. Still, this submarine brought the familiar sensations roiling to the surface.

"I don't feel so good," she murmured, leaning more heavily on Remington than she wanted to.

"It was a long ride last night. Perhaps you just need some rest and something to eat," he said as he pulled her in closer to his side, supporting her weight with the strength of his arm around her waist.

"Rest. Yes. Maybe that."

"Can you show us to our berths?" Remington asked the first mate. She gave a curt nod and spun on her heel, leading them up a flight of stairs to the deck above.

The spaces of the submarine became instantly smaller and more confined the moment they left the cargo area. The hallways were almost narrow enough that Remington had to walk with his shoulders to the side since they brushed each wall, and there was only one way to walk down the halls—single file.

"Watch your step," Monica said as she stepped over the rim of a portal door leading them from one section of the ship to the next. "Your berths will be here."

She opened a door in the hallway to show a room where bunks were built into the walls, separated by curtains that drew across each berth. They were as large as coffins and had only enough head space between them for a person to sit up, well at least for her to sit up. China wasn't sure Remington could. Panic welled up in her throat, making it suddenly harder to breathe. She didn't want to sound ungrateful, but she needed to know if there was anywhere else she could sleep. "Do you have anything . . ." She chose her next words carefully. "Less confining?"

One of Monica's brows arched upward. "Afraid of tight spaces, are you?"

China barely nodded. It was all she could manage until her body regained some kind of equilibrium, surrounded by all this metal.

"You can sleep in the map room if you prefer. I can have a cot set up there."

China offered her a feeble smile in response. "Anything would be appreciated."

Monica went back out the door they'd passed through and continued down the hall and up another flight of narrow metal stairs until they were on the top deck of the ship.

Once they reached the map room China sagged into a sitting position, propping herself up against one of the walls. Remington crouched beside her. "Are you sure you're okay?"

China glanced around at the metal walls. "Too much iron in these walls. It messes with my powers."

He nodded. "I suspected it was something like that. Let me see what I can do to get you something to eat. That might help too."

She gave him a weak nod, then watched him straighten and walk out of the map room. Rolled maps nested like wine bottles in a complex set of cubbyholes that covered one wall. The center of the room was occupied by a table that was bolted to the floor. A case against the far wall contained what looked like navigation equipment, sextons and all sorts of gauges and compasses.

"Excuse me," a male voice said from the portal. China turned. "Captain said to deliver this cot and bedding to you." The crew man was of average size and dressed in regular clothing rather than any kind of uniform.

China stood and gripped the table to steady herself. "Thank you. Put them over in that corner."

He nodded and did as she requested, setting up the cot and placing the bedroll of blankets on it. China wobbled her way to the cot and opened the bedroll, spreading out the blankets before she sank gratefully to the cot and stretched out, shutting her eyes. The horrible nauseous feeling eased slightly. This was going to be a long trip, even if it was only a few days.

Remington returned with some bread and cheese on a plate to find that China was passed out and fast asleep on her cot in the map room.

"She's not much of a sailor," Monica commented.

"Shifters rarely are."

She shrugged. "Too bad. I had something splendid to show you both. Now I suppose only you will get to see it."

Remington set the plate of food down on the table so it would be there when China woke. "What is it?"

"My father sent ahead instructions to have a Spider Walker put on board for you."

Remington tensed. He didn't care much for mechanical walkers, mechanical horses, or other forms of travel, even preferring to travel by stagecoach rather than train when it could be helped. "Spider walker?" he said cautiously.

"He said Marley Turlock had made it for him some time ago to help navigate the jungles that make up the interior. It can get over just about any terrain." She marched at a quick pace back toward the cargo hold, and he followed, matching his stride to hers. Beneath their feet the hum of the engines vibrated through the flooring.

"And what about if there's trees? Jungles tend to have a lot of those, I'm told."

She rolled her eyes. "Marley knew what he was doing."

"He always does."

"It can climb through the trees if necessary. It's very adaptable."

They reached the cargo hold, and Monica stripped off the duck-cloth sheets from the large mounds China had asked about when they'd arrived on the submarine.

The eight long, tubular metal sections looked like long legs. "I thought you said it was a walker, not just the legs? We don't have to attach those to ourselves or something do we?" He wouldn't put such things past Marley.

"The Spider Walker comes apart in pieces so it can be easily stored in our hull. Over there is the main pod of it." She marched over and yanked the covering off the bulbous shape. The distinct abdomen and cephalothorax of a spider came into view, but rather than many eyes, the front of it sported one single large glass canopy through which he could see two seats.

"The abdomen houses the water tank and steam engines. You two sit up front." She motioned with her hand.

"Has it been tried before?" Remington was smart enough to know not to use Marley's inventions, especially anything this large, without having them tested first. The last thing he wanted was to go up in flames or have the machine explode while he was in it.

She smiled at him, a look of understanding passing between them. "Don't worry. We've used it several times. It's safe."

He nodded.

"Do you really think it's necessary?"

"You're going to be headed across the narrowest part of Mexico, but also one of the most treacherous. There's jungles and mountains. Without the Spider Walker it could take months to travel on foot to the other side."

"And with the Spider Walker?"

"A few days at most."

Then she was right. They needed the Spider Walker if they were going to get to the temple in time to beat Rathe to the Gates of Nyx.

Monica bumped her fist against the side of her thigh a few times. "Mr. Jackson, I wondered if I might ask a favor of you."

Remington nodded. "If I can grant it, I will."

"Do you still have my uncle's map?"

His hand strayed to his breast pocket over his heart. "Yes."

"And the codex he gave you?"

He nodded.

"I'd like to work with you on decoding the codex to find the place names for the map, and, in exchange, perhaps you can give me the codex and map when you return."

They'd mean more to her than to him once his mission was accomplished. "Certainly."

She gave him a warm smile. "Thank you."

"If we're going to figure out the particulars on your uncle's map based on the codex, we need to get started."

"Precisely what I was thinking."

The next two days passed far more quickly than Remington anticipated. Without him knowing if it was day or night, they blurred together as he worked by lamplight on the codex and map. He ventured out of the room where they worked only to stretch his legs, and while he ran into China a time or two, he was too preoccupied with finishing the map to talk to her much. He didn't need the distraction, so he kept things as civil and polite as possible.

China couldn't wait to get out of the machine. The tight confines of the submarine did not offer a lot of places where one could find solitude. Especially in human form. The heavy iron content of the metal kept her from being able to shift into something smaller. Only the round portholes offered any relief, and they simply looked out into an endless field of deep sapphire blue. And the deeper they went, the darker it became outside.

Not only did the rounded walls of metal seem to be constantly closing in on her, but the small spaces and tight places meant she was forever bumping into Remington. Now on their third full day in the machine, she'd had enough.

After what had happened in the mountain pass, she wasn't sure how to talk to him. Things had become awkward again between them. Oh, he'd been kind—thoughtful even—at the time, but his eyes had been so vacant, so cold, she couldn't help but feel that some of the spark she'd sensed between them had died there amid the carnage as well.

Perhaps that was for the best. If he ever discovered the truth behind how she was connected to Rathe, all hope of his trusting her would burn up faster than a match tossed in a haystack. Worse, having a Hunter's help, *this* Hunter's help, would even her odds of appeasing Rathe. She didn't want Remington to know that she needed him perhaps more than he needed her.

No, it was much better if she just avoided him and the slippery sensations he caused.

As if summoned by her musings, he passed through the portal, blocking the way with the broad expanse of his shoulders. Immediately her traitorous heart kicked up the pace. Just being around him was enough to set off her senses in all the wrong ways. "Ah, China, I wanted to speak to you. I've been looking through Diego's codex."

Oh, joy. How on earth could he read while bottled up in this tin can? Just the constant rumble of the engines that shook the ship and the thought of being under the endless expanse of blue made her feel woozy. The soft trace of his Bay Rum aftershave infused the air around her, adding to the dizziness, making her light-headed, but for a whole other reason.

"Would you mind looking at these with me?"

Yes, she minded. Because it meant she had to be close to him. But if he could act all cool and collected-like, as if there were nothing there between them, dammit, so could she. "Sure." She followed him into the next room, lifting her troublesome skirts, careful to step over the raised edge of the connecting doors between compartments. Each door had a huge locking wheel in the center of it. Monica had said it was to keep water contained if the submarine sprang a leak, something China didn't even want to contemplate.

He laid the codex on the table, his finger tracing below the section he was reading. "It says here the way in is through a sacred underground entrance."

"Fantastic," she said without enthusiasm. Sometimes the traits of her strongest and most frequent animal shifts tended to leak into her human form. An intense dislike for large bodies of water and swimming were among them. And she was more sensitive to it after having assumed her mountain lion form previous to boarding the submarine.

Just beneath the codex he spread out the map he'd been sketching. "I believe the entrance will be about here. In the Veracruz area, based on the longitude and latitude notes from my mother's diary. The captain—"

"Monica—" China said, absently watching his lips move as he talked. And watching his lips made her remember how the man could kiss. Lord, could he kiss. And thinking about how he and Monica had been so chummy and talkative on the trip from Caborca to the submarine made her angry.

Maybe he liked the submarine's captain because she was human, not a Darkin. Either way, she didn't care. He could have the girl.

"The *captain*," he continued, "said if we make land here, we will need to cross over the bottom of the Sierra Madre del Sur mountain range to reach Veracruz."

"And how are we going to hike across all that jungle in such a short time?"

Remington grinned, and it was breathtaking. The man could power a whole town with the intensity of his smile alone. "You haven't seen what they've got down in the hold, have you?"

"I didn't make a point of sneakin' around and bein' light-fingered if that's what you're askin'." Sure, it sounded a bit snide, but she was in a twist. Nothing had felt right since she got in this tin can. Monica had made it clear from the moment they'd stepped on board that this was her domain and she was in charge. That was pain in the ass number one. China didn't like people telling her what to do. Especially a beautiful woman who looked at Remington like he was her next meal.

Pain in the ass number two came from the tin can itself. Truth was she'd been so seasick, walking around only made it worse, so she'd confined herself to her makeshift cabin in the map room as much as possible and avoided the mess hall and any smells of food. Since one had to pass the mess hall in route to the hold, she hadn't bothered.

He ignored her rebuttal completely, just like he'd mostly ignored her for the past three days. China suspected he'd been spending his time talking with the "captain" and looking over his books. Other than a polite howdy-do in the confined passageways of the ship, he'd mostly kept himself too busy to spend any time talking to her, but seemed to be somehow constantly in her space regardless, as if he were checking on her.

"They have one of Marley's Blasters and a Spider Walker." She had no idea what he was blathering on about, but his eyes were so bright and his manner so genuinely excited, like a kid on his birthday, that she became infected by his enthusiasm.

"A Blaster, huh? That some sort of gun?"

"It's based on the technology Marley used in Colt's Sting Shooter." China was familiar enough with that little weapon to know it could blow a hole clean through a man from ten feet away with nothing more than an electric shot produced by a Tesla coil. It was like having lightning in your pocket. Dangerous, unstable, and highly effective.

Now he had her attention. "A Blaster sounds like it might be a bit bigger than a Sting Shooter."

"It is."

China gave him a cat-in-the-cream smile. It sounded promising. "How big is it?"

"Big enough to shoot a man-sized hole clear through the metal hull of this submarine."

"Perfect."

His face turned deadpan. "You're not shooting the submarine."

Damn. She'd been hopeful that she might be able to once she was off of it. "Well, not while we're in it. But I'm sure there's at least one or two things we'll need the Blaster for in the deep, dark jungle."

"Hopefully we'll be able to travel right over the mountains and jungle in the Spider Walker."

China screwed her face up. She'd changed into a lot of things before, but never a spider. She didn't like them. All those eyes and spindly little legs gave her the jitters.

"You all right? You look a little green, like you swallowed a bug."

China glared at him. The last thing she wanted was for their first major conversation in days to be about how horrible she looked. "How sure are you this Spider Walker thing will work?"

Remington shrugged. "Haven't any clue. But most of Marley's inventions are utterly brilliant."

"Or a horrible failure," she shot back. "I saw the scars Colt had from a close encounter with one of Marley's mechanical cacti that Colt says he's got as security around his place." She shook her head. "Those were nasty scars." She intentionally didn't mention they were on Colt's ass. Things were already weird enough between her and Remington without bringing up his brother's intimate body parts.

Remington knew precisely where Colt had his scars from the mechanical cacti. He'd helped Marley pull the metal barbs out and had held his brother down while Marley stitched him up. His insides curled with a strange, burning heat. What in tarnation was that? Jealousy? He absently rubbed at his stomach, hoping to ease the uncomfortable sensation. "I know the ones."

Since when had he ever been jealous of one of Colt's many conquests? Never. That's when. Usually their taste in women was so completely different, it hadn't mattered. He liked smart women with a bit of spunk. Colt wasn't as picky. He liked women so long as they were available and pretty.

She stared at him with those wide gray eyes fringed in

sable lashes. "You do?" She swallowed, and he watched the movement down the length of her neck.

So what was it about this Darkin that intrigued him so? When she'd bent over the table, staring at the map, even without a bustle, her derriere had a luscious curve to it. He fisted his hand to keep from touching her. He liked that China wasn't built like a rail. She had very feminine curves. The dress revealed the silky valley between her breasts. Her skin looked like cream and smelled like vanilla, and he wondered if the spot would taste just as sweet.

Ever since he'd kissed her, inappropriate thoughts had intruded at every opportunity, and he was starting to think he'd never think of vanilla the same way again.

"Why are you staring at me like you want to eat me for dinner?" she asked, her tone breathless.

Remington turned and took a step toward her. China took a step back, putting her smack up against the metal hull of the ship. He stepped in, bracing his palms on the steel wall on either side of her head, trapping her there for a moment in the cage of his arms. But he was well aware caged animals were dangerous.

"You're an intelligent woman. Why don't you tell me?"

Her soft pink tongue nervously slicked a trail over her bottom lip. "I think it's better if you just stop this right now, Jackson. We ain't fit for one another. You're a Hunter, I'm a—"

"I know exactly what I am, and what you are," he growled. "That doesn't change a damn thing. Neither does the fact that you were with Colt. Are we clear?"

"Crystal cl—"

He fit his mouth over hers, hot and intense. The scrape of his teeth against her bottom lip nearly lifted China up off the floor. Muscle memory flooded back, and her body went from stiff and annoyed to pliable and needy in mere heartbeats.

In a single, mind-bending kiss, he was able to reach in, take her heart, and twist it inside out.

His hand slid from the wall to the bare expanse of her shoulder, where he spun slow intimate circles over her skin with the pad of his thumb. Each spiral undid her resolve a little more. He pulled back and gazed into her face, his eyes twin points of blue flame that seared away her common sense. She wanted him to kiss her, to touch her.

But it would only lead to heartbreak, her common sense insisted. Colt had proven that. Even if Hunters and Darkin occasionally dallied with one another, it never lasted. It couldn't. But wouldn't he be worth it? Just once, her body argued back.

"Do you have any idea how difficult it is to ignore you?" The rough timbre of his voice crept beneath her reserve and made her quiver. No. She would not give in. Being stubborn was one of her best traits.

So ignoring her *had* been deliberate. Interesting. Perhaps Remington Jackson was not as hard and cold as he appeared to be. Perhaps an actual heart beat beneath that broad chest. But it was too little too late. She spread her fingers on his chest, intending to push him out of what little air space she had left, and instead felt the rapid, hard knock of his heart against her palm.

"Look, we can do this the easy way or the hard way, and personally I always found the easy way works best for me. You can let me go, or I can make you let me go." She said it with more bravado than she felt. She was perilously close to the edge of giving in.

He laughed at that and leaned down, bringing his fantastic mouth a hair's breadth away from hers. "Maybe when I'm done with you, China McGee, you won't want me to let you go." Remington brushed his lips back and forth against hers, so lightly she found herself leaning in for more.

He moved before she could kiss him, his mouth trailing

searing kisses across her cheek and jaw, then down her throat. They grew hungrier and more demanding the farther down they went. Try as she might to rein her body in with her mind, her determined libido was having none of it.

China squirmed. "And what if I resist you?"

His hands spread and flexed on either side of her rib cage—a most inappropriate and welcome corset, his thumbs brushing against the soft underside of her breasts in unison. She gasped at the sensation, wishing once again that she wasn't wearing a dress. Her breasts tightened, waiting for and wanting his touch, the points becoming hard. Desire flared in his eyes.

She found her legs giving way, her body sagging against the wall for support. His hands moved lower, resting against the indention of her waist, holding her up, lifting her against him. His eyes had grown softer, sexier, as the lids dropped partially down.

"You won't resist," he said, his tone half cocky, half a rumble that amped up her need to feel him against her. "You want to know how I know?"

She leaned into him, her hands twining about his shoulders, and nodded. "I have tells?"

He chuckled. "You mean besides the blush that turns your skin to strawberries and cream or these?" He reached up and gently rolled a hardened nipple between his fingers. China arched her head back at the onslaught, barely able to breathe. "I know because when I kiss you properly, you start to fall apart in my hands."

He followed up on his assessment with a practical demonstration of his talents as he kissed slowly and with deliberation down the length of her neck and across the tops of her breasts. The warmth of his mouth shot a surge of heat spiraling through her from the tips of her breasts to the apex of her thighs. China was beginning to realize that as cold as Remington had been in the midst and aftermath of battle, he was equally as hot now—all intensity.

The whirr of the engines made the air within the submarine vibrate with a hum she could feel to her very core. The throbbing sensation intensified, a most pleasurable discomfort. Remington cupped her bottom in his hands and in one smooth motion lifted her up and spun around, brushing the charts aside with a sweep of his arm and sitting her neatly on the table. He kissed her again, muddling her mind and making her hyper-aware of the flavor of him.

China scooted to the edge of the table, letting him step in between her legs. She wrapped her legs over his butt and rocked against him to ease her torment. It didn't work. All it did was make it worse.

"So what are we going to do about it?" She barely managed to get the words out, her voice husky and heavy with need.

His sinful mouth tipped up at the edge in a way that made her stomach swoop. "Let me show you."

Chapter 13

Remington's hands disappeared beneath the black fabric of China's skirt, inching it up higher to pool around his forearms as his fingers skimmed up along the dainty turn of her ankles and the sweet curve of her calves. He didn't need to see to be able to feel . . . and he only needed to feel to imagine.

Her bare skin was silky and hot, especially behind her knees. She shivered beneath his fingers, and her hot, sweet breath fanned his face. "Maybe this dress wasn't such a bad idea after all," she murmured.

"I know." He kissed her lightly, touching his forehead to hers and looking into her eyes. They were fierce and bright, desire bringing a delightful blush to not just her rosy cheeks, but to her neck and the pale skin of her plump breasts. He really couldn't resist any longer.

"You are exquisite."

China gave a husky laugh, the movement of her body rasping her damp heat against him. "I ain't ever been called that before."

"A shame. Especially considering how perfect you are." Though she looked as fragile and beautiful as a porcelain doll, her skin as clear and smooth as any doll's, China was far from breakable or brittle. She was pliant and soft, and he sought out her lush mouth for another kiss, like a thirsty man in the desert needed water.

"Now you're just sweet-talkin' me, 'cause I know I ain't perfect."

"You're perfect for me."

Just her touch, the fragrance of her skin, the small sounds she made as he skimmed his fingers along her inner thigh made him hyper aware of how much he'd been missing when it came to women. Oh, he'd enjoyed them, yes. But none had given him a sense of power, a sense that he could change their world with a flick of his fingers. And yet it wasn't the power that humbled him, but the sense that he wanted to please her like no one else ever had. It was an itch he couldn't scratch, a need he couldn't satisfy until he saw her come completely undone in his arms.

He moved his hand from beneath her skirt and slid it over her shoulder, slipped the strap that held her bodice firm in place down her arm. China made a low growling sound deep in her body that resonated through his chest and trebled his desire to touch her. He was hot and so damn hard he could have chopped wood. He didn't want to ruin her gown, but he wanted it out of the way, the sooner, the better. Somewhere in the recesses of his logical mind, he realized he had her up on the chart table, and that anyone could happen upon them if they merely opened the door. Another part of his mind reminded him how dangerous she could be. She was still Darkin and he was taking a tremendous risk, leaving himself vulnerable to a possible attack by her.

He didn't give a damn. Not now. Not when she was shimmering in his hands. One slow, persistent pull on the upper edge of her bodice bared her right breast. As he'd suspected the hardened peak he'd felt earlier was a soft rosy pink. Score one for his imagination. Her lashes fluttered shut as she tilted her head back, her mouth open, her breath coming in pants.

He filled his hand with her breast, indulging himself with

the warm silky weight of it. But if one was good, two were better. He slid the other strap off her left shoulder and exposed her left breast to his hungry gaze as well.

There was no point in resisting; the pulse thrummed so loudly in his ears, he was deaf to all other sounds. He laved the hardened nub of her breast with his tongue, enjoying the sweet, salty taste of her skin on his lips. China rose up off the table, arching, her heat rubbing against him, making him flex and buck in response. He wanted to sink in deep and wrap himself in her wet heat and never leave.

His kiss wasn't soft, nor was it slow, but revealed the full fury of the raging inferno inside him. He moved to tear the dress from her, to feast on her. And China gave as good as she got. Her nails scored his skin straight through his shirt, and she nipped at his bottom lip then suckled it as she drew him up flush against her, her bare breasts pressing against his chest.

"Jackson!" Monica called out. Remington stiffened as if he'd been hit. "Jackson, we've made land." The captain's voice echoed on the metal hull of the submarine. He and China broke apart, both breathing hard and fast. They locked gazes, and the lightning there between them could have burned the place down had it not been made totally of metal.

"What in the hell was that?" China said between breaths.

"The captain."

"I know it was her! Where? Has she been watching us the whole time?"

He glanced to the door and shifted his position, making sure China had time to cover herself as he waited for the wheel on the door to turn, expecting Monica to step through at any moment. When she didn't, he frowned in confusion. He'd plainly heard her, just as China had.

"Mr. Jackson, I know you can hear me. Everyone on the ship can hear me. Please pick up the speaking tube." He swiveled, glancing up, and realized a brass horn, rather like the horn on a gramophone, was positioned on the wall just behind his head. He could only assume Monica meant the long, black braided chord attached to a smaller version of the brass tube. He picked up the smaller horn and spoke into it. "Jackson here."

"Finally. I thought I was going to have to come and locate you. We've made the point. I can get us close to shore here, but you'll need to assist with unloading the Spider Walker."

He glanced at China. Her gray eyes sparkled like diamonds, bright with desire. Her lips were bee-stung and swollen from their kisses, and her bare breasts rose and fell with the fast rhythm of her breath. He wanted to tell Monica to go to Hell, or at least wait an hour.

But dallying with China wasn't what he was here for. He was here to recover Elwin's piece of the Book of Legend. "I'll be there in five minutes." He could not resist kissing her just once more. Five minutes wasn't going to tip the fate of the world.

The engines slowed, the constant *thrum* growing slower and slower until the hulk of the ship came to a stop. He hadn't realized the motion of the ship had affected him so, but now that they were simply bobbing about like a cork, his limbs had an uncharacteristic lightness to them, as if they'd somehow fallen asleep. But perhaps that had as much to do with having touched China as it did with the machine. She sure affected him more.

He walked briskly toward the top decks of the submarine. Monica came wheeling around the corner and joined him as they marched to the entrance hatch.

"We should be able to see the coast from here and determine the best place to lay in so we can unload." She gave a hand signal to her crewman, who began to twist a series of wheels on the wall.

With the mechanical clank and click of several gears, the secondary entrance hatch used when out in the water, opened above them. Natural light flooded in, making them all squint at the unbridled brightness. Monica ascended first. He followed, climbing the metal rungs quickly. They stood together on the narrow teak platform and stared out at the ridge of land before them.

It was an endless stretch of pale golden sand and jumbles of gray and tan rock, turquoise and sapphire surf rolling into lacy white waves, and verdant jungle as far as the eye could see.

"Welcome to the Gulf of Tehuantepec," Monica said with a touch of pride. "See, I told you I could get us here."

Remington heard the rustle of fabric behind him and saw China had climbed the rungs to join them. "How can you tell we ain't just washed up on some deserted tropical island?"

Monica arched a brow, the breeze buffeting her dark hair about her face. "I run these waters with my father once every month. My instruments give me bearings. And the sea floor starts to climb just past this point and becomes much shallower. This is the best point for us to bring the submarine closer in to land."

The deep blue waters split before the bullnose of the submarine, peeling apart into frothy white waves that formed a V-shaped wake. The smell of brine above mingled with that of engine oil coming from the staler air below. China shivered, and Remington put his arm around her and tucked her into his side.

Monica lifted her chin into the wind and pointed to a spot where the water was darker around the rim of land. "We'll pull onto the beach there and open the forward hatch. We should be able to pull out and assemble the Spider Walker quickly." She glanced at them. "Then you two can be on your way."

Remington placed a hand on Monica's shoulder. "You don't know how much your help has meant, Captain."

Monica shrugged and looked back at the beach. "Don't be flattered, Mr. Jackson. I didn't do any of it for you, or for Miss McGee. I did it because my Uncle Diego dedicated his life to restoring the Book of Legend. For him, my father and I have made this journey and helped your cause." She flicked her suddenly fierce gaze at him. "Do not disappoint us."

She turned and headed back down the rungs, leaving Remington and China alone on the upper view deck. "Do you think it's even possible?"

"Assembling the Spider Walker on a beach or reuniting the Book of Legend?" he teased.

China swatted at his chest. "Reuniting the Book, of course."

"If there's one thing I've discovered as a Hunter, it's that anything is possible."

They pulled the individual mechanical legs of the Spider Walker out of the hull one at a time, each one requiring four people to move it. The bulbous body and brass-rimmed glass canopy that topped it each came out separately.

China grimaced. "Are you certain we need this thing?"

Remington smiled. "I take it spiders aren't your favorite thing."

"It would have been easier if they'd had a giant mechanical jaguar or even a mechanical parrot for us to fly. Besides, I thought you didn't like mechanical things—like Tempus."

He shook his head and laughed. "A horse is a far different thing. I'd take a real one of those any day over Colt's mechanical version. But I'll mention the jaguar and parrot to Marley next time I see him. Until then I can be quite satisfied in this machine. I don't especially care for it, but this should help get us up those hills."

Farther inland stark gray and tan points rose up out of the lush green vegetation. Monica wiped the sweat from her brow with the back of her hand. "Here, Miss McGee; make yourself useful." She handed China a wrench.

China grumbled beneath her breath. She and mechanical things rarely got along well. Give her a good gun, a few explosives, and some inside information on how to sneak into a place, and she could accomplish far more than she could with a dozen wrenches and screwdrivers.

She bent down and started turning the lug nuts on the bolts Monica had indicated. They spun off and fell into the sand, causing China to curse as she dug through the gritty sand to find them and brushed off the metal rings on the hem of her black dress. Monica sighed. "Righty tighty, lefty loosey," she admonished.

China shot a glare at her the minute Monica's back was turned. *Righty tighty, my ass. How about a nice right upper cut? That would fix things nicely.* It would make her feel better at any rate. The nut became harder and harder to turn. "This ain't working," she muttered loudly. China frowned at the wrench. She knew it wasn't Monica's fault she didn't possess a drop of mechanical skill, but it felt better to rail at her in her mind all the same.

Truth was, China didn't like feeling as if she were the outsider. Of course that had been a near constant state her entire life. Among the humans she was an outsider because she was a bastard. Among the Darkin she was an outsider because she was marked by Rathe. She was a thief. She had no family.

Remington's large hand covered hers. China glanced up into his face, and every touch came rushing back with a vengeance, making her shake. "It's just cross-threaded. Here, let me help you."

He used his strong fingers to twist the nut back, freeing it up. Somewhere deep inside her a small flicker of hope kindled into a flame. No one had ever watched out for her before. It was something so refreshing, so utterly new that she was afraid to believe it was real. "Thank you," she said softly.

He offered her a patented Jackson smile that could charm a habit off a nun. "My pleasure."

China's heart sped up, and her cheeks heated. A soft step of a boot in the sand caused them both to look up.

"How's it going? We've got two more legs before we can raise up the body pod."

"Almost finished here," Remington replied.

Monica's mouth turned down at the edges. "You'd better get her out of the sun. She looks like she's burning."

China muttered underneath her breath and attacked the rest of the nuts and bolts on the mechanical leg with renewed vigor.

Remington grabbed hold of her hand, keeping her from using her wrench. She glared up at him. "What am I doing wrong now?"

His mouth cracked a lopsided smile. "Not a damn thing. I just wanted to tell you not to take the captain's criticism personally. She's that way with everyone, not just you."

"It doesn't feel that way."

He chucked her under the chin with his finger. "Chin up. You've got other skills she can't possibly match. And they're ones I need far more."

The compliment hit China all wrong. She didn't want to be accepted or appreciated because of what she could do—or who she was or wasn't. She wanted to be appreciated for just being herself. She nodded stiffly and returned to work.

It didn't take them too much longer to get the rest of the Spider Walker assembled. Small metal steps stuck out of the Spider's front legs like stiff hairs, allowing China and Remington to climb up into the body pod, which housed two cushion seats in black leather with high backs, a panel full of brass levers used to maneuver the machine, a special transponder unit to communicate with the submarine, and the bulbous glass dome that hinged down over them and locked in place with a curved bolt lock. A hole directly behind the chairs in the pod wall was designed to fit the Blaster. It would power up the boiler, which comprised the majority of the spider's abdomen. Their supply packs were stored beneath their chairs.

Monica and her crew disappeared back into the submarine, taking their tools with them. They looked as if they were climbing into the gaping mouth of the thing, then the hatch closed up behind them.

"Well, this is . . ."

"Comfortable?" Remington suggested.

"Yes. I suppose," China replied, but the greenish tint to her skin suggested she wasn't pleased with their transportation.

"A damn sight better than walking, that's all I know."

She nodded stiffly in agreement, but her lips were pressed together tightly.

"And you've got to be glad to be off the submarine."

Her eyes met his. "Yes." Her tone was resolute. "Yes, I am glad of that."

Up ahead was a wall of green. The vegetation soared upward, taller than any building Remington had ever seen. The massive trees knit together into a solid canopy of green. A sudden sinking feeling hollowed out the pit of his stomach. When Diego had said this mission was impossible, he'd been generous. This wasn't finding a needle in a haystack, it was more like finding a particular grain of sand at the bottom of the ocean.

"How the hell are we supposed to find anything in that?"

China lifted her chin, her eyes narrowing. "You don't feel it?"

Remington glanced at her. "What?"

"The pull right about here." She placed her hand on the flat of her stomach.

"Are you sure it's a sense of direction and not just hunger?"

China rolled her eyes. "Very funny. And before you ask, it isn't a female condition either."

Remington shrugged. He had been thinking of that, but had sense enough not to comment. "Well as long as we have a map, how about we use that instead of your instincts?" He slipped the map carefully out from between the pages of the codex and unfolded it.

China closed her eyes and inhaled deeply, as if scenting the air. She pointed, then opened her eyes. "It's that way." She glanced back at him, her finger still extended. "Are you sure you don't feel anything?"

He just shook his head. Oh, he felt plenty—just nothing to do with the location of this fabled forbidden entrance. He wasn't about to tell her about the hot tight sensation she created in him every time he looked at her, especially after the incident in the submarine. He wasn't about to tell her his fingertips tingled just thinking of the hot silk texture of her skin. Remington double-checked the map. The direction she pointed in was the right way. He adjusted his hold on the levers of the machine into a more comfortable position.

"Well let's get going. We don't have much time to find Elwin's piece of the Book."

Chapter 14

Armed with the map, they struggled through the jungle. Remington had been right about the Spider Walker's offering them a distinct advantage in this terrain. The dense canopy of the jungle turned the sky overhead a mix of green and vibrant points of orange, brilliant pink, and yellow from the exotic flowers that seemed to grow on spindly stems and dangle from the very branches of the lush vegetation.

The stifling humidity made everything slick with a layer of moisture. Beads of water dropped from the leaves and streaked the glass dome of the Spider Walker, making visibility difficult. Inside the pod, the air was stifling, thick, and cloying, making it a challenge to breathe without feeling as if she were drowning.

China pushed back the damp strands of hair sticking to her forehead and throat, blowing out a heavy sigh. She plucked at her damp clothing, but it just sucked back down to her skin the instant she let go.

Monkeys chattered and howled, jumping from branch to branch to follow their noisy progress through the trees.

China watched it all with a kind of detached interest. She was trying hard to focus in on the small tug in the center of her gut, knowing it was a way to double-check the map until they reached their goal. But pressed into the confines of the Spider Walker control pod with Remington, concentrating was damned difficult, if not impossible. The odor of Bay Rum had long since faded from his skin, leaving him with clean sweat and male musk.

Remington's skin was shiny with perspiration, and his white shirt was transparent as it stuck to his damp skin. She could see the curvature of his shoulder and biceps as he worked the levers. The uneven terrain required his constant attention as he adjusted the eight individual legs of the machine.

China tried hard not to think about what he looked like without his shirt on at all. The damp fabric clung enough to give her an intense flash of memory of how his back had looked, bronzed skin poured over his well-sculpted physique, when he'd removed his shirt the day before to haul water for the boilers. She squirmed against the insistent throb that she got whenever she remembered their interrupted moment on the submarine too vividly. China crossed her legs and squeezed.

"Why does it have to be so damn hot in this thing?" she muttered a little breathlessly, fanning herself with her hand. It did no good to assuage the throbbing sensation and only circulated the humid air.

"Look, we've gotten much farther than we would have on foot. Another day and we'll be in Veracruz province."

He was right, of course. But that did little to stem the ache in the small of her back or untie the knots in her legs caused by the continual wobbling, clanking stride of the Spider Walker as it clamored over obstacles. Even with the glass dome, the machine was too small of a confined space for a shifter. The only time they'd taken a break was to replenish the water in the boiler tank. Remington had even insisted they sleep during the last two nights in the contraption for safety's sake.

"I need out of this thing."

Remington glanced at her. "We'll stop in an hour."

China glanced at the dials on the control panel. "We need

more water anyway. Besides, I have to make a stop." She fidgeted a little in her seat to prove her point.

"Fine. Just let me get to that sandy clearing up ahead."

Small rivulets wove through the jungle, trickling and merging here and there into larger streams. She suspected this had once been a bed for one of those streams that had diverted elsewhere, maybe because of an enormous downed tree or some other natural obstacle. Remington could stop this machine anywhere he wished as long as he let her out for a respite of the heat—both the weather and the internal heat he generated without even being aware of it.

He pulled back a lever on the control panel, and the machine slowed to a crawl then stopped. He unlatched and pushed open the glass dome. She shimmied down the metal foot pegs in the spider's front leg until she reached the ground and took her first deep breath of fresh air in hours. Sure the machine had bellows that puffed in air from outside, but somehow it wasn't the same. It had a metallic taste to it.

Outside the sweet scent of orchids perfumed the air and competed with the moldy odor of decaying vegetation. China gave a relieved sigh and stretched, just happy to be out of the machine and to wiggle her toes in the earth.

Until her feet began to sink.

The soft, wet soil swelled up around her ankles. She tried to take a step and found it to be a sucking pull that wouldn't let go. "Remington?"

"I'm coming. Just let me get the Blaster and our packs." He insisted that any time they left the machine to gather water, food, or take care of other necessities, they take protection with them. But she was sinking fast and couldn't wait.

"Remington! Something about this ground isn't right." She looked up at him and saw that the Spider Walker was listing to one side, and he was holding on as it tilted. The ground had risen—or had she sunk?—to around her calves.

"It's quicksand!" The worry in his voice only made the situation worse.

While she'd heard tales of it, she'd never actually seen it before. "Are you sure?"

"The Walker is sinking, isn't it?" His tone, clipped and impatient, irritated her.

"So am I!" she added indignantly, annoyed he hadn't noticed.

He pulled a length of rope from the pack on his back and quickly formed a lasso, which he flung at a nearby tree branch. The lasso snagged tightly on the limb, and the rope vibrated with the tension as he rappelled down the length of the spider leg still well above the quicksand and held out his hand to her.

She reached for his hand, but only her fingertips skimmed his. He was just out of reach. Panic welled up in her throat, making it hard to breathe, and the more she struggled, the tighter grip the viscous wet sand took on her, sucking her down to her thighs.

"Come on, grab hold of me!"

It wasn't as if she weren't trying, dammit! She closed her eyes, letting her body grow warm, and imagined her arm stretching out like a monkey's, long and lean. Muscle and sinew pulled, and she felt the hard clasp of Remington's hand around hers.

"Relax and let me guide you to the edge where you can crawl out."

One hand on her, one hand on the rope, he hopped down from the leg of the spider toward the base of the tree he was leashed to.

The quicksand had worked its way up to her waist, and she tried to relax, just as he'd said. The hard pull of the ground on her subsided. He hauled her up and out of the quicksand, and for a moment they both lay on the ground breathing hard.

Blup . . . blup . . . blup. Bubbles rose and burst on the

surface of the quicksand as the Spider Walker sank farther. It was half buried now in the muck, only two of its legs visible and the entire abdomen of the spider submerged.

Remington cursed beneath his breath. "There's no way we'll get it out now. Marley is going to have my hide for losing it."

China sighed. "Even if you did get it out, it would never work right again. All that sand, grit, and water in the mechanics will freeze it solid."

"At least I saved this." He reached into his pack and pulled out the Blaster.

China hugged him hard around the neck. "A man after my own heart."

The press of her body against him was welcome. He'd damn well been thinking about it two out of every four seconds round the clock since they'd climbed onto the deck of the submarine two days ago. But there was a fine line between doing what was desired and what was necessary.

And while Remington desired a great many things, and often bent the rules to his favor, he always did what was necessary first. Lives depended upon it.

This was no different. The search for Elwin's piece of the Book had to come first, before any personal agenda. He stood up and climbed the tree to retrieve the rope, then coiled it neatly back together and stuffed it into the pack, which he heaved onto his back.

"You wanted plenty of fresh air. Now you have it," he commented dryly. "Let's push on."

Down on the ground the vegetation the Spider Walker had seemed to glide over was a daunting barrier to movement. One didn't walk through it; one inched.

Remington dug deep into his pack and pulled out the blade gauntlet Marley had suggested he carry with him at all times.

As with all of Marley's inventions, there was a fifty-fifty chance the first time you used it that it would either perform better than expected, or maim a piece of you. Since the gauntlet had proven its use against the viperanox without damaging him somehow, he was happy to use it again.

The device had a brown leather glove, reinforced along the back with articulated metal plates that extended into a set of leather bands encasing his forearm. A lethal machete blade of sharp Toledo steel, locked between the layers of leather, extended over the top of his hand, making it perfect for hacking away at anything that got in his way—be it Darkin or in this case the thick swaths of wide leaves and dense vines that made walking in the jungle nearly impossible.

"You'd better stand back."

China didn't argue; she took two paces back, paused, then took two more.

With a loud series of grunts punctuating his swings, Remy hacked and hewed at the foliage, creating a path for them through the understory. His arm, shoulder, and back began to burn with the effort. Sweat plastered his hair to his head and trickled in a stream down his back, turning his clothing into a sauna. He didn't want to admit it, but China had been right. This explorer's uniform was a pain in the ass, and he looked like an idiot.

He paused long enough to shuck off the pith helmet and linen shirt, leaving him clad in jodhpurs and boots. Only the boots were worth a damn in this climate and the jacket had been lost when the Spider Walker sank.

"Do you mind putting these in the pack?" A small, cat-like, knowing smile curved her lush mouth. She didn't say I told you so, because she didn't have to. He could tell she was just a bit too pleased with herself for being right.

Four hours later he was sore, sullen, and exhausted. There

was no way they were going to make it to Veracruz in time like this.

"Do you mind hurrying this along a bit? At this rate it's going to take us months to reach the temple."

Remington turned around and glared at her. "Fine. You think you can do better? Here you go."

He unlatched the machete from his leather gauntlet and slid it out, handing it to her.

China stared for a moment at the blade, then set her chin, gritted her teeth, and snatched it out of his hand. Her arm jolted straight down at the sudden and unexpected weight of the machete. He threw her a triumphant look, which only fueled her determination more.

She let the transition take her, shaping and molding her body, her spine growing curved and longer, her arms stretching down to the ground, and the hairs on her body growing into a dense, thick pelt. She breathed for a moment after she'd changed, and the air smelled different, somehow greener. She could smell ripe bananas and mangoes, breadfruit, and the other edibles in the forest ahead. But she wasn't here to eat.

She turned back and grunted at Remington. His eyes were wide, and he'd stepped back a pace.

"I didn't know you could change into a giant monkey."

China huffed and grunted at him. She was a gorilla. Surely he knew the difference. In her thick black hand the machete now seemed like a toy. She whacked and slashed at the pathway before them, ripping down the limbs and small saplings that she couldn't shove easily past.

What she couldn't hack down with the blade she snapped in her massive hands or trampled. Moving through the jungle was vastly easier in this form than as a human.

The jungle seemed to part around her, like prairie grasses

before the wind, offering little resistance to her force. But regardless of their progress, the air was stifling with both heat and humidity, and the dense fur on her body only amplified the discomfort.

She quickly tired, and was so thirsty she thought she might expire on the spot. But as tired as she was, she didn't want to change back into the dress that hampered her movements.

Still, being a gorilla wasn't all that wonderful. She was hungry, horribly hungry, and the thought of food drove her mad.

China tossed the machete to the ground, letting her body transform back into its usual shape once more.

"Had enough?" Remington teased.

"At least I bested your time by a half hour," she threw back at him.

Remington frowned. "I think it's about time for us to eat." He glanced around.

"What are you doing, looking for hams hangin' from the trees?"

"Not ham, fruit." He pointed upward. "Does that look edible to you?"

China took a deep draft of air into her lungs. Her stomach rumbled. Her gorilla sense of smell still hadn't completely faded. "Smells good enough to eat. And the monkeys seem to like it."

Remington pulled off his pack, snatched the machete from the ground, clamped the blade between his teeth, and began climbing the tree. He looked like a pirate. The muscles in his back gleamed with sweat, and without his shirt China had a great view of him. Monkeys chattered and screamed, swinging wildly through the branches as he came closer to the fruit. China backed up a step, then another, tilting her head to try to get a better view as he climbed higher.

He whacked at a branch, taking off a cluster of the round,

brownish fruit with his machete, and held it high. "Ready? Catch!"

China walked a few more steps backward, holding up her arms to catch the falling fruit. Suddenly the ground disappeared beneath her feet, and she was the one falling. "Remington!" she screamed, thrashing wildly as her stomach swooped up into her chest and the darkness closed in around her.

Chapter 15

One second there was solid earth beneath her feet, and the next she was falling. China waved her limbs wildly, searching for any purchase as she gained speed, but the sides of the sinkhole were slicked with damp green moss and too far apart for her hands to grab hold of anything.

Her scream echoed off the rocks, freakishly magnified as she plummeted inexorably faster and faster. The pool of light above her grew smaller and smaller. A terrified glance below showed what waited for her at the bottom: jagged points of rock, spearing upward toward her through a pool of water.

Shift! Shift! Shift!

Her scream altered as she concentrated, letting the change take her, until her arms grew light, her face hard, and her body hairs stiffened into brilliant red feathers.

She squawked and pulled up from the free fall, using her body until it burned. China soared upward toward Remington, who leaned dangerously forward over the rim, a dark visage against the light that surrounded him. "China!"

Even as she crested the edge of the hole, she flew higher, until she was in the canopy of the giant trees, their foliage a wash of brilliant green. She was free of danger, but at this moment she needed something more. She needed to reassure herself she was still alive.

Her avian body naturally sought out the spaces between the branches, allowing her to go even higher until she broke through into the brilliant sunlight. With each downward beat she glimpsed the red tips of her wings. China let the rush of energy and pure joy fill her, making her lighter than air as she flew.

Of any of her forms, besides human, this was what she enjoyed most—being a bird. In parrot form she reveled in the freedom and the brilliance of her red and yellow plumage. From up here the jungle looked far different. It was a dense, rolling sea of green that stretched far toward the horizon where it met a band of turquoise water that glittered in the sun. But off in the distance to the north, she spotted an inconsistency. Something looked different. A flash of white stone among the treetops.

A mountain perhaps? And if there was a mountain, perhaps there was a spring or water, or possibly even shelter. China pumped her wings hard and flew. She didn't want to leave Remington alone too long. There were dangers in this jungle neither of them could fight off alone.

She dipped the tip of one wing and wheeled back toward him. The leaves rushed by her, the sound of the wind rippling them filling her ears as she sped past, down through the layers of the canopy.

"China!" She heard him call her name and zeroed in on the source of his voice far down below in the thickness of the jungle. She banked left and came to rest in a tree near him. Her arms were burning, but it was a good feeling to stretch and work her muscles hard. She gripped the branch with all four toes as she walked sideways along its length.

Remington walked to the base of the tree, narrowing his eyes as he glanced up. "China, is that you?"

She cocked her head. Perhaps she ought to stay in this form for awhile. It would be much easier to lead them to the mountain if she could occasionally fly up above the trees to check their progress, but then she couldn't tell him about what she'd seen. *Choices. Choices.*

She squawked at him in response, and he smiled.

"You'd talk back to me even if you were a turtle, wouldn't you?"

She chirped a series of calls that sounded like a harsh approximation of a human laugh, then flew down to the ground and let the heated flow of transition take her back to her human form.

The moment she stood up from her crouch, Remington wrapped her in a fierce hug. "I was afraid I'd lost you in that hole, that something awful had happened to you."

They stood near the edge of it, holding each other. "There's water down there," she said matter-of-factly. "It must be an underground river of some sort. And when I was above the tree line I saw something else."

He pulled back and locked gazes with her. "What?"

China frowned. "I don't know really, but it was white and as tall as the trees. It seemed out of place somehow. I thought it was a mountain."

"Or the lost temple of El Tajin."

"Is that what we're searching for?"

Remington nodded. "The codex said the Totonacapan were among the first peoples to meet the Spaniards when they came to Veracruz. And when war arose between the Aztecs and the conquered Totonacapan, the Totonacapan sided with the Spaniards against the Aztecs, hiding Elwin's piece of the Book in their sacred place—the Temple of the Niches or El Tajin."

"Why does that sound so much better than the horrible rivers and trials Diego told us about?"

"Getting to the temple is only the beginning of a more perilous journey."

Oh joy. China shook her head. Why did everything with Hunters have to be glorious, mad, scientifically-enhanced warrior death? Why couldn't they do anything the easy way? *I'd like to close the Gates of Nyx. Oh? Here's the key. Return it when you're done. Have a nice day.* Easy. Simple. She liked life simple, and Remington, his brothers, and the rest of Hunters were anything but simple.

She glanced at the sinkhole and thought about the quicksand. "Now I see why Diego lost more than half his men. This is an impossible task even for a Darkin to undertake alone."

Remington tipped her chin up and brushed her hair back from her temple as he stared down into her face. A sudden tenderness softened his features. "But we're not alone. We have each other."

"How can you be so optimistic?"

Remington shrugged and smiled genuinely at her, and it was enough to boost her confidence in their capabilities too. "Sometimes optimism is all you have. And in that case, why not take it all?"

There were so many times that Remington seemed like such a complete contradiction. She'd made up her mind he was a tough and rugged Hunter, cool under pressure to the point of being ice-cold when he was focused, and then he'd do something like this where he revealed he had a tender heart and filled her with hope. The duality of him awed China. What awed her even more was how he seemed to genuinely care for her.

Only her mother had ever shown concern for her well-being. Her father in turns terrified her and beguiled her, but there was never love there.

Remington's brow furrowed. "Are you all right?" Concern colored his tone. "You didn't get hurt in the fall, did you?"

She waved away his concern even though it touched her heart. "You ain't got to worry about me none. I know how to take care of myself."

"I never doubted that for a moment," he assured her as he kissed her cheek, then pulled away from her. He reached over and picked out a piece of the brown-colored mamey sapote fruit he'd climbed the tree to retrieve for them. They were dry and rough to the touch, like a cross between peaches and sandpaper. He cut one open with the machete to reveal a creamy soft pink-orange interior with a single big seed. "Why don't you eat something, then we'll go search for the lost temple you saw."

The entire time they ate, Remington could only stare at her. China McGee was one hell of a woman. And he'd almost lost her. Well, thought he had at any rate, which was enough to make him reconsider his position on Darkin—one Darkin in particular. In fact, Remington wasn't so sure he even thought of her as Darkin anymore. He thought of her as China—just China.

Once they'd finished their hasty meal, they packed what remained so they'd have it for later. Remington was pretty damn sure there weren't any towns close by, or handy dry-good stores to be had between here and their destination. They were on their own, especially since he had no way to contact Monica to retrieve them now that the Spider Walker had sunk.

He'd salvaged what he could to help them on their journey, but he didn't have the heart to tell China the odds weren't in their favor. Even if they found the Book, he had no idea how they'd get it back in less than two weeks before the night of the new moon.

They walked for the rest of the afternoon, but the heavy

vegetation, humid heat, and endless whacking to create a path had left them both exhausted.

With his machete Remington scraped dry remains from the inner bark of a dead tree to start a fire. They didn't need the warmth, but it helped to dry their things, give them light, and deter curious animals as the jungle shadows grew and darkness fell.

Even in the desert at night there was light from the stars. Here in the jungle the dense canopy of trees blocked out even that, leaving them in inky darkness. Insects by the dozens buzzed and hummed around the edges of the firelight. China huddled close.

"What will happen if we don't make it back?" she asked as she threw chips of wood into the smoking fire.

He didn't know for sure. No one did. Remington wrapped his arm around her, both to give her a comfortable place to sleep and to keep her close. "Marley's been researching this for a year or better now, trying to help Colt. As best as he can tell, if the Book of Legend isn't reunited, then according to the prophecies, Rathe will be able to permanently open the Gates of Nyx, leaving our world vulnerable not just to the Darkin here, but to any in the universe."

"You mean like a portal between worlds?"

"Of a kind. Marley said it has more to do with the way matter and energy relate to one another. For example, this wood is physical matter, but if I chuck it into the fire"—he matched action to words—"it becomes light and heat as the energy in it is released. Apparently humans serve that same function for some other forms of Darkin that are kept out by the Gates. They see humans as fuel."

China frowned, determination flashing in her eyes. "Then we really don't have any choice. We have to do this, no matter what."

Remington nodded. "It's tempting to think about what life would be like without all this sometimes. To just be ordinary."

China would have given anything to have been born in his kind of ordinary world. She snorted. "My ordinary isn't anything people would want to start with." For one thing she'd discovered her Darkin powers early. Her mother had been startled and afraid to find a cat in her baby's crib, and terrified when she discovered her baby *was* the cat!

Remington moved his hand along her arm in a distracted circular motion that soothed her frayed nerves. "But your mother loved you."

Her mother had tried to love her, but it was hard because China's mother always kept a distance between them. Perhaps she hadn't been able to adjust to the idea that her daughter shifted at random times into other things. "Yes, as best she could."

"And your father?"

She paused for a moment, considering the best way to answer his question as honestly as possible. Her relationship with her father was . . . confusing. While she had been under his power, she'd come to crave spending time with him, even if he frightened her with how he might harm her. But being away like this, having Remington treat her with kindness and tenderness, caused a crack in her thinking. Other ideas started to leak in. What if bringing the Book of Legend together and giving it to Rathe wasn't the right thing to do? What if gaining his approval no longer was what she craved most? What if those Darkin Remington mentioned came through the Gates of Nyx and wiped out humanity all because she couldn't get over her own complex and confusing issues with her father?

She pulled her knees up tight to her chest and rested her chin on them. "He was never around much. And when he did visit, it was always to take what he wanted then leave, not caring how we fared without him."

Remington shifted, laying his cheek against the top of her head. "You didn't have much of a family, did you?"

She gave a weary sigh. "That's why your family is so fascinating to me. You all seem so close to one another."

His body shifted slightly beneath her shoulder and hip as she leaned into him and the comfort of his arm around her shoulders. "It looks that way from the outside, only because no one ever saw the way Winchester and Colt fought like Hunters and Darkin over things when we were kids. Winchester was Pa's boy and Colt Ma's. I was pretty much left on my own."

There was a heartbreaking edge to his voice. The sound of a small boy forgotten, who'd grown up thinking he didn't fit in or matter. She knew that feeling so well it called out to her. Perhaps she and Remington were more alike than she'd ever dreamed.

"I remember. You said you're the smart one. Where'd you go to school?"

He sighed. "Back east. Harvard University. It's a different life back there."

"Do you miss it?"

"Sometimes."

"It gave you polish your brothers ain't got."

He smiled against her head; she could feel the movement of his lips against her hair. "Polish isn't everything. Certainly it doesn't count for much with most Darkin."

China frowned. There was one Darkin who found polish like the kind Remington had to be exactly what he preferred and emulated himself—Rathe. She didn't like making the comparison, but there it was. Rathe was always dressed like some fancy English lord. But unlike Remington, it didn't enhance what he already had. Instead it was like putting an expensive dress and makeup on a whore. It didn't fit, and the dark depraved depths of him still shone through all the highfalutin clothing and fancy manners. But she didn't want to think on Rathe, or his sadistic ways, or how it tangled her up inside wanting his approval, yet dreading seeing him. Not now, not while she was in Remington's arms.

Her eyes were growing heavy as the fire's light waned. An orange glow flickered and danced in and among the glowing hearts of the coals. Remington flipped another piece of wood on the fire to keep it going, and she snuggled into him as they took turns sleeping and keeping watch through the night.

Early morning birdsong woke Remington from a stupor. He was stiff all over, and none of it in the right ways. Their clothing and hair smelled of woodsmoke. It wasn't unpleasant, but neither was the warm vanilla scent he loved on China's skin. He kissed her on the forehead and woke her.

She yawned and stretched, rubbing her eyes. "Are you always this much of a morning person?"

He grinned, just to goad her more. "Aren't you?"

She didn't even bother shaking her head. She just glared at him in response.

"I'll take that as a confirmed no. In the meantime, how about more fruit?"

He pulled some from their packs and cut it open, handing it to her. "We've got a long walk ahead of us. You'd better eat up."

They took care of what was necessary and headed off again. The days to complete their mission were quickly dwindling away. They were well into the jungle when the soft earth, spongy and dark from the litter from the trees and vegetation, shivered beneath their feet.

China glanced at him as he placed his hand on her arm to halt their progress. "Earthquake?"

"Doesn't feel like any earthquake I've ever experienced. You?"

She shook her head as the ground vibrated beneath their feet, making leaves and twigs on the ground dance and branches high above them shimmy. The rustle of leaves alone indicated something unusual. Monkeys chattered excitedly high above them, and in the distance the sound of a big animal rang out a warning to the denizens of the jungle.

The hair on the back of Remy's neck lifted in warning.

Not an earthquake, he thought, keeping his senses open, trying to pinpoint direction and what the impending danger could be. The animals around them knew to get the hell away. Birds scattered like buckshot from the trees, and swoops of orange butterflies flew south like well-organized confetti.

This was more like some giant thing or a huge group of little things was digging its way out of the soil like a coterie of prairie dogs. But bigger and a lot more dangerous.

Remington's gaze darted across the open areas among the trees. The dirt and detritus began to split open in a dozen places, making it impossible to watch them all at once. Shiny bits of smooth white material speared upward from the soil.

China shifted to stand closer to him. "What the hell are those?"

"If I didn't know better, I'd say they were bones." A bulbous skull pushed through the soil, its sightless eye sockets and gaping nose hole pulling level with the dirt. It was really too bad that he wasn't wrong more often.

One by one the skeletons emerged from the soil, crawling their way out of the earthen crypts. The bones were animated, humans without muscles or flesh, unseeing but apparently determined to wreak havoc.

"Oh!" China jumped forward, knocking into his back. "There's more!"

He spun around and glanced behind them. They'd been so

stumped by what was happening in front of them, they hadn't realized the skeletons had them surrounded. Each held an obsidian blade, spear, or Aztec war club in bony hands, all tips pointed inward toward them. Blast.

"Any thoughts on how to best them?"

China huffed. "I've never fought off the dead before."

The bone warriors continued to sprout up out of the soil, their arms outstretched. Their gaping maws letting out a collective bloodcurdling, dust-dry wail. Remy took a swing at one and it busted apart, the skull flying off and shattering as it hit the trunk of the massive tree to the side of him. China flinched as the chunks of bone scattered, nicking her skin.

But the blow didn't stop the warrior. Headless, it kept coming as if nothing had happened. Its hands wrapped around Remington's throat. The skeleton was surprisingly strong and its fingers hard, bruising the skin as it pressed off his airway.

Remington grappled with the thing, pulling at the wrist bones at his throat. Nothing broke its hold. Stars floated and popped in his vision. Time to use a different tactic. He swung his arms around, throwing them down hard on the forearms of the skeleton. The arms broke away at the elbow from the rest of the skeleton, but still the fingers squeezed the living breath from him.

Zzzot! A bright blue flash of light filled the clearing, and the main body of the skeleton disintegrated into ash. The bony hands fell away, and Remington whipped around to find China armed with Marley's Blaster. Her eyes were bright and her smile almost a leer. "Did you see that?"

"Of course I saw it. You almost hit me!" He ducked as another bone warrior took a swing at him with a wooden club covered with obsidian spikes. He hadn't tried the Blaster before because frankly he hadn't been sure he'd survive. But now that he knew it worked—"What are you waiting for? Follow me and keep shooting! We need a path out of here."

China charged up the Blaster again, the electric hum of it filling the air like a swarm of angry bees. "Brace yourself!"

Remington knocked two bone warriors sideways, toppling to the ground with them as she aimed and fired another blast of blue electricity. *ZZZZot!*

A charred path led straight out of the clearing, small tendrils of smoke curling about the edges of it. Remington didn't waste a second. He grabbed hold of her hand, and together they fled into the jungle.

Shhhunk! A fast-moving brush of air caused Remington to glance sideways. An obsidian blade lay half buried in the trunk of the tree next to his head. Holy hell. It was a good thing those skeletons weren't more accurate. Then again, if he didn't have eyeballs to spot his target he supposed he'd miss now and again too.

His legs pumped hard and fast. Massive leathery leaves slapped him in the face and chest as he and China barreled down what looked like some sort of animal path. The rattling sound of bones knocking together and dry wails didn't abate. He glanced back and saw the skeletons were still hot on their trail.

The roaring sound of running water—a lot of it—pricked up his ears. "This way!" Without body mass, he doubted the skeletons could swim. If he and China could just make it across the river, they'd be safe. For the moment.

He dodged left, dragging China along behind him. Her breathing was harsh and fast. "Slow down; this thing is heavy!"

"Not a chance." He grabbed the Blaster from her on the run and shoved her ahead of him. "Go, go, go! They're right behind us!"

The roaring grew louder. China came to a dead stop in front of him, and he plowed into her. "What the hell are you—"

He looked in front of their feet at the edge of the ravine

that dropped off into space. A waterfall plunged fifty feet down to rocks below.

Shhhunk! Another deadly black glass blade missed them by mere inches.

"Jump!"

"What? No! I hate water! I can't—"

Remington gave her a shove off the ledge just as a bony hand clamped around his throat and squeezed.

Chapter 16

Shift!

Before she could change into another bird, or a fish, or even a butterfly, China's arms pinwheeled. Screaming she tumbled down in a freefall off the cliff toward the roaring bottom of the waterfall and churning river below. Spray from the waterfall soaked her well before she plunged into the ice-cold water.

Shift!

Instantly her skin stung and burned from the impact, and the water closed over her head. The rolling current of the river, pushed by the waterfall, kept shoving her under as she tried to climb to the surface.

Shiftshiftshift!

China kicked and writhed, her lungs burning. She rose to the surface, sputtering and coughing. Just then another wash of water slapped over the top of her as a big object fell into the river beside her.

She gasped, her arms flailing, barely able to keep her head above the surge of the water. A strong arm came from somewhere below and wrapped around her middle, just beneath her breasts, keeping her head up above the waterline. *Remington*.

Droplets of water sprayed from his hair as he shook the

water from his eyes when he broke to the surface. They were carried downstream through rapids. He did his best to shield her from the rocks with his body. As the water slowed, he moved them closer to the edge. With powerful legs and long sweeps of his arm he swam to the riverbank, keeping her tucked against his side.

They both crawled onto the wet rocks and lay there for a moment, just breathing, which was harder for her than for him. China turned to her side and coughed, her throat scraped raw and her chest sore as water came up.

He laid a warm hand on her back. "Just keep breathing. It'll get easier."

"I can't swim," she rasped. "I tried to tell you but you didn't give me a chance."

"You did see the army of skeletons after us, didn't you?"

She turned her head and gave him an incredulous look. "Well, yes—"

"Then you know why I didn't listen. I was more interested in keeping you alive."

"By drowning me?"

He looked up at the sky and muttered underneath his breath, something about perverse points of view, before he turned and speared her with a hard gaze. "Look at it however you want to, but you're still alive." He stood up and offered her a hand. Water still trickled down him in rivulets, making dark streams on the gray rocks. His shirt and pants were plastered like papier-mâché, outlining every rock-hard curve of his impressive body.

If her body hadn't felt capable of moving before, it certainly didn't now that her bones had turned to the consistency of jelly. "You actually expect me to move after all that? I just started breathing normally again."

He quirked a sleek, dark brow upward as if to say, *of course you ninny; now take my hand.*

China sighed and slipped her hand into his. It was a perfect fit, and it took hardly any effort for him to lift her up in one clean, fluid motion from the rock to a standing position right next to him. She grew instantly aware that her clothes were as wet and clingy as his, and that the tips of her breasts were hard as pebbles. His gaze dipped down for a moment, and when their eyes met again, a slow, sly smile crossed his sinful mouth.

"I'm cold," she said, even as a blush began to heat her cheeks.

The smile got slightly bigger. "Naturally."

China berated herself for being so insecure about it all. After all, the man had already seen her breasts completely bare; why did it matter if he noticed her nipples were erect? But it did. A lot.

The chemistry between her and Remington was different than anything she'd come across before. He pushed her buttons, but he also had the capability of soothing her too. Hot and cold. All intensity. "Which way would the temple be from here?"

Remington patted down his pockets. He shoved his hand into his pants and came up with nothing but a sodden piece of paper. He gingerly peeled apart the folds of the map, but it was no use. Ink smeared and dripped from the page. The paper began to sag and tear. The map was ruined. He tore off his pack and found the codex equally wet, but slightly more intact. But until it dried out, he wasn't about to pull the fragile pages apart. "What in the blue blazes do we do now?"

China cocked her head to one side. "We find our way there."

"Fantastic," he said, his voice heavy with sarcasm. "How?"

China closed her eyes and sought out the familiar tug in her gut that she'd had from the minute they'd reached land after being cooped up in the submarine. Surrounded by all that metal, her shifter senses had been dulled, but on land she could more easily access them. She'd been using them as a double-check to Diego's map, but hadn't told Remington.

There was no need to share more with him than necessary about her Darkin abilities.

The shimmering pull came from the northeast. She swiveled around until it tugged at the center of her gut, then opened her eyes and pointed. "It's that way."

They trudged on through the jungle. Remington made use of the machete gauntlet again because the Blaster had gotten wet. It made going slow, and as the afternoon wore on, their clothes became only marginally drier than they'd been when Remington and China had come out of the river.

"How does anyone survive in this humidity?" China grumbled, swatting at the mosquitoes that seemed to appear in clouds now and again.

"They simply sweat. Judging by the mosquitoes, we must be closer to fresh water. Lots of it."

Oh joy. Just another reason for her to hate the little blood-suckers.

He stopped in his tracks, turned, and narrowed his eyes at her. "You don't have to growl about it."

"I didn't growl."

The hard, firm line of his mouth said he didn't believe her. "Well, if you didn't growl, who did?"

Raw-awrr! Grrrrrr. From between the large, shiny leaves appeared the massive black head of an enormous jaguar the size of a hellhound. Its black lips were peeled back, revealing lethal white canines, and it stalked, low to the ground, shoulders rolling, tail twitching as it came closer. It growled low and deep, and she could feel the vibration of it straight through to her spine.

Remington grabbed her arm hard. "Do we run?"

China could barely shake her head. "It'd kill you in one pounce."

Remington knew the machete wouldn't do more than scratch it and give it another reason to bite them into meat treats. The Blaster was useless until it dried out. He had more chance of killing himself with it via electrocution than of killing the giant jaguar.

"That's not a normal jaguar, is it?"

China sniffed the air and subtly shook her head. "It's Darkin." She moved slowly away from him. "I'm gonna try somethin'."

Remington's gut clenched. He hoped like hell she knew what she was doing. "What are you doing?"

"I'm going to shift. See if you can keep it distracted long enough for me to complete the change."

"No! Are you crazy, woman?" He kept his eyes on the beast, seeing its coiled muscles beneath the sleek black fur. The low, deep-throated growl grew in intensity. The six-foot long tail whipped back and forth, back and forth. "You're at your most vulnerable in between forms." Shifting into a predator large and vicious enough to scare away the giant cat made sense, but not if China ran the risk of being devoured when she was half her and half something else.

"You're wasting time. Hurry up!"

Shit. At this point Remington had to wonder, what exactly did one do to try and attract the attention of a massive cat without increasing the chances of dying painfully? Shouting seemed the answer.

"Hey! Over here, you big furball!"

Ggggrrrrrr. The jaguar took a measured step on paws the size of Thanksgiving platters toward Remington, and it took every ounce of guts Remington had not to take a step back.

"That's right. I'm the one you're interested in. I'm the threat to your master, Rathe."

Raw-awrrr!

Good God that thing had razor-sharp teeth six inches long that were most visible when it roared. Its golden yellow eyes the size of his fists were dilated, befitting a predator on the hunt. China had better be damn close to changing into whatever it was she planned to be.

Raw-awrrr!

Remington looked out of the corner of his eye, not wanting to look away from the direct threat bearing down on him. Another giant black jaguar stepped from the jungle vegetation. *Let it be China. Let it be China. Please, let it be China.*

It swiped a huge paw, lethal claws extended, at the hindquarters of the other jaguar. The first cat swung around and slapped back. A riot of hissing and spitting, growls and roars filled the air as the two battled each other. They clawed and bit and moved so fast, Remington had to shimmy up a tree to make sure he didn't get trampled.

The two jaguars seemed to reach a stalemate, each circling the other and breathing hard, their growls still low and mean. The second jaguar glanced up at him in the tree, and Remington saw the flash of silver eyes. It was China!

Instantly his gut took a dive. She was bleeding. He couldn't let her continue to fight without help. He hoped like hell the Blaster was dry enough to work properly.

He pulled it from the pack and fired it up. The angry buzz of the machine caught the first jaguar's attention, and it flicked its gaze to Remington's spot in the tree. It pulled back its lips and hissed, striking out with a paw to swipe at him.

He was grateful he was out of reach. He checked the gauge to see if the Blaster was ready and fired. For as big as the cat was, it moved lightning fast. The blast scared it momentarily, but missed.

Below the tree China in jaguar form growled, baring strong white razor-sharp teeth. He didn't know what she wanted, but their distraction would only work for a short time. He hurried down the tree and approached her cautiously. China rubbed her massive black, furred cheek against him, nearly knocking him to the ground.

"We don't have much time. We need to get out of here."

She bent down, bringing her belly to the forest floor, and nudged him with her nose.

"You want me to ride you?"

She blinked at him.

The foliage stirred as the other jaguar began to pace the clearing, watching them. Time had run out.

Remington questioned the sanity of the idea in his mind, but climbed onto China's back all the same. He flung one leg over her broad back—as wide as a horse's, but lower to the ground. Her muscles shifted and bunched beneath lustrous thick, soft fur. He secured himself by grabbing fists full of fur, and tapping lightly with his heels, he indicated he was ready. More than ready. The other animal was growling low and deep, the swishing tail like a lash.

She roared a warning to the other jaguar, a sound that shot straight up, rattling from his tailbone up to his skull, then spun on her paw and bounded off into the jungle.

Everything became a blur of green, color, and shadow as she moved swiftly. Despite her enormous size she was lithe and graceful, her muscles bunching and pulling with each stretched-out stride as she ran at top speed. It was all he could do to hold on tight. He'd thought a lot about riding China, but had never imagined this would be how it turned out.

The crashing of branches and the growls told them the other jaguar was in hot pursuit, but had fallen far behind. But they could only move so fast on the ground. China was beginning to tire, and the trickle of blood at her neck was still flowing, shiny and dark, matting her black fur. She slowed, trotting and panting, sides bellowing in and out.

Remington leaned close to her massive furry ear. "You're losing blood. I can't patch you up until you're human again." She chuffed in response and came to a stop, slumping down to the ground. Remington eased off of her big feline body and watched with renewed appreciation for her skills as she transmogrified, her shape blurring and shrinking into the familiar petite form he'd come to appreciate most.

He bent down beside her and lifted her head to the side,

looking at the scratch marks on her neck. "Well, the good news is, the marks are all in proportion. Looks like you got into a scrap with a house cat instead of a cat the size of a house."

China gave him a weak smile. "Still burns like the devil."

He strained his senses and listened intently to the sounds around them, trying to hear if the jaguar was close. Only the twitter and squawk of birds, the hum of insects, and the sound of the wind in the leaves filled the air.

"I don't hear it anymore."

"Maybe it gave up the chase."

"Maybe." But he doubted it. Darkin didn't just give up as a general rule. Not when they were ordered by Rathe to kill something. He cleaned her up as best he could using water from their canteen. Her black dress was torn, her skin marred by deep red scratches on her neck and back. He wished he could do more to soothe her wounds. Guilt burned a hole in his stomach. He should have been the one to take those. Not her.

China leaned back on her hands and stared up at the canopy. Every bit of her ached, or stung, or both. She might have been a match for the giant jaguar, but fighting it had taken a toll. A chill had settled deep in the pit of her stomach, and China knew she wouldn't be shifting again anytime soon. It would take hours to recover, maybe even a day or two.

"Thank you." His simple words startled her.

"Whatever for?"

"It's not often a Hunter has his life saved by another. We usually are in the business of doing the saving. I sincerely doubt I could have battled that giant jaguar on my own. So, thank you." He brushed a kiss against her forehead that made the aches start to fade.

"You never told me what you would have been if you hadn't been a Hunter."

He shrugged. "An attorney. Most likely the most boring man you'd know, with a lovely house, a few prime horses, and several children."

"And what about a wife?"

His forehead wrinkled, and his eyes flicked away from hers. "Yes, well, I realize that would be part of the mix, but we are talking about something that will likely never happen, aren't we?"

"You don't think the world will change at the Gates of Nyx?"

His potent blue stare returned to her. "Oh I have no doubt a great many things will change, if we reach the Gates in time, but I'm not about to pin my hopes to them."

"Sometimes dreams are all that keep a person alive when things get hard."

He arched one dark brow in response. "You sound as if that came from personal experience."

She nodded, then rested her head against the tree behind her. "At least you've had your brothers to rely on. The way I grew up, I had no one."

The wind blew the tops of the trees, and she caught a glimpse of something white. She sat up, a sudden burst of energy soaring through her. "Remington! I saw white! The stones!" She got to her feet, and Remington pulled the pack on his back, then donned the machete gauntlet on his hand and forearm.

"Means we're getting close to the temple," he said as he whacked at the foliage, trying to create a footpath for them. China wished she could volunteer to help, but she'd done enough shifting for one day. Just walking was an effort.

The white stones, now easily distinguishable as squared stones stacked atop one another, formed a massive stepped pyramid above the tree tops. They were close!

The ground beneath their feet began to shiver.

China looked at him, terror streaking through her. They were both thinking it. More bone warriors.

Points of white polished bone began to poke up through the soil. "Blast! Don't those things *ever* die?"

"Do you ever get the feeling that perhaps those bone warriors were letting the jaguar herd us here?"

Remington narrowed his eyes, taking in their surroundings, looking for a means of escape. He didn't need to bother. She could have told him there was none.

"Remington, are you even listening to me?"

"Uh-huh."

"What did I say?"

"Herds of jaguars." But he wasn't even looking at her; he was looking at the ground. More and more of the bone warriors sprouted up out of the soil, forming a solid blockade around them.

Remington had his feet spread, his knees bent, and his arms akimbo, like a man ready to wrestle. He frowned. "They aren't attacking. Why?"

"Don't look a gift horse in the mouth. If it's a standoff, that's fine with me."

But it wasn't.

In a few minutes the warriors closed in tighter, until they formed a wall around them. China and Remington were stripped of their packs and weapons, but not physically harmed. Slowly the bone warriors began marching forward, pushing China and Remington along with them.

China grabbed Remington's hand, holding on tightly, terrified they'd be separated. "Where do you think they're taking us?"

They rounded the bend, and there before them the flat ground started to dramatically rise upward, a mix of gold and green and white. It took a moment to realize that this *was* the temple. She could barely make out the squared steps of the pyramid-like structure and the carvings through the layer of vines that had taken root and tried to reclaim it. Along the outside of it were rows upon rows of small rectangular windows on each step level. A long, angled stone staircase rose straight up the middle of the building.

Remington's steps slowed as he stared openmouthed at the temple. A prod in the back with a sharp spear point was enough to get him moving faster again, even though his legs ached and burned. Up ahead a dark square entrance was cut into the white face of the stone, and they were headed straight for it.

"Looks like we're getting to the temple just like we wanted."

"I didn't want to come in here like this!"

It took a moment for his eyes to adjust to the darkness. Inside the thick stone walls, the temperature was twenty degrees cooler and the air much dryer. His sweat evaporated quickly, leaving him chilled. China's hand felt very small in his, her skin, cold and clammy.

Lit torches lent a flickering light to the squared hallway that seemed to stretch into the bowels of the temple. Remington eyed the bone warrior up ahead. The thing had the Blaster strapped to its back. If he could just get close enough to get his hands on it, they might have a chance of ditching these strange creatures and delving into the secrets of the temple themselves to find Elwin's piece of the Book. "Don't worry. It'll be all right."

"How?"

"I don't know. I'm working on that."

"Work faster, dammit!" The bone warriors didn't seem to care about their raised voices. They just marched them steadily through the stone hallways decorated with painted carvings of sacrifice scenes, where bloody heads rolled away from the bodies and hearts were pulled from the victim's chest and held high to the skeletal god looking down from above.

"They mean to kill us."

His control finally snapped. "I know!"

The hall continued until it opened into a massive central room with a raised stone dais at the far end. High above it loomed a huge stone replica of their skeletal god, his ribs forming a cage and his bald bone head crowned in an array of stone feathers.

"Is that a sacrifice altar?"

The blood on the altar was dried in flaky, rust-colored patches, but certainly not hundreds of years old. In fact, if he had to guess, he'd say it was far more recent, perhaps even from within the past few months. "Don't panic."

"Don't panic? Don't panic! You can't be serious! They're gonna sacrifice us, and I'm just supposed to remain calm?"

He flicked his gaze in her direction. "Just keep calm and I can get us out of this. Trust me." Remington hoped they weren't famous last words.

Chapter 17

The great stone rib cage of the skeleton god opened with a harsh grating noise. The sound scraped her already frayed nerves raw, making China shiver. Goose bumps of trepidation prickled her skin, as the sharp poke of a spear in her back propelled her forward through the opening in the sternum.

The two halves swung closed with surprising speed, sealing them inside the cavity where she imagined giant lungs and a heart might have been. The convex bones, thick as her wrist, were carved of tan stone, and even a hard shake with both hands didn't budge them. Too close together to squeeze through, too hard to break. They were trapped inside the cavity that was their prison.

For the first time in millennia, if ever, the stone god had two beating hearts inside his chest. But for how much longer?

A quick glance around the space showed it was no more than a ten by ten cell. There were several man-height rock formations protruding from the ground, making the floor space limited.

She glanced at Remington. He'd made himself comfortable, sitting down on the cold stone floor, knees drawn up, head resting back against the rock. His eyes were closed.

Irritated, China kicked his foot to get his attention. "How can you be so relaxed at a time like this?"

He opened one eye. "I'm thinking of how to get us out of here."

"You could look like you're actually trying, instead of taking a nap."

With an easy smile he closed his eyes again. "A nap—not a bad idea—but not going to help us much at this point. We have to wait for them to start fighting one another."

China snorted. "You really think that'll happen?"

He opened both eyes and locked his intense blue gaze on her. "I'm a student of human nature. If they revert to their warrior roots, they'll want to sort our things and portion them out. That's bound to cause conflict." He closed his eyes again. "Just be patient."

But these damn things weren't human. They weren't exactly Darkin either, at least not Darkin she was familiar with. His relaxed appearance put her even more on edge. China put her hands on the rib bars of their cage and peered out at the bone warriors milling about the temple, preparing for their sacrificial ceremony. Remington was right. Now that they'd been incarcerated, the ordered behavior of the bone warriors seemed to dwindle.

Four of them were digging through China and Remington's packs, pulling out items, shaking them, and running their bony digits over them. They seemed to squabble in another language as they sorted. Three more were playing tug-of-war with the Blaster, their dusty voices rising as they talked louder and louder. Clearly arguing.

"What are they doing?"

This time he didn't bother opening his eyes. "I told you. Arguing."

"Over what? Us? Over our stuff?" Were they arguing

about what to do with the prisoners? Kill them, or . . . ? China rubbed the chill on her arms.

"Over spoils of war. They're warriors. This makes perfect sense."

She glared at him. Patience wasn't one of her stronger attributes. "How's that escape plan coming?"

He grumbled under his breath. "If we wait long enough, we might not have to do much." He glanced at her, a sly smile lifting the corner of his mouth. "Care to place a bet on how long it takes one of them to figure out how the Blaster works?"

At the thought of the bone warriors blowing themselves apart with Marley's invention China returned his easy smile, suddenly feeling much better about their chances of escape. "You're hoping they'll destroy each other?"

"Destroy themselves, create a distraction, I don't really care which as long as it gives us a chance to find the entrance to the caverns Diego said run under this temple."

She rubbed the center of her bottom lip with the point of her index finger in concentration as her gaze slid over the room. She was growing antsy in the confines of the cell and needed to occupy her mind with something. Looking for means of escape seemed the best choice. "We need to look for clues. Diego must have left some sign when he came through."

"Look for the Hunter's cross, a lion, raven, or palm tree, anything that might indicate the Legion," Remington suggested as he rose from the floor and dusted his hands off.

If his prediction of the warriors' behavior was right, it wouldn't take long. Time to find the mark was in short supply. While he ran his broad hands along the walls of their cell, she used her Darkin-enhanced vision to scan the rest of the huge room.

It was immense. Each stone from ceiling to floor looked like it fit perfectly against the next. And while the outside had seemed neglected because the jungle had reclaimed most of it, here inside the temple, time had stood still. The paint on the intricate stone carvings decorating the walls was still vivid, the whites and blues, reds, yellows, and greens, all enhancing the grisly detailed scenes. She looked at each one, searching for some of the Hunter insignias, but found nothing.

She pulled back, rubbing her burning eyes, trying to rid them of the dust-dry sensation. She blinked and sighed, looking at the sacrificial altar, a short distance beyond the bars of their cage.

She'd avoided looking at it, not wanting to think about what would happen to them if Remington's plan didn't materialize. The tug-of-war between the bone warriors became more intense. They were growling and wailing in dry, skin-scraping shrieks at one another as they wrenched the Blaster back and forth between them.

"Remington!" He turned.

"Look at the altar!"

He joined her at the bars, squeezing his face between the ribs so he could get a better look.

"Just there, in the center on the back side of it. Do you see that lion fighting a jaguar? There's a triple cross on the lion's shoulder."

A buzzing hum filled the air, and the hair on her skin lifted with static electrical charge. One of the bone warriors had powered up the Blaster. They both looked up at the same time. The bone warrior who had managed to pull it away from the other two rested his hand near the trigger. The large cylinder on the front of the Blaster was glowing with pulsing blue electrical charge. The other two tried to grab the Blaster back.

"Here's our chance." Remington pulled her back with him behind the cover of an outcrop of rock.

ZZZott! A blinding blast of blue light, like a lightning bolt, filled the room, followed by the sound of shattering stone. China coughed at the haze of acrid smoke and sharp ozone that filled her throat.

When the dust cleared a huge black scorch mark the size of a train car marked half the interior of the chamber. Where there had been bone warriors, there were now bits of ash, charred stone, and curls of smoke, and the vile stink of burnt bones in the air. The remaining skeletons scattered in confusion, their bony feet clattering against the stone floor. The Blaster still hummed. The warrior holding the Blaster turned the device to look at the business end.

Remington picked up a stone from the floor and took aim and threw it like a skipping stone. The stone hit the weapon, triggering it. *ZZZott!* The bone warrior got a big electrical charge that vaporized his upper body.

"Move!" He shoved her hard, slamming her body up against the back wall of their cell, covering her with his body. The Blaster clattered to the floor. *ZZZott!*

He pulled away from her. China winced. Her whole back ached. "What were you think—" She stopped mid rant the instant she spied the smoking remains of their cell. Marley's weapon had blown apart the half where she'd been standing. Without Remington's quick reflexes, she would have been incinerated. Her eyes flicked up to lock with his intense blue ones.

He smiled. "You're welcome."

Remington didn't waste a precious second. He dashed out of the smoking remains of their cell and snatched up the Blaster from the floor before any of the other confused bone warriors had a clue what was going on. For now, they had scattered from the main chamber. Some fled down the long entrance hall; others had disappeared into the niches that lined either side of the temple. He crouched on the floor, using the altar as a shield, pulling China down beside him.

Her cheek was dark with a smudge of soot. "That was impressive."

He gave her a superior look, even though their escape had just been by chance. "I know."

China rolled her eyes. "See, you had to go and ruin a compliment by being a know-it-all."

He smiled. "I'll admit I don't know everything. I just know enough." He jerked his head at the abandoned packs on the floor. "We've got to get our packs before we go any farther. They've got Diego's transcript of the codex, the stone statue, and our supplies."

China nodded. "I'll get the packs. You stay here and figure out how we use the lion to get out of here."

Remington frowned, but nodded. "Be quick about it. They won't be scared off long."

He looked at the altar, running his hands along the detailed carvings that had to be hundreds of years old. And yet there it was, the triple cross of the Legion of Hunters inscribed on the lion's shoulder. The outline along the lion was deeper and more distinct than the one chiseled around the jaguar.

Remington pushed on the lion, and the sound of grinding stone made him step back. The altar slid toward the front of the chamber and away from him, revealing a stone staircase that disappeared down into the darkness. "China!"

She came barreling around the corner of the altar, breathing fast, her eyes bright and a pack on each shoulder.

"That fast enough for you, Jackson?"

He gave her a nod. China glanced down at the steps, then back at him, her eyes wide with terror. The lively pink color in her cheeks drained away. "We're not going down there, are we?"

"We don't have much choice. Not if we're going to get to the Book."

She worried her full lip between her teeth. "I don't know if—"

"We have to. This is our only way out."

The rattle of bone on bone and the dry wails of the warriors were growing louder. The warriors were coming back. She was hesitating, and he didn't understand why. She'd been so brave, thus far. What about those dark stairs frightened her so? He could see it in the slight tremble of her body, the downward turn of her mouth, and the extra shine in her eyes that looked like she might cry.

He grabbed her hand and held it in his and realized how small it truly was. Strong, but small. "I'll be right there beside you. We're in this together."

Her gaze met his, and the air between them charged. It raised the hairs on his arms, neck, and scalp. Something had shifted between them in a profound way. Danger had a way of doing that, but this was different. He could see the trust in her eyes. Deep down a part of the protective shell he'd always kept over his emotions cracked. In this moment they were each truly all the other had. It was only the two of them, live or die, and Remington realized he had to trust her in equal measure if they were to survive. He would have to trust her to guard his back as he'd guard hers.

It went against everything he'd been trained to do, everything his Hunter education taught, but right now he was going by his gut to keep them alive—and his gut said trusting China was the right thing to do.

"Promise you won't leave me down there alone?"

"Promise."

She nodded.

"I'll even head down first."

China squeezed his hand. "Just don't let go of me."

Remington pulled a coil illuminator from the pack. Marley had assured him the brass tube with a glass lens at one end would provide ample light if it was shaken. He'd filled it with magnets coiled with wire. There was a fifty-fifty chance it would work beautifully or disfigure Remington somehow. He hadn't been eager to find out, but the situation demanded a source of light, the sooner the better, and there were no torches around. It was getting hard to see the steps as they descended, and for all he knew they could just randomly drop off into nothing, a trap of Hunter design.

He shook the coil illuminator. *Clack. Clack. Clack . . . Rumble. Rumble.* Overhead the altar began to slide back into place, sealing them in the stairwell. China grabbed onto him, her body coming up flush against his as the darkness welled up around them and swallowed them whole.

She could barely breathe. It wasn't that there wasn't enough air; it was that her lungs refused to work. They'd frozen, just like the rest of her. The second she'd looked down those dark stairs, the smell of smoking skin and burning flesh had filled her nose. It was memory. She knew that in her head, but it didn't stop her body's violent reaction to it.

The brand at the base of her spine would forever remind her of her link to Rathe. That he had claimed her as his property and forbade all others to give her sanctuary or help in the Darkin realm until he allowed it. And he would not allow it until she came crawling back to him and won his approval.

Her body shook, and it took a moment for her to realize a voice was calling her name. "China! China! Wake up!" The press of warm hands to her chilled face brought her back to the present. A blue glow of light lit the stairway, and Remington was holding her close. In the strange glow that uplit his face, his brows were bent, deep lines scored around his mouth, and his eyes and his jaw ticking. "Can you hear me?"

She nodded. The tension in his face eased, and he kissed her on the forehead. "You were almost catatonic."

The shivers wracking her body grew more intense, making her teeth chatter, but she could do nothing to stop it.

"What happened?" he asked.

She shook her head, her lips and jaw trembling, unable to speak. Even if she could get her tongue to function properly, she couldn't tell him the truth of why this place made her get lost within herself.

He pulled her into the solid warmth of his chest, asking no more questions, stroking her hair. "It's all right. You don't need to tell me. Whatever happened was horror enough for you. I've been there myself a time or two, especially when I was young. I wasn't meant to be a Hunter like Pa. It was too much for a child to take."

A comforting hand rubbed up and down her back, draining away the fear and the pain so she could function again. His strength during her moment of weakness meant more than he would ever know.

China pulled her head up from his chest and looked into his face. "I'm sorry. The dark stairs. I remember stairs like those before . . ." She stopped, the thickness in her throat making it hard to speak. She swallowed hard.

"It won't be dark as long as we have Marley's coil illuminator. And I will be with you."

She glanced back above them, but she could see nothing but darkness. The space smelled of damp earth and mildew, and a faint trace of sulfur carried on damp air. "We won't get back out that way, will we?"

"I don't think we were meant to. But if Diego found a way out, then so shall we."

They moved forward, cautiously, but as quickly as they

could. The days and hours were counting down, and every minute was precious, not to be wasted. Up ahead the stone staircase leveled out into a smooth floor. The chisel marks revealed it had been carved out in the rock by the hand of man, not nature. Three separate tunnel entrances branched off from the landing.

"Which way do we go?"

Remington narrowed his eyes and moved the light of the coil illuminator over each tunnel opening. "I don't know."

He ran the rim of light from the coil illuminator over the rock above the tunnels, looking for some sign. There, chipped into the stone was the triple cross. He jerked his head to the tunnel on the left. "That way."

China didn't argue, just stuck close to him, her step determined, her head held high. They wandered for hours through the stone tunnels, and with their trudging steps and the relative quiet of the tunnels, it seemed interminably longer.

Finally China broke the silence. "You spent an awful lot of time reading your mother's diary and Diego's codex on the submarine."

"Are you trying to strike up a conversation with me? It really isn't necessary."

"I was getting to an honest question. I wanted to know if you found anything in the diary that might help us."

"Ma's diary said a lot of things. It talked about the differences in the Hunters my father worked with. It talked about how the Legion was beginning to crumble as men gave up trying to fight what they saw as a losing battle after centuries. It talked about her fear that her three sons were spoken of as the answer to the age-old prophecy that would end the threat of the Darkin to our world. My mother didn't want us to be the Chosen." But most important Ma's diary had told him about something that had little to do with Hunting or Darkin. It had contained insights into how she'd loved her husband and her boys.

A pause stretched out between them as China nibbled on her bottom lip. She turned to him, curiosity in her eyes. "What did she want for you?"

"She wanted us to have normal lives. To find a woman someday who could handle the life we were raised to lead as Hunters." He'd closed the diary after he'd finished it and realized what a special person his mother really had been.

"So what kind of woman is that?"

"Well it isn't anyone I associated with at university, from the upper echelons of society back east, I can tell you that much."

"What about a hearty western frontierswoman who'd be able to handle being married to a Jackson? I doubt they'd wilt under the tough and dangerous circumstances you and your brothers face as Hunters."

He frowned at her. "Now you make it sound like I'm looking for oxen. No thank you." He wanted a woman who was both intelligent and tough, with beauty and a sense of humor. He'd begun to think that kind of woman didn't exist—until he'd met China. Granted, she wasn't totally human, but that was beginning to matter less and less to him. He appreciated her humor even in the darkest of times. He appreciated her intelligence and her natural beauty. Most of all he liked that no matter how hard things got, she forged forward, never questioning the importance of her purpose. In that way she was very like him.

"The light's getting low." He shook the coil illuminator to regenerate the flow of energy and glanced at the woman walking along beside him. Her blond hair tumbled down her back, and the now ragged edges of her black dress swung around her booted feet.

She caught him staring at her. "What, do I have something stuck in my hair?"

He grinned. It was tempting to tease her, but they'd already been through enough for one day. "No, I was admiring your beautiful hair; it's like cornsilk."

China snorted. "Do you really think those rivers Diego mentioned are real?" she asked, quickly changing the subject. "They could just be Hunter exaggeration."

"I don't think he was exaggerating. What could he hope to gain?"

"He might have thought to scare us off."

Remington gave a brittle laugh. "Diego knew my pa better than that. He ought to know Cyrus's boys were just like him."

"So if he wasn't exaggerating, then that clacking I hear can't be a good thing."

"Never is." Remington ran his hands along the butt of the Blaster and lightly traced the trigger to know exactly where it was. The clacking and skittering sounds grew louder, like a malevolent whisper echoing on the stone walls.

"What do you think it is?"

They turned a corner, and Remington stopped dead. Nothing could have prepared him for this. The River of Scorpions was an actual river bed that cut the chamber in two halves down the middle, filled with hundreds of thousands of scorpions of all shapes and sizes.

Despite Diego's description, the writhing mass of scorpions chilled his blood. Next to snakes, scorpions were some of his least favorite creatures.

"How do we get across?" China's voice wavered, which strengthened his own resolve to get this over with and press on. He couldn't let his own irrational fears keep them from moving forward.

"Diego was pretty damn specific. Go in on foot and you'll

drown in the things." He resisted the urge to shudder, thinking of all those legs and the sting of a million tails.

"We could blast them," she suggested, then gave him a manic grin.

"I think you like that gun too much. Besides, you might kill a good chunk of them down the middle, but then it would only get the ones remaining fired up enough to sting anything within striking distance."

China was being awfully quiet. She wasn't still contemplating using Marley's Blaster was she? He glanced back just to be sure. Her head was tilted back, and she was staring at the ceiling of the cavern. "What are you looking at?" He cranked his head back and narrowed his eyes in the dim light to see if he could see it too.

"Don't those look like steps to you?" She pointed at a row of symmetrical lines that carried over from one side of the cavern to the other.

"Upside down steps, maybe. Isn't any way we could walk on them." The longer he stared at them, the more his perspective shifted. "Maybe those aren't stairs at all; maybe they're handholds."

China frowned, pulling her bottom lip in between her teeth and gnawing on it. "It's worth a shot. Not like we got any other options here unless you wanna spend the next few months building a bridge."

He raised a brow. "You could just fly across."

A wide smile instantly brightened her face. "I can, can't I?"

Remington double-checked the straps on his back to ensure they were secure, then rubbed his hands together. He started climbing the roughhewn steps in the wall. At first it was easy enough. He could use both his hands and his feet. But the more horizontal the surface of the cave wall became, the more he had to rely on just his arms. His shoulders and forearms burned from the exertion, and his fingertips were raw, scraped, and throbbing from digging into the rock.

"I'm going to fly over to the other side," China called up to him. Her voice echoed off the stone walls. The sound threw the scorpions into an even bigger frenzy. *Don't look down. Don't look down. Don't—*

Remington heard the increased clacking of their hard bodies moving against one another and their claws snapping. He glanced down and saw the undulating tide of arachnids. His navel shrank back to meet his backbone. God, he hated the things. He cursed under his breath and kept going.

A bright flash of color and a loud squawk came from the opposite side. China turned back from a parrot to her human form and leaned her shoulder up against the rock wall. "How long you plannin' to hang out in here?" Her tone held just enough gibe that he started moving faster.

His grip wasn't as sure as it should have been. And he slipped, dangling one-armed fifteen feet over the swarming scorpions. His stomach dropped not just to his toes, but out through the bottom of his boots. China's cry of alarm didn't help any. After all he'd been through and done, he sure as hell didn't want to die in a writhing pit of pain, stung to death by those things.

A curious grinding sound started to shake the steps above him. He grabbed hold of the rock step above him and hung on as the ceiling started lowering toward the scorpions. His muscles screamed, and his fingers began to grow damp and slip.

"Remington!"

"Not now!"

"Remington!"

He glared at her. "Holy hell, woman, not now!"

She returned his glare, threw her hands up in the air in disgust, then pointed. "Listen to me dammit! It's a bridge! You're on the underside of a bridge!"

For the first time Remington looked up instead of down.

The steps were part of an arched bridge of stone that lowered slowly downward from the ceiling of the cavern toward the dark living river of pain below. His arms were just about to give out. With one last heave he swung his body weight and managed to kick one leg up on top of the steps. The shaking of the bridge made his hold tenuous at best. *Snap!* The strap on his pack suddenly gave way, throwing his body off-balance and threatening to dump the remainder of their meager supplies—and more important Diego's transcript and the small stone statue—into the River of Scorpions.

China nearly nibbled her fingernails to the quick as he clung to the underside of the bridge like a baby monkey to its mother, the pack dangling off of him. The stone bridge was lowering in channels in the walls, bringing him close enough to the scorpions that she was certain he was going to drop the pack, fall in, or both.

Remington grimaced as he scrambled to the topside of the stone bridge. The weight on his shoulder shifted as the pack slipped. His Hunter reflexes served him well as he grabbed it and swung it up onto the steps. He lay there for a moment, the air sawing in and out of his lungs.

The bridge came to rest with a heavy *thunk* on the ground below. China ran to him. His chest and belly were scraped raw and red from the stone.

"You did it!"

He gave her a weak smile. "How'd you find the bridge?"

"It was more like it found me. I leaned up against one of the carvings on the wall, because I spied what I think is an exit, and the carving sank into the wall and the bridge started to move."

Remington rolled to his side and sat up. "Better than landing in a pit of scorpions."

China carefully leaned over the edge and looked down. There were no rails on the bridge; it was simply an arch of stone steps, and she didn't want to fall in any more than Remington.

The scorpions writhed and twisted, their claws clacking and their tails arching as they snapped and stung at one another just five feet below them. She shuddered.

"Let's get out of here."

Remington got to his feet and held out a hand in invitation. "Ladies first."

Chapter 18

The exit China had discovered was cleverly hidden between the folds of rock on the far side of the River of Scorpions. From the opposite side it couldn't be seen. Only if you managed to survive the river was it possible to find it at all.

"What in the blazes were they thinking to hide Elwin's piece of the Book in such a place?" Remington muttered.

China ran her fingers along the walls, trying to keep her bearings as the narrow passage twisted and turned upon itself, coiling back and around until she had no sense of direction. "I'm sure they thought if it was the local's version of Hell, then no one would try to steal it. That, and they probably had guides who knew this place."

Remington gave a humorless, dry laugh. "And never mind about the poor bastards who'd eventually have to come down and get it out to save the world."

She speared him with a glance. "Didn't the three brothers who hacked it apart intend for it never to be reunited?"

He gave her half a smile. "Know your Hunter lore, do you?"

"A little."

"Then you know when Cadel, Haydn, and Elwin separated the Book of Legend, they did it because the Gates of Nyx had cracked open, and they feared the Book would be taken by the Darkin. Problem is, the only thing that can close the Gates back again—"

"Is the whole Book. I know."

He quirked an eyebrow at her, telling her without words exactly what he thought of her retort. China quickly changed the subject. "What else did Diego's transcript of the codex say we were in for?"

"Diego didn't lie, if that's what you're asking. It mentions both a River of Scorpions and a River of Blood. Something about a room with a wind of blades, which didn't make a whole lot of sense, a place of biting cold, and the house of fire."

"Well at least there's no more water. That's a relief."

"China McGee, you aren't like other girls. Only you would think what's ahead was mild compared to another swim."

He gave her a brilliant smile that made her stomach do a backflip. China pressed a hand to her belly to quell the sensation. Her feet seemed to stick to the floor.

She glanced down. Her feet *were* sticking to the floor, and the walls were starting to grow shiny and smooth the farther they walked down the passage. The odor of rotten eggs permeated the air, making her want to gag. "What the hell is that stink?"

The acidic bite in the air was enough to make Remington's eyes water. "I think we've found that River of Blood Diego mentioned." The passage widened, opening into yet another cavern split in two by a wide river. This one flowed from an opening in one wall and out the other. It was a bubbling rust-red color, and twists of white steam eddied over the surface. A weird silver-white slime seemed to drip from the ceiling and coated the rock walls, making them look like they'd been plated in silver. It was weirdly beautiful and disturbing all at once.

The edges of the stream bed were black, smooth, and slick. A human skeleton lay half in, half out of the river, its fingers dug into the rock as if the person had died trying to crawl out. China shuddered.

"You don't think that's one of those bone warriors do you?"

"Let's be sure." Remington shoved the rest of the skeleton into the river with his boot, where it smoked and quickly sank beneath the surface. Damn. That stuff was lethal.

China whistled. "Looks like sulfuric acid. It's eaten the rock down to the layer of volcanic glass beneath."

Remington glanced at her. "Is that a guess or based on your extensive in-depth study of chemistry?" he asked, a note of sarcasm in his voice.

"Darkin, remember? If it smells like sulfur and looks like it could eat your hand off, chances are it's acid."

Remington smiled. "You're smart, I'll give you that. If we ever get out of this hellhole, remind me to introduce you to Marley. He'll like you."

"Even if I'm Darkin?" she challenged.

Remington shrugged. "Point taken. I'll tag along to referee." He surveyed the space looking for weird stairs, points of rock that could be possible levers, signs of the Legion, anything that could potentially get them across. "Now how do we get across it?"

"I'm not sure I can shift again so soon, otherwise I'd fly across." China narrowed her eyes and stared at the slime. "How do you think that stuff survives in here?"

He turned and peered at the wall. "What? That gelatinous glop? It's not even a living thing. It doesn't have to survive anything; it just is."

China got closer to the glistening silvery white material that covered nearly every surface in the chamber. "I think it's more than that."

She pulled a piece of the mamey sapote fruit from one of the packs and dipped half of it into the slime.

"Dear God, what do you think you're doing?"

"An experiment."

She approached the reddish bubbling river with caution, taking care to hold her breath, and she lightly dipped the slimed section of the mamey sapote into the river. It steamed a little, but when she pulled it back, the fruit's outer brown skin was still intact, and the slime slipped off of it, far more thin and watery than it had been before.

China grinned at Remington. "Look. It works!"

He frowned. "Are you sincerely suggesting we coat ourselves in that goo?"

"Did you have another suggestion, other than spending years building some sort of air flotation device to ferry us across?"

Remington opened his mouth then snapped it shut, making his teeth click together. He paused for a moment. "No."

"I didn't think so. Come here and I'll cover your back."

This was not at all what he'd had in mind when he'd been thinking of them covering one another's backs. China swept her hand over the surface of the rock, collecting a handful of the gelatinous muck. She slapped it onto his back and shoulders and began to spread it out. It clung to his skin and clothing, oddly warm and slippery feeling.

"For the record, this is disgusting."

China snorted. "And getting sprayed down with viperanox guts isn't?"

"I didn't say that."

"Turn."

The only good thing about having China smear the slime over him was that she touched nearly every inch of him. Every gliding touch of her hands amped up his physical attraction to her another notch. "Make sure you get a nice thick layer on me," he said as she rubbed the substance over his thighs. He was hoping she'd go higher.

She arched a brow at him. "I think you can get the rest yourself. My turn."

For the first time since they had passed the River of Scorpions he had a reason to smile. He scooped up a handful of the nasty mucus. It oozed through his fingers and clung to his hands. He smeared it over her form, taking extra precaution to make sure there was a good layer of the stuff on her very nice breasts.

China wrinkled her nose. "Ugh. Now I'm wishing we had water."

"Then it *does* bother you more than you were letting on."

China glared at him. "I'm doin' my best to make do with our situation. You could try the same."

The river was narrow enough, not more than a ten-foot stretch, but it was still too wide for a man to just jump across. Remington took their packs and threw them across. One made it; the other didn't. It dissolved into a thin brown ooze on the surface of the acid.

China groaned. "Please tell me that pack wasn't the one with the codex and the statue."

"It wasn't. That was our food supply." He tossed the Blaster as well, landing it safely atop the remaining pack. He let out a sigh of relief.

China caught his gaze. Panic was showing in her eyes. "How deep do you think it is?"

Remington frowned. There was no way to really tell. "As long as this stuff works, it won't matter. I can swim across . . . with you."

But that first step was a doozy. If the slime didn't protect them, if it had just been a fluke, then he was likely to lose a limb and die a swift, horribly painful death. Of course, considering their surroundings, if he didn't try it he was going to die a long, agonizingly protracted death by boredom and starvation.

He glanced over his shoulder at her. "Any last words you wish to say to me before I leap to my death?"

Her mouth trembled a bit, and he instantly felt like a cad for teasing her. "Don't say things like that. We're going to be fine. We're going to survive."

So much for being lighthearted, he thought. He made sure even the bottoms of his feet were covered in slime before he lowered his foot slowly into the river. The liquid was hot, but it didn't sear his skin.

He slipped his other foot in, prepared to tread water until she got in so he could swim across with both of them. His feet touched bottom, and the liquid reached up to his chest. Remington glanced back at her. "Come on in, the water's fine." He was braced for the mucus to wash away, and his skin and bones with it. "Hurry up."

China snorted. "If you don't mind, I'll hold back on hoopin' and hollerin' about it until we reach the other side."

She sat on the edge of the riverbank, took a few fast, deep breaths, then one big long draw of air, and held her breath as she slipped into his arms.

Remington swam as fast as he could with a one-armed stroke across the river and hoisted China up on the bank. The slime dripped off of her, running in rivulets and puddling around her in silver pools. A burning sensation in his legs told Remington his own coating of slime was wearing off quickly.

He pulled out of the river and looked at his legs. His pants were disintegrating below the knee and his boots were steaming. "That stuff worked better than I expected, but not quite good enough."

He tore off the boots and his socks, leaving his feet bare. "If Diego's right, we've got a few more tests before we can reach the Book."

China groaned.

The walking got tougher as they went on. The tunnels twisted, rose, and fell. The slime had dried to a thin crust that she picked at as they walked, trying to peel it off her skin. China was so damn hungry her stomach growled nearly as loudly as a hellhound, and they'd long since run out of both food and water. Her body was feeling the lack of food, and her feet were beginning to drag.

The floor dipped below her foot, making China's ankle roll under. At first she thought it was just the uneven surface of the paving stones. But as she caught herself to keep from stumbling, she heard something out of place in the cave-like room they'd just entered.

Click.

"Remington . . ."

He turned and looked at her, swinging his coil illuminator in her direction. "Did I just hear something click?"

She nodded and moved closer to him, grasping his arm as the rumble of stone grinding against stone echoed behind and above them. A limestone slab slid down and blocked the doorway behind them. From the ceiling dropped a series of shining obsidian blades on either side of the room. They began to swing in opposite directions, crisscrossing paths in the middle, making it impossible to dodge between one swipe of a lethal blade and the next.

Remington held her back behind him, watching the movement of the blades that flashed each time they passed the beam of the coil illuminator. "We should have anticipated this and been more careful."

"So this is what the wind of blades meant," China muttered. "At least they named it accurately." The air puffed into her face, blowing her hair back each time a blade swung by.

Remington watched the blades move, analyzed them. "There's a space between them in the arc of their swing. If we time things just right, we should be able to make each space and move between them."

He grabbed her hand and crouched into a running stance. "We'll make a run for it on the count of three. One. Two."

"No!" She yanked her hand from his. "There's no clear path. Our movements have to be to a precise beat to make it through the blades." She began to hum a tune as she watched the blades.

He crossed his arms. "And you have a better method?"

A glint of amusement lit her eyes. "I think we should go *dancing*."

He glanced at the blades and frowned. "Dancing? Now?"

"It'd at least make death a bit more fun."

Remington sighed, grasped her hand lightly, and spun her about, putting his hand at the base of her spine and holding her arm extended to the side to waltz with her.

"This what you had in mind?"

"Well, it'd be better without the swinging blades of death, but I suppose it's the only chance we'll get."

He tracked the movement of the blades. "Keep humming that tune."

She obliged, and together they began to sway. Remington glanced at the blades, counting silently in his head to the time of her tune. One. Two. Three. One. He moved them forward. Two. Their feet came together, and he pressed his hand against her waist, signaling her to quickly turn as the first blade came swinging back. Three. He took a quick step backward as the blade finished passing behind them, waiting a beat before moving forward on the next step. The stream of air caused by the blade ruffled the back of his hair. That was close. Too close.

Over and over they repeated their waltz step and turn, slowly dancing across the room in time to the soft hum of her voice. Beneath his hand her body relaxed into the rhythm, and China closed her eyes, content to follow his lead.

It would have been easier to get caught up in the moment, to believe they were just dancing at some social soirée among his college friends in the midst of a ballroom aglow with gaslight. Remington wished he could relax into it as she did, but he kept the relentless, repetitive count going in his head. Their very lives depended on it. So he did the next best thing and looked his fill at the smooth planes of her cheeks and the dark fan of lashes resting against them. She looked, in a word, angelic. His gaze dipped lower to the lush mouth pressed into a near kiss as she hummed.

And with the passing of each blade he realized how much he liked having China in his arms just like this. Enough that he could easily imagine them in a different place and time having a life together. Pure fantasy, but why not indulge himself if he was more likely to get hacked to pieces than have it become reality. Five more blades to go.

Her body was so light, so agile, and fit his hands so perfectly. They moved in sync, their bodies understanding the motion of the dance now, so he no longer had to count. And for a brief bit of time, Remington relaxed into the moment too.

The last blade passed them, and he bent to capture her mouth in a kiss. Her lips buzzed against his as she hummed. Her eyes flew open at the touch of his mouth against hers as they came to a stop. Even though she'd stopped humming, the buzz moved through his system. He wanted her. Plain. Simple. Now.

A confused and bewildered look flitted through her eyes, and she pushed back from him. Her reserve fell firmly in place. "You're a fantastic dancer," she said, her voice soft and a bit wistful.

"It helps having a good partner who's light on her feet."

A blush infused her cheeks. She turned and started walking down the tunnel on the other side of the room of blades. She turned. "Are you coming?"

"Just taking a moment to catch my breath."

The truth was Remington was enjoying the view. He watched the fabric of her dress shift over her ass as she moved and decided maybe her winning an argument now and again wasn't such a bad thing after all. It had gotten them through the room without being cut to shreds or losing anything vital—that had to count for something.

But he was growing tired of the journey. He was tired, hungry, and cold. He stopped in his tracks for a moment. Cold? That didn't seem right at all.

"Hey, Remington . . ." she called from up ahead in the tunnel. "You might want to come and see this."

The moment they entered the next chamber, he knew something was off. The walls themselves seemed to glitter, and the floor was slick. There was no exit. It was a dead end. At least to the untrained Hunter that's what it would look like. Remington knew better. There had to be an exit. Somewhere. "Watch your step. I think it's ice," he warned.

China exhaled, and her breath turned into a cloud of white. Her skin shrunk, and a shiver wracked her frame. But Remington was far worse off. Without his shirt his chest and back were exposed to the bitter chill as were his bare feet. "What is this?"

"I'm guessing it's the place of biting cold."

Her jaw began to quiver, her teeth clicking together. "Looks like Hell frozen over."

Remington shot her a smile. "Then we must be getting close to the Book."

But it was no laughing matter to her. Unless they got out of this ice box and soon, they'd freeze to death. Her stomach was already quivering, despite her rubbing her arms with her hands to create frictional heat. "How do we get out?"

Remington's lips looked different. They were losing color. Turning blue.

"Until we can figure that out, come here." He motioned with his hand for her to come closer.

China didn't hesitate. Desperate to conserve heat, she cuddled into him. "I wish we were in Arizona right now." Her body wouldn't stop shaking.

"Think of the sunshine warm on your back." His voice was so smooth, so inviting that China closed her eyes and imagined the warmth of the sun hitting her back and her neck. She drifted off for a bit, relaxing against the heat.

Remington was fairly certain his balls were about to freeze off completely. If it hadn't been for China snuggled up against his chest and groin, they very well might have. He shivered as he kept looking for some sign, any sign marking the exit.

He nestled his cheek against her head, curling himself around her to keep her warm. And if he were to be honest, because she felt damn good. Her hair still smelled faintly of vanilla, but also of the water from the river and of woodsmoke from the torches the bone warriors had used to light the temple. He couldn't do anything about their situation, but he could enjoy what he could of their current predicament.

He rubbed his hands over her arms. Even when freezing cold they were silky smooth. She fidgeted, moving a little, her thigh brushing up against his groin. The heat there was instant, and he grew hard just thinking about the texture of the skin on her thighs. *Stop it*, he firmly told himself.

Kissing her on the submarine had been a bad idea. Hell, this entire trip had been a bad idea, but he was stuck now. Well and truly stuck. And the only way out was to keep pushing forward.

He slid his foot back and forth over the ice, brushing the layer of frost away from the ice beneath. A faint shadow caught his eye. Remington straightened, jostling China awake with the movement.

"Wh-what is it?" she said, her voice thick with sleep.

"It looks like a triple cross, just down there. Or am I seeing things?"

China breathed on the spot on the ice, rubbing it vigorously with her hand to get a better look. "It is!" Buried there in the ice was a wooden triple cross.

"So what do we do?"

Normally Remington would have said dig, but there was no point. "Hand me the Blaster."

China dug it out of the pack and handed it to him. Remington fired it up and waited for it to charge. The hum alone made him feel warmer. He took aim at the spot in the floor, made sure she was back away from where the edge of the blast would hit, took aim, and fired. *ZZZZoottt!*

The floor collapsed in a rush of water, sending them spinning down as if they were in a drain. They came to rest on a smooth stone floor, sopping wet.

Remington laughed. "You wanted water to wash off with. There you go."

China smacked him on the arm with her hand. "You did that on purpose!"

"How? Did you see any other means of getting through that floor?"

"No."

"Then what are you complaining about? We got out didn't we? You're not cold anymore, are you?"

"No, but I'm wet."

Remington did have to admit she was right in that regard. The black dress molded itself to her body, outlining every dip and curve of her very female form. A gnawing hunger that had nothing to do with food bit hard in his belly.

He forced himself to focus. "The sooner we get up and get moving, the sooner we'll be out of here." His tone was short, abrupt even, but he didn't like losing control of himself around her.

"How do you know that?"

He whipped around and glared at her. "I just know."

"You think you're so superior!"

"Not at all. Quite the opposite, in fact. I spent all my efforts trying to measure up."

She stared at him blankly for a moment. "Measure up?"

He gave her a boyish grin. "Winn was the oldest—the apple of my pa's eye. He could always run faster, shoot farther, and was stronger."

"Well, of course, he was *older*."

Remington brushed aside her comment with a flick of his hand and kept going. If she was going to understand this, she had to hear all of it. "Colt was my mother's favorite. She made no bones about it, and neither did my pa. He was the one my pa let stay home. She'd bake Colt cookies when I was with my pa and Winn out on hunting trips, field-stripping weapons, cleaning their gear, knee-deep in battling Darkin."

China's face fell. "You never saw how much they loved you."

"Oh, I *knew* they loved me, intellectually speaking, but I didn't always feel it. And since I couldn't be the center of either of their affections, I decided I'd be the best educated of my brothers. The most in command of myself and my destiny. I would not be dictated by the Legion like Winn, nor would I strive to be the spitting image of my pa, like Colt. I was going to be my own man."

"That's why you're so damn hot and cold."

He locked gazes with her. "I beg your pardon?"

"When you're killin' things in the hard places where death puts on a staring match with you, you turn ice-cold. Vacant. It's like all the life gets sucked right out of you, and your eyes look like nobody's home."

Remington frowned. He had never looked at himself at those times, so it was difficult to argue the veracity of her claims.

"And when you kiss me . . ." A delightful blush infused

her skin. "Well, you're just about the hottest thing there is. All intensity. Like staring at the sun. Both sides of you are deadly—just hot and cold."

"I've always been in the middle. I was born there."

China grabbed hold of his arm and looked up into his face. "But it doesn't make you less. It makes you more. Don't you see? Colt is ruled by his passions and doesn't always think before he acts. Winn is too busy thinking everything through to commit until it's nearly too late. You are the balance. You complete them." She paused for a moment, her eyes turning a shimmering silver. "You complete *me*."

Her comment floored him.

He'd never considered them together as a couple, if only because she was Darkin and he was a Hunter. But what if? What if it were possible?

Perhaps if they'd been in a different time and place it would have been. He liked her. He truly did. And she certainly knew how to engage his baser instincts, as well as his intellect. But was it enough to close such a huge gap? Because despite all those things, he didn't know if he completely trusted her.

He gave a heavy sigh. "China—"

She bit her bottom lip and held her finger to his mouth to stop him. "Don't say it. I can see it in your eyes." Her finger dropped, leaving him feeling oddly bereft of her touch.

"Let's just keep going so we can get to the Book." She turned on her heel and marched on ahead of him down the tunnel, leaving a sodden wet trail in her wake.

Remington ached. Why did he feel like he'd screwed up even though he was trying to do what was right?

Chapter 19

The tunnels beneath the ice were just as much a warren as the previous ones. Trying to get her bearings down here without daylight or dark, or any kind of way to feel her way through made it impossible to tell which direction they were headed any more. Her anger had come down to a simmer and then lost steam altogether. What did it matter if he'd gotten her wet? What did it matter if she wanted him? The chances of escaping this place intact were slim to nill just as Diego had predicted.

Suddenly the tunnel came to a dead end. Green and black flames writhed over a glistening pool of what looked like congealed blood. The dark, viscous surface reflected the screaming faces and tortured images revealed in the flickering flames.

"What in blue blazes is that?"

"Darkin fire. Magical flame." She edged closer, placing a hand on his arm, absorbing strength just from touching his hard muscles and knowing he was there beside her.

"Deadly?"

She gave him a sardonic look. "Isn't everything in here deadly?" *Even you.*

Remington flashed her a smile that melted her bones. "We seem to specialize in deadly. What do you propose?"

China shook her head. His famous Jackson smile alone gave her plenty of ideas she could propose, most of them involving his clever hands, and wickedly wonderful mouth, and never leaving a prone position again. But that was for another time. If there ever was another time, the possibility of which was growing dimmer and dimmer.

As for the Darkin fire, there was nothing that could penetrate it. It was magical. Evil. Pure. It had no weaknesses that could be exploited.

"Can we fight fire with fire?"

She gazed up at him. The flicker of light from the flames threw the solid planes and angles of his strong face into stark relief, making a slow sizzle snap and spark along her veins. Just being near him did that to her. "How so?"

"You can change into anything, right?"

"Almost." *Anything but a plain, boring human woman who could have your heart.*

"What about a phoenix?"

China frowned. A phoenix. A Darkin creature made of fire. It just might work. It was genius. But there was just one problem. She placed her hand on his chest, felt the strong and sure beat of his heart beneath all that muscle. "The fire won't let anything but Darkin pass, and I won't go on without you."

He grasped her around the shoulders and looked deeply into her eyes. "You might have to."

In those blue depths China saw something she'd never expected: trust. It shook her to the core. Remington Jackson might not love her, but he trusted her, which was almost as good—almost. More than that, he appreciated her, and that was something she'd never gotten from Rathe. Ever. And in that moment something deep within her shifted. The iron grip Rathe had held on her fell away. She no longer cared if she received his approval. Not when something she longed for far more was in sight—love.

But all that responsibility on her shoulders made her uneasy. China shook her head, her sweat-dampened hair sticking to her skin. "I'm not the Chosen. *You* are. Your brothers are. It's you who has to get the piece of the Book of Legend. Not me. You who must put it together to stop Rathe."

He tipped up her chin, slowly brushing her bottom lip with the pad of his thumb. Sparks of need flared into a full-blown flame. Her entire body grew hungry for him, wanted him, needed him, but China held herself back.

"I can't do it without you," Remington admitted.

"Why?"

He glanced at the wall of green flames. "That, for a start, and because you're part of this legacy, China, whether you know it or not. All of us knew we couldn't reach the piece of the Book on our own—we always knew it took Darkin powers. You are my Darkin."

His touch was so tender, so loving, her heart fractured a bit. *His* Darkin. His *Darkin*. She didn't want him to see her only as a child of the night. She wanted to be so much more. She stared up into the mesmerizing blue of his eyes and let her gaze stray lower to his mouth and the indention in his chin. With a sinking sensation born of past heartache, China realized she loved him, every inch of him, and she knew she was headed for heartbreak once more.

She pulled back from him and turned away, unable to bear being so close to the object of her affection, yet knowing it would all come crashing to an end sooner than later. Once he knew her terrible secret. "You'll have to leave everything here. It won't go through the fire."

His mouth twitched. "Everything?"

"Your clothes, the pack, the Blaster."

"But that means we'll be leaving the codex, the diary and the statue behind."

"We no longer will need the codex. We've found our way, haven't we?"

"But the statue—"

She pressed a finger to his lips. "It's a sacrifice we'll have to make. Everything must be left behind."

"Can I assume that would include your clothing too?"

Heat engulfed her from her scalp to her toes—a full-out body blush. "Yes." But in the back of her head she was loathe to expose herself fully to him because it would be harder to conceal her awful, damning brand.

"Shall I help you?" The undertone in his voice was sensual. China's heart pounded hard in her chest. She wanted to take him up on the invitation; Lord, did she want to. But there was a risk he'd question her.

He began unbuttoning his pants, and her mouth went dry. His bronzed skin was taut over an impressive chest dusted with hair just as dark as the thick hair on his head. The hair arrowed down past his navel toward his waistband, leading her gaze lower still. There a distinct ridge gave evidence of his desire. *If he asks about it, lie,* her libido whispered insidiously inside her head. Her desire won out over common sense.

Truth was she was glad to be rid of the black dress. Her fingers trembled as she unfastened the small buttons along her back. But she couldn't get to all of them.

"Let me help." His words were warm against the nape of her neck and sent a delicious shiver down her spine. His deft fingers made short work of the persistent buttons, skimming along her shoulder blades as he spread the bodice apart and slid the short sleeves down her shoulders. The dress fell with a whisper of fabric to the floor, leaving her in her corset, chemise, and bloomers.

He kissed the back of her neck, then beneath her ear, and across the slope of her shoulder as he unlaced her corset. China closed her eyes, absorbing the sensation—the smooth heat of his mouth, the gentle sweep of his damp tongue as he tasted her skin. She let it fill her up and radiate out through her body like sunlight reaching in to dispel the shadows that had haunted her for so long.

The pressure released around her ribs as the corset loosened, and the walls she'd built around her heart crumbled. He slid the corset down enough to reach around from behind her and cup her breasts in his warm, roughened palms. He drew her back to him, her bare back against the heat of his chest, his hair-roughed thighs brushing the back of her legs. China gasped at the sensation. Somehow in the time it had taken her to fiddle with her own buttons, he'd removed the rest of his clothing. She leaned her head back as he rolled the points of her breasts between his fingers.

Through the thin cotton of her bloomers, she felt the hard length of him pressed against her. It flexed, and the throb that had started when she saw his bare chest turned into a full-blown aching need that made her slick. She arched her back, pressing herself against him.

Remington growled deep and low, the reverberation of it vibrating through her back and making her breasts tighten further. She pulled open the fasteners of her loosened corset and let it fall to the ground. She reached for the strings on her bloomers.

He settled one hand on the curve of China's hip. "Don't."

The intense heat of the cavern amplified the spicy sweet scent of her. He inhaled, letting it imprint on not just his mind, but on his soul. No matter where he went or what he learned, he would never forget how she looked, how she felt, the scent of her skin and hair in this moment. She turned in his arms. Her body warm and pliant, her skin damp from the heat. Her thin cotton garments clung to her damp skin, revealing almost as much as they concealed.

"Why?" Her voice was soft, breathless, her eyes shimmering.

"I just want to look at you."

A glorious pink suffused her skin, making her breasts rosy and her areolas even rosier. He pulled her closer, bringing the damp slide of her heated skin against him.

A sultry smile curved her lush mouth, and he fixated on it, wanting desperately to kiss her, his hands kneading the flair of her hips.

"I thought all you wanted to do was look," she teased.

"Semantics," he answered, his voice husky and ragged with need. "Pretend I'm blind and I need my hands."

Her eyes widened with delight. Her full lips parted slightly. He threaded his fingers into the damp hair at her nape, cupping the back of her head, indulging in the silken feel of it as he kissed her. Her lips were sweet and soft. She opened for him, her mouth welcoming him with a sensual moan that made him want to hold her tighter. The soft mounds of her breasts pressed against his chest. She was so damn soft against everywhere he was hard. Her body fit his to perfection like matched pieces from a puzzle.

He'd kissed women, plenty of women, but this with China was different. She reached inside him and twisted him up, made him want things he couldn't have, desire things he shouldn't. And damn, did he want more.

He pulled the strings just above her navel and felt the fabric of her bloomers relax and slip down her legs. He bent down, pushing the fabric down as he kissed the soft, smooth skin of her belly and nuzzled the fragrant curls at the juncture of her thighs. He remembered the smoothness of her thighs beneath his lips and the tension, already a throb he couldn't ignore, increased, until his penis ached so badly he gritted his teeth.

"So perfect," he murmured against the skin of her thigh as he gently lifted each dainty foot in turn and pulled the bloomers from first one ankle and then the other.

He stood and kissed her, his erection brushing the soft damp curls, and he flexed against the red-hot animalistic instinct to drive himself into her. She lifted up on her toes, the slide of her body against his mind-numbing. He circled her waist, intent on lifting her up. China tangled her arms around his neck as her kiss deepened, her tongue sliding over his teeth. Remington wasn't sure how much he could take. The flames around them soared higher, a match to the inferno raging inside him.

But in the heat of the moment, none of it mattered, not the caverns and tortures of the temple, not finding the Book or his brothers. There was only him and the goddess in his arms, his alone for a moment that stretched into eternity.

For as long as she'd been around Remington he'd found a way to keep himself clean-shaven. But here in the bowels of the temple, his beard had grown, leaving his skin abrasive as he kissed her. The light scrape of his beard down her neck and over her breasts made the tender skin even more sensitive and responsive to the caressing touches that followed in the wake of his mouth.

"We need—" she panted.

"More time?" he growled against her breast as he pulled it into his mouth.

She groaned at the spike of sensation that shot to her toes. "A blanket."

He slowly let her slide down the length of him, her body memorizing every ripple and roll of his muscled torso as she moved against it. Remington quickly pulled a blanket from his pack and spread it over their clothing, trying to pad the hard stone floor. "I'm sorry it's not more comfor—"

China placed an index finger on his lips, then slid the finger downward over his sculpted bottom lip to trace the indention in his chin. "If I wanted comfortable, I wouldn't be here with you, now would I?"

Hunger flashed and burned in his eyes. She followed the path of her finger with her mouth, swirling her tongue in the divot of his chin. She pulled him down with her as she lay on the blanket. Inside her everything flexed and tightened. She wanted to feel him inside her. Needed it. If she couldn't have his love, she could have this one moment of perfection with him.

The green light of the Darkin fire highlighted his hair and the blue of his eyes, making him look even more intense. "I don't know if this is the right thing for either of us, China, but I can't stop myself."

"I know." She kissed him hard, putting everything she couldn't say into her kiss. His heated weight on her body felt secure and strong, allowing her to let go and just ride the wave of need crashing over both of them with him. The hard, solid length of him slid home, and China cried out as her body responded with unbridled pleasure. Fireworks exploded across her vision, and sparks shot out along every nerve ending. Her hips lifted, taking him in farther. She wanted more. Everything he could give her, she'd take.

The need between them intertwined, until it was a living, breathing thing unleashing its fury on them both. Her body spun higher and higher, until it shattered, leaving her boneless and damp with sweat.

Remington rolled to his side beside her, breathing hard. His hair stuck damp to his cheek. He looked wild and untamed, nothing like the properly-dressed attorney who'd gotten her out of jail what felt like a lifetime ago. He turned his head to the side and gazed at her, his eyes softer now.

"I think I could die happy now."

She smothered a laugh. "That's good. We might have to do just that."

He touched her hair, taking a piece of it and smoothing it between his fingers. "At least we'll do it together." He kissed her tenderly, and all the explosive warmth China had felt coalesced into a small ball in the center of her being.

His clever fingers kneaded along her skin, soothing away her cares. It felt so damn good. China closed her eyes and let herself relax into the sensation of being pampered by someone for the first time in her life.

His hand smoothed along her skin, slick with perspiration. China tried to roll onto her back so he wouldn't touch the brand. She didn't want to think of it. Especially not now. Not in this place.

But Remy held her close, her body pressed deliciously against his, his fingertips tracing a shivering path down the length of her spine. His kisses soothed her, made her forget not only this hellish place they were in, but who she was, for just a moment.

And then his hand stopped on the curve of her buttock. His fingertips brushed the edge of her scar, and everything within her froze in an instant, rigid and hard. Her throat filled with her heart, making her choke. She pushed away from him.

Suddenly the air was even more stifling than it had been. They were both breathing hard and fast.

Remington's eyes narrowed as he propped himself up on his elbow, the sheen of sweat on his skin making it glisten. "That's a hell of a scar. What happened?"

"Accident." She could barely get the lie out between her gritted teeth.

His blue gaze bore into her, but his voice was calm and level. "Tell me the truth."

Sitting up, she curled her legs up against her body, wrapping her arms around them and putting her chin on her knees. "I'm one of the marked."

"Marked?"

And here was where everything between them would crumble and die. Once he knew, there was no going back.

He'd know precisely who and what she was and that he never should have trusted her. She would lose him.

The searing pain in her chest spread, like a vicious attack on her body, making her ache all over. She let the curtain of her hair fall around her as she placed her forehead on her knees. But there was nothing she could do to hold back the tears.

Remington, damn him, made it all the harder by gathering her up against him, his strong arms about her shoulders as he caressed her hair. Every touch drove the pain that much deeper. "Darling, what is it?"

"You're going to hate me," she said between sobs. "Rathe didn't just torture and murder my mother. He's the one who branded me. I'm marked because—" It was so damn hard to get the words out. She hiccuped. "Because he's my father."

Chapter 20

For a moment Remington wasn't sure he could breathe. Or that he'd heard China correctly. He pulled back and gripped the back of his skull with his hands to keep from throttling her. "You're Rathe's *daughter*?"

China bit her lip and nodded, her gaze slowly rising to meet his. Uncertainty fill her eyes. She expected him to push her away. China wasn't just any Darkin. She was Rathe's spawn. Had everything sweet and tender between them been a lie all along? Had she used her Darkin powers to manipulate him into falling in lo—into *caring* for her? Remington didn't know what to believe. How in hell was he supposed to trust her knowing that?

Remington closed his eyes to give himself space to think in the confines of the room, where there was no door he could walk out of, no window he could open to let in some fresh air. It was just him and her. Alone. And no foreseeable means of escape. He could come to terms with this right here, right now, or potentially die here with a woman who'd been trained since birth to be his enemy. But he didn't hate her. He didn't despise her. He ached for her, bone deep.

His inner attorney whispered in his ear, challenging his Hunter self. Since when could a child be responsible for who his or her parents were? Yes, this made her an even bigger liability to his mission than he'd realized, but on the other hand, it also made her potentially an even bigger asset. Regardless, his trust in her was shaken, but it was still there. Dammit, he'd told her they were in this together and they were, for better or worse.

She'd given everything she had to get this far. That spoke of her courage. She'd endured far more than he ever had. That spoke of her determination and a deep wellspring of strength. And she'd never taken anything from him.

Except his heart.

Remington let the confusion and anger drain away, centering himself. He opened his eyes and glanced at her. His calm demeanor seemed to calm her, too. The furrows in her forehead and the worried lines around her eyes eased, and her shoulders relaxed to a more natural position.

"It's the real reason my blood runs red. Only the marked Darkin have that trait. By the way, an archdemon lord makes a lousy father."

Remy couldn't help himself. "How so? Let me guess. Never around much?"

China shook her head. "I wished he'd never come 'round at all. When my mother wouldn't hand me over to the demons he sent for me, he had her tortured to death in front of me. He branded me too so that all other Darkin would know to shun me. He left me dependent on him, on his every whim. And if I didn't behave exactly as I should, I was punished. But it was my fault."

Remy swallowed hard against the acidic bile spurting up in the back of his throat. Jesus. Her fault? Given what little he knew of the sadistic sonofabitch, nothing could have been her fault. She had every right and then some to hate the bastard, and he suddenly felt outraged on her behalf. He brushed the small scar. So small to have such hideous meaning. "How old were you?"

"Six."

His mouth dropped open. He had to swallow a few times to get his tongue working again. Dear God. She had been tortured, orphaned, and then abandoned? "You telling me you've been on your own since you were six?"

China nodded.

Well that just put her in a whole new light. She had to be one of the toughest, most resourceful people he'd ever met. Her habit of stealing was a survival tool she'd learned young. Remington raked his fingers through his hair. "Holy hell."

He blew out a fast, hard breath, trying to get his lungs to expand again. He didn't know any Hunters who could have done as well as that, orphaned at six, with a demon for a daddy—literally. And she'd been a girl to boot.

China McGee earned a measure of his respect right then and there.

She stood, buck naked, and walked to the edge of the dark pool, her blond hair a curtain of fine pale silk down her back, and that damn black scar marring her otherwise flawless skin.

He rose to follow, but before he could step any closer she turned and held her hand out to stop him. "Stand back. I don't want you to get burned if this doesn't work."

"What do you mean if it doesn't work?"

She shrugged. "I've never tried to become a phoenix before. It's not absolutely certain I'll be able to change back into myself afterward. I may just burn up."

Remington cursed under his breath and cupped the back of his head, pacing back and forth. "Don't do it. We'll find another way."

"There is no other way, Remington. You know there isn't." She cast a glance at the wall. "It's what needs to be done if we're going to get to the other side. And I don't want to try and get back through all of that, do you?"

"Hell no."

"Well then. Here goes everything." China closed her eyes,

letting the heat flow through her veins, pulsating energy that filled every cell. Fire erupted in her heart, and from there she became engulfed in flame. It burned, but she was no longer just flesh, she felt the energy, the power of the fire dance through her veins and flicker across her nerves. Her fingers extended to become elongated bones of a wing, her ears shrunk into her head, and her neck extended and her breast-bone stretched and grew as she took the shape of a graceful gold and red bird, covered in flame.

Remington stood back and watched her transform with awe. While he'd seen her change into many shapes, nothing compared to this. She was magical. Her blond hair transformed and became gold feathers covering her body, shimmering as the flames danced along their metallic sheen. As a phoenix, she was intense beauty and lethal power all rolled into one. He had no clue if it would work, if he could even touch her and survive. But right now he didn't want to think. Couldn't think about the implications of what might happen. The different levels of this place had stripped that away from him. All he knew was that if he were to make it out of this place alive, it would have to be in her arms.

Remington held his breath and stepped toward her, nervous as hell, but determined. But as he glanced up into the bird-like features, he saw something that settled his worries. Even as a phoenix she retained those translucent gray eyes that connected with him. And those same eyes were full of trust, hope, and faith and left him humbled.

"You are truly amazing."

Just keep your eyes on mine. I won't let go of you. Her voice spoke inside his head. For a moment he was shocked. He and Winn had been schooled on guarding their thoughts from Darkin as part of their Hunter training, but being linked so closely with her, those guards had fallen by the wayside.

He kept his gaze fixed on hers as she wrapped her wings about him to protect him from the Darkin flames. Heat, like standing out in the noonday desert sun, seared his skin, but didn't burn as the phoenix fire caressed his skin. The fire licked along his body. It consumed everything, took everything, leaving him naked against the soft feathers of her as they walked across the surface of the dark liquid and passed through the wall of green flame together.

The green Darkin fire mixed and hovered on the edge of her golden flames but didn't overtake them. They were surrounded by light and heat; a kaleidoscope of colors swirled around them. In her phoenix form there was nothing to keep him from her, not a scrap of fabric, not the boundary of skin. She was more than that. She was fire, energy, pure soul, able to mingle with the very essence of him. Able to touch his heart.

He couldn't see how something so beautiful, so pure, so full of light and life, could be claimed to be a thing of darkness. A crack formed in the beliefs that had sustained him. Darkin as a whole were not the enemy—just those that threatened humanity. In the whole scope of things they were just as much a balance of light and dark as humans.

He was hardly aware they'd reached the other side until China began to shift once more. She unfurled her wings and let him step back from her flaming form. Like a breath of wind across a field of wheat, her golden form rippled and began to change. The enormous wings shrank into lithe arms and her body came back to its feminine form, flames still licking along her bare skin. Her golden hair fanned out around her shoulders and waist, caught up in the heated wind coming from the green wall of flame.

She reminded him of an image he'd stared at for hours in an art textbook in the college library: a Renaissance painting of the ancient goddess Venus rising from the sea. At that moment China was every inch a goddess, golden and beautiful, the embodiment of power and sensuality rising above the dark surface of the pool.

The room on the other side of the wall of Darkin flame was far smaller than he'd anticipated. In fact it wasn't much larger than a parlor in someone's home. But there was nothing inviting about it. The only thing in the room without windows or doors besides the edge of the dark pool and the wall of flame was a huge mirror of volcanic black glass set into the rougher stone. Their naked images reflected in the dark surface, the wall of flickering green flame the background behind them.

Suddenly the image shifted, and instead of being bare-naked, with China standing behind him, like some sort of twisted Adam and Eve minus the helpful fig leaves, he was clothed in something straight out of medieval history. His reflection revealed his face, but in the uniform of a knight, his arms clad in chain mail, his chest plate dented and scored, bearing a red triple cross—the insignia of the Legion of Hunters. The image shimmered again.

Reflected now on either side of him were the images of Winn and Colt, both clothed as he was, like knights. Each of them held a set of what looked like ancient vellum pages in their hands. Remington's eyes narrowed, and he glanced from side to side. China was still standing there to his left, her face pinched with concern. "What is it? What do you see?"

Remington rubbed at his eyes, just to make sure he wasn't so tired his mind was playing tricks with his vision. But straight ahead of him the image remained. Three men. Three pieces of the Book.

Remington raised his hand. His image in the middle of the mirror sandwiched between his brothers did too. What in blue blazes was this?

He turned to China once more. "Do you see my brothers in the mirror, or just us?"

She bit her lip and reached up to feel his cheek. "You're not fevered."

"What do you see, China?"

"Just us. Standing here, side by side." She slipped her hand into his and squeezed it, silently giving him her support. "What do you see?"

"Me, between my brothers." He frowned, and so did his reflection. "But we're all dressed like knights from the earliest crusades."

"Do you see anything else?"

"Yes. We're each holding a bunch of what looks like pages."

"The Book," she breathed. "Reach out and see if you can touch it."

He turned and gazed at her. "Don't be ridiculous. It's a reflection and a distorted one at that. That can't be right."

She squeezed his hand. "For once, don't worry about if it's right or not and just trust me."

He raised his hand. So did the image in the mirror. He reached forward until the image of his hand holding the pages and his real hand touched. Suddenly his hand was slipping through the surface of the obsidian mirror.

China gasped. "You're doing it!"

The sensation was like cold aspic, thick and gelatinous, but pliable. His arm was sunk halfway to his elbow in the dark surface.

Something dry and rough brushed against the tips of his fingers. His gut told him to grab it. Even though it went against his Hunter training, he did, not knowing who or what it was that he took hold of or what would happen next.

His hand closed around something. It was papery on one side, smooth on the other. "I've got ahold of something."

"Pull it out of the mirror!"

Remington locked gazes with his medieval reflection. "Here goes everything," he muttered to himself.

Slowly he withdrew his arm from the gelatinous mirror, and as it emerged from the dark surface, he did indeed have something in his hand. His heartbeat thundered in his ears. Was this it? After all this time, had he finally found the Book? Or was this a sly trick, another obstacle to finding what he sought? It was old, far older than anything he'd seen in the libraries in the college, or in the museums. The pages were softer than paper, thicker and covered in neat handwritten lettering in dark ink. Rich colors and gold leafing embellished the image in the top corner of the page. The back of it was a leather book cover. "It's Elwin's piece of the Book!"

China gasped, her eyes widening with delight as she looked at the mirror. "You know what this means?"

Remington glanced up at her, reluctant to tear his gaze away from the piece of the Book of Legend. "We've accomplished our mission."

She turned and snorted. "You wish. No, we've almost completed our mission. Our mission is to return with this piece of the Book and reunite it to take down Rathe and seal the Gates of Nyx. And I think I may have found a way to do it."

"What are you talking about?"

"This ain't just any mirror."

"I'll say. It was concealing the Book."

"No. That's not what I meant. If it can conceal the Book, then it has other Darkin powers as well. I think this may be a scryvoyager."

"A what?"

China snorted. "Did I find a word too big for you?"

Remington frowned. "What does it do, woman?"

"It's a portal. It can take us back to Tombstone, or Bodie,

or wherever we need to go as long as there is a mirror on the other side."

A big smile lit up his face. "It can?"

China nodded. "It's probably how the original Hunters who placed it here got out safely, so they could later write down their notes in the codex."

"How many of them are there?"

China shrugged. "No one knows. They're Darkin magic, like the flames we passed through. Cortez must have bound a Darkin to his service or had one of the locals manipulate one to install the Book in the scryvoyager and erect the wall of flame, and then escaped."

"It's worth a shot."

"We need to pick a destination and focus on it, then walk through to the other side."

One of his brows rose as if to say, you simply must be mistaken; that's too simplistic.

"If you don't trust me, toss a rock through or something."

Remington picked up a rock from the floor of the cavern and bounced it in his hand like a ball. "Just concentrate on a destination, huh?"

He closed his eyes and took a deep breath, holding it for a moment. His eyes snapped open, and without ceremony he tossed the rock into the dark glass-like surface, then flinched, expecting it to shatter.

Instead the rock disappeared, and the glassy surface rippled like a still lake hit by a stone. He opened first one eye then the other. "It worked!" There was the sound of shattering glass a moment later, but the surface of the dark mirror looked undamaged.

China sighed and shook her head. "What destination did you pick?"

Remington shrugged. "My law offices. Why?"

China snorted. "I think you may have just broken a window." She grabbed his hand. "Ready?"

"Everything is an adventure with you, isn't it?"

She gave him a wide smile. "At least you can't say I'm boring."

He gave the mirror a dubious look. At least they were going to his office. It was about as good a place as any to travel to when they were both still buck naked. Everyone knew he was gone, and he had extra clothes in the wardrobe there. "After you."

Chapter 21

China gave a heavy sigh. "After all we've been through in the last few days and you're scared of a scryvoyag—" She stepped into the dark surface and disappeared along with his hand.

Remington wasn't sure what to think, but he held his breath and plunged in.

It wasn't unlike swimming in a pool of chilled aspic. Not something he'd ever chosen to do. He wasn't a big fan of aspic in the first place. But it was soft and semi-solid, yet it gave way easily around their movements.

He felt the warmth of sunshine on his hand before he emerged fully on the other side. Remington blinked against the brightness of the light. He was back in his office in Tombstone. His desk—actually everything in his office—had a light layer of dust on it. Clearly he was going to have to talk to his cleaning lady, whom he paid a weekly sum to come whether he was there or not. He glanced back at the plain full-length mirror on the wall inside his personal office.

It looked no different than when he'd seen it two weeks ago. He touched the surface and found it solid, his fingers leaving prints on the glass. "That's the damnedest thing. It's like Alice in Wonderland going through the looking glass."

China was leaning up against his desk, her arms crossing

over her breasts, causing them to swell in a rather enticing manner. She jerked her head to the side. "Told ya you broke a window."

Glittering shards of glass littered the floor. Remington swore under his breath. His landlord was going to have words for him. But that could wait. Right now he needed to get to the telegraph office and quickly.

He grabbed China around the wrist. "Come on."

"We just got here! Can't we get something to wear first? Where are we going?"

He glanced down at himself, a slight blush coloring his skin. "You're right. Clothes first, then to the telegraph office. If the codex was right, then there's no way the Gates of Nyx are in Bodie like my brothers think. I need to wire them to meet me at Marley's so we can put the Book together and then figure out where the Gates might be."

China stared at him. "I know a way we can find out."

"How?"

"I'll ask dear old daddy."

He whirled around, a vein pulsing hard in his temple. "No!" From the glint in his eye she could tell he didn't trust she'd return. He went over to a wardrobe closet he had in his office, opened the doors, and began flinging out garments and an oilcloth. He chucked a shirt and a pair of pants and suspenders at her and gently wrapped the piece of the Book they'd brought with them in the oilcloth.

"If anyone would know where the showdown is going to be, don't you think it'd be Rathe?" she said as she slipped on the shirt and began buttoning it.

"Of course, but you can't risk it." He shoved on a pair of pants himself, then stalked over and grabbed her about the shoulders, his fingers digging into her flesh.

China threw off his hold, angry. "Why? Because I'm not a Hunter born and bred like you and your brothers?"

"No."

"Then why?"

"Because I'm not strong enough." He closed his eyes and bent his head.

"You aren't strong enough? You mean to defeat Rathe?"

"No. I know I can't do that on my own. That'll take me and my brothers." He shook his head and turned from her. He paused, and the silence stretched out between them. "I'm not strong enough to . . . lose you."

China stepped around and cradled his rough cheek in her hand, her thumb caressing the deep divot in his chin she loved to kiss. No one had ever given her what he had: his trust and true concern for her welfare, even above his own. He'd made her feel important, valued, not for what she was, or who she was, but simply because she existed. She hesitated to label such a thing love. She'd had so little experience of it to go by in her own life, it was hard to know for sure, and risky to make the assumption.

"Let me do this for you. It's one of the only things I can do to help."

"I don't like it, but I also don't see how we have much choice. There's barely a week until the new moon rises." He kissed her fiercely. "You are the bravest woman I know. If there were such a thing as female Hunters, you'd be one."

She gave him a weak smile. "If I were a female Hunter, then I wouldn't be Darkin, and I wouldn't have the direct connection to Rathe that might make this shortcut possible." She reached out and touched his cheek. "I'll always find my way back to you. Trust me."

China finished dressing as best she could. Nothing fit; it was all far too large and made for a man, but that was fine with her. It didn't need to fit for where she was going. She reached beneath the baggy shirt that smelled of Remington's Bay Rum and placed the tip of her middle finger on the center of her brand and let the sluggish, sticky sensation wriggle and creep through her veins. She hadn't wanted Remington, or anyone else for that matter, to touch the scar for a good reason. It was one surefire way to locate Rathe, anytime, anywhere. A direct line to her father, not something to be tampered with lightly or even by accident. Not something she wanted.

Normal Darkin could only transport to places they'd been before, but because she was marked by Rathe, she could return not just to a place she'd been before, but to a person with whom she shared a connection. Her body began to fall apart, but not in the same way it did when she shifted. Instead of the welcome rush of heat and the sparkling sensation that filled her, this was cold, sticky, and vile like congealed blood. Dark particles consumed her from the feet up, turning her into nothing but smoke and ash as she transported to Rathe's hall of horrors.

She'd been there twice before. Once as a terrified six-year-old to watch her mother die and to receive her brand then be held against her will for six months before he cast her out into the world, and once when he'd ensured she had her virginity taken by force by one of his incubi. China couldn't breathe; the suffocating sensation made her lungs and nose burn, then just as suddenly dissipated.

Without opening her eyes she could smell the stench of burnt flesh and decay in this place. Beneath her hands was something hard and cold, the familiar black marble floor on which she'd broken her first bone. The light from the lava on which the floor floated glowed red through her eyelids. Still she hesitated to open her eyes, knowing that Rathe sitting upon his monstrosity of gleaming glass-like obsidian, would be waiting to greet her.

"I see the prodigal child has come home." The sound of his voice, unctuous and superior all at once, grated on her nerves and made her palms instantly damp. Her heart pounded out a mad tattoo, like it was as desperate as she was to leave this place.

China lifted her head and glared at the archdemon from Hell who'd sired her, locking her gaze on him as she slowly stood, bare feet braced wide apart. The deathly pallor of his face picked up the reddish glow from the lava that lit the edges of the enormous rock cavern that was his throne room. It was really a torture chamber as far as China was concerned. She could hear the clink of the rusty chains and massive hooks overhead that disappeared into the infinite darkness above them.

He was dressed like a dapper Englishman, all spanking clean and pressed, from the crease in his pinstriped trousers to his matching vest and coat, and crisp, high-collared, snowy shirt. In many ways he wasn't dressed all that differently from Remington on the first time she'd seen him. The big difference was while it looked good on Remington, it made Rathe appear overdone and gaudy—like a whore trying too hard to look like she'd risen above her profession and become respectable. The bloodred silk tie was overkill. So was the golden watch chain strewn with the shrunken, gilded heads of his enemies.

China refused to let her body shudder. She'd deliberately waited a moment to answer him back. "It's not as though you've put out the welcome mat," she answered tartly.

The reddish slash in his face that passed for a mouth flattened into a grim line. "I see your manners have not improved." The fingernails on his hands changed, elongating and sharpening into black talons, like those on a bald eagle.

China had tried to shift into a bald eagle once. The feel of talons, that big and that long, extending from her fingertips had made her think too much of being like Rathe, and she'd never done it again.

"Didn't feel there was anybody here I needed to impress."

Rathe steepled his fingers, the talons clacking against one

another. "Then, if not for a social call, why are you here, daughter? Surely you didn't hope to receive a matching brand for the one you already have."

China flinched before she could stop herself. "I came about the Chosen."

"Ah, the Chosen. One of my more favorite topics of conversation as of late. And how are they, my dear?"

"I wouldn't know. I've only been tagging along with the middle Jackson brother since the younger one left me buried in adobe brick and rotting in jail."

Rathe leaned forward. "And did Remington Addicus Jackson recover the final piece of the Book of Legend?"

China gave one curt nod. "Thanks only to me," she replied.

"You didn't expect me to make it easy, did you? I wanted them to feel a sense of accomplishment before I snatch it all away and open the Gates of Nyx wide to the rest of my brethren, and bring about a new world order."

Her heart clutched in her chest. The age-old wound broke open deep within. She'd wished he cared even a fraction of that much for her. But the days of seeking his approval were over. "Why do you care if they have a sense of accomplishment?"

His ice-blue eyes turned yellow and hungry like living flame. Only the vertical slit remained the same, and even that widened with anticipation. "The more accomplished they feel, the more agony they will endure when I take it all away and they realize all their sacrifice, all their lives, and those of their ancestors have been in vain. Worthless. A waste."

He was one sick, cold, evil demon. But then, that wasn't anything new. She just hated being reminded of how ruthless and sadistic Rathe could be and how heavily she'd relied on him, feeling helpless and hopeless when he'd branded and discarded her.

China swallowed down the bitter bile tainting the back of her tongue and searing her throat. She hoped like hell this touching family reunion was worth it. As long as she could find out the location to the Gates of Nyx, she could return with her head held high.

Rathe rose from his throne and stepped down from the dais, moving slowly toward her like a pit viper. "Do you know how all this began—Darkin and Hunters, the prophecy of the Chosen?"

He was close enough now that the reek of dead things coming off of him made her eyes burn. "You were all bored to tears and decided to screw up the world for entertainment?"

He slapped her full force, making her neck snap as her head swung with the blow. China had been hit before, but not like that. Never anything that made her face go numb from the pain and started to swell her eye shut instantly.

"Insolent child. I never should have let your mother keep you."

Least she never laid a hand on me, China thought bitterly. She would have spit out the words, but she still couldn't feel her jaw, and the blood collecting in her mouth was choking her.

I heard that, my pet.

Joy. She hadn't let anyone in for so long, she'd forgotten powerful Darkin could read one another's thoughts. And there was none more powerful than Rathe.

His yellow gaze bored into her, the vertical slits in his eyes widening like a cat's the instant it scented prey. *I've a plan for you. You are going to help me annihilate the Chosen.*

And why should I? You're going to kill me anyway.

His mouth, if it truly could be called a mouth, stretched slightly, a dark, lipless maw in his pale, waxy, dead-looking skin. The sharp points of his teeth just barely visible. "You can either serve me or be destroyed; that is true. But if you serve me, the end will be far less painful for you."

So the choices are die, or die painfully?

The vertical slits in his eyes narrowed. "You are not afraid to die, are you?"

China refocused her gaze, letting it rest on the spot just behind Rathe. She didn't want to see his face. Didn't want to be reminded that this Darkin had branded her skin when she was a defenseless, frightened child. The searing smell of human flesh and the blinding black pain had been equally branded on her memory.

"But you do value the lives of the Chosen. Do you not?"

It took everything within her not to flinch, not to change the pace of her breath. She looked Rathe straight in his dead yellow eyes, gathered all her power to shield her thoughts from him, and lied.

"What happens to them is none of my business. I only look out for one person since you killed my mother—me." It was really more of a past truth than an outright lie. Up until she and Remington had been pulled together by their journey to the center of the earth and back, she'd not known a man could be so kind, so tender and loving, while at the same time strong and decisive.

His gentle, kind side didn't make Remington weak; rather it made him even stronger. Something Rathe would never understand. Remington might have a weakness for always wanting to be right, but his strength was that he did the right thing, regardless of what it cost him. There were so many ways he was like Rathe and yet totally different. Her heart squeezed at the realization.

"All I wanted to know was where I should be for the best view when the showdown happens."

Rathe's golden gaze bored into her; the corner of the red slash that marred his skin as a mouth lifted in approval. "Well, that's a change. Could it be that my spawn is finally willing to take up the mantel of her station as one of the noble among the Darkin?"

China stiffened. She could do this. She *had* to do this.

"The Gates of Nyx are never in one place long. They change their position at sundown. When the Book of Legend was torn apart, our forces poured forth in the north of the Island of Britain. But when we meet the Chosen?" He rolled one of the small gilded head fobs decorating his watch chain between his fingers, and it squealed in pain. The dark slash of a mouth widened, revealing the points of his teeth and a bit of black gums. "Who knows? It could be anywhere."

A sinking sensation filled her chest, making her feel as if she were drowning. Coming here had been for nothin'. He wasn't going to tell her. She could hardly draw a breath.

Rathe's face changed, his perfectly sculpted black brows drawing down in the center, making his expression lurid and vile. "Go back to the Jackson brothers, my pet. Tell them to come to me."

She swallowed hard in order to force words past the thickness in her throat. "How?"

"They will find another book, that of my once brother, the archangel Jezriel. In it they can find the means to locate the Gates of Nyx on the rise of the new moon." He balled his hand into a fist. "And I will crush them and begin my reign as ruler of this world."

China still hadn't returned. She'd disappeared in a swirl of dark particles. He'd long since passed worry and entered into the realm of panic. Where the hell was she? What if Rathe wouldn't let her return? Deep down he knew he had to trust her. If anyone could escape Rathe's grasp, it would be a thief of her caliber. But was it enough?

The sun beat down, the air shimmering with the heat of it, as he walked his horse up the zigzagging dirt road to Marley's house. It sat apart from the town on a bluff overlooking a deep gorge and was the strangest place Remington had ever seen. A large brass telescope, various cranes, and a few weather vanes Remington suspected were for attracting lightning during a thunderstorm, were among the objects that protruded from the roofline of Marley's house. Some moved unexpectedly at odd intervals, giving one the sense it was not so much a building as an enormous living mechanical creature.

Among the flora and fauna on Marley's property were glints of metal. The mechanical spine-shooting cacti and mechanical eyes Marley had scattered throughout the landscape so he could both warn and then defend himself against unwanted visitors.

Marley would know he was there before he ever reached the front door. Remington dismounted from his horse and moved to knock on the wooden front door, but it opened before he even touched his knuckles to it.

"Remington!" Marley stuck out his hand in greeting, his brown eyes magnified to the size of dinner plates behind the special lenses of his unusual goggles. Cottony tufts of white hair blew about in the wind. He was a sight for sore eyes.

"It's good to see you, Marley." Remington took Marley's hand and instead of just shaking it, used it to pull the smaller man into a bear hug. "Damn, it's good to see you."

He pulled back, and Marley looked a little dazed, but gave him a big smile, which pushed his goggles up a notch on his nose. "It's good to see you in one piece. I had my doubts. Were you successful?"

Remington held up the oilcloth that covered the precious pages. Marley's eyes lit up like those of a kid on Christmas morning. "Brilliant!"

"I just hope the others lived through it. I barely did," Remington said.

Marley's dark brows drew together and disappeared behind the rim of his goggles. "I've heard from Winchester, but not from Colt. Things have gotten worse since you Jacksons have been gone." Remy didn't like the uneasy tremor underscoring Marley's uneasy tone. Marley waved Remington inside and took a quick glance around outside before he shut the door. Inside he locked a series of padlocks and bolts that ran the length of the door. Some of it was new. If Marley was beefing up his security, then things had definitely gone from bad to worse.

"What's happened?"

Marley pulled the goggles from his head, leaving a red rim around his eyes and over the bridge of his nose. "Earthquakes for a start, then wildfires and dust storms, and that's only the natural disasters. I was accosted in my own home by a shapeshifter disguised as Colt. Darkin have been found running amok in several cities all over the country, if my sources are correct."

Marley's sources were always correct. Remington pulled off his hat and ran his fingers through his sweat-damp hair. "Rathe's pushing open the Gates as far as he can. Crack only has to be a little bit wider to let even more Darkin through."

He looked for a place to sit down in Marley's parlor, but everywhere was piled high with stacks of books and boxes of gears, wires, tubes, and glass piping. Marley was worse than a desert pack rat. He saw a use for everything.

Remington picked up a bust of President Lincoln off the edge of the piano that looked like it had been exploded apart and glued back together with some sort of adhesive, giving the piece irregular golden lines all through it. "Did you research how to put the Book of Legend back together?" Not like this, Remy hoped.

Marley nodded. He turned to a desk buried beneath stacked volumes of leather-bound books. He tapped his bottom lip with his thumb as he searched through the stacks. "Now where did I put that volume?"

He picked out a particularly old book with a black satin ribbon marking a page and cracked the volume open to the marker. "I say, old chap, are you certain you are ready to go through with this?"

Remy narrowed his eyes. "You say that like you're asking if I'm ready to meet my Maker." Which, if all of this didn't work, would be exactly what would happen in a week.

Marley bobbed his head in such a fashion that the white tuft of hair on his head waved wildly about. "Well, as much as I hate to say this, it's distinctly possible." He peered at the book, running his finger down the page. "All indications point to a blood sacrifice by the Chosen."

A long silence stretched out between them. Marley finally looked up.

"A blood sacrifice? How much blood exactly are we talking about here, Marley?"

Marley frowned. "That was difficult to pinpoint. We won't be able to tell until the pieces of the Book of Legend are all in one place, ready to be reunited. And once they are reunited, there is still the matter of finding exactly where the Gates of Nyx are located." He waved his hand about in the air vaguely. "I've searched through every bit of Hunter lore I've been able to get my hands on and still haven't been able to pinpoint where the Gates are located or determine how to go about closing them for good."

The knowledge that this last piece of information might be the final nail in the coffin of the free world made Remy's stomach knot. He and his brothers had endured so much. He didn't even know if Colt had found the other pieces of the Book, or if they were still searching. Was the mysterious, unknown location of the Gates what was going to make them lose the game at the eleventh hour? "Blast."

"I was hoping you or your brothers might have come across the information during your journeys."

Remington shook his head. "Nothing we came across gave us any clue. The codex Mendoza had only indicated the Gates wouldn't be in the same location as one of the hidden pieces of the Book, which nixed it being in Bodie. But China is trying to find out where the Gates might be."

Marley worried his lip again, muttering to himself.

"You have something else to tell me?"

His old friend looked intently at him. "Are you certain, Remington, absolutely certain, that you and your brothers are the Chosen?"

Remington gripped the edge of the table nearest him and the stacks of boxes teetered, but didn't fall. He had doubted it for a long time, but there had been no doubt after the vision he'd seen in the scryvoyager in the temple. "There's no need to guess. I know. We are the Chosen, Marley. We must defeat Rathe or the world will fall to him."

Chapter 22

It was only a matter of time until his brothers arrived at Marley's. It would take all of them, together, to bring down Rathe and seal the Gates of Nyx; he knew that now. And with China's help they would know where the Gates were located. *If China returned.*

It was ironic that one Darkin could turn the tide against another determined to end the world as they knew it. He glanced at Marley. "Do you think my brothers know what will happen when we reunite the Book of Legend?"

Marley took off his glasses and removed a thin white cotton handkerchief from his breast pocket. He cleaned the lenses in slow, small circles as he considered the question. "It's difficult to tell. I'm certain that they've faced challenges just as you have, but there is no way of knowing if they've come to the same conclusion regarding your joint status as the Chosen, or if they've recovered the other pieces of the Book as you have."

Remington shut his eyes and took a deep, still breath. The resonance was still there, deep inside him. The disjointed pieces of the Book were coming closer together. The vibration of it in his bones was now a constant, pleasant hum in his system. "They have them. And they are getting closer. Look!" Remington pointed out the window.

On the stretch of horizon a dust cloud rose, a tan plume against the piercing clear blue of the desert sky. "It's either a steam carriage or he's on Tempus," Marley said softly.

Colt's mechanical horse could cover more ground than any ordinary horse without the need for food or water, but it had a downside. One bit of gravel, one worn gear or spring, and the internal clockwork of the thing would seize up, leaving it useless. Technology was a wonderful thing, but unlike Colt, Remy didn't like to rely on it too much.

And until China, he hadn't wanted to form permanent attachments to anything beyond his brothers and Marley. It had seemed a waste, knowing that the end of the world was possibly at hand. There was no future. Not unless they closed the Gates.

Remy and Marley both headed outside and watched the plume grew wider. Regular, rhythmic thump of hooves could be heard pounding against the desert valley floor. The familiar black-and-white cowhide covering that made Tempus look like a paint horse, instead of a machine, became easy to see. Colt was riding double, with Lilly behind him.

They slowed to a trot and quickly transitioned to a walk as they approached Remington and Marley. Colt waved, and they both waved back.

"Got your telegram. I thought we were all going to meet up in Bodie," Colt called out as he dismounted from the horse and helped Lilly down.

"We were until we decoded what I found in Diego's codex. Turns out the location of the Gates of Nyx is still a mystery. China has gone to find out if she can nail down that information."

Colt tipped his hat up. "Marley, you mind if Lilly gets out of this heat inside?"

Marley gave Lilly a familiar and easy smile that she

returned, her green eyes sparkling. "Not at all. You know where everything is, don't you, Miss Arliss?"

"I do. Thank you, Marley. It's good to see you again."

Lilly glanced between the two Jackson brothers, a soft, knowing smile on her lips. "Boy talk, huh? Fine. I'll get you a drink too, while I'm at it. I have a feeling you're all going to need one before the day is out."

Colt watched her sashay into Marley's house, then turned and scowled at Remington. He lowered his voice. "Didn't I tell you not to get mixed up with that thief shifter?"

Remington shrugged. "You mean just like I suggested to you?"

Colt rolled his eyes. "You ain't gonna bring that up again, now are you?"

"Nope. Knowing what I know now, can't say I blame you."

Colt eyed him, his gaze narrow and assessing. "I'll be damned. You and China are together now, aren't you?"

Remington could hardly deny it, but he refused to give Colt the satisfaction of being right, so instead of answering he just gave him an inscrutable smile.

"You ain't gonna fess up to it, are you?" Colt pushed.

Remington glanced at Marley. "You said Winn would meet us here as well?"

Marley adjusted his wire-rimmed glasses. "The mechanical messenger bird I received stated he was on his way here with the vampire's piece of the Book of Legend in hand. It also stated that he was bringing something else we'd need."

Remington raised one brow. "What else could we need? We'll have all three pieces of the Book of Legend."

Marley shifted his weight from one foot to the other. "We'll need all three pieces, and all three of you brothers, but we also need the instructions on how to bind the Book back together. And those are in the Book of Jezriel."

"Never heard of it," said Colt. He looked at Remington expectantly. "You're the smart one; you ever heard of it?"

Remington shook his head. "Me either."

"You'll likely wish you never had," Marley replied. "Believe me, it's one of the things that got me lured into this entire Hunter existence." Beads of perspiration dotted Marley's high forehead.

"Then how did you come across it?"

Marley sighed. He pulled a handkerchief from his pocket once more and mopped his brow. "That is a long story for an entirely different time, when we've closed the Gates of Nyx, defeated Rathe, and are old men ensconced by a nice fire with a bottle of brandy."

Colt chuckled. "You got some imagination, you know that, Marley?"

Marley smiled and stuffed the cloth back in his breast pocket. "From the likes of you, I shall endeavor to take that as a compliment."

"What the devil is that?" Remington squinted, looking into the too bright sky. The dark dot in the air appeared to be growing larger. "It can't be."

He'd never seen anything like it.

"It looks like a goddamn ship," Colt muttered. And indeed it was a full-size galleon, the style from a hundred years ago, with billowing white sails, rope rigging, and a wooden hull, descending upon them. Two shimmering copper wings extended from either side of the ship, glaring in the harsh sunlight, and a twin set of propellers hung off the aftdeck. Its hull came to rest with a groan against the edge of the bluff that bordered Marley's property.

"Ahoy there!"

The voice sounded familiar. Remington put his hand to his forehead and peered up to the edge of the galleon's deck. His brother Winchester waved his black Stetson at him, his goggles glinting in the afternoon sunlight. Remy shook his head. Leave it to Winn to fly out on a vampire's airship and come back home on something even more out of place.

"I say, that's a most intriguing vessel," Marley said, as he pulled down his goggles to take a better look.

"Winn, you taking up a hobby riding strange airships?" Colt called up.

"At least I've had a more interesting time than you the last three weeks," he answered back.

"I doubt it," Colt retorted, not to be outdone.

Remington cleared his throat. "Would you two stop trying to outdo each other. We've got a world to save here."

"I have to agree with Remington, chaps," Marley added. "Regardless of how intriguing this all may be, we must focus our efforts on reuniting the Book."

Beside Winn appeared a shorter person, whose face was shadowed by a wide-brimmed hat accented with ostrich feathers that had seen better times. The individual's billowing white shirt, black britches, and high boots made it difficult to discern if it was a man or a woman. But whoever it was looked like a pirate.

"Let down the ladder!" The high voice left no doubt it was a woman.

A chorus of other female voices answered. "Aye, captain!"

Remington looked at Colt, who looked at Marley. A ship with a female captain and crew? Perhaps Winn's adventure *had* been more interesting than his brother's. Winn started down the rope and rung ladder and was followed by the small woman in men's clothing. She was agile on the ropes, Remington gave her that.

Colt whistled long and low. "Would you look at that," he said under his breath. "I think I'm liking this trend of women wearing britches." Remington glared at him as did Marley.

Colt shrugged. "What? It's an observation."

Remington shook his head. He couldn't understand how his little brother could remain aware of women when he had a succubus waiting for him just inside that could literally seduce the soul right out of a man. But then again, this was Colt. He'd have to be dead *not* to notice women.

Personally, Remy was just glad to have all his brothers together, alive and all in one piece. Winn and the pirate captain reached the dirt, and Remington jogged up to clasp his brother in a hug. "God, it's good to see you, Winn."

Winchester smiled at him. "Good to see you too, brother."

"You're the last to the party, I'm afraid. Colt beat us both to finding a piece of the Book."

Colt gave Winn a smug grin. "That's because I'm fastest."

Winchester raised a dark brow and ignored his little brother's comment. "He had the least distance to travel I imagine. I've been to Transylvania, France, and London to get my hands on Haydn's piece of the Book." He put his hand to his forehead. "Where are my manners?" He gestured to the small woman beside him. "Captain Le Renaud, may I introduce you to my brothers, Remington and Colt, and to my good friend Marley Turlock."

The captain swept the broad-brimmed hat from her head and gave a bow from the waist. *"Enchanté, messieurs."*

Remington gave a slight bow. "The pleasure is mine. And thank you for returning my brother to us in one piece."

"And Haydn's piece of the Book," Winn added.

Remington glanced at the cloth-wrapped oblong object Le Renaud held with gloved hands and nodded to it. "That it?"

He reached for it but Winn grabbed him by the wrist. "Don't touch it without gloves on."

Colt frowned. "Why not?"

"We had to take some precautionary measures to keep it away from Rathe. Keeping it simple, you touch it with your bare hands, you'll die from cyanide poisoning." He pulled a pair of gloves from his hip pocket and pulled them on, then the captain handed him the oilcloth-wrapped parcel.

"How did you manage that?" Marley asked, his face alight with curiosity.

Remington glanced at Marley. "We're going to have to discuss how it had become poisoned some other time."

Marley's shoulders slumped a little. "Yes, yes. Rightly so. Time is of the essence. The sooner we figure out how to bind the pieces back together, the better."

Captain Le Renaud cast an amused glance between each of the Jackson brothers. "The family resemblance between the brothers is most intriguing," she said as she made eye contact with Marley.

He swallowed hard, and nodded vigorously. "I believe it's due to a rather strong gene inheritance, if Gegor Mendel's work is to be believed."

The captain's smile broadened, as Marley's reply intrigued her. "If you gentlemen will *excusez-moi* for the moment, I have duties on my ship to attend to if I am to raid the gold fields of California." Her eyes met Winn's and he winked at her.

"Pirate," he said by way of explanation. Each of them nodded in turn at the petite captain, touching the brims of their hats. Marley moved to grasp her hand and the captain pulled it out of his reach.

"Cyanide traces on the gloves," she said as she removed the glove from her right hand and held it back to Marley. He smiled and grasped her hand lightly in his, brushing a kiss over the back of it.

"*Adieu, Messieur* Turlock," she said as she mounted the ladder and quickly climbed back aboard the ship.

Winchester glanced up the ladder. "Tessa will be down any moment."

Remington narrowed his eyes. He'd already been surprised by the pirate airship captain. Had Winn picked up someone else as well? "Tessa?"

"The Contessa Drossenburg."

He had a nickname for the vampire? What the hell had happened on his trip? Perhaps it was a good thing. At least they still had a vampire on their side when it came to fighting Rathe.

"The vampire?" Colt said.

Winn's face grew both sad and fiercely proud, if that were possible. "Not any longer. She gave up her powers to save me from Rathe."

It took a moment for that to roll around long enough in Remington's head to fully sink in. "She's not a Darkin anymore?"

Winn nodded. "Pulse and everything. As flesh and blood as you or I."

"Fascinating," Marley said, rubbing his hands together.

"Blast." Remy ran his fingers through the edges of his hair beneath his hat and gripped the back of his skull. "That's awful."

Winn arched one brow. "I thought that was a good thing."

Remington sighed, letting his hands fall limply to his sides. Their advantages were slipping away one by one, and their showdown at the Gates of Nyx was becoming a more dangerous proposition by the minute. "Means she's more in danger. We all are. It would have been useful to have another Darkin on our side. That leaves us with just China."

Winn frowned. "And the succubus."

Colt shook his head. "Nope. She's changed back to mortal too."

Winn's frown deepened into a scowl. "Damn. That does put us at a disadvantage."

"Hold up now. That's not exactly true," Colt said, putting his hand on Marley's shoulder. "We got Marley too. One great inventor can sway a battle."

Winn's mouth split into a wide smile, making his mustache broaden. "How about two?"

Remington flicked his gaze to Marley, then his older brother. "What?"

"Octavia's part—well, *was* part—of Le Renaud's crew. Her chief mechanic. But she's come to meet Marley."

Down the ladder shimmied a slip of a girl, in mechanic's pants and shirt, her hair a froth of copper red curls.

Beside him Marley started making a choking sound. Remington stared at the inventor. His mouth hung open, and his eyes looked larger than ever, which was saying something since he looked so damned bug-eyed with his special goggles on anyway. He'd never seen Marley stunned like this before.

"Sephie?"

The girl pulled her goggles down around her neck and gave him a wide smile. "No. My name is Octavia. Octavia Turlock." She held out a hand and Marley frowned, confusion flitting through his eyes.

"I'm your daughter."

Marley's mouth opened and closed, but no sound came out. He cleared his throat and ran his finger under the edge of his collar. "My daughter?" His voice cracked.

"It's the truth, Marley," Winn said. "And if I do say so, she looks an awful lot like you."

"I'll tell you who she looks like. She looks just like Balmora, that code machine of Marley's," Colt said as he tipped back his hat.

Marley's eyes darted from Octavia to Winn to Colt and back again. "That's because I based my design of Balmora on Sephie—the Lady Persephone Hargrieve. Wherever did you find this girl?"

"She was crewing aboard Le Renaud's airship," Winn said. "And she's got your flair for inventions. Apple don't fall far from the tree on that one." He clapped a hand on Marley's shoulder and gave him a good-natured grin. "Congratulations, Marley. You're a father."

Remington snorted. Colt outright laughed. It was a rare treat to see Marley out of words. The man almost never stopped his long-winded explanations. Figured that having a kid would be the one thing to flummox him.

Marley turned to Winn. "But how?"

"My mother assured me it was in the normal way," Octavia stated, a hint of humor to her voice.

Marley looked at his daughter. By gum, Winn was right. The family resemblance was there in the stubborn tilt of her chin and the intensity of her eyes.

"But why did she never contact me?"

Octavia's blue eyes grew misted. "She said you'd made yourself crystal clear. You were going to America, and you didn't want her to follow."

Marley pulled at the tufts of his white hair, making them stand out in an even more crazy fashion, and began to pace back and forth. "That was because I was disgraced! She was supposed to marry some chap her parents could approve of! She was supposed to find a doctor who could cure what ailed her. But she never said she was with child! Never!" He stopped and grasped Octavia by the shoulders, his face suddenly turning solemn. "I never would have left had I known. You must believe me. Your mother was the love of my life. The only woman I've ever loved."

Octavia laid a tender hand on Marley's cheek. "She felt the same about you." For a second Remington felt embarrassed to be there during such a personal moment, but he didn't want to ruin it by distracting either of them from something so monumentally important, so he stood stock-still and remained where he was.

"Where is she now? How is she? Did she recover from her sickness?" Marley frowned. "Does your mother know you were crew on a pirate airship?" He tossed his hands in the air and began pacing again. "How could she have let this happen?"

"Father . . ." The one word stopped Marley in his tracks. "She's been gone a long time now. She died when I was only ten. She told me if I ever found you, I was to give you three things." She handed him a metal box with a complicated locking system, then fished out a small key on a chain around her neck from the folds of her shirt and pulled it off and handed it to him. Last, she reached deep into her pocket and pulled out a ratty piece of faded black velvet. She pulled the frayed fabric back to reveal a miniature mechanical King Charles spaniel. The sun glinted off of its copper and silver curls.

Something within Marley broke. There was simply no other way to describe it. He took the toy dog from Octavia with a shaking hand and clutched it tightly. Remington had never seen him this way before. He slumped to the ground, and Octavia crouched beside him.

He looked at her, his eyes sadder than Remington ever recalled. Then suddenly the spark of life reappeared in them. He bolted upright like he'd been electrically shocked. "Ten? Ten! Why on earth are you not with your grandfather, girl? You're the granddaughter of a duke!"

Octavia's mouth hardened into a firm line, and her eyes sparked with defiance as she straightened. "He shipped my mother off to some far-off property the moment he discovered she was with child and forbade her to come back to London. And once I was born, he said the only way they would take her back into the family fold was if she married that horrible Lieutenant Frobisher. She refused."

Marley sighed and paced. "That sounds like Persephone. Stubborn to the core, and absolutely right to do so."

"We lived in a cottage on the edge of the town of Falstone, alone. There was no one else to tend her except me once she came down with consumption. And when she died, we buried her in Northumberland. And I went to London on my own. When I came to the address she'd given me for my grandfather's grand house, I knocked on the front door, and the butler informed me that the duke didn't have a granddaughter and slammed the door in my face. I roamed the streets, living off what I could until I picked Le Renaud's pocket. She took me on her ship."

Marley thumped his fist against the side of his leg, clearly unsure of what to do. "Well, I suppose you'll have to stay with me then," he said, his tone sheepish. "If you wish to," he added.

Octavia ran at him, practically bowling Marley over in a bear hug about the neck. "Thank you! Thank you! That's all I've ever wanted since mother passed away."

Marley gingerly wrapped his arms about the girl, as if she were fragile glass. Maybe it was because he felt so fragile in this situation.

"I think we ought to leave these two alone to get better acquainted before we go into battle tomorrow," Remington suggested. Winn and Colt nodded in agreement. Family was sometimes all a man had. And to discover that he wasn't all alone in the world had to be a big jolt for Marley.

Glancing at his two brothers, one on either side of him as they walked toward Marley's house, Remington realized how important the bond he and his brothers shared really was. It had sustained them when their parents had died. It had given them a shared mission that had brought them back together when times were toughest. And in the end it would be all three of them who had to sacrifice to close the Gates of Nyx.

Remington wasn't sure he wanted to tell them that part yet. Tomorrow would come soon enough.

Chapter 23

China couldn't wait to get out of Rathe's personal domain. The moment she could, she'd focused on Remington and the ethereal thread that connected them so she could locate him and transport herself there.

Her body reformed from the dark particles of transport on a desert bluff at mid-afternoon. The welcome familiar scent of creosote and desert sage tinged the air, and the sun beat down on her hair and shoulders, warming the chill that had seemed to seep into her bones while she'd been in Rathe's presence.

She peered at the strange house with hooks and telescopes and mechanical arms that stuck out of the roof every which way, and the even stranger galleon airship docked nearby. She shook her head and smiled to herself. "You gotta give them credit for bein' a different sort of family." But it was the difference that appealed to her; it was what made Remington special.

With caution she approached the door. If Remington's stories about Marley were right, the inventor had Darkin detectors galore around his place.

As if on cue, a siren began to blare, and a panel in the roofline slid open. Out of it rose an enormous gun that looked like the big brother of the Blaster. The hum and buzz of it powering up to full strength shook the ground. Didn't Marley realize if he shot the thing he'd likely collapse the entire hillside and start a landslide that would wipe out the town in the valley below? A female mechanical voice began a countdown. *"Ten. Nine."*

The door opened, and Remington came strolling out and swept her up into his arms, swinging her around. "You made it! I'm so glad to see you."

"Eight."

"I, yes, um, Remington, the cannon?" She nervously glanced up and pointed at the Tesla cannon now aimed at both of them, the barrel throbbing with blue light.

"Seven."

"Marley! Your cannon is about to fire," he yelled.

"Six. Five."

In the doorway appeared a wiry man a bit shorter than Remington, with a stained leather apron over his work clothes and snow-white hair that didn't match his dark brows or the youth of his face.

"Well of course it is; she's bloody well Darkin, isn't she?"

"Four. Three."

Remington set her down, firmly wrapping his arm around her waist. "She's also on our side."

"Are you absolutely certain?"

"Two."

"Yes!"

"Fine." Marley pushed a button by the door, turned on his heel, and walked back into his house, leaving the door ajar behind him. Remington shook his head, and his warm gaze connected with hers. "Trust me he'll warm up to you once he gets to know you."

"That's not what Colt said."

"Colt likes to *think* he knows everything."

China raised a brow. "And you don't?"

His eyes sparked with mischief. "Ah, but that's the difference. You see, as soon as you tell me about the Gates of Nyx, I will know everything." He brushed a kiss on her forehead, and her heart sped up in response. Just having him touch her made breathing easier again. "Have I told you how glad I am to see you?"

She gave him a smile that came straight from her heart. "You might have mentioned it."

He laughed as they walked together into Marley's house. "Welcome to the strangest home on Earth."

Inside, Marley's house was packed to the gills. Bits of his tinkering and experimenting lay piled up and stacked on nearly every surface, leaving a trail between teetering stacks from one room to another. "I thought you said this was a home. It looks more like a laboratory exploded everywhere."

Remington gave her an affectionate squeeze. "The man's work has been his life until now." He steered her into the kitchen. There, sitting around a great oak worktable on bar stools, were Colt, Winchester, and Marley. With three big men in the kitchen, plus her and Marley, it was a cramped space.

Colt pulled at the brim of his hat. "China. Good to see you in one piece."

China snorted. "You're just saying that 'cause I brought your brother back in one piece."

He grinned. "True."

Remington glared at his little brother. "We've got more important things to discuss. Did you get anything out of Rathe?"

China gazed at the Hunter who held her heart. She wished she had better news; she really did. But she offered him everything she could. "He said the location of the Gates changes daily at sunset."

Remington cursed and slammed his fist down on the table, making Marley's instruments jump. "Then how are we supposed to locate the damn thing?"

"The Book of Jezriel," China and Marley said in chorus.

They looked at each other, surprised to have such knowledge in common.

Marley pointed at her. "You know about the Book of Jezriel?"

China shrugged. "Rathe said his once brother archangel had written down how to find the Gates. I guess he's like some anti-Rathe."

Remington noticed Marley's fingers close around the small iron key Octavia had given him. "You'll all excuse me for a moment." He hurried out of the kitchen, leaving them to stare across the worktable at one another.

Winchester locked gazes with him. "What do you make of that?"

"I think Marley's a bigger piece of this than we realized." He glanced at China. "You're absolutely certain that's what Rathe said?"

She nodded. "Where are the other Darkin?"

"Tessa and Lilly are aboard the airship, pulling together weapons and preparing for us to travel to the Gates, once we know where they are."

There was a great crash. They all ran. Marley was sitting on the floor. From the look of the chaos surrounding him, he'd knocked over a stack of boxes, which had toppled an array of cogs and gears into a selection of brass tubes and metal plates, sending all of it scattering like dominoes.

Remington offered Marley a hand up from the floor. "Marley, you need a housekeeper."

"Not a chance. I'd never be able to find anything, old chap. Did I ever tell you I was always the neat one in the family, until I lost Sephie?" Marley shook his head and frowned at the toppled boxes. "What the devil were those boxes doing there?"

Octavia's face peered around the edge of a doorway in

Marley's hallway. She bit her bottom lip, her blue eyes big and worried. "I'm sorry. I was trying to get to the power coils you had on the shelf," she said softly. "I didn't put the boxes back in place."

Marley twisted and looked at her with affection. "Not to worry. It's precisely what I would have done. Octavia, can you join us for a moment?"

He carried the locked, battered metal box to the table and laid it down. *Thump.* Octavia followed on his heels. The girl was wrapped in a work apron several sizes too large for her.

Marley glanced at her. "Did you ever see your mother unlock the Book of Jezriel?"

Her eyes darted between Marley and all the rest assembled there, and she shifted uncertainly on her feet. . . . "Are you sure—"

He laid a hand on her shoulder. "If it is to be of any use in saving the world, this is the time." He pulled the chain with the key she'd given him off his neck and handed it to Octavia.

She inserted the key into a keyhole in the box and twisted it twice to the right, then pushed a button cleverly hidden in the etched design of the box, and turned the key once counterclockwise. A series of metallic clicks sounded. *Snick.* The lid unlatched.

Marley didn't make a move to lift the lid. He glanced at them, each in turn. "Persephone was the keeper of the Book of Jezriel. Maybe the Hunters have had the knowledge of how to close the Gates far longer than they realized, but were waiting for the Chosen to do it."

"That's a damn sorry-ass excuse for not saving the world," Colt muttered.

Remington pinned his little brother with a look. Colt could be flippant because he didn't know that putting the Book of Legend back together required their blood sacrifice.

Winn leaned in closer. "So this will tell us how to reunite the Book of Legend and how to find the Gates of Nyx?"

Marley nodded.

They all held their collective breath as he lifted the lid of the box and pulled out the fragile pages. The book was like nothing Remington had ever seen. Instead of being written on paper, it was written on thin metallic sheets of gold, held together by rings.

"I can see why they boxed it up," Winchester said softly. "That's not something you just let lie around without people taking notice."

Marley carefully flipped the pages and frowned. "I can't read this. It's in some sort of code."

Remington groaned.

"What about Balmora? Could she decode it?" Colt suggested.

Everyone turned and looked at him. "What? It's a good idea, ain't it?"

Marley clapped him on the shoulder. "It's bloody brilliant." He turned to Octavia. "Can you transcribe these pages onto paper for me?"

She beamed. "Of course I can." She dashed out of the room and brought back parchment and a fountain pen and sat down at the table.

Colt stretched. "Well, looks like all we can do for a bit is wait it out."

Remington frowned. "How long do you think this will take, Marley?"

Marley's brows drew together over the rims of his glasses. "Once we have the transcription, I should be able to feed it into Balmora's decoding apparatus, and given the complexity of the coding, and the initial scan of—"

"How long, Marley?" Remington persisted, cutting off Marley's long-winded explanation.

"A few hours."

* * *

China sat on a tiny corner of a dusty settee in what must have been Marley's parlor before it had been taken over by his collection of experimental materials and books. There wasn't room in the kitchen with all the men, and she wasn't about to go make friends with the other Darkin ladies, so she'd left about the time Marley had gone to retrieve the Book of Jezriel.

While she'd been curious, she didn't doubt that her contributions at this point would be minimal. Better to give them space to do what they needed to. Despite what Remington had said while they'd been in the caverns below the temple, *they* were the Chosen. And they certainly didn't need her to finish the job they were destined to do.

Colt ambled out of the kitchen, stretching his long, lean body, arms over his head. He navigated the paths between the piles and stacks toward her. An uncomfortable embarrassment slid through her gut as he approached.

She'd pursued him so hard; it was ridiculous when she thought of it now. He stopped in front of her and crouched down, bringing them face-to-face.

"How you holdin' up?" he asked.

She gave him a weak smile. "Goin' to Rathe didn't help us much."

He grabbed her hand and gave it a squeeze. The zip she had once felt when he touched her was no longer there. It felt more . . . brotherly.

"Now don't go talkin' like that. It helped. You got Remington to Diego and, by the looks of things, a whole lot more. But I've been meanin' to talk to you since the airship took off in Tombstone." He glanced sideways as if trying to figure out how best to phrase his words. "You and me, we weren't right for each other."

China just stared at him. She knew that. Now. What she'd had with Colt had been only an illusion of intimacy and a relationship. A kid playing at being in love. But with Remington it was different. It reached soul deep and resonated within every cell in her being. She would do anything, be anything, to keep him alive and well. It wasn't a competition; it was a joining of forces, and it made them both stronger than they were apart.

"I know," she said simply without explanation. How could she tell him all that had passed between her and Remington? How she loved his brother. China realized with a start that it was the truth of it.

She loved Remington. And perhaps for the first time she felt loved in return, regardless of whether he had actually said it.

His eyes widened a bit with surprise. "Okay. Good. That's real good." He lifted a brow. "You're in love with my brother, ain't you?"

She couldn't stop the smile that spread across her lips. "There's just somethin' about you Jackson boys."

Colt chuckled. He lifted a hand as if taking an oath. "I tried to warn him about you, I swear."

Remington found China talking to Colt. But unlike before, when there was a snap to the air, this was easy, light. Old friends. He hadn't realized his stomach had hardened into a Gordian knot until it released.

"We're getting ready to try the code in Balmora."

Puffs of dust wafted into the air as China rose from the couch. She coughed and waved her hand about to dispel the dust. "I hope Balmora is better kept than Marley's house."

"Oh, I wouldn't worry about that none," Colt said. "He kinda fancies Balmora."

China shifted her gaze to Remington, questioning him with her eyes. He lifted his hand. "You'll see. She's really quite marvelous as far as inventions go."

Remington slipped a hand around China's waist as they

followed Colt through the stacks and down a hallway to a back room guarded by a bank vault door. China paused for a moment to look at the door. "That's some pretty heavy hardware to protect an invention."

"You haven't seen Balmora yet." For that matter neither had he. He'd only heard over-flowery descriptions from Marley as he'd worked on the machine.

Besides the glass-fronted bookcases that lined the walls, this was the most vacant room of Marley's home. In the center sat something large beneath the covering of a pristine white sheet.

Marley whipped the sheet away to reveal a mechanical woman who sat at an elegant polished cherrywood table. China gasped.

"She's beautiful," she murmured.

And she was right. Marley had outdone himself. Balmora was more art than machine. Flawlessly smooth silver skin formed a set of aristocratic features looking eerily similar to those of Miss Octavia, even down to the wide blue glass eyes. Her fat copper curls were held in an elaborate cog and jewel clasp. And while she was dressed in the fashion from twenty years ago, it was refined, made of polished brass, right down to the elegant edging of detailed brass lace. Set into her chest sat a red, heart-shaped jewel that began to glow once Marley had set the clockwork in motion by turning the large key behind Balmora's chair.

Her head lifted, and she blinked.

Marley came around from the back and clasped the papers in his hand. "Good day, Miss Balmora."

She turned to him in recognition. Over the sound of gears and clockwork clicking, they heard a tinny but musical female voice. "Good day, sir."

"We have a puzzle for you in code. Can you please translate? American English, please."

"Yes, sir."

Marley fed the papers one by one into the narrow slot on the top of the cherrywood table. The gears and clockwork whirred, and everyone held his or her breath.

"She's amazing," Octavia said, her voice full of admiration, her eyes fever bright. "And she looks so very like Mother."

A slight mist clouded Marley's eyes, making Remington's chest ache for him. Clearly Marley had created Balmora after his memory of his lost love. It was a bittersweet thing.

Balmora cocked her head to the side and blinked as if listening intently to something. "It is not in code, sir, but another language. Language: unknown. Shall I continue to translate?"

"Yes, please."

"The sooner the better," Colt muttered under his breath.

China shushed him with a finger to her lips. Remington tried not to smile.

There was the clacking sound of typewriter keys flying over paper. It fed up through the slot in the table into Balmora's metallic hands. "Shall I read the first page, sir?"

Marley glanced at Octavia, taking in her reaction, and nodded. "Proceed."

"And at the dawning of each night, the Gates of Nyx shall arise anew, so that none may use such power to their advantage over the mortal worlds. But on the day of the dark moon, when the Gates of Nyx be closed by the Chosen among all mankind, they shall rise up on a mountain in the sea. A mountain of fire by the name of Krakatoa. And there shall be the battle of all."

Chapter 24

For a moment, none of them said a word. They didn't even get to page two of the translation. They were stunned that the Book of Jezriel was so specific about the location of the Gates of Nyx. The only sound in the room was of their mingled breaths and the continued whirr and click of the mechanical Balmora as she continued to translate pages.

"Krakatoa? Where the hell is that?" Colt muttered.

Winchester shifted his weight from foot to foot. "We need a map."

"Follow me!" Marley barreled out of the room and down the hall with everyone in his wake. He stopped only briefly to rifle through a series of rolled maps stuffed into a large blue and white Chinese vase in the corner of his living room before continuing to the kitchen. He spread a map on the table, tracking his finger across the Pacific Ocean to a spot just north of Australia. "Krakatoa is a small island between the Sundra Islands of Java and Sumatra in the Dutch East Indies."

Remington whistled long and low, then looked up at his brothers. "How are we going to get there in time?"

"We fly," Winchester said matter-of-factly.

"I didn't know you intended to sprout wings."

"Very funny, Remy. We fly on Le Renaud's ship, the *Circe*. It can take us that far before the moon goes dark."

"That great hulk of a sea vessel with sails sitting out in the desert?" Colt asked.

"The very same. It got me and Tessa here; it can get us to Krakatoa."

They had a full complement of crew when they boarded. In addition to Marley and his brothers, the contessa, Miss Arliss, and China, Monica Nation and Captain Nation had arrived by horse, and both came aboard and were introduced to Octavia and Captain Le Renaud.

Since they possessed intimate knowledge of the Darkin realm and of Rathe's weaknesses in particular, the contessa, Miss Arliss, and China were all dispatched to concentrate on creating tactical plans for eliminating Rathe and the different Darkin they might encounter.

The Jackson brothers, Marley, and Octavia went to the workroom in the belly of the *Circe* to reunite the Book of Legend. And Captain Nation and his daughter were to work with Captain Le Renaud to strategize on the defenses of the ship.

China went with the other Darkin ladies, but found it difficult to sit still for long around the contessa and Miss Arliss. Both ladies looked so damn proper, and comfortable, in their long dresses. China was just happy to be back in pants again. The familiar garments were like long-lost friends she'd sorely missed while on her trek to the temple and back with Remington.

The contessa and Miss Arliss chatted together like familiar friends, leaving her to feel once again rather an outsider even in this small of a group. China cleared her throat. The contessa slowly shifted her glance in China's direction. "Did you have something to add, Miss McGee?"

"Look, I know that being Darkin and all you both think you have an idea of what Rathe will do."

"Oh I have a better idea than most," Lilly shot back. "I sold my soul to the bastard and served him for decades."

"And neither of us is actually Darkin any longer; we've both been stripped of our powers," added the contessa.

China's heart took a double beat. "You what?"

"I traded my powers to Rathe in order for him to spare Winchester," the contessa answered.

"He took mine in a bargain with Colt."

China bit at her lip. She *really* didn't fit in. They were mortal, human, once Darkin but no longer. "I-I didn't know such a thing was possible," she stammered.

The contessa poured out a measure of tea for each of them in the cups that were precisely laid out on the table before them in the small galley area of the *Circe*. "It is, but it is a terrible price to pay. We can no longer be of help to the Chosen by using our powers, so we must use what knowledge we have to defeat the enemy."

Screw that. China shoved back from the table. "You'll have to excuse me. You two might not be able to do anything with your powers to get back at Rathe, but I still can." She left the two mortals to their tea and scheming and stalked off to find out what the brothers were planning.

Once the Jackson brothers, Marley, and Octavia were all crammed into the workroom Octavia used aboard the *Circe* to mend and invent things, Marley and Remington cleared a space on the wide wooden workbench for the three pieces of the Book and the materials Marley would need to bind it back together.

"According to the Book of Jezriel, we'll need blood from each of you to form a paste that can bind it back together," Octavia told them briskly as she brought various jars and implements and laid them out on the workbench. The brothers hadn't stayed around long enough to hear the entire translation of the Book of Jezriel. That had taken hours. They'd left it to Marley and Octavia to sort out.

"How much blood?" Remington asked. He didn't mind giving some, but he didn't want to be too weak to simply fight it out if the whole Book thing fell to pieces.

Marley frowned and glanced over Octavia's shoulder at the text. "It doesn't specify. It only says that the blood must be added in order of birth and gives a specific mixture of mastic, gold, and herbs to mix into it."

"Sounds like a bunch of hocus-pocus to me," Colt muttered.

"It worked well enough when I sent you back to Rathe's domain to fetch Miss Lilly," Marley countered tersely.

"You went to Rathe's?" Winchester scowled at Colt.

Colt pulled back his shoulders and leveled his gaze at Winchester, challenging him. "I sold half my soul to Rathe to save Lilly."

Remington's chest contracted around his heart. Colt was half Darkin? Holy hell. The world really *was* ending. It was a damn good thing Pa wasn't around to see this happen; it would have killed him all over again.

Winchester shook his head. "I warned you, boy. There's no goin' back on something like that."

Colt's jaw jutted as he clamped his teeth together and stared Winn down. "Worth it. Can we get back to what's important here?" Colt's demeanor was a mixture of dare and regret. It was clear to Remington he didn't like what he'd done, despised it, but would do it again in a heartbeat if it meant saving the woman he loved.

"Look, I did what I had to do, and I wasn't asking your permission."

Remington clamped a hand on his little brother's shoulder. "You had your reasons," he said softly. He couldn't keep the ache out of his voice, but he wanted to let Colt know he accepted his choice.

"What is wrong with all of you?" China blurted. "This is fantastic! This could change everything!" All three Jackson brothers turned in unison and stared at her as if she'd just sprouted out of the earth fully grown. She'd in fact slipped in when they weren't paying any attention since she'd felt more at home with the brothers than she did with their mates.

"When you use that Book to seal the Gates, they will fall, and there will be hell to pay. There's no way a regular Hunter is going to survive that. And since it must be one of you to close the Gates, then as half Darkin, Colt is the logical choice. He's the only one of you who has a chance to survive."

The Jackson brothers glanced at one another, a silent communication passing between them. They were hesitating, not knowing if this would be the last they'd ever see each other once this was over. There wasn't time to ponder and debate the decision; they only had a short time to plan!

China speared Colt with a direct stare. Looking at him now she wondered how she'd ever been attracted to him. Compared to Remington, Colt was a rough imitation. "You said if I made it through, protected your brother's back, and found the last piece of the Book that we'd talk about what you owed me. Well, time to pay up."

His lip curled. "And you want me to risk my *life*. That's your price?"

"Not my price, Colt. *The* price. There was never any question that closing the Gates of Nyx would require sacrifice. You gonna be man enough to do it?"

His eyes narrowed, determination streaking through his blue eyes. "I was always man enough, but now I'm Darkin enough too," he shot back.

China gave him an approving nod. "Then we'll do it

together." She turned to Remington. "I'll stay with him and we can transport back to the ship."

Remington grabbed hold of her, his hand sliding up to cup her cheek in a touch so tender it almost broke her heart. His body was stiff, as if he were in pain, and his fingers trembled against her cheek. His eyes said everything he couldn't. Anguish filled him that he couldn't protect her. He feared for her.

Loved her.

The recognition that it was there in his eyes, even if it still went unspoken, both shocked and thrilled her.

"You don't have to do this."

"You know I do." China placed her hand over his, holding his cold fingers against her cheek, breathing in the familiar scent of Bay Rum, possibly for the last time. "I'm the only one who can."

The hell of it was she was right. "I know, but that doesn't mean I have to like it."

"I'm not asking you to like it. I'm asking you to let me go."

There was nothing harder than letting the woman you loved go into danger and knowing there was damn little you could do to protect her. Remington pulled her close. "I can't until I take care of something."

"What's that?"

He pulled her up tight against him, bringing them flush together from chest to toe.

His mouth captured hers like she was his last breath. He poured his heart and soul into the kiss, trying to tell her without words what he'd only just discovered: he loved her. She was the best thief that ever lived because she'd managed to steal the one thing he'd been certain no one ever could: his heart.

Her lips, soft and pliant, turned demanding. All the pent

up frustrations, the worry, the fear unleashed in a storm of want and need. The realization that he loved her made him pull back and take a good long look at her. His heart fractured when he realized this might be their last kiss. So he kissed her again.

"You two about done? We got a world to save, and we're on a tight schedule," Colt taunted.

Remington held her close for just a moment longer, then took a deep breath, spiked with the scent of vanilla and something uniquely China, and reluctantly released it. "Let's go."

Ten minutes later Marley had them lined up, forearms bare beside the workroom table in the belly of the *Circe*. Marley sliced a small line on the right forearm of each of them, collecting the blood in a black bowl. "Here, put a bit of this on the cut so it'll stop bleeding and heal faster," he instructed as he tossed a vial of black powder to Remington.

"What's in it?"

Marley gave him a pulsating glare. "Do you really think now is the time to worry about such things? My Uncle James was a pharmacist. Just use it."

Marley turned away and worked with Octavia on mixing the binding blend.

He smeared the black, viscous paste on the binding edge of each piece and on the strip of imprinted leather he'd laid out on the table. "Each of you pick up the piece of the Book you brought with you. Careful of the binding blend; we need every drop."

"Winchester, you'll need these," Octavia interrupted, handing him a pair of leather gloves. "Don't want to touch the pages bare-handed."

Colt took a step back. "I vote Winchester goes first."

"I second that motion," Remington chimed in.

Winchester shook his head, but there was a touch of humor in his voice. "Yer both yellow."

China was shocked at how these big men could be so careful with their hands when necessary, as each of them gently picked up a piece of the Book, cradling it like it was as fragile as a newborn. Remington's and Colt's pieces each had a piece of the original leather cover of the Book still attached. Winchester held his section of pages with care. He gently placed it, binding side down, on the center of the long strip of leather.

"I'll hold this in place while you boys put yours together. Remington, you next."

Careful to avoid touching his brother's pages, Remington placed his section of the Book on the leather, then carefully raised it up until it was flush against the middle section. Winchester slid his fingers out of the way. "Colt, your turn."

Colt carefully placed his part of the Book at the end of the leather strip, and like Remington pressed it slowly upward toward the center until it was flush with Winn's section. Winchester removed his gloves with help from Octavia.

Marley clapped his hands together, then rubbed them with satisfaction. Remington didn't miss the bead of nervous sweat that rolled down his friend's lined brow. "Excellent. That's half of it."

"Half? What's the other half?" Remington asked.

"We have to fold the leather around the Book and use the incantation from the Book of Jezriel to finish the binding."

Colt cut in. "Then what? Your Jezriel fella got anything to say about how we use it to shut the Gates?"

Marley blinked. "No. I suppose that might come from the Book of Legend itself once it's bound back together." He carefully smoothed the strip of leather over the spine of the three pieces as the brothers held them in place, and slowly began to chant.

It wasn't a language Remington recognized, but the fluid cadence of it charged the air with power. The small hairs on his skin lifted in response.

"Anyone else feel funny?" Colt muttered. All three of the brothers let go of the Book.

Beneath Marley's hands the Book of Legend began to glow with golden light. He backed up a pace as the Book levitated off the table and the pages began to flip rapidly, as if moved by an invisible hand.

"What's happening?" Winchester said under his breath.

Marley grinned. "It's working!" The pages stopped moving, and the Book came to rest on the table. There on the open page was an image of large, wrought-iron gates leading to a wall of Darkin flame.

Marley adjusted his glasses, pushing them up his nose a little farther. "If I'm reading this correctly—and my Latin is rusty, so you'll have to bear with me—it says the Gates of Nyx can only be sealed when the Chosen form an unbreakable bond between themselves and Darkin. The three guardians of the Gates must be placed at left right and center before the Book is thrown into the Darkin flames."

"What's that mean?" Colt prodded.

"We throw the Book at it," Marley said. "Literally. As for the unbreakable bond, and the guardians of the Gates, it isn't as clear."

"I wonder if the guardians are those squat stone statues?" China murmured. All eyes turned to her.

"But we lost the one," Remington said. His tone agitated.

China turned to Marley. "Are you sure it only says three guardians?"

Marley adjusted his glasses and looked again. "Yes."

China glanced from Marley to Octavia and back again. "Did Captain Nation bring his statues with him?"

"He did," Octavia said.

"We're going to need them," China said.

Remington glanced at the thick, completed Book of Legend. "And that's it? The completed Book, the statues and we're done?"

"Technically speaking. The Book must pass through the door to the other side to ensure it closes and is permanently sealed. The trick will be getting close enough to the Gates to place the guardians in position, then make sure the Book makes it through and into the Darkin flames."

"You're expecting opposition from Rathe?" Remington countered.

Winchester grumbled. "Of course Rathe is goin' to keep us from closing those Gates. He wants them flung wide open."

"We'll close them." Colt's tone brooked no argument.

"Well, there is another potential outcome," Marley said, shifting his weight from one foot to the other.

Winchester's gaze narrowed. "Out with it, Marley. What's the problem?"

"According to Jezriel, there's the potential of opening a rift. It's the reason the Gates were never fully closed. It's why the guardians are necessary."

A cold sensation slithered down Remington's spine. "Rift? What kind of rift?"

Marley glanced at him. "A time rift. A tear in the fabric of the universe, which could cause massive destruction."

The nasty feeling was correct. This wasn't good. In fact their efforts could likely cause a whole different set of problems. But then again, would there be a world for them to inhabit if Rathe were allowed to run it as he saw fit?

"Wait," Colt interrupted. "So you're tellin' us we either throw that Book in and tear up the universe, creatin' this rift thingy, or we don't throw it in and Rathe gets to let a bunch of his human-killin' children of the night through, and it all depends on a couple of stone statues?"

Marley rolled his eyes upward for a moment as if searching for the answer overhead on the beams of the ship. He looked Colt in the eye. "Yes. That's about the best approximation."

Winchester's face hardened, his jaw flexing. "We can't let the more dangerous Darkin through. You boys don't realize that the Darkin who are here ain't the bad ones. The ones we're familiar with, werewolves and vampires, shifters and demons are chicken feed compared to what he's got on the other side."

"We'll all go together to close the Gates," Remington said resolutely.

"Can't this ship go any faster?" Colt demanded of Octavia, his fingers curving over the butt of the revolver holstered at his hip. "Dark moon's rising tomorrow night."

"We'll be there in time," Marley assured them.

And true to his word, they arrived just before the sun set the following day. Tensions were running high. They could all feel it—that sense that Hell itself was about to be unleashed.

Remington and Colt leaned over the rail of the *Circe*. The sea below was a clear aqua blue that met in a level line with the vibrant orange and red band of the horizon of the sunset. Islands, some smaller, some quite large were scattered everywhere and clothed in a vibrant pattern of black volcanic rock and lush green vegetation.

"How the hell do we even know if it's the right island? There's so damn many of them," Colt groused. "It ain't like they're labeled like they are on the map."

"Look for the Darkin clustered around it, and you'll find it easily enough," Remington said, his tone flat as his eyes scanned the land and water below the ship.

In the distance he could see an oily blackness that surrounded a very small island between two much larger ones. Remington pointed. "I think I see it. Looks like Rathe has called them all to the party. Tell the captain it's time to take us down."

Orders were shouted across the decks and the brass wings that collected water folded into the ship's hull, letting the sails take them down as they billowed overhead, slowing their descent. The smell of brine grew stronger, along with the stench of sulfur.

"Easy on the main sail!"

"Aye, captain!"

The sun was setting, casting the white sails in shades of pink and coral. And the closer they got, the darker and more pervasive the Darkin presence became. They were in the water and the air; they occupied the land like a stinking, writhing plague.

Winchester had joined them at the rail. "They're all waiting for the Gates to appear, aren't they?" he muttered.

The sun slipped lower as they came to rest with a splash in the waters fifty yards from shore. Surf from the ocean pounded up on the rocks, sending a shower of salty cool spray through the air. The red rim of the sun sank beneath the edge of the darkening ocean, and a flash of brilliance from the island caused them all to hold their hands over their eyes.

Standing thirty-feet tall, the Gates of Nyx looked like they were made of wrought iron. They stood at the mouth of the volcano that spluttered and fumed, letting off great belches of steam and dark smoke.

"I'll be damned. It's real."

Winn glanced at Colt. "You doubted that?"

"Didn't doubt so much as had a shred of hope it was all some grossly misleading joke."

"Well if this is a joke," Remington said, cupping a hard fist with his other hand, "let's be the punch line."

Chapter 25

The men prepared to go into battle, loading up their weapons with Marley's special Darkin-killing ammunition. They grabbed a new Blaster, Colt's Sting Shooter, and anything else they could get their hands on. But when it came time to climb down the ladder and into the dinghy, Remington found their path barred by six women. China stood shoulder to shoulder with Lilly, the contessa, Captain Le Renaud, Octavia, and Monica Nation.

"You aren't going without us," Lilly said, blunt as could be. Her folded arms and grim expression showed their stance was nonnegotiable.

"Have you seen what's on that island?" Winchester shot back. "You'd be killed in no time flat. You aren't Darkin anymore. You're mortal."

The contessa came up to him toe-to-toe, nose to nose, her shoulders squared. "Have *you* seen what's on that island? You need all the help you can get, and while I may not be Darkin any longer, I know how they think, I know how to fight, and I know my brethren will listen to me still."

"Your . . . *brethren?*"

Suddenly the decks filled with spirals of dark smoke as

vampires began popping out of the ether faster than rats could multiply on a ship stocked with cheese.

A big grin spread across Colt's face. "Now that's more like it!"

Winchester glared at him, then fixed his gaze back on the contessa. "I don't want you to go."

"Do you think any of us wants any of you to go?" China snapped, looking right at Remington. "This isn't just a Hunter's battle; this matters to all of us." Behind her, several of the vampires nodded in agreement, crossing their arms.

Remington looked at them all. Well, if they were going to do this, then they might as well do it together. He climbed to the edge of the ship and held fast to the rope rigging. His clothing rippled and flapped in the evening breeze, ripe with the sulfuric stench of the multitude of Darkin waiting on the shore, ready to tear them to shreds.

"My friends"—his gaze drifted to Captain Le Renaud, to Captain Nation and his daughter, and to Marley—"my former enemies"—he nodded to the vampires—"my brothers." Remington locked eyes with Winchester and Colt. "Tonight we fight for our very existence. We fight not because it is easy, but because it is right. We join together in victory or in death!" A great roar rang up from the decks of the *Circe,* and it shook Remington to his core, swelling in his chest, filling it. He looked to China. She only had eyes for him. His whole world shrank for one second to the color of her eyes.

"To battle!" cried the vampires, and they began to puff into dark swirls of smoke. The moment between them was gone and replaced by a frenzied rush for the boats to go ashore, and in it somehow Remington grabbed China's hand, holding fast.

The closer they got to the shore, the quieter everyone became. Captain Nation and his daughter stared straight ahead. They held the three stone statues inside leather packs on their laps. Lilly entwined her fingers with Colt's, and Winchester wrapped his arm around the contessa, but no one spoke. The base of the Gates of Nyx, the hills, teemed with Darkin of all shapes and kinds. China stared at Remington. She'd only seen one person turn ice-cold in a similar way— his eyes going dead before he started killing everything in his path. And that person was Rathe.

The fact that there was *any* similarity between Remington and the archdemon lord forced a surge of bile up into her throat. She couldn't think of the man she loved being anything like the evil entity who sired and tormented her. Refused to. Remington would *never* be like Rathe. He would never harm her. At one time she'd thought that the absence of pain and humiliation was love, and now she knew differently. But the emotionless smoothness of his face, and the flat, faraway look in his eye made her shiver all the same.

Whatever switch had been flipped, Remington was now a killing machine.

"Let's go." He stepped from the boat into the warm surf, but there was no heat inside him. No warmth to be found. His belly was tight and cold, his mind focused on one thing and one thing only—destroying Rathe and closing the Gates of Nyx. A close third was survival, but he might not have that option. So be it.

His brothers flanked him, each of them carrying one of the guardian statues in a pack on his back. Behind them was a force of vampires bent on removing Rathe from power. It wasn't so much, Remington suspected, that the Darkin wanted to fight their fight with *them*; it was that they were more afraid of the unknown that Rathe was about to unleash. Their very existence might depend on siding with the Hunters. At least for now. Remington wasn't sure which side the Darkin would be on when it came down to who was about to win, and who was about to die. Their allegiance, he suspected, could be swayed.

They marched, two lines toward one another on the battle-field. Behind Rathe's forces rose the Gates of Nyx. A shimmering ethereal blockade that looked as if it were an elaborate, black iron gate. It stood ajar, the intricate scrollwork laced with magical, writhing green flame. It twisted and moved, like a living, breathing thing, huge and formidable. Through the narrow opening and out of the wall of flame behind the Gate poured more Darkin.

"How do we get close enough to throw the Book at the Gate?" Winchester shouted over the noise of shrieks and war cries and the crackle of flames.

Remington's heart pounded loudly in his ears and muffled the cacophony. He tightened his grip on the revolver in each hand. "We fight our way through."

"We're screwed," Colt muttered.

Remington lashed out at the oncoming Darkin forces, werewolves, demons with solid yellow eyes, shape-shifters, scoria soldiers, hellhounds, and fire wraiths. He killed whatever he could.

The brothers worked in unison like a finely tuned machine—one reloading his guns while the other two laid down a hail of Marley's special bullets into the oncoming Darkin. Marley's Gatling gun was a wonder, mowing them down into nothing but dust, but it wasn't enough.

By the wee hours of the morning, they pulled back, unable to take any more losses. Darkin could kill Darkin. None were immortal in this fight. The onslaught was too much and far greater than they'd feared, and they hadn't been able to get close enough to the Gates to place the guardians in position or throw the Book through the narrow opening.

Remington scanned the faces of both enemy and ally on the battlefield, looking for a trace of China. He spotted her blond hair flying in the wind as she shot down a hellhound and then two werewolves. The woman was fearless.

She caught his gaze. Her cheeks and clothing were smeared with black Darkin blood, and cuts that bled scarlet, which was her own. He motioned to her, and she came zigging and zagging through the battle toward him.

Before he could even utter a word, she kissed him hard, full on the mouth. He cupped her head, deepening the kiss, taking it like water to his parched soul. God he wanted to win. For her. For all of them. But it wasn't possible.

He released her, and she pulled back, checking the deep, gouged lacerations in his side. "Those don't look good."

"They're fine. I'll be fine," he lied. "We need to call a truce."

She bolted back from him, her eyes angry. "What?"

"We have to be strategic. Look around you; there's far more of them than there are of us. We're not making headway. The only thing that will stop any of this is if we get the guardians in position and Book through those Gates, and we must do it before sunrise. They aren't overrunning us because they are stalling. Time is running out."

China frowned. "What do you want me to do?"

"I want you and Colt to meet one-on-one with Rathe."

China thought about it. Two Darkin against one. Given, Rathe was an archdemon lord with a ton of tricks up his sleeve, but she was smart and resourceful, Colt had quick reflexes, and both of them had Darkin powers. It just might work. Especially if they played to Rathe's ego.

"Winchester and I will stay behind and—" Remington said.

"No. You won't."

He frowned. "I'm telling you how the plan is going to go."

She put her hand up. "And I'm telling you, if this happens, you and Winchester and any other mortal you give a damn about needs to be as far away from this island as the ship can fly. Colt and I can transport in an instant, but we won't be able to take anyone else with us in our weakened conditions. You stay, you die. It's that simple. At least Colt and I have a chance."

His frown deepened. "So we're all just supposed to fly away and watch from a distance?"

She gave him one curt nod.

Remington gathered her up into his arms and held her tight. "You're smart. I know you can do this. I know"—his voice cracked—"I know you can win."

A half hour later their forces had reassembled on the decks of the *Circe,* and preparations were underway for the ship to fly away from the island. The boilers were humming, and the huge propellers at the aft deck made a steady *whop,whop,whop.* Captain Le Renaud shouted orders at her crew, and the large brass wings of the airship were extended as they prepared for liftoff. The smell of smoke and sulfur, blood and gore hung heavy in the air around the island.

China wished she too were going far, far away, but instead she locked her gaze on Colt. He held the Book. She had taken the packs with the statues. "When we go to meet Rathe, you need to act like we're a couple still."

Colt frowned. "Now why the hell would that matter?"

"Just trust me on this."

"China, tell me what's going on."

"Rathe doesn't just want the Book, he wants to destroy the Chosen, especially you. I'm guessing your little deal with him pissed him off, and now he's expecting payback. He'll have taken the ship's leaving as a surrender. You and I are going in to talk terms."

Colt cursed under his breath. "I should've expected this. You get me into the worst situations, you know that?"

"It's a hard habit to break. But I promise, I'll get you out of this one too."

As the ship lifted into the air and the wind buffeted them, Colt clasped her hand. The instant their skin connected, they both began to dissolve into oily dark particles of smoke that twisted and moved off the ship and toward the mouth of the volcano—and the Gates of Nyx.

Particle by particle her body reformed itself. She hated to travel by transport, but there was no other way to get to the Gates without risking their mortal lives. And it had to be a Darkin in league with the Chosen to close them. Only then would there be balance, a chance to make the world right again.

Rathe waited at the Gates. They were halfway open now as the new moon rose. The wall of green Darkin flame filled the slowly widening gap, and his Darkin minions crowded around on either side.

He stood between China and Colt and the Gates, wearing a black top hat and a spotless black greatcoat. Beneath that was a tailed tuxedo jacket and an impeccable, crisp white shirt. He looked to all the world like a highbrow English lord about to go out for a night on the town. She could even smell the starch in his shirt over the vile scent of decay and death that permeated the air. China despised him. The waxy pale skin of his face stretched over his bones, making him look more like one of the walking dead than an archdemon lord.

"That form don't suit you, Rathe," she said, her voice full of distain and loathing. "You look like a sick old man rather than Lord of the Darkin."

One brow arched up in a questioning fashion. "Is that any way to greet your father?"

Colt stared at her, his mouth hanging open, confusion and doubt flitting through his blue eyes like bolts of lightning. "He's your goddamn father? You could have told me that!"

Ah, yes, but if I had, your reaction wouldn't have been

genuine. "Damned, yes. Father, no. He's merely the man who raped my mother then came back to try and enslave me after he'd tortured and murdered her."

Rathe smiled as if her recollection of the situation pleased him enormously. "I can see I left quite an impression on you."

China forced herself not to wince at his double entendre. The scar at the base of her spine throbbed. God how she hated him. Every fiber of her being pulsed with it. The urge to brand him straight in the forehead throbbed like a second heartbeat in her body, taking over her mind and pounding right behind her eyes.

"How delightful, my prodigal child by blood and my half-born Darkin returned home to give the Book of Legend to their father."

"Not. A. Fucking. Chance. In. Hell," China ground out.

A rumble of worried voices washed through the Darkin crowded on either side. Rathe squeezed his hand into a fist, and her airway closed off as her feet rose up off the black volcanic slag, lifted by a massive invisible hand. He shook her like a rag doll. "You will give me the Book or you will die. Both of you, and the rest of the Hunters and those who blindly follow them. You will all die, a slow, *excruciating* death. I will see to it personally." He waved a violent hand in demonstration.

China went flying to the side, her body slamming into the ground in a red-hot flash of pain. She struggled to her hands and knees, fighting the stars and blackening edges of her vision. Blood streamed into her eyes. A cheer shot up from the Darkin amassed there. She scrambled for the packs, feeling them with her fingers to make sure the statues were still intact after the blow. Her heart sank. One of them was smashed to bits by her fall.

"And you, Colt Ambrose Jackson, were your brothers surprised to find you were no longer one of them?"

"We didn't figure it mattered much."

Rathe's gaze snapped up, his vertical slits growing wide

with anticipation and delight. China gasped. Standing right behind Colt were Remington and Winchester. "Just because my brother is half Darkin doesn't mean he isn't all Jackson," Remington continued. "And just because we're not Darkin, doesn't mean we can't transport with a little scientific assistance."

Behind Remington two more people appeared. Lilly and the contessa. The men turned, looking surprised at their appearance.

"What are you two doing here?" Winchester growled.

"We know what needs to be done," the contessa answered as she stepped up beside him. "The unbreakable bond. It's love."

Rathe laughed. It was vile and repugnant, a harsh and grating sound that seeped into one's ears and slid oily and thick down one's back. China wanted to shut it out, wanted that familiar chill to leave.

"How very droll. Oh, China, you've done well. You've brought me all the Chosen, their feckless Darkin whores, *and* the Book of Legend. How splendid, daughter."

Colt and Winchester both glared at her as they grabbed hold of their women beside them, but Remington stepped away from his brothers. Winchester grasped him by the sleeve of his shirt, but Remington shook off his grip and came to stand beside her, taking her hand in his. "Don't even think about it. She's mine. I love her." He said it as much to Rathe as he did to his brothers.

Rathe's gross approximation of a smile grew even larger. "And to have them divided right when they need to be one, even better. I couldn't have asked for more." His malevolent yellow eyes, with the thin, reptilian vertical pupils, turned to her. "And now, since our bargain is complete, my dear, you may die."

Her gaze bore into Colt. "Throw it! Now!"

Colt hesitated for a moment, frowned, then twisted his body and released the Book of Legend, catapulting it end over end toward the Gates of Nyx. Pages fluttered as it shooshed toward the opening. A collective gasp rose up from the Darkin hordes.

China rushed forward trying to put the remaining guardians in place but was blown back off her feet by an invisible barrier. Rathe levitated and caught the Book in his hand. He made a mocking tsking sound and shook his head at Colt as he came back down to rest on the ground. "A nice throw, but hardly the stuff of legend." The Darkin cheered.

But the Book had come close enough to the Gates to change the Darkin flames, or perhaps it was because they were all united now, each of the Chosen with his mate. China wasn't sure which, but it didn't matter. The Gates creaked shut, sealing the Darkin portal between their world and Rathe's realm.

Now, instead of a wall of green, a blue vortex, twenty feet tall, swirled before the closed Gates. Was it the passage to other dimensions Marley had warned them about? There hadn't been time to put the remaining guardians in place before Colt threw the Book.

A fire wraith fell before Rathe at his feet. "Master! The Gates have sealed. What will we do?"

Rathe squeezed his hand into a fist, and the fire wraith toppled to the ground, struggling against an invisible force suffocating the life from it. The flames faded from its form, leaving nothing but a dried husk of ash behind. "Impertinent fool. The object was never to open the Gates permanently, but to open ourselves to even greater powers." He lifted his hands high into the air, and the blue light of the vortex pulsed like a heartbeat.

The brand on China's lower back began to throb and then burn. She arched forward, grasping at it with both hands, and screamed against the searing pain that ricocheted through her body, setting all her nerves on fire. Remington caught her as her knees buckled. "China, listen to me. We have to get you away from here. Away from Rathe."

Her whole body shook, racked by the pain, but she stood up, her hands balled into hard, whitened fists. She would not let him win this time. *"No!"*

China took the pain; she stuffed it down. It was how she had survived before; it was how she would survive now. She let the terrible pain create a burning fire within her, then focused that fire and let the transition take her. Remington backed away as her body morphed and changed into that of a giant hellhound. She was bigger than a locomotive, more powerful and pissed as hell.

The smug look on Rathe's face faded, the slash in his face falling into a grim line. "So is that how it is to be, daughter? You would use the power *I* gave you, what *I* made you, against me? I created you, you filthy half-Darkin bitch, and now I will do what I should have done long ago and destroy you, and the Chosen."

She relied on her mental communication with Remington to speak within this form. *I will kill him. Now. You, Winchester, and the ladies must leave.*

She reached down deep inside and pulled what energy she could and tried to transport Winchester and Remington back to the *Circe*. But in her current state it was too much of a draw. She couldn't maintain her hellhound form and transport the two of them.

She bellowed out an anguished howl of frustration and lowered her head, squaring her massive shoulders. She'd head butt that sadistic bastard into the next dimension. She charged at Rathe, and he dissipated into a curl of dark particles, leaving her to skid to a stop before she barreled straight through toward the vortex.

"I could have told you that wouldn't work," Winchester

called out. "That's how the bastard made sure I shot our mother."

Both Colt and Remington stared in disbelief at Winchester. "You shot Ma?" Colt sputtered. Lilly gasped.

Winchester's brows drew together. "Not intentionally. I was young, inexperienced, and aiming for him. We'll talk about it later, *if* we get out of here."

Remington gripped his shoulder in a show of support. It didn't matter what had passed. They were still family. No matter what had happened. He wanted to know, but it could wait. "*When* we get out of here," he shot back. Winchester glanced at Colt, and Colt nodded an affirmative.

Rathe reappeared, floating in midair as if he were seated on a chair, his legs crossed. "How touching, to see such family unity." He glanced in China's direction. "Nothing like our family, is it my darling?"

China roared, and chunks of rock from the rim of the volcano came loose and tumbled to the ground. Behind Rathe the Gates shook, and the vortex grew larger, the ominous blue swirls spinning faster and faster.

Fine. If the only way the Book would go through the Gates was if she took Rathe in too, so be it. She lowered her head, ready to charge, then started running.

"China, stop!"

At the sound of Remington's voice, she slid to a stop. *ZZZoott!* The blue bolt of electricity that came shooting out of the Blaster missed her hellhound nose by mere inches, slamming into Rathe. He went flying backward, carried by the blast into the vortex, clutching the Book of Legend in his hands, his mouth an open scream. The vortex exploded outward in a giant wave of electrical discharge as he disappeared.

The resulting shockwave blew them flat on their backs.

Winchester rotated his head and glared at Colt who was holding the smoking Blaster. "Why didn't the vortex disappear? Marley said throw the Book at it and it would shut!"

"We weren't able to put the guardians in place. They must have been what would prevent the rift from happening when the Gates shut!" Colt snapped.

The ground shook. Remington sat up, and so did the others. "I don't know, but something tells me we'd better not stick around to find out."

China let the transition warp through her system, shrinking and pulling her body back into its normal shape and size. And there was Remington, holding her up as her knees wobbled.

"How did they get here?" she murmured.

"Marley got us here. He has some evaporative transponder machine he used to get Colt into Hell. He reconfigured it to take us to wherever Rathe was."

"Can you use it to get back?"

Colt shook his head. "Nope. One-way ticket in."

"Then how do we get them out?" she muttered, then looked up into Remington's face. "I don't know if I have the ability to transport all of us."

"Looks like we have bigger problems than getting off this rock," Colt muttered. The Darkin masses had closed in around the six of them. There were no more coming through the Gates, but there were too many for them to fight alone and survive.

Remington set China on her feet and stood slightly in front of her. "If you want her, you'll have to go through me first."

"And me," Colt added.

"And me," Winchester said as the three of them stood shoulder to shoulder, a wall in front of the women.

China got up on tiptoe and looked over their massive shoulders. A werewolf came forward, ears pinned submissively against his head, tail between his legs, and knelt before them. "Sire, we only want to pledge our allegiance to our new queen."

"New queen?" Colt muttered.

China shoved between Remington and Colt and looked

down at the werewolf and then out at the crowd of Darkin that covered the island. Like a wave washing across the Darkin, they all sank to their knees and bowed their heads. "What is your will, Your Majesty?" the werewolf asked, baring his neck in a sign of submission. The ground beneath their feet shook and rumbled.

"I'll be damned," Colt murmured. "She's their queen now that Rathe's gone."

"Whatever you are going to order, you better make it quick," Remington said softly.

China lifted her head and took a regal stance. "Darkin, you are ordered to live in peace with the mortals and to disperse from this place." Like a forest fire, the air filled with hazy smoke as they began to twist and dissipate into dark particles.

Remington gazed at her with total confidence and kissed her hard. China let the welcome tingling sensation of it seep all the way to her toes, wiping away her pain, her doubts, and her fears. "Have I told you lately that I love you?" he said.

She smiled at him. "No, but I like the sound of that." He kissed her again for good measure.

"Do what you can. Get them back first, and we'll live with the rest." The trembling grew worse, and a loud cracking sound ricocheted off the stones as threads of red began to crack the surface of the molten rock beneath their feet.

"Colt, have you ever transported anyone before with your Darkin powers?"

He gave her a smug grin. "How hard can it be if you can do it?"

That sounded like Colt. "Good. You transport Winchester and Lilly, and I'll take Remington and the contessa." She pulled all her power together at her core and grabbed hold of Remington and the contessa. A renewed level of power sang and hummed in her veins. She was stronger than she'd been before, more powerful than she'd ever been. "Close your eyes; it'll help."

Remington laid a kiss on China's lips as they twisted apart into a spin of dark particles. When they came back together, they collapsed in a heap on the deck of the *Circe*.

The explosion, with the sound of a thousand cannons firing at once, rocked the ship backward several hundred feet on a blast of hot, sulfuric wind. Remington groaned and scrambled to his feet, then staggered to the ship's railing to peer out across the ocean. A black mushroom-shaped cloud billowed out of the heart of the volcano, glowing red lava covering what was left of the island, visible for miles even in the darkness. Most of the land mass was gone, and a rain of burning fire, brimstone, ash, and pumice fell from the sky. The searing heat of the air, the suffocating stench of sulfur stung his eyes, nose, and throat. The black spread out, devouring everything in its path.

Remington turned. "Captain! If you want to live, get us the hell out of here! Fast!"

The *whop whop whop* of the *Circe*'s engines grew faster, *whipwhipwhipwhip,* until the deck below them hummed and vibrated with their power. The sulfurous wind cut across the deck, buffeting them with gale force, so that they had to cling to anything they could to prevent getting blown overboard.

"Jumpin' Jehosophat. Did you hear that thing blow?" Winchester yelled, hair blowing wildly about his head as he staggered to the rail to join the others.

"I think the whole world heard it," Remington replied.

Colt, shirt billowing and hair whipping around his head, came up alongside them. "Do you think the vortex closed?"

"What?" Marley asked from behind them. "The Gates of Nyx didn't close?"

They all turned. He was worrying his hands, muttering to himself something that sounded like calculations.

Colt pulled off his hat and clutched it in his hand to keep

it from blowing away. "The Gates closed. We threw the Book in, just like you said. But we couldn't get the guardians in place in time."

"What do you mean? Are the Gates still there?" Marley asked, his gaze bouncing back and forth between the six of them.

"There was an odd swirling kind of blue spot between them," China offered. "Like a whirlpool of energy."

Marley frowned, his white hair waving about manically in the wind. "How big?"

"About twenty feet in diameter," Remington told him. It might have been larger, but he'd been too damned worried about China to pay that much attention. He looked at her, loving the smudges on her face and the triumphant glow about her.

"Twenty feet? Twenty feet!" Marley threaded his fingers through his already wild hair, making it stand askew even more.

Octavia tugged on Marley's sleeve. "It could very well be a time rift!"

Marley glanced at her. "I think you may be right!"

Winchester cleared his throat. "Well, I don't know if it makes any difference, but Rathe and the Book got blasted right into it."

Marley looked a bit startled. "I thought you threw the Book into the Gates?"

"They closed because of the unbreakable bond. The Book went through the vortex because Rathe just happened to be holding it at the time," Remington explained with a grin.

Marley mumbled. "Most intriguing. This could require further research."

Remington looked over his shoulder at the red glow that lit up the sky from the island. "I don't think there's anything left, Marley."

"What heading, Mr. Jackson?" Captain Le Renaud asked.

"Take us home, Captain." He had never really thought of Tombstone as home; home was not anywhere really. But things were different now. He was different. The idea of putting down roots in one place without the constant threat of Darkin appealed to him.

China leaned on the ship's rail, staring out at the chaos on the horizon as it became smaller and smaller. He walked to her and she slid her fingers into his and gifted him with a smile that could break a man's heart. The wind caught her blond hair and sent it spiraling out behind her head like a golden sail.

He used his hold on her to pull her into his arms and clasped her lightly about the waist. "You make one impressive hellhound, and an even more impressive Darkin Queen."

A bubble of laughter welled up from inside her. "Don't you forget it."

He kissed her lightly, just a brush of his lips over the silk of hers, but it made him remember just how spectacular making love to China could be. "I thought you were in love with my brother."

"So did I. Once." She brushed her fingers gingerly through the hair at his temple. "But I realized it was only a silly competition between us—who could best the other, who could win."

Remington flinched. "I don't like to lose. You know that, right?"

She offered him a sly, knowing smile. "But that's just it. With us it isn't a competition. It's a joining of forces. We're stronger together than we are apart."

"Two halves of the same whole?"

She laughed and kissed him. "See, we're even beginning to share a brain."

"Oh, don't ever accuse me of that. I can't hope to understand the way you think."

Her gray eyes turned misty and soft and full of love as

she laid a hand tenderly against his cheek. "But you at least try. That's more than anyone has ever done for me."

Remington brushed his thumb over her bottom lip, marveling at the softness of it, at how this woman could be so tough and resilient and yet still had the biggest heart he'd ever known. She was smart, strong, and sexy, and she brought out the best in him. "It's because you're special, China McGee. There isn't a woman on the planet like you."

"I know."

He laughed. "You're part of us now, you know, this crazy, mixed-up family of mine. Are you sure you're up for the challenge?"

She glanced at Colt who was holding Lilly about the waist, his hands fisted in her flaming hair, and at Winchester who whispered things into the contessa's ear, and at Marley who had his arm around his daughter's shoulders. "Yes, we are a family, aren't we? A crazy, mixed-up family. But you know me, I'm always up for a challenge."

Remington hugged her close, and he never planned to let go. "That's my girl."

"I *am* yours. *All* yours."

"I know."

Author's Note

In every bit of fiction there's hidden a kernel of truth. In the case of the Chosen, submarines were in use far before 1883 during the Civil War. While my version is a little more advanced (taking on some qualities of those built a bit later during 1914), the basics, including pressurization under water at depth, air scrubbers, and more were already in use before my story would have happened. If you'd like to know more, check out www.navyandmarine.org/ondeck/1862 submarines.htm

And while they didn't have a name at the time for the psychological difficulties China endures in respect to her relationship with her father, Rathe, where an abused individual identifies and can even defend his or her abuser, we know it today as Stockholm Syndrome.

The Temple of Niches aka the Temple of El Tajin, where I have the last piece of the Book of Legend hidden, is in fact a real place, once occupied by natives who were eventually subdued by the Aztecs. These natives did help the Spanish conquistadors in a plan to bring down the Aztecs, which ultimately failed before their culture was overtaken. For more, start here: http://en.wikipedia.org/wiki/El_Tajin

And there are many, many accounts of the explosion of the now famous Krakatoa on August 26–27, 1883, which killed more than 36,000 people and was at the time the loudest explosion ever heard, with about 13,000 times the nuclear power of the Little Boy bomb that annihilated Hiroshima, Japan, during World War II. I imagined if I were going to make something seem like the end of the world at that time, this would have been the closest thing to it.

Keep reading for THE INVENTOR,
a bonus novella
previously available only as an eBook.

Sir Marley Turlock doesn't normally bother with flirtation. He's an inventor, a scientist, not a gadabout. And the floor of the inaugural London Aeronautical Exhibition, just before he presents his groundbreaking new device to the Queen herself, is not the place to change his habits toward the fairer sex.

But Lady Persephone Hargrieve has her delicate fingers engaged in the innards of his device before Marley can catch his breath at her beauty. He's never met a woman like her— with a fiery intelligence to match his own, a genius for mechanics, and more secrets than he can guess.

Of course, Sephie's secrets aren't all innocuous tricks to make the gears spin smoother. It's no coincidence that she's turned up to investigate Marley's machines—if they're good enough, if he can be trusted enough, they might save the country. Even if along the way she ends up losing her heart . . .

Chapter 1

London, 1868

It was all wrong. Horribly, horribly wrong.

Marley Turlock fisted the missive into a ball in his pocket. Her Royal Majesty, Queen Victoria informed him that she was looking forward to seeing his work on the Sound Transmission Auditory Ranger device.

A prestigious honor to be sure.

Unfortunately, he couldn't make the damned thing work.

He flipped another lens down on his specially designed goggles to peer more closely at the complex maze of tubes, wires, gears, and pistons within his machine. The buzz and hum of voices in low, excited conversation reverberated throughout the expansive space of the Crystal Palace. The sound bounced back from the translucent panes of glass making up not just the walls, but the ceilings of the exhibition hall. Everyone was excited about the world's first Aeronautical Exhibition and the possibility of manned flight. He would be thrilled as well, if he could get the damned device to work as it should. He'd been working so hard on his airborne electrical transmission enhancer that he'd not spent quite enough time on the STAR.

Early morning sunlight, buttery and soft, illuminated his display area and the walkways at the southern end of the great building. The odors of grease and new paint mingled with expensive cigar smoke and heavily perfumed humanity. But none of it sank in. Marley was too focused on getting his invention up and running before they opened the doors to the mass of people waiting outside, tickets in hand.

Clearly in between disassembling the complex device in the laboratory and transporting it to the Crystal Palace, either something had gone missing or been damaged. Marley pulled back the spectro-photometric oglifiers from over his eyes and stared at one of his recent inventions, the one that was supposed to launch his career to a whole new level. The extended brass goggles with their various additions and multiple lenses made him feel a bit like a demented horned beast.

"Damned and blast. Just wait until Her Majesty sees this. I can wave fare-thee-well to becoming the top candidate for her lead royal scientific advisor for certain," he murmured to himself as he wiped the thick, dark grease from his fingers.

"Is that so?"

Marley cringed, knowing from the tenor of the voice alone that he'd sworn in front of a woman, a most ungentlemanly thing to do. He whipped around. No one who wasn't an exhibitor at the great inaugural Aeronautical Exhibition was supposed to be within the inner sanctum of the Crystal Palace yet, and he sincerely doubted there were any females displaying inventions at the event.

Burnished copper curls framed a heart-shaped face and made the young woman's eyes turn an intriguing shade of cornflower blue. Her chin was stubborn, but her features aristocratic. The smell of flowers—hyacinth, he thought—perfumed the air around her. While he could create mechanical marvels, he could not manage to link two cognitive words together in response to her comment.

The sensation taking over his body was not unlike being

woken from a particularly vivid dream. He'd heard his cousin talk of women who stole one's ability to breathe, but until this moment he'd never met such a paragon. He managed to gather enough moisture in his mouth to respond finally. "Sir Marley Turlock, at your service, and whom do I have the pleasure of addressing?" His pulse roared so loudly in his ears, he wasn't sure he'd be able to hear her.

She glanced quickly over her shoulder and held up her pristine white-gloved hand to partially cover her mouth, as if she spoke a most important secret to him. "Lady Persephone Hargrieve. I really shouldn't be here as yet. My father is currently putting the finishing touches on his own display, but your machine looks utterly fascinating. I couldn't resist finding out more about it. What is it?"

Marley wasn't the only inventor showcasing new ideas or even plans for ideas not yet built. "It's a Sound Transmission Auditory Ranger device."

"And what does it do?"

"The STAR functions as a sonic tracking and wind measurement device for guiding air flight carriages."

"Air flight carriages?"

"Yes, well, gazing about it's not hard to see there will be scads of them flying groups of people about in the not too distant future. What we lack, however, is the means to prevent them from colliding with one another while in flight and the means to determine the wind strength and flow while they are airborne. Now, this device, based on the internal ear of a bat, reconfigured mechanically to—" Marley stopped himself mid explanation.

By the look in her wide blue eyes, he could tell she was interested, but that vivid sparkle in her eyes indicated far more. Inventor's heat they called it, that unique quality among those so dispensed to invention that their brains became fevered by the rush of ideas.

"Is there something you noticed?" He glanced back at his

machine and readjusted the audio projection tube that looked as if it might have tilted out of place.

"If this is bat-like, then does it emit high-pitched sounds?"

"It both emits and receives them, my lady."

"And that bit, there." She lifted her pale blue skirt in a thoroughly unladylike manner, enough to step over the thick black velvet ropes that separated the walkways from the exhibits. In the process she completely exposed her neatly little buttoned up white boots and shapely ankles beneath layers of ruffled petticoats. His body took notice. "Does that rotate the emitters and receivers?"

Marley swallowed hard. Blast. He hadn't considered that. Rotation would have been most useful. "No, but it should."

She worried her soft, rose-colored bottom lip between her even white teeth, then flicked her inquisitive gaze to meet his. "Do you mind if I take a closer look at it?"

He was still so fascinated by her mouth that it took him a moment to realize she'd asked him a question and another for him to respond. "Are you sure you want to? You'll likely mar your gown and gloves."

She waved her hand in dismissal. "Pish tosh. A little bit of good grease never harmed anyone."

Most unusual for a lady. His own bevy of six aunts had made it abundantly clear on several occasions that such things were precisely what females concerned themselves with. Marley hesitated an instant. He'd never let anyone other than his cousin Thadeus assist him with his inventions before. But then, to be honest, he'd never met any female quite like Lady Persephone Hargrieve before. She was a heady combination that left him stunned.

He wasn't at all sure what to make of her. Most ladies wouldn't be caught dead with a mechanic's wrench in their hands or dark grease marring their pale skin. He'd thought that might dissuade her. Apparently not. Clearly his Aunt

Lydia, Thadeus's mother, had never met a woman like Lady Persephone either.

"Of course, if you wish, please take a look," he finally said.

She ripped off her white kidskin gloves, stuffed them into her beaded reticule, which she tossed aside, then began tearing at the wires and snatched up a wrench, tweaking at the bolts to rework his machine. Her hands were so slender and dainty that she was able to easily reach into places between the gears that would have required an extendable wrench for him to access. She worked so fast, Marley barely had an opportunity to do more than gawk stupidly, enjoy the fragrant scent of her, and hand her tools to assist as she tinkered with his invention.

She was brilliant. That was the thought that crowded out nearly every other in Marley's mind for a full minute. Everything she was doing made perfect, logical sense. Not only did she create rotation of the mechanism, she managed to find the connection he had missed. A wire deep within the machine that had lost the bolt holding it in place.

"You're absolutely right. If we modulate the frequency here, and make it rotate, then we could easily determine not just what is in front of the air carriage, but what is to either side, behind, and below it as well. Well done, my lady."

Persephone glanced at him, her skin growing warm from the color creeping into her cheeks. No one had ever complimented her tinkering skills before, quite the opposite in fact. Having someone as accomplished and brilliant as Sir Turlock give his approval to her work was a wondrous thing. Little bubbles of joy fizzed and welled up in her bloodstream like fine champagne.

"Thank you. It's not often I get a chance to work on a new invention."

Marley grinned, and he was twice as handsome when he looked pleased, and Sephie found herself growing far too warm.

"This is nothing," he said as he handed her a towel to wipe her hands. "You ought to see the grand project I'm working on in my laboratory right now. It could bolster the industrial revolution in a whole new way, provide electricity to thousands based on extracting static electrical energy from the atmosphere over water and then transmitting it in a concentrated charge. Enough to supply several villages and factories at once." From the glint of determination in his eyes, she could tell his mind was fevered with inventor's heat even as they stood in the midst of one of the most fascinating exhibitions of the decade.

He was close enough now that she could detect the faint odor of Bay Rum aftershave on his skin. The smoothness of his well-shaped jaw and chin was evidence he'd shaved only a few hours ago. She fidgeted, wondering what they might feel like beneath her fingers, perhaps even her lips.

She hadn't expected to be attracted to Sir Turlock. Far from it. From the description her father's protégé Lieutenant Frobisher had given her, she'd expected a mousey little man, all glasses and intellect. Instead, Sir Marley Turlock was a man who appeared lean, fit, and strong—able to move the great machines he built with his own power. And he was a good head taller than she was. In short, he was very different from the wealthy and titled men with Legion connections who had been parading before her nearly her whole life. His fierce intelligence and easy smile were far more attractive to her than any number of stories of military skirmishes.

She caught his curious brown gaze, flecked with the most interesting bits of gold, and realized he was waiting for a response from her. What had he said before she'd gone all featherheaded for a few seconds? Grand Project. Supply. Electricity for everyone.

"Electricity? Why ever would people want that, to electrocute themselves?"

The inventor shook his head. "I think one day soon, people will run entire factories on it; it's far cleaner than steam or coal-fired engines. No more foul-smelling oil or coal smoke, no more candle fires. Just think of it. Electricity pulled right from the air."

Preposterous, and yet, possible. She supposed that those without an abundant supply of water for a good supply of steam power in places like the great deserts of Africa or far inland from the coasts would find it useful. Perhaps even people in the highlands of Northumberland. Perhaps that was why her father had encouraged her to check on Sir Turlock's machines. She pursed her lips and tapped her chin. "That's an interesting thought. I would love to see your laboratory some day."

Marley glanced around, and by the puzzled then agitated look on his face he must have seen it was already far later in the morning than either of them had realized. People were already milling about through the exhibition, paper programs and exhibit maps in their hands. He took off his stained brown leather apron, casting it aside, then pulled the pocket watch from his elegant brown and gold brocade vest and flipped it open. "I think we've quite lost track of time."

Heat flooded her cheeks, and Sephie was suddenly aware of the people staring curiously at her. Her father would be furious. She was to have remained as unobtrusive as possible. That was the mission. She should get back to him as quickly as possible. "Oh dear."

"My lady, is something the matter?" His genuine concern was touching.

"Oh no. No, no. I find your work fascinating. It's just that . . ."

"That what?"

"My father. He won't approve of my interest." Specifically her interest in Sir Turlock, rather than his machines. Especially if she considered her father's grand plans to marry her off to his protégé, Lieutenant Frobisher. She snatched up her reticule, pulled out her gloves, and quickly began smoothing them onto her hands. There was no time to think on such things now. Her father would be waiting on her.

"But you're a brilliant mechanic."

Sephie couldn't help herself. She smiled, and her heart beat a little faster. The open, honest look of his face said more than his words. He wasn't the kind to needlessly flatter a woman. He meant precisely what he said. The slight coloration to his face creeping up from beneath his neck cloth told another story. He'd been bolder with her than he normally was with females. He was simply charming.

"That's kind of you, Sir Turlock. Not many would have allowed me the opportunity to work on such a personal project, and for that I shall always be grateful."

"But surely your father recognizes you have a talent for this."

She buttoned up the small ivory buttons along each wrist, encasing herself once more in the guise of a perfectly genteel lady. "He sees my preoccupation with mechanics and science as extremely discomforting, but occasionally indulges me nonetheless. Like today in bringing me along to the exhibit. He's one of the Queen's primary advisors. He thought it would be educational for me to see how our great monarch is protecting the empire's position by supporting science and aeronautical invention."

A thick lump formed in the back of Marley's throat, making it difficult to swallow his own saliva. Chances were good that he'd already compromised his chances of getting into the Aeronautical Society of Great Britain by allowing this young woman to tinker with his work. From the state of his hands alone he knew he likely had dark grease smears on his face.

"What are those?" Her eyes glittered as she nodded toward the specially modified goggles atop his head. Just having her lean close again brought another assault of improper thoughts.

"Spectro-photometric oglifiers. I use them to detect leaks and as protection when welding or soldering on piping."

"Are those your own design as well?"

Marley smiled as much as a schoolboy locked for the night in a sweet shop. "Of course."

"Lady Persephone Hargrieve, please report to the rotunda." The commanding boom rattled the glass panes of the Palace.

Several people stopped and gazed about as if wondering where the enormous sound had come from. Lady Persephone sighed. "My father. His voice amplification device. He's planning for the future of communication between airships."

Marley nodded. He was loath to see her go, but at the same time very aware he had a job to do. He could not ask her to stay. "Very sensible of him."

Lady Persephone picked up the edges of her ruffled skirts and turned to leave, but hesitated. "It was lovely to meet you, Sir Turlock."

"You as well, my lady. I hope we meet again someday."

She gave a small nod and an encouraging smile in acknowledgment, then turned, stepped over the rope, and blended into the growing crowds, the powder blue of her gown disappearing among the black and brown suits and occasional wide skirts.

A heaviness settled in Marley's chest that he didn't recognize. He was sad to see her go. It wasn't often that he saw someone who showed the same preoccupation he did with invention. But it was more than that. He'd never believed all the balderdash about love at first sight spouted off by poets, but perhaps there was something to their fanciful thoughts after all. He'd certainly never been so affected by a woman in his life as Lady Persephone Hargrieve—and he craved more.

It wasn't until later in the afternoon that a very well dressed older man, with perhaps the tallest black top hat Marley had ever seen, approached him. His great white mutton-chop sideburns and an equally large waxed mustache added to his impressive look. The crowds parted then flowed back in his wake as if a sea before the prow of a legendary ship. People whispered behind gloved hands and stared at the man's back.

Marley suddenly had a reason to calculate what his association with Lady Persephone might cost him. His heartbeat picked up tempo, pounding hard at the base of his throat. She walked a step behind the gentleman, and they shared the same shape to their noses and chins. It had to be her father, or another close male relation. Either way a sense of foreboding swished in an oily slick sensation through his stomach. The man smelled of expensive tobacco and gunpowder, and looked deadly serious.

"Sir Marley Turlock?"

Marley tugged at the edge of his top hat in deference. "I am, sir. Whom do I have the pleasure of addressing?"

The gentleman extended his hand. "Lord Hargrieve. Pleased to make your acquaintance."

"The honor is mine, my lord." He took Lord Hargrieve's hand and found his almost crushed by the older man during their brief handshake.

"My daughter has been telling me in some detail about your work." He glanced at Lady Persephone. "I hope she wasn't a bother with her questions earlier."

Marley's gaze flicked to her. What exactly should he say? Her white gloved hands were gripping one another tightly enough to pucker the fine white kidskin that covered them. She was as uneasy and agitated as he was.

"No bother at all, I assure you."

Lord Hargrieve glanced back at his daughter and then locked gazes with Marley. An invisible electrical current to the air raised the hair on Marley's arms and neck. Clearly her father thought there was more going on between the two of them than seemed proper. And while Marley might have considered such things in the privacy of his own thoughts, he'd certainly never voiced them aloud. Lord Hargrieve's daughter was beautiful, but Marley had his own ambitions and no time for the distraction of female company, even if she was the most stunning combination of beauty and brains he'd ever seen.

"I understand you are currently one of Her Majesty's favored inventors," Hargrieve said.

Marley straightened his shoulders a bit more, pulling himself back to focus on Lord Hargrieve. "I aspire to become the head scientific advisor to Her Majesty."

Beneath the wide white mustache, Hargrieve's lips twitched. Marley hoped it was either amusement or approval, but he couldn't tell for certain.

"Excellent, sir. Most excellent. I should like an opportunity to talk to you further about your ideas for electricity. Would you be available on Monday?"

Marley bent his head slightly, forcing his gaze to remain fixed on Lord Hargrieve rather than stray toward his daughter. "Of course, my lord."

Lord Hargrieve reached into the double-breasted fold of his dark suit jacket and pulled out a gold card case with an enameled top featuring a scene of hunting hounds. He pulled a cream-colored card from the case and handed it to Marley. "Give this to my butler when you come by."

Lord Hargrieve and his daughter turned nearly in unison and disappeared into the crowd. There was a sudden rush of eager and chatty onlookers at Marley's exhibit, firing questions off like rapid gunfire about his machine.

He answered as best he could, while still seeking out glimpses of Lord Hargrieve and his daughter. The chatter was silenced moments later by an even more impressive presence than the Hargrieves. He could hear her approach before he even saw the Queen as whispers of "Your Majesty" rippled through the crowd. Bows and curtsies ebbed and flowed about the Queen and her scarlet-coated guards as they passed.

Marley whipped his black top hat from his head and went down on one knee as the Queen approached. "Rise, Sir Turlock. Is this the mechanical wonder of which you wrote to us?"

He stood, and his gaze lowered so he could connect with hers. It was hard to imagine that a woman so tiny was the ruler of half the known world. She was a conundrum. A widow who still ruled society. A powerhouse whose empire spanned the globe, and yet a good foot shorter than himself. "It is, Your Majesty."

She paused for a moment, her keen gaze roving over the machine. "It looks very impressive. Have you tested it as yet?"

"Not this version, Your Majesty. There have been modifications made only recently that I think will even better serve Your Majesty's requests. I was hoping to do so in conjunction with the test of my latest invention that is designed to create an airborne power source to fuel engines, factories, and even towns."

"Quite so. Please see to it you inform us of your test plans. We are very interested in your work, Sir Turlock. Very interested."

A giddy wash of delight sparked through him, like the shock off of an electrical wire. The Queen liked his work. He still had a chance! "Of course, Your Majesty. I am ever your servant." He bowed again.

The crowd parted before her as she swept away to another exhibit in the hall.

Now the crowd clamored even more. Before the end of the day Marley had several orders for other inventions of his as well as design requests for a few things he'd never considered. Thadeus was going to be elated when he heard. Their fledging operation was certain to get support now, giving both of them a reason to be free of their mothers' worrisome diatribes on trying something more suited to a gentleman.

Today might have started out horribly wrong, but it was definitely looking up.

Chapter 2

The next day, Marley and his cousin Thadeus should have been working, but instead Marley was toiling and Thadeus was peppering him with questions. They were in their somewhat damp laboratory in the basement of Bostwick House, which belonged to Thadeus's father.

Thankfully they weren't dependent on the weak sunlight that struggled through the ivy crawling up the high windows as it took over the outside of the house. Brilliant light from an arc lamp powered by an electromagnetic dynamo generator lit their space as brightly as the midday sun, even at midnight. Their workbenches were surrounded by neatly ordered coils of wire, bright metal sheeting, and canisters of oil, grease, and flux needed to weld pieces of metal tubing together. Shelves and cabinets held their large glass jars of gears, screws, and other small bits needed for their mechanical experimentation.

The pleasant scent of toast, coddled eggs, and kippers still filled the air even though they'd eaten every morsel, and their empty plates were stacked on a small table near the dumb-waiter awaiting a trip to the kitchen.

Marley had just about had his fill of his cousin's questions. Thadeus, who was three years his junior, was a complete and utter moron when it came to pretty females. He lost all common sense, daydreamed about them, and spent far too much of his time thinking about how to gain their attention rather than working on the project at hand. He leaned his chin on his fist and asked, "Is she quite beautiful?"

"Yes. I suppose." Marley readjusted his glasses, his irritation at the question evident in his tone. For some inexplicable reason Thad's keen interest was more disconcerting than usual.

"You suppose?"

Marley glared at him. The family resemblance was evident. Boring brown eyes and dark brown hair, only he wore wire-rimmed glasses and Thadeus didn't. Their similarities extended only to their features, though. Thadeus was hopelessly messy, whereas Marley found he liked things in neat, organized order, as evidenced by their worktables, which faced one another, Thadeus's detritus of materials spilling into his own neat workspace.

Their social skills were as different as could be as well. Thadeus reveled in talking to people, while Marley found himself more suited to solitarily creating machines and avoiding interaction as much as possible.

"Well, it wasn't as if I were cataloging her characteristics. We were working together on the STAR."

Thadeus looked both aghast and curious at the same time. "She was working with you on your machine?"

Marley smiled. "Yes." He did recall her vivid blue eyes and quick lithe fingers as she tinkered with the gears and wiring. Watching her work on the machine had been the highlight of his experience at the exhibition. "She'd make an excellent lab assistant."

His cousin stared at him, his mouth opening and closing soundlessly like a beached fish gasping for water. "Lab assistant! Lab assistant? Marley, have you gone off your rocker? Do you even know who Lady Persephone Hargrieve is?"

Marley frowned. "I suppose she's a fan of aeronautics and science."

Thadeus rubbed his hands over his face. If he'd already rolled up his sleeves to work, he would've left his visage streaked with great grease marks. As it was he just looked disgruntled. "She's the only child of Lord Harrington Hargrieve, who married Catherine Percy and is next in line for the title of Duke of Northumberland once his father-in-law passes."

Marley just stared at Thadeus dumbfounded. He wasn't exactly certain what Thadeus was nattering on about. Social rank was not one of the things that occupied his mind any more than gear ratios or the potential for focused light beams interested his lordship. "Oh."

"Oh?"

"Well, it's just, she has rather a sharp mind and a mechanical talent, hardly the hallmarks aspired to by a lady of quality. I wouldn't have suspected she was the daughter of a soon to be duke."

Thadeus scurried around the worktables and grabbed Marley by the upper arms, giving him a shake. "Marley, you great dunderheaded trout! Don't you see what this means? If Lady Persephone Hargrieve is interested in your work, her father might become the sponsor you need to launch you into the Aeronautical Society. The Queen's interest is lovely, but she cannot sponsor you. Only a current member of the society can. Lady Persephone could be our golden ticket."

Marley's frown deepened. "That's so very crass of you, thinking of a bright young woman as merely a ticket to something else."

Thadeus just shook his head and muttered something under his breath about social normalities, marriage, and idiot buffoons. Marley was inclined to ignore him, in particular because his work on the autorotation cuff for the resonating device was just about finished, and he dearly wanted to have it complete before he met with Lord Hargrieve.

"It's not as if I'll be discussing the matter of their support over tea this afternoon."

A heavy wrench fell to the flagstone floor with a great clank that echoed in the laboratory. "Lady Persephone invited you to tea?"

"Well, it really was more Lord Hargrieve who issued the invitation to come and speak to him. Lady Persephone kind of just stood there."

Thadeus stared at him.

"I say, are you sure you aren't coming down with something? You seem rather peaked today," Marley said by way of observation.

"Please tell me, cousin, that you've at least thought of a gift to take her."

"A gift? Whatever for?"

Thadeus groaned, tilting his head back and peering at the huge exposed wooden beams overhead. He closed his eyes for a second, then shook his head, his gaze landing squarely on Marley. "You know, for as brilliant as you are, you have absolutely no bloomin' clue when it comes to women, do you?"

"Well, I suppose if I studied the matter—"

"Studied the matter? One does not study women. One hopes to appease their hysterical natures and not arouse their wrath."

Marley didn't try to suppress his grin. "Are you certain you're talking about women other than Aunt Lydia?"

Thadeus laughed. "Out of the two of us, my good fellow, I have far more experience with the fairer sex, I assure you. Trust me. You'll want to bring her a gift. It would be the proper thing to do after the help she gave you with the machine."

But Marley wanted to do far more than just offer up a gift. What he really wanted was to discuss the possibility of courting her. Perhaps if her father were impressed enough with his work, he'd consider the match, even though she was in a far different strata of society. Marley had never courted a woman before—never had the desire to. But there was an indefinable quality about Lady Persephone that lured him, like an inventor to the spark and flash of a shiny new idea.

"What does one get as a gift for a lady of quality? Gloves?"

"Too personal."

Marley worried the end of his wrench, his finger tracing the curve of it. "Flowers?"

"Too romantic."

Marley chucked the wrench down on his workbench, making it clatter. "Then what the devil do you suggest?"

Thadeus glanced around their basement work area. There was a cabinet filled with small mechanical toys he and Marley had been crafting for their little cousins' stockings at Christmas. He strode over to the cabinet and opened the glass door, then ran his finger along the lineup of toys, past automated mice, little mechanical birds, a metallic ferret, and mechanical dogs. "This one should do." He snatched up a little toy King Charles Spaniel, no bigger than a teacup, with green glass eyes, its wavy coat a combination of silver and brass.

"It's a toy, Thadeus. She's quite beyond the nursery and certainly not interested in toys."

"No woman can resist a cute little dog."

Thadeus brought him the little mechanical dog and wound up the key on its back. Inside, the clockwork gears clicked and hummed. The eyes lit from within, glowing green as it sprang to life. The ears lifted, and the small, articulated brass tail began to wag as the little toy's head tilted to one side. Marley smiled. Perhaps Thadeus was right. It was a brilliant piece of mechanical ingenuity. She might indeed appreciate it—if she didn't take it all apart first to see how it worked.

* * *

Sephie couldn't wait for the day to be over with, and it had only just begun. She had lost her appetite the moment she'd entered the dining room for breakfast and found Lieutenant Frobisher at the table.

He was dressed in his military scarlet, the coat specially tailored to his broad shoulders. Most women swooned at his feet because they found his chiseled jaw, wavy dark hair, and commanding presence alluring. All of it only underscored the reason she disliked him.

He rose from his seat when she entered, but all the politeness, good manners, and breeding in the world didn't make up for his misplaced ambition. She refused to be a mere pawn in the machinations of the Legion.

"Good morning, Lady Persephone."

"Is it?" she returned. Prickly of her, she knew, but then he annoyed her to no end. She'd rejected his advances, endured his smothering kiss a time or two, and still he persisted in trying to act as though there were some chance that she'd actually marry him, even though they both knew it wasn't her he was interested in as much as the chance to become the next leader of the Legion.

"Sephie, manners," her father warned from behind the folds of the morning paper.

She resisted the urge to roll her eyes and instead glanced at the silver chafing dishes and decided none of it looked appetizing and opted instead for a cup of hot Earl Grey tea. Ever since their Northumberland neighbors at Howick Hall, the Earl and Countess of Grey, had given a small tin of it to her as a gift, it had become her favorite. She settled in her seat at the table and let the hot brew with its heady citrus fragrance warm her. With Frobisher here this early in the morning, she knew that cup of tea could very well be her only comfort of the day.

"Your father tells me you made contact with the inventor at the Aeronautical Exhibition."

She nodded.

"And what did you think of his work?"

Clearly she was not going to get to enjoy her tea. She settled her fine bone china cup into the saucer with a slight clatter. Just thinking about Sir Turlock made her head spin and her stomach do an odd little flip-flop. "He's brilliant. Whatever it is you and father want him to create, I'm sure he's capable."

"It's good to know your awkward interest in machines has a use," Frobisher murmured as he stuffed a helping of eggs and toast into his mouth.

Sephie pressed her lips together to prevent the unladylike retorts running through her head from spilling out.

"I've asked him to come for an interview this afternoon," Lord Hargrieve said, still not looking at either of them from behind the shield of newsprint. It had become his habit, as a way to endure these unfortunate breakfasts when his protégé was at the table with his daughter.

Frobisher wiped his mouth with his napkin and set it aside. "Are you certain he's ready to learn about the Darkin, my lord?"

Her father bent one corner of his paper and locked gazes with Frobisher. "William, he's got to know what he's being asked to destroy; otherwise how can he create weapons to do so?"

Frobisher gave a slight bow of his head. "Of course, my lord."

The corner of the paper flipped back into place, and Sephie covered up a snort of laughter with her napkin by pretending it was a sneeze. Frobisher glared at her. His ego was almost enough to fill out the seating at the twelve-person dining table.

One thing was abundantly clear to Sephie: she needed to find a way to escape Frobisher's intention to marry her, no matter what it required.

Chapter 3

Later that afternoon, Marley approached Lord Hargrieve's London townhouse with a sense of trepidation. The gray granite façade, barricaded by a sturdy black iron fence, was three stories tall and at least three windows wide on either side of the main entrance.

If he'd had such a grand house, he likely would have equipped it with a great spying glass mounted to the roof and perhaps a trapdoor beneath the front step to ensure unwanted visitors didn't call again soon. Seeing no such equipment, he supposed Lord Hargrieve didn't need to dissuade visitors who might interrupt his work.

The small mechanical dog clicked and whirred in his leather satchel. He never should have let Thadeus wind it up again before he left. For a second Marley wondered what Lady Persephone would make of the little toy, but then he ruthlessly reminded himself of his purpose at the great house. He might want to court her, but he had far greater aspirations on his mind.

The experiment he planned to test his airborne electrical transmission enhancer was to be a crowning achievement. Her Majesty had already drummed up enthusiasm for it among her cabinet members. It could spur an industrial revolution by providing power in ways never dreamed of by those who relied on coal-fired furnaces and simple piston machines. Electricity was going to replace steam. Marley just knew it. All he needed was someone like Lord Hargrieve to give his endorsement.

His hand slid over the small mechanical spaniel in his satchel, and it wriggled at his touch. He wanted to thank Lady Persephone for her intervention yesterday. It had set him on an entirely new path in his work, and he at least owed her for the insight.

Marley lifted the great brass lion-head knocker and tapped it against the door three times, each drop of it creating a loud, echoing *thump*.

Presently a well-groomed, if dour, butler with salt-and-pepper hair and great, sagging, bulldog-like jowls opened the door. "May I help you, sir?"

"Sir Marley Turlock here to see his lordship." Marley pulled the calling card from his pocket and held it out to the butler.

The man plucked it from his grasp with a white-gloved hand and then peered down his nose, clearly looking over Marley. "His lordship will be with you shortly. You may wait in the parlor."

Marley took a deep breath, pulled back his shoulders, and ventured into the house. While the Turlock family was extensive, their holdings were nothing compared to those of the future Duke of Northumberland.

He followed the butler, but hardly took in his surroundings. His mind was too busy thinking on a dozen things at once, and the most distracting of those was what he should say to Lady Persephone when he gave her the little dog so he didn't appear either too forward or a bumbling idiot.

"In here, Sir Turlock." The butler pulled back the partially open door, and Marley stepped inside.

He'd thought he'd be alone and would have further time to

contemplate his choice of words. He'd been wrong. Inside the room, with its pervasive color scheme of royal blue, white, and gold, were three people. All conversation stopped the moment he crossed the threshold as Lady Persephone, a maid, and a gentleman Marley had not met before all rose at his entrance.

The powder blue ruffled confection of yesterday had been replaced by a more somber, dark rust-colored gown today, with identical rows of brass buttons down the front and a heavily pleated black underskirt. The color brought out the red highlights in her curls and turned her eyes from cornflower to sapphire. Every inch of his skin contracted, and his heart threatened to crack a rib with its sudden hard thumps.

Lady Persephone started forward with a warm, genuine smile that made his head very rummy. Tucking her hand about his arm, she led him to a comfortable if overstuffed chair. "Sir Turlock, how good to see you. Allow me to introduce Lieutenant William Wallace Frobisher. Lieutenant Frobisher, this is the brilliant inventor, Sir Marley Turlock."

The man was military. From his black hessians that could reflect an image as well as a mirror in the hall to the cut of his scarlet coat over his massive shoulders, the man's appearance left no doubt of his occupation. He was all brawn, and Marley suspected not much brain. Marley nodded in greeting, but said nothing.

"So you're the bloke Lord Hargrieve is so eager to talk to," the Lieutenant said as he rocked back on his heels. "Have any actual flying experience?"

Marley adjusted his spectacles. "Yes." He didn't feel the need to expound on his experience simply to appease the man. He was far more interested in delivering the mechanical toy to Lady Persephone before her father took him elsewhere.

Marley pulled open his worn leather satchel and pulled out the bit of plain black velvet tied with a blue bow. The bow had been his idea. He thought the satin ribbon would match the color of her eyes. The dog must have wound down again, because it was no longer wriggling. "A gift for you, Lady Persephone, for your assistance at the exhibition."

Her eyes widened, and her face lit with delight. "For me? Really? You didn't need to, Sir Turlock."

"What exactly did she do?" Marley didn't like Frobisher's annoyed, angry tone one bit.

Lady Persephone's gaze never strayed from Marley's, and they both ignored Frobisher's question. The instant she took the gift from him her hand dipped with the sudden weight. "It's heavy." She sounded surprised.

"I hope it's to your liking."

Her fingers eagerly plucked at the bow, gingerly peeling the fabric apart and revealing the gleaming little mechanical dog.

Frobisher leaned in closer to inspect it. "What the devil is that?"

Persephone glared at him. "Language, Lieutenant. And clearly it's a dog."

His face grew thunderous, his dark gaze shifting to Marley; he had the unmistakable look of a man whose territory has been trespassed upon by a poacher. "A toy?" he scoffed.

Marley tried his best to ignore him. "It's just a trinket, really. My cousin Thadeus and I make them for the little ones in the family, but I—we thought you might enjoy this one."

Her slender fingers caressed the little dog, then took hold of the winding key and twisted, bringing the creature once more to life. "Oh!" The sound of her genuine laughter, bright and delightful, filled the room as she set the small dog down upon the tea table and watched it with fascination. "Oh, Martha, come and look how she lifts her ears and twists her sweet little head! She even sits and wags her tail. Isn't she precious?"

Frobisher took a step, inserting himself as much as he could between Lady Persephone and her maid and Marley.

"Thank you for your gift. I'm sure my fiancée appreciates it." His tone was low and threatening, almost a growl.

Marley's chest contracted for a moment. Lady Persephone was affianced? She had not uttered a word of this to him. He felt a crushing pressure on his chest at the thought that she was in love with someo—with *Frobisher*. The thought of such a capable and brilliant young woman being attached to such an obvious buffoon stuck like a bit of sand where one ought not to get sand, grating and irritating in the extreme. He lifted one brow. "Many felicitations to you both," he said with no genuine enthusiasm.

Lady Persephone picked up the little dog and held it close in the crook of her arm. "We are not engaged." Her firm and resolute tone eased Marley's discomfort some.

Frobisher gave her a hard stare. "We are intended, and that is enough until your father decides we should declare it formally."

Her nostrils flared slightly, and Marley found the blue flicker of fire in her eyes most enchanting. "We shall see about that." She turned to her maid. "Martha, I feel a sudden headache." She glanced at Frobisher and then at Marley, her body vibrating with restrained anger he could nearly feel shimmering in the air of the room. "Will you gentlemen please excuse me?"

The men bowed as she swept from the room.

Frobisher waited a second after she'd left before he flopped himself down on the settee, making himself at home. "I thought she hated dogs."

Marley's eyes burned inexplicably. She hadn't seemed disappointed in his choice. Was she just being kind as a hostess? She didn't seem the type to offer false flattery.

Frobisher grabbed up three little finger sandwiches at once and stuffed them all in his mouth and chewed. "Bit of a fireball, isn't she? I'll soon have that corrected."

Marley swallowed hard. He might not know as much as

Thadeus knew about women, but he knew enough to tell when one was truly angry versus just playing the coquette to earn male attention. "She doesn't seem to take well to the idea of your coming nuptials."

Frobisher brushed the crumbs from the front of his jacket onto the fine hand-cut wool carpet beneath his feet. "She'll get used to it. Love isn't always necessary in these arrangements, is it?"

At that moment Marley was quite sure of two things. One, given the right opportunity, he'd like to light Lieutenant Frobisher up with a great wallop of an electric charge just to watch him bounce about on the ground like a beached fish; and two, Lady Persephone Hargrieve deserved better than this big lout for a husband.

Marley pulled back his shoulders, stretching himself to his full height, and glared openly at Frobisher. "Perhaps the arrangement isn't necessary at all. She might have more than one suitor to choose from."

Frobisher rose to his feet, his face turning red, his fists bunched by his sides, arms slightly bent, as if he intended to throw a punch. Marley stood his ground, refusing to budge. Let the oaf do his worst. He'd find a way to make him pay in spades.

"Don't go getting ideas about Lady Persephone, little man. She's mine. And if you get in my way, I'll squash you. You haven't the skills it takes to protect her."

"I'd say that matter is up to the lady."

A deep clearing of the throat from the doorway had them both turning to see Lord Hargrieve staring at them. "Is there a problem, gentlemen?"

Frobisher's stance changed immediately. "No, my lord. No problem at all. Just giving our inventor some useful advice."

Lord Hargrieve gave Frobisher a pointed look. "He's not our inventor yet, Lieutenant. We might want to be more cordial to him in the meantime." The man looked over his shoulder. "Wattly, please show Sir Turlock to my study."

"Yes, my lord." The butler edged around Lord Hargrieve and inclined his head to Marley. "This way, if you please, Sir Turlock."

From the alcove in the great hall, Sephie spied Sir Turlock following Wattly to her father's study. She'd found pleading a headache or some other sort of feminine ill was the easiest way to extract oneself without too much questioning from a room full of men. There'd been many such occasions in her father's house, and since her mother's passing, she'd had to act as his hostess, even in the most tedious of social situations.

Her hands were still shaking. Overhearing the exchange between Frobisher and Sir Turlock had left her giddy. In her own flights of female fancy she'd imagined that the looks Sir Turlock had given her were more than his approval of her mechanic skills. Now that she knew he might even offer for her, she was beside herself with joy. Not only was Sir Turlock fascinating, he found her passion for machines a wonderful thing rather than trying to quash it as Frobisher and her father did. How marvelous would it be to be one's self with one's spouse?

She held up the adorable little dog he'd brought her, her heart swelling with emotion. She'd been given so few toys as a child, and had never been allowed to have a dog because of her allergies to them, despite her fondest wish to have one. In one fell swoop, Sir Turlock had given her both and made her smile from the inside out. But her happiness was drowned out by low and angry voices coming from the parlor where Frobisher and her father argued.

"He has intentions toward Persephone," Frobisher ground

out. Sephie huffed. He was complaining as if she were his property already. The great oaf.

"You will not undermine my authority in this, Lieutenant. He is not to be harmed until we have the weapon from him. It could make all the difference in our battle with the Darkin. We need him. Do I make myself clear?"

"And what if his energy cannon doesn't do what he thinks it will?"

"Then that will change matters. But until that time, if he wishes to court Persephone, then I shall allow him to."

Anger filled Frobisher's voice. "And what of our agreement? You promised her to me!"

"I promised you could court her, Lieutenant, and I've made every effort to place her in your presence so that you could convince her of your sincere interest. But you know as well as I do how headstrong she can be."

Sephie ducked back behind the edge of the alcove as her father stalked back to his study.

"Perhaps you ought to beat that stubbornness out of her," Frobisher muttered as he stamped out of the parlor toward the front door. "I know I would."

The front door slammed behind him, and Sephie shuddered and held the little dog closer. She knew the risks her family took. Her father thought Frobisher could protect her from the hideous things they hunted and were in turn hunted by. But Sir Turlock was smart. If he knew the truth, perhaps he could think of ways to protect her that Frobisher never could.

Marley waited in Lord Hargrieve's study. Since it was midsummer there was no fire in the grate, but the odor of cigar tobacco clung to the room along with the mellow scent of the old leather binding the hundreds of books in the room.

Every wall of Lord Hargrieve's study was covered in built-in shelving. Much of the shelving contained books, and other shelves were covered in far more curious items. Marley stared at the rows of glass bell jars on the shelves. Some held displays of unusual dried flora and fauna; others were filled with preserving liquid in which strange creatures floated in limbo. Marley was surprised to think of Lord Hargrieve as a naturalist. Certainly it was a hobby many appreciated, but Lord Hargrieve seemed more a man of industry.

"May I get you anything, sir?"

Marley started and glanced back at the butler, unaware that he'd slowly walked to the near middle of the room. "No. No, I'm fine. Thank you."

"Very good, sir." Wattly closed the door, leaving Marley alone with the bizarre collection. One jar in particular caught his attention. It was a smaller jar, inside which were what looked like they could have been a set of human teeth; but upon closer inspection, Marley decided they had to be animal in nature. The canines were far longer, more suited to a large predator like a wolf or big dog. He bent closer to look.

"I see you've found my collection."

Lord Hargrieve's voice startled Marley. He jerked up. "I—yes. Most unusual. You have quite an extensive set of specimens."

Persephone's father settled himself in the large, upright chair behind the massive mahogany desk. He leaned forward and pulled over a humidor, flipping it open and pulling a fat brown cigar from it. "Would you care for a cigar?"

Marley shook his head, unable to keep his eyes from straying to the odd mandibles in the jar. "No, thank you, my lord."

"Please take a seat."

Marley dutifully sat down in one of the two overstuffed chairs facing Lord Hargrieve.

The man took several puffs on his cigar, held his lips closed for a second, then blew out a stream of fragrant smoke.

"Sir Turlock, I assume you know of my interest in your work. But what you may not know is why I have an interest."

"I assumed it had to do with your involvement in the Aeronautical Society, my lord."

"Quite. But there are other, more pressing reasons for my interest and that of my colleague Lieutenant Frobisher. We are part of a special group of the military that answers only to Her Majesty. We deal with things of a questionable nature and are always looking for new ways to defeat our enemies."

"And what, may I ask, has that to do with my aeronautical display at the exhibition, my lord?"

"We think you might be a very useful part of our cause."

Marley's skin prickled with apprehension. Somewhere deep in his gut something told him this was no normal interview. Whatever Lord Hargrieve was involved with, along with that Frobisher chap, was serious business.

Chapter 4

Thoughts of secret societies and strange rituals swirled in Marley's head. What exactly was Lord Hargrieve into? He swallowed past the thick lump swelling in his throat to address the older man seated behind the enormous mahogany desk.

"What is your cause, if I may be so bold as to inquire, my lord?" Marley tried to minimize the tightness in his voice.

Lord Hargrieve tapped the gray ash from the end of his cigar into a small brass tray on his desk. "We are called Her Majesty's Hunter Service."

"And what, do you, um, hunt, my lord?"

Hargrieve chuckled and wedged his cigar back between his lips, giving it a few great puffs. "What we hunt isn't mentioned in polite society, Sir Turlock. It isn't fit to grace the hunting lodge walls. And if people knew, they might panic."

"You mean big game from Africa, my lord?"

An odd twinkle sparked in Hargrieve's eyes. "No. Something far deeper and darker than anything that continent could provide. The creatures we hunt are Darkin. Werewolves, vampires, ghosts, demons, and such. But that's not the point. The point is, are you up to the challenge of assisting us in weapons development, to annihilate these creatures?"

Marley could tell from the look in the other man's eyes that this was no jest. No alarmist musings. "Such things actually exist?" Marley asked, mouth dry as his fingers gripped the smooth wood of the chair arms.

Lord Hargrieve leaned toward him, his dark blue eyes intense and serious. "I saw you eyeing my set of vampire fangs earlier."

Marley shifted uncomfortably in his chair. A shiver shot down his spine. Vampires. Werewolves. Demons. Ghosts. Fae. If all the dark things he'd thought were only the vestiges of unscientific mythology and lore were actually real, what did that mean for their society? What did it mean for science? How did one possibly fight against things one couldn't comprehend?

"We have training, Sir Turlock, knowledge that is kept within the society on how to effectively attack and resist the Darkin. We will share that with you, but we need weapons. We need your scientific mind to help us break the stalemate between our forces and the Darkin. Will you do it?"

"I suppose it would depend on what kinds of weapons you wanted, my lord." He hadn't the faintest clue what one would use to defeat any of the Darkin Lord Hargrieve had just mentioned.

Hargrieve rolled the cigar to the corner of his mouth, his lips spreading into an approving smile that calmed Marley's nerves slightly. For a moment he had been certain Lord Hargrieve was going to tell him they hunted humans or some such strangeness.

"Excellent, Sir Turlock. Now we'd like to begin by having you test your electrostatic transmission ray in a demonstration for us in North Umbria."

"My device? But how—"

Hargrieve raised a hand to stop his question. "Suffice it to say Her Majesty is well aware of your experiments, Sir

Marley. We're particularly interested in the transmission ray. We believe it could have use as an electrical cannon of sorts."

Marley shifted uncomfortably in his chair. "Yes, my lord. But it isn't yet fully operational."

Hargrieve pulled the cigar out of his mouth and set it to rest on the edge of the brass tray. "That may be, but Her Majesty and I have full faith in your skills. We'd like a demonstration of it by next month. Will that be sufficient time to ready the device?"

A cold, prickly sweat broke out on Marley's brow and upper lip. It would be possible for him to get it done, but he'd have to work night and day to make it happen. But Marley knew an opportunity when it was presented. He didn't dare pass it up. "Certainly, my lord."

"Excellent. Then I'll inform Her Majesty. And as compensation, following a successful demonstration of your device, shall we say five hundred pounds and admission into the Aeronautical Society?"

Marley practically sprang out of his chair. That was far more than he'd anticipated. "Very generous, my lord."

Hargrieve extended his hand to shake Marley's on the deal, then rose from his chair, signaling their interview was at an end. "I'll have the papers outlining our expectations sent round, and I look forward to your demonstration," he said.

Marley stood and gave a slight bow of his head. It had been the strangest half hour of his life. "Thank you for the opportunity, my lord." Marley hesitated one moment, his heart practically climbing out of his chest and into his throat. It was now or never. "Lord Hargrieve, if I may be so bold, would you allow me the honor of courting your daughter?"

Lord Hargrieve stared long and hard at him, and the moment seemed to stretch on into what felt like infinity. "You know she has a suitor already, don't you?"

"Yes, my lord, but if she is willing to entertain my suit as well, I shall give her every reason to be happy for it."

Hargrieve nodded his head and rubbed the white whiskers on his right cheek. "Very well, then. If you know the risks and are still up to the challenge, you have my permission."

"Thank you, my lord!" Marley gave a quick bow of his head. He left Lord Hargrieve's study feeling utterly elated, but he made it only a few steps before a hissing sound stopped him. Marley, his nerves now on edge, knowing there were dark things lurking about, nearly jumped out of his skin.

"Psst."

He turned and peered into the dark recesses of the hall to find Lady Persephone ensconced in an alcove between her father's study and the turn to the entrance hall. She waved with her hand, motioning him to her.

Marley glanced at the hallway to make sure they wouldn't be seen conversing unchaperoned. "Yes, my lady?" he said, his voice barely above a whisper. "Was there something you wanted?" He wondered for a moment if she was aware of the oddity of her father's profession and that of the lieutenant.

Lady Persephone nodded and nibbled at her bottom lip as she stepped out of the alcove. "I want to thank you for the little dog. I'm horribly allergic to real dogs. I've wanted one for so very long. It was the most thoughtful of gifts. Thank you."

And before Marley had a clue what was happening, Lady Persephone reached up on tiptoe and pressed a warm, velvet kiss to his cheek. Heat spread through his system from the point of contact, making him tingle all over. Her unique scent—a mix of heady hyacinth and sweet female— overwhelmed his senses, indelibly imprinting her on his brain.

She glanced up at him, her blue eyes huge and sparkling, then turned away without another word, which was fine by Marley because he was too tongue-tied to say anything. Other than his scores of female relatives, no woman had ever kissed him before.

But the moment was spoiled almost instantly. A thunderous crash and the sound of shattering glass came from Lord Hargrieve's study. Marley whipped around and shoved Persephone behind him as a precaution.

There was a great yell and a sharp report of gunfire. Marley only made it two steps toward the ruckus when Lord Hargrieve burst into the hall with a deadly looking blade in one hand and a gun in the other. His white hair was askew, his face florid.

"Demon! Turlock, get her out of here! I haven't time to load another salt shot, and there'll be more!"

For a second, panic overtook Marley. What the devil did one do to defeat a demon? His feet seemed rooted to the polished floorboards.

Hargrieve spared him only a glance as he hastily tried to reload his gun with shot and gunpowder and what looked like rock salt. "Move, Turlock! That's an order!"

Self-preservation and common sense took over. Marley turned, grabbed Lady Persephone's hand in a firm grip, and ran for the front door.

At the juncture of the hall she dug in her feet, nearly yanking his arm from its socket. "No! Not out the front! They'll be expecting us out the front!" A swirl of what looked like dark smoke began to leak from beneath the front door, growing denser, into what Marley thought were feet. The watered silk on the walls began to shred and ooze blood, and the crystal vase full of flowers on the front table exploded, sending glass shards like bullets to stick into the opposing wall.

Marley held up his arm to ward off the explosion and swore. What the devil was going on?

"Come on!" She pulled him toward the back of the house at a run, her skirts swishing around her booted feet. They burst into the kitchen. "All of you! Stations! Demons!" she shouted.

The cook's face screwed up, and she set down her wooden

spoon. "Lizzie, get the salt and holy water!" The scullery maid rushed to the larder and pulled out a canister of salt, which the cook began pouring out onto the floor in the doorway.

Marley could pause for only a second at their odd behavior before Persephone pulled on his hand. "Come on! They know what to do. This way!" With quick footsteps she led him down into the cellar.

A dark cellar was not his idea of a good escape route. In fact, he was rather concerned that there might be more to worry about being trapped in such a place. "Your father said I should get you out of here."

"I know. This way." She pulled him, as if by memory, through the dark, through the rows of shelving. The musty odor of dank earth, wood, and fresh onions and garlic lingered in the air. Over their heads feet scuffled across the floorboards, and there were unearthly screams and the crashing of crockery and glass. The floor seemed to be sloping upward, and Marley nearly tripped over his feet in the dark.

He tugged on her hand, stopping her headlong race across the stone floor. "Lady Persephone, I must protest. This is most dangerous. We need to go back upstairs and help!"

"My father wants me out of here for a reason. He told you to help protect me."

Marley muttered a curse beneath his breath. "If we're going to get out of here before those things come after us, we need a light." Persephone let go of his hand. Before he could protest, he blinked at a sudden burst of brilliant sunlight. She'd opened a door at the back of the house that seemed to be hidden behind a screen of tall shrubbery. From the smell of hay, horse, and fresh manure, Marley guessed they were close to the stables.

"That enough light for you?"

Marley blinked. Smart girl. She'd found them an exit. The moment he let go of the door, it swung shut, as if on springs.

Marley couldn't see more than the crease outlining the door. There were no handle or hinges to be found, no way to open it from the outside. They pushed through the foliage, the grass beneath their feet hushing their footsteps.

Inhuman screams and more crashing could be heard from inside the house, and Marley hesitated. "Run! I'll go back and assist. They need help."

Persephone put her warm, damp palm against his cheek and turned him to face her, locking her serious gaze with his. "We do as my father said. We leave. Now. We need to find someplace safe. I have to make sure this isn't taken." She pulled on the golden chain around her neck and withdrew a small, iron key.

He had no idea what lock the key fit into, or how he'd gotten caught up in this insane twist of reality, but all he could do now was carry on. Marley pressed his mouth into a firm line and nodded. "We'll go to my laboratory."

They raced through the stableyard, through the alley and into the street and grabbed the first coach for hire they could find. Marley glanced back at Lord Hargrieve's house as they drove away. Other than the broken front window, it looked utterly placid. From the street in front nothing seemed amiss, and one couldn't hear the screams. Lady Persephone sat across from him but stared out the window.

"Are you certain they'll be all right?"

Persephone nodded. Her gaze flicked briefly to him. "Father has plenty of devil's traps molded into the plaster designs in the ceilings. Chances are they'll all get caught in one; then father, cook, and the others of the Legion can dispatch them."

For a second Marley simply stared at her. She knew all about her father's occupation and didn't seem ruffled about it in the slightest. How was that possible?

Deep in his own chest his heart beat at a manic pace, suiting a man who had just been scared out of his wits and run for his very life. He glanced down at her hands. Her fingers caressed the small mechanical dog, which had gone still, unwinding in their daring escape. She'd kept hold of the dog during absolute bedlam. Amazing.

Marley struggled to collect his scattered thoughts enough to form rational words. "How long have you known about all of this?"

Her piercing blue gaze, so like her father's for an instant that it unnerved him further, locked with his. "My father has always been in Her Majesty's service. Few are called, Sir Turlock, but it is a proud tradition handed down from father to son."

"And what of you? Is it handed down to daughters as well?"

Her teeth nibbled at the edge of her lip. Marley had the insanely curious urge to kiss her then and there, but he resisted. "We are not Hunters, as the boys are." Her fingers twisted in the chain about her neck, making the key catch the light. "We are Keepers. We tend to the histories, the knowledge of the Legion. I'm not sure how much of this I can share with you, Sir Turlock."

Marley leaned forward and wrapped his hand over her slender fingers. "Given all that's transpired this morning, don't you think we're well past such formalities? I think you should call me Marley."

Her lush mouth widened into a smile. "I should like that. And you must call me Sephie."

Sephie. He liked the sound of it. Rather like an exotic flower from Egypt or some other such faraway land. But darker thoughts intruded.

"How will we know that your father and the others are safe?"

"They will send word."

"But they don't even know where we are going."

Sephie arched a delicate brow, an incredulous look on her face. "Marley, do you really think that father would have asked you to take me to safety if he didn't already know everything about you?"

Marley stiffened. He didn't know if he liked the idea of any man prying into his personal affairs without his consent or knowledge. He tended to be more of a private man, steeped in his work. He didn't socialize like Thadeus. Focus was critical if he was to complete his work.

"Do you actually have any interest in aeronautics or mechanics or were you merely sent over to capture my attention?"

Sephie broke her direct eye contact with him and sighed. Her gaze dropped to her lap and the little dog in her grasp, before she looked back up at him. "He didn't say anything about helping you with your invention. That was purely my curiosity and your kindness."

His shoulders relaxed a bit. "I meant what I said yesterday. You're very good."

She shook her head, making the riot of fiery ringlets about her face dance. "Father is dead set against me inventing anything. My first responsibility is to marry into the Legion and perform the duties of a Keeper." The sad, hopeless sound of her voice reached into his chest and gave his heart a sharp twist.

"That's why he's made an arrangement with the lieutenant, isn't it?"

She nodded, her eyes growing shiny with unshed tears. Marley chose his words carefully. "You aren't . . . fond . . . of him, are you?"

She rubbed her fingers over the smooth metallic coat of the little spaniel. "He's a formidable Hunter. One of the best of the new young ones in Her Majesty's service. But being an excellent Hunter doesn't necessarily make one good marriage material."

"Have you told your father how you feel?"

Sephie sighed, the glistening tears beginning to spill down

her cheeks in such perfect little drops they looked to Marley like translucent pearls. Lady Persephone Hargrieve even cried prettily. She hastily swept the tears away with a brush of her hand. "You must think me a silly chit to cry over such things."

Marley reached out again and covered her hand with his. "What a woman feels is never silly."

She gave a hiccup and a sad little bubble of laughter. "I've never heard a man talk like that."

He offered her a gentle, genuine smile. "Perhaps that's because the men you've been around have been fighting the unthinkable instead of having an army of well-meaning aunts see to their instruction." He reached up and brushed one of her perfect tears away from her cheek with the pad of his thumb.

Sephie gave a delicate sniff and a tremulous smile. "I rather like the difference."

Lady Persephone Hargrieve was a conundrum. In the midst of bedlam, she'd been sharp and strong, focused and brave. But within her was a keen intellect as bright as any arc light, balanced with a sweet, feminine heart as fragile as glass.

His pulse thrummed hard in his chest, spreading out until it filled every cell. It was as if his whole world tilted off its axis for a moment, wobbling. He'd never met a woman who'd thrown him off balance like Sephie.

"Marley?"

He leaned in closer. "Yes," he whispered.

She blinked the damp fringe of her sparkling lashes, turning her eyes into a lake of blue. Marley felt himself falling, drowning there. "Are you going to kiss me?"

For once, Marley found words perfectly unnecessary.

Chapter 5

The rocking of the poorly sprung hackney cab and the steady clop of the horse's hooves on the cobblestone streets faded into the edges of Marley's awareness. All he could focus on, all that filled his senses, was Sephie.

Marley closed the space separating them in the seconds between one pounding heartbeat and the next. His hand slid around the indent of her waist. Beneath his questing fingertips he felt the crisp cloth and regular intervals of the boning in her corset. Hard when he wanted soft. He wondered if she was just as soft there beneath all the artificially constructed barriers as her cheek had been when he'd touched the satiny smoothness of it.

The heady fragrance of hyacinth and warm female wound about his brain, making his heartbeat extend to the very tips of all his extremities, mostly notable the one between his legs. In the back of his brain a warning claxon blared. He shouldn't kiss her. It could ruin everything for them both. He'd never kissed a woman properly before, but her lips looked as lush and ripe as a strawberry picked fresh and sun-warmed from the field.

She was irresistible.

His lips touched hers, gliding and pressing against the

inviting softness, seeking out her warmth. Sephie's eyelids fluttered shut, and she made soft noises as she leaned into him, her fingers wrapping possessively around his neck and threading into his hair. Her eager response wound his need into an even tighter coil, a spring waiting for release.

For the first time he understood why Thadeus could be so smitten by females as to lose all his common sense. Deep down Marley wanted the moment to freeze, to never end, but continually replay over and over so it could always be like this. The warmth of her against him, the feel of her beneath his hands, the taste of her on his tongue, the fragrance of her skin filling his senses.

Sephie thought she might come out of her skin, or at the very least out of her dress and corset. Every inch of her skin felt alive with flame. Unlike Frobisher's hard, punishing kisses that left her feeling like she were bruised and drowning, eager to get away, Marley's kisses were smooth and seductive, luring her deeper into his arms until she was practically atop his lap, her skirts bunched up about her hips.

His hands, warm and firm on her waist, had skimmed up higher, the edge of his thumb tracing along the soft, sensitive underside of her breast, making the tip pebble and ache for his touch.

She wanted to taste him. Sephie tentatively touched the tip of her tongue against his lips. He immediately responded, opening up to her, his kiss deepening in an erotic slide that reduced her insides to a quivering mass of aspic. A persistent throb at her core grew into an unbearable ache. Sephie brushed herself against the broad expanse of his thigh to assuage it. Marley growled deeply in response.

The hackney came to a jolting halt, causing them to nearly slide to the floor. Sephie realized how close she'd come to compromising herself in a way that could never be recovered.

Something about Marley made her forget herself far too easily. She pulled back from his touch.

"We've stopped."

A look of hurt flickered through his eyes for a moment, but then he too seemed to come out of the sensual fog that had shrouded them both in the half an hour it had taken to get to Bostwick House.

Marley opened the door, and she moved to climb out, but his hand wrapped in a no-nonsense fashion about her wrist. "You'd best wait in here until I can determine if it's safe," he said.

Sephie nearly laughed at the absurdity of his comment. She'd been the one raised as the child of a Hunter, and she knew precisely what they were up against and had come prepared, unlike Marley. But she held her urge to laugh in check, realizing from the frown on his face that Marley was deadly serious.

"If you must. Just be careful," she said. He gave her a curt nod and shut the door.

Her finger tapped out an impatient tattoo on the leather seat while she waited. It was ridiculous. Of the two of them she'd been more closely associated with the Legion of Hunters far longer. She knew what could stop a demon in its tracks and how to outsmart a vampire. Marley had only learned of the existence of the Darkin a mere hour ago, if not less. Still, it spoke well of him that he considered her safety above his own.

"How long can a look around possibly take?" she muttered under her breath to no one in particular. She knew they hadn't been followed. The emergency exit through the cellar had warding spells and seals upon it, not letting any through but those alive and breathing, so she knew no Darkin had followed them across town. But in the event that they had been followed, the small sachet of wolfsbane in the pocket of her skirt would ward off curious vampires who could become paralyzed by the stuff. For demons and werewolves, she had a vial of holy water, and if a ghost came too close, she could swing the nearest iron implement and take care of it temporarily.

Marley poked his head back in the hackney and a rush of relief filled her. She'd begun to worry about him.

"It looks safe enough." He held out his hand to assist her. Sephie was only too glad to have another excuse to slip her hand into his. The smooth, dry whisper of his skin against hers sent a fresh thrill shooting through her, making her tingle in places she'd never considered all that interesting before.

The waning light of evening cast the entrance to Bostwick House in shadow, making the residence seem far more foreboding than it had when she and her father had driven past to inspect the place during his investigations of Marley a month before.

Overall her father was a cautious man. He didn't choose associates indiscriminately. Her Majesty's Royal Hunter Service wasn't considered the top of Europe's branch of the Legion for nothing, and her father intended to keep hold of that legacy as long as possible.

"Do you think anyone is home?" she asked as the hackney clattered off into the gathering gloom of the street. The lamplighters were making their way along the streets with their long-poled lighters as people returned home to dress for various elegant events. The Earl of Sedgwick's ball was tonight, she remembered. Not that she'd wanted to go. She'd rather be here with Marley than swirling about a ballroom with anyone else. Lieutenant William Wallace Frobisher in particular.

The ivy crawling up the great brick walls of Bostwick House shivered slightly in the warm evening breeze. The muddy scent of the Thames contrasted with the floral freshness of summer roses and lilies in bloom on the grounds. Against the twilight, lights blazed in a few of the windows; the human presence making the house seem welcoming enough at a second glance. "With six aunts and four uncles, there's always someone home at Bostwick House," he grumbled.

"You have a large family, don't you?"

"Too large. And far too nosy."

"I always thought a large family would be a comforting thing."

"Not when you are trying to maintain secrecy."

Rather than walking her up the front steps, Marley steered her toward the side of the house and indicated the bright glow of light coming from the basement windows. "This way." He led her around the side of the house. "For the sake of propriety, it's best if we use the outside entrance to the basement. It'll cause fewer questions later, I assure you."

"You don't like your family knowing what you're up to, do you?"

Marley offered her a good-natured, lopsided smile. "If you lived with them, you'd understand; it's less complicated this way."

Sephie nodded. Anything would be good as long as they got indoors quickly. The prickling of the small hairs on the back of her neck told her Darkin were close. "Whatever you wish. You certainly understand them better than I do. But let's hurry."

Marley grabbed her hand and gave it a squeeze. "Trust me, if I were to walk in with you in tow, they'd immediately begin peppering us with questions about when we were going to announce our engagement. And it would be doubly hard to explain why I'm alone with another man's intended without spilling an awful lot of your father's secrets and upsetting a family blissfully unaware of Darkin in the process."

Eyes narrowing, Sephie glanced around as if suddenly aware that they were alone in the semi-darkness. Marley tightened his fingers around hers to reassure her. She was safe with him. She'd always be safe with him. But he now had enemies he didn't know or understand. These Darkin, whatever they were, were dangerous. He'd seen Hargrieve's reaction to them. But how could he possibly hope to build a weapon against something he didn't know how to fight? He glanced at Sephie as they opened the gate in the wrought iron fence. He might not know about the Darkin, but she certainly did. And as brilliant and gifted as she was, she could help him formulate not just weapons, but a plan for altering his electrostatic power generator into the electric shot cannon Lord Hargrieve had requested.

"We'd best get inside now," she said softly. "It isn't safe to linger out here in the open too long."

He should have let go of her hand, but he didn't. But in his defense, she didn't seem eager to let go of him, either. "This way," he said, leading her back around the gravel path through the lush, half-overgrown garden, filled with the fragrance of lilies and roses and freshly cut grass. Crickets chirped in the warm evening air. A perfect summer night, if they hadn't been running from Darkin.

They came to what looked like a potting shed overgrown with climbing red roses. Their heavy sweetness infused the air and disguised the odors of ozone and chemicals that came from the lab below. He and Thadeus had planned it that way to ensure no little cousins inadvertently found the secret back entrance to their laboratory. They figured if it looked like it might involve hard work with rakes, hoes, and clippers, the little ones were likely to stay away. So far they'd been right.

He pulled his key from his pocket and opened the lock on the door. The familiar scents of potting moss, earth, and lye filled the air. The potting shed was dark, but there in the floor one could see the outline of a large square indicating the trapdoor. Marley pulled her inside. There was hardly enough room with the two of them in the confines of the little shed to open the trapdoor. "I'm sorry, but you'll have to stand closer to me if we're to open the door."

She gave him a saucy smile, her pretty teeth white in the gloom. "You say that as if you think I'll mind."

Marley swallowed hard. He'd enjoyed kissing her, but it muddled his thinking, and now was not the time for being wobbly about the brainbox. It was best if he didn't lead her on—or give in to further temptation himself.

She moved until she was right next to him. The warmth of her, noticeable even in the heat of a summer evening, made him positive he had too many clothes on for comfort.

Focus, man. Focus.

He crouched down, fingers brushing the floor, feeling for the recessed metal latch in the wood. He found it and gave a great pull, lifting the trapdoor and letting the light of the tunnel connecting the shed to the laboratory in the basement fill the shed.

"Careful. The steps can be slippery if they're damp." He held her hand tightly as he helped her navigate the steep descent of the stone steps leading down into the tunnel.

As soon as they were clear, he pulled the door shut over them.

"This is extraordinary," she murmured, her voice echoing as she ran her fingertips over the stone walls and walked beside him down the hallway, wide and tall enough to accommodate a horse-drawn carriage. The temperature was slightly cooler than above, and the hall was lit by the ambient glow coming from the arc lamp in the laboratory just up ahead.

He walked side by side with her, enjoying the moment of being able to hold her hand in his. Mixed with the familiar must of the damp stone was the sharp tang of ozone, a by-product from some of his experimentation. She turned and glanced at him. "Did you and your cousin build all this?"

Marley shook his head. "We added and modified, but some of these tunnels have been here for ages. The Turlocks tend to be a creative lot. My cousin Thadeus and I used to get lost for hours mapping out the hidden rooms and passages in the house when we were children."

"And your mother didn't mind?"

"She always encouraged our curious nature."

She gave a great sigh as they reached the bend that turned the tunnel toward the house. "I wish I could say the same. My father has kept me practically under his boot heel since I could toddle."

"Probably with good reason. It looks as though what he fights is very dangerous."

She stopped and locked gazes with him. "But that's just it. I know the dangers better than most, so why not let me fight against them with my mechanical creations rather than just relegating me to record kee—"

A great grinding *clunk* cut off what she was saying. The sound was followed by a whirring then another *clunk*.

"Blast!"

"What is it?"

"Thad must have left Binky on guard."

"Binky?"

Just then a gigantic mechanical construct, its shoulders wide enough to stretch from one side of the tunnel to the other, its head nearly grazing the roof, with hands the size of wheelbarrows, came lumbering into the space before them, its red glowing eyes fixed firmly on the two of them.

"You two named that monstrosity Binky?" Most women would have run at the sight of the mechanical creation, but Sephie stood her ground, her eyes narrowing as if she was picking it apart and assessing it. "Why Binky?"

"Thadeus thought it funny. He once had a stuffed toy rabbit named Binky."

"Your cousin has an unusual sense of humor, doesn't he?"

Marley didn't get to answer. "Who goes there?" The tinny mechanical voice scratched and vibrated out the words.

"Halt, Binky."

"Who goes there?" it repeated.

"Sassafras," Marley said sharply.

Whirrr. Clunk. The construct kept coming toward them, its massive hands raised and poised either to mash them flat into the floor or crush them to paste against the wall. "Bloody hell, Thadeus has changed the password."

Her eyes grew a little wide. "What will it do?"

"Try to kill us most likely." He frowned. "Pumpernickel." *Whirrr. Clunk.* "Kipper." *Whirrr. Clunk.* They backed up a step toward the stairs. "Spotted Dick." *Whirrr. Clunk.*

"I think you're just angering it now."

"Let me think. What other dish would Thadeus order?"

"Those are your passwords? Food?"

"He's a growing boy," Marley shot back.

Whirr. Clunk. Rechetchetchet. The construct took a swing at them, and Marley shoved Sephie to the side of the tunnel just in time to keep from being smashed. Rock dust coated his glasses and hair, and particles of stone stung his skin. He gathered her in close beside him, trying to spare her the worst of the debris. "Are you all right?"

She nodded, grabbing ahold of his shirt. "Think of the password before that thing kills us!"

Gears whirred and clicked as Binky raised his massive fist again. *Rechetchetchet.* They were out of room to retreat. The man-sized hammer of a fist hit the top of the tunnel's arc and began to swing downward toward their skulls.

Chapter 6

They were out of time and in danger of dying at the massive mechanical hands of his own creation before they ever reached his laboratory.

If Thadeus's favorite foods weren't working as passwords to stop his monstrosity, perhaps Marley needed to think of something Thad hated.

"Haggis!" Marley shouted.

His construct's massive metal arm froze in mid motion. Marley sagged with relief against the stone wall and breathed a silent prayer, his pulse so hard it throbbed behind his eyeballs.

"Welcome home, sir," Binky ground out as he stiffened to attention.

"Guard the back entrance," Marley instructed. "Unless it's family, kill anything and anyone that gets through."

"Yes, sir."

He was going to have words with Thadeus once he got hold of the blighter. What could have possibly made him think changing the password and activating Binky in attack mode while he was in the lab would be a good idea?

They scooted past Binky and headed for the laboratory.

Sephie kept throwing worried glances over her shoulder. "You're certain it won't malfunction and sneak up on us from behind?"

"There'd be no sneaking about it. And I'm as certain as I can be about a mechanical thing. There's always a chance it will fail, but if we stopped every time there was a chance of failure, we'd never succeed."

They rounded the corner into the main laboratory. Thadeus was nowhere in sight. The small hairs on the back of Marley's neck rose—and from the lack of crackling sound Marley knew the phenomenon wasn't caused by an electromagnetic field.

"Thadeus? Thad, are you here?" he called out.

No one answered. That worried him. It wasn't like his cousin.

"Perhaps he's gone upstairs to have dinner with your family," Sephie suggested.

"Not this close to a breakthrough. He's as driven as I am. We'll work through the night and use the voice tube to have meals sent down on the dumbwaiter. I wouldn't have even come out of the lab myself at this juncture, except that your father insisted." And now he knew why. *Darkin.* Fascinating to consider—academically at least—the possibility of dark forces swirling around humankind on this earthly plane.

Sephie gasped, which made him whip around.

"What's wrong?"

But she wasn't in danger from another of his inventions; instead, her eyes grew round with wonder. "These are amazing!" she said as she pressed her fingers to the glass doors of his curiosity cabinet and gazed at row after row of the little mechanical constructs he and Thadeus had created for the younger cousins.

Marley had never brought anyone into his lab before. Sephie's excitement and wonder were infectious, momentarily distracting him from the more pressing matter of drubbing his cousin once he found him.

She flitted from one cabinet of creations to the next, inspecting them as if they were cabinets of fantastical wonders at the South Kensington Museum in the heart of London. "So intricate and artistic. You and your cousin really do have a flair for making things lifelike."

"You're kind."

She turned and stared at him. "Your tone suggests I'm coddling a child. And I think we both know you are hardly that." A twinkle in her blue eyes made his gut contract with longing. "Father said you make weapons as well."

Marley nodded. "He's asked me to make some for the Legion."

Her brow furrowed slightly. "I know. That's why he asked me to go and look at your work and assess it at the exhibition."

Marley stopped for a moment and stared at her. "You were spying on me for the Legion?"

She nodded and worried her lip between her teeth, giving a dainty shrug of her shoulders. "You aren't mad at me, are you?"

Marley sighed and shook his head, then started chuckling. "No, but I do find it funny. You're far more than you appear to be, aren't you?"

Her eyes glittered, and for a second Marley wasn't certain if she was about to cry. The thought that he might make her cry struck him like a physical blow to the gut. "You're the first man to really appreciate all my skills."

He reached over and brushed the back of his hand over her cheek. "How could I be angry when I find you so intensely fascinating?"

Her lips spread into a tremulous smile. "Thank you for that."

"Anything for you, my lady," he said with sincerity. The

moment grew too tense, and Marley turned away. "Now where were we? Ah yes, weapons."

He took her hand and steered her toward his armory within the lab. "I'm afraid the collection I have isn't extensive." The collection included the modified Amanarath crossbow from Germany he'd refitted to reload bolts automatically, a few long-range pistols he'd augmented with special sighting scopes that gave the user tremendous range, and a wrist weapon that housed a series of Oriental throwing stars. "Weapons aren't normally my focus. My efforts thus far have been trained on flight and the use of electricity."

"These are very good. I should very much like it if you'd make me a gun." Her finger traced over the sharp tips of the bolts in the Amanarath crossbow.

"You shoot?"

She nodded. "You didn't really think all a Hunter's daughter knew how to do was serve tea, did you?"

He gave her a lopsided grin. "I knew there was more to you than that the moment you stepped across the velvet ropes and began to tinker with my machine."

A blush infused her cheeks. "You make it sound very risqué."

His smile got even bigger. "What kind of gun would you like?"

Sephie clasped her hands together. "You're very good with electricity, and you're the only inventor I can think of who could create such a thing. What I'd really like is a gun powered by a Tesla coil. One that shoots bolts of electricity rather than bullets or arrows."

"A Tesla coil shooter . . ." Marley murmured. "I hadn't ever thought of applying electricity in that manner, but it has potential."

Her broad smile lit up the room, making the very air seem to sparkle. His heart twisted. Marley realized he'd give anything to see her smile like that every day for the rest of his life.

"I'll be happy to work on one for you. But it might have to wait for a few months. Thadeus and I are planning to test our great airborne electrical transmission enhancement machine, and we must finish it. In the meantime, I'm being a horrible host. May I order tea? I know I could use something after our greeting from Binky."

"Yes, please. Tea would be lovely." She tilted her head to one side as he went to the voice tube that led to the kitchens upstairs and ordered tea for the two of them.

"Is the invention you and Thadeus are testing the one my father is so interested in?"

Marley nodded as he returned to the edge of his work desk. "I'm planning on testing it in North Umbria."

"Where exactly?"

"Ullswater."

"That's a fairly large lake. In fact, it borders one side of one of the family's country estates."

A tight knot swelled in Marley's throat. "It does?"

She nodded.

He had best be certain the invention would work. The last thing he wanted to do was anger Lord Hargrieve or any of his relations.

A small brass bell rang three times, providing a very welcome distraction. "That should be the tea. Cook is most excellent about making sure there's always something about for Thadeus and me no matter what time of day it is."

He walked over to the wall and slid up the wooden door of the dumbwaiter. Inside the wooden contraption sat a silver tea service and three china plates on two trays, one heaped with sandwiches, one with scones, clotted cream, and strawberry jam, and another with sliced fruit and boiled eggs. He picked

up the trays, balancing them two on each arm as he carried
them over to his workbench.

The back of Sephie's mouth began to ache and water, and
her stomach took the opportunity to growl. She pressed her
hand to her stomach to quiet it. She'd missed any chance of
having something to eat when Frobisher had rudely shown up
uninvited at their home that morning, as he did far too often.
He usually consumed everything from the tea tray, leaving
her little besides the comfort of a cup of hot Earl Grey tea.

She picked up one of the sandwiches and bit in, enjoying
the crisp, fresh taste of the cucumber and the green bite of the
watercress, along with the sweetness of the soft butter. It was
simple enough fare, but she was hungry and so it tasted as
good as any of the fourteen-course meals her father had their
staff serve on important occasions.

Marley poured her a cup of tea and added a generous helping of sugar. "I didn't ask, but I hope you like your tea sweet.
It's how I take it."

She offered him a grateful smile. "It's perfect." It could
have been the weakest, most pathetic cup of tea in the realm
and she would have thought it special, only because he'd
poured it for her. It had been a very long time since a man had
treated her as something other than a featherheaded female
or—worse—a china doll to be wrapped in tissue and cosseted
away in a drawer for fear of breaking it. Marley was attentive,
yet believed in her strengths and reveled in her intellect.
Sephie decided he was a most unusual man. Brilliant, but
with a tender heart, and a fierceness when it came to protecting others.

He peered at her over the edge of his teacup, his great
brown eyes the color of dark tea, but flecked with bits of gold
that seemed to make them sparkle. Marley set the cup down.

"That key you're protecting," he said, nodding at her, "what does it go to?"

Sephie lifted the dark metal key that hung about her neck and stared at it. The black iron was pitted and in truth it looked as old as it likely was, but the metal was still warm from the heat of her own body. "Doesn't look like much, does it? This little key unlocks a chest that holds a very special book."

Marley snorted. "Your father sent you away from his home and risked his life battling demons to protect a book? Surely he has libraries full of them!"

"Yes, but the Book of Jezriel is one of a kind. It tells how the archangels and their followers came to be, and how some of them fell, becoming the most powerful dark forces in our world."

"And am I correct in guessing that you are its keeper?"

Sephie smiled. "I knew you were astute."

"Is that why Frobisher wishes to wed you so badly?"

She shrugged. "That, and he wants to be the next leader of the Legion. He hopes if he aligns himself with my father by marriage it'll be more likely. But that's up to the Legion leaders to decide, no matter how he manipulates the situation."

Marley glowered into the dregs in his cup. Just by the stiff set of his shoulders and the way his great dark brows drew together in a frown, she knew he was agitated. He hadn't even shown her his invention, which didn't seem like him at all.

"You're still worried about Thadeus, aren't you?"

He gaze connected with hers. "This isn't like him. Cook said he hasn't been home since this afternoon. He left about an hour after I did." He plucked the round watch from the small pocket in his vest and checked the time.

Sephie racked her brain. She didn't know where Thadeus had gone or why, but it was clearly distressing Marley. Until they received the notice that things were safe from her father, she needed to stay here and keep Marley here as well. It was just safer for both of them.

"Perhaps he was working on the invention and needed something," she said. "If we go and look it over you might see what happened."

Marley's mouth flattened into a line of resolute displeasure. "I suppose you are right. No use fretting like a mother hen, is there?"

He wiped his mouth with his napkin and stood, straightening his vest. He waited for her to rise. "The machine is this way." She followed a step behind him, eager to see the electrical machine that could pull current from the air. She'd heard only snatches of the conversation between her father and Frobisher. If Marley was truly as brilliant as they both believed, this machine might be altered into an electrical cannon, capable of being flown in the skies to destroy their enemies with a focused beam like a lightning bolt.

A scraping noise of a door opening at the far end of the laboratory and heavy footfalls on the wooden stairs leading down from the house upstairs stopped Marley in his tracks. "Thad? Where the devil have you been, old chap?"

He stepped toward his cousin, but Sephie gripped him hard on the arm and held him back.

"It's all right. It's just Thadeus."

"No, it's not." Her face was white and drawn, her lips pressed together in a thin, tight line, and her body stiff. "Look at his eyes," she whispered.

As Thadeus emerged from the shadows of the stairwell, Marley could see his eyes were not the familiar brown he'd known but a dark, golden yellow. The raw, prickly sensation of something unnatural that one felt walking through a graveyard at night coiled and twisted in Marley's belly like a ball of worms. Sephie's reaction and his own intuition told him whatever had happened to Thadeus wasn't normal.

"He's been possessed by a demon. We need to leave. Now." Her tone was hushed but urgent.

"Where are you going, Marley?" Thad's voice echoed as if more than one person spoke with his vocal cords at the same time.

"I have to see our guest home."

"Rude of you not to introduce us." He tilted his head to the side, a gruesome smile stretching his mouth. "But then, we don't need much of an introduction, do we, my dear?"

Sephie shuddered, and her hand grew instantly clammy against Marley's skin. She tugged harder on him. "Now, Marley."

Marley didn't stop to think. He went with his instincts.

He dashed for the outside exit, pulling her with him. He hoped if they approached Binky, he'd obey the order to kill anything coming into the lab, but allow them to go out unharmed.

Sephie screamed, and Marley felt the both of them yanked viciously backward. "I want that key!" Thadeus hissed.

She scrabbled with her clothing, reached into her pocket, and pulled out a vial of clear liquid. With one smooth movement of her thumb, she popped the rubber stopper out and tossed the liquid at Thadeus. He let go, howling in protest and clawing at his face as chunks of flesh turned first into a bloody pulp and then charred.

Marley spied Binky clanking and whirring in their direction. Rather than take a chance he'd be inclined to mash them flat, Marley doubled back toward the lab, past his writhing cousin, Sephie in tow behind him.

"Where the blazes are you going? The exit is that way!"

"Yes, and the airship is this way."

He pulled down a huge lever in the wall, and the large

seam in the center of the smaller room off to the side of the main laboratory began to widen, opening to the night sky. "Help me get the tarps off!"

Together they pulled at the heavy canvas sheeting that covered his machine, which had a gondola the size of a phaeton. Part aeronautic carriage, part dirigible, part energy manipulation machine, it was their best chance to get up and away from whatever it was that had taken over Thadeus and seemed to be relentless in pursuing Sephie and the key she wore.

"Get in!"

She scrambled over the wicker edge of the gondola in a flurry of petticoats and rolled into the basket beneath the balloon. Marley climbed in and fired up the propellers. Using electromagnetic energy to heat the water for the steam boilers ensured the water heated almost instantly, providing ready access to steam.

Thadeus came limping toward them. Bile rose bitter and acidic in the back of Marley's throat to see the damage his cousin had suffered. Out of habit and curiosity he leaned toward him, but Sephie grabbed Marley's arm, jerking him away as she said urgently, "He's trapped in his own body right now. The demon controls him. He'll kill you with his bare hands and not be able to stop himself. Don't think for a moment the demon will allow him pity or remorse. It's here to do a job: kill us and take the key."

Marley stiffened his resolve and his upper lip and removed the anchor rope holding the craft down as the balloon swelled upward. It grew until it was ten times larger than the gondola and lifted them out of the open hatch into the night air.

He had to carefully adjust the direction of the propellers to keep the balloon from snagging on the wrought iron edging and ragged bits of slate that fashioned the roofline of Bostwick House.

While Thadeus cursed and jumped, scrabbling for a hold

on them, Marley noted the dark shadows shifting through and filling the gardens. They weren't ordinary shadows, of that he was sure.

Sephie peered over the edge. "More demons," she muttered. "It looks as though your laboratory isn't as safe as we thought."

"Clearly." He peered sharply at her. "What will become of my family?"

"The Legion will be here shortly and help them. I'm sure that the minute Father dispatched the demons at our home he sent word for us to be followed and protected."

They rose still higher, the gas streetlights of London barely visible through the pervasive coal-smoke haze that perpetually hung in the air. Fog rolled in off the Thames, and as they climbed still higher, they lost sight of the city altogether.

A strong breeze whipped along the gondola, and the steady *whop, whop, whop* of the wooden propellers created a soothing noise that made their daring escape seem that much more surreal.

Sephie wrapped her delicate hands over the wooden rails of the wicker gondola, looking down on a world that seemed much more peaceful, more serene than it should. The shroud of dark, smoky air beneath them gave way to clearer skies over the country as they headed north.

The warmth of Marley standing behind her kept the shivers at bay. Their escape had been by his ingenuity and her knowledge of Hunter lore. The countryside spread out beneath them, making her very aware just how lucky she was to be with the one man in all of England who could outsmart the Darkin without any Legion training. They would be a fine pair, once she convinced her father to let her marry Marley— if he proposed.

He placed a hand on either side of the rail, holding her in the circle of his arms. "Are you certain you aren't hurt?" he asked softly, dipping his head to speak softly beside her ear.

"Nothing but a few scratches."

"That's good. I couldn't bear if anything happened to you."

She turned to face him, putting their mouths within inches of each other. Her lips tingled at the memory of what kissing him was like. The moonlight, unfiltered by fog and soot-laden air, cast his strong features in stark relief.

Sephie had never had a man give her his full attention in this way, as if she were the sun and the planets all revolved around her. It was quite a heady thing. "Have you come to care for me that quickly?"

"More than you know." His gaze dropped for a second. He shoved his right hand in the small upper breast pocket of his vest and pulled out a bit of white tissue paper. The edge of it fluttered in the breeze. "I meant to give this to you this afternoon at your father's house. I asked his permission to court you."

He carefully peeled back the folded layers of tissue, exposing a simple gold oval locket on an elegant chain. "I wasn't positive how your father would take my request, especially after learning he entertained Frobisher's suit for your hand."

"But I don't want Frobisher," she interrupted. "You know that."

"I do. But the question remains if your father will see me as a suitable match for you after all this. I think it'll rest on the success of the electric cannon."

Sephie huffed. "I don't think it will matter. He hasn't a choice now, has he? We're together. Alone. Unchaperoned. After we spend a night together traveling to Northumberland, I hardly think he can in all good conscience reject a proposal, no matter how your experiment goes."

Marley's sculpted lips spread into a genuine smile, the kind a boy gives when his dearest Christmas wish has been fulfilled. "I know this isn't a ring, but I thought you might wish to choose that for yourself."

Sephie lifted the locket from the paper. The golden oval wobbled back and forth in the breeze. "Marley Turlock, are you making me an offer of marriage?"

"I certainly am. I know I'll never meet another woman who has your combination of kind heart and inquisitive mind. You are truly one of a kind, and I love you and want you to be my wife."

Her stomach flipped and a giddy, fizzing sensation spread out to every cell. This was what joy and freedom felt like. Pure, undarkened, unbridled. She smiled, reaching up on tiptoe to brush her lips against his.

He pulled back slightly. "Is that a yes?"

She kissed him harder. "Of course that's a yes, no matter what befalls us. Will you put the necklace on me?"

Marley unlatched the chain and slipped the locket around her neck. "I thought we might put a picture of you and me in it to keep the pictures of us close to your heart."

Sephie smiled warmly at him, her fingers slipping over the locket. "You just remember you're mine while you're at those fancy royal balls and bestowed with honors, once you test that invention of yours and become world famous, and we have all these amazing adventures together. I'm one in a million, Sir Turlock, and I loved you even when you were just a mere inventor."

"How could I ever forget? I doubt you'll let me," he teased in return.

"You're right. I never will." This time Marley cupped her cheek in his hand and kissed her soundly.

Sephie could barely breathe. She didn't want to. She wanted this moment to last. But when he finally broke the connection between them she gazed up in the warm chocolate eyes of the man she loved. "What was that for?"

He gently took a curl of her hair and smoothed it between his fingers, adoration in his gaze. "Because, Lady Persephone Hargrieve, I'll never get enough of you."